FLORIDA'S FRONTIER

The Way Hit Wuz

Mary Ida Bass Barber Shearhart

Florida's Frontier
THE WAY HIT WUZ

Mary Ida Bass Barber Shearhart

ISBN 10: 1-886-104-39-5
ISBN 13: 978-1-886-104-39-6

The Florida Historical Society Press
435 Brevard Avenue
Cocoa, FL 32922
www.myfloridahistory.org

P•R•E•S•S

Title page by author's daughter, Virginia K. Barber McLamb

To My Twin Brother
Need "Buddy" Bass

I Could Not Have Done This Without You

That Which Has Been Is Now,

And That Which Is To Be

Hath Already Been;

And God Requireth That Which Is Past.

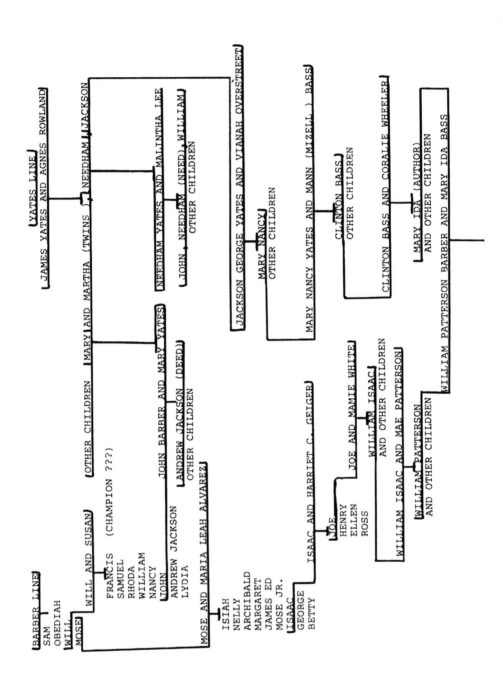

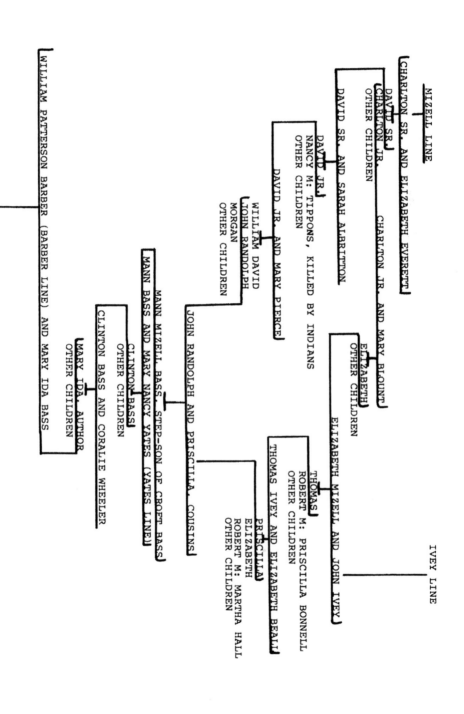

PROLOGUE

The lakefront park was crowded that day. The Florida sunshine outdid itself as sunbathers basked in its rays. Bikers, walkers, and an occasional jogger filled the boardwalk that ran along the water's edge. The majority were elderly retirees like myself, out for their daily exercise routine. But unlike me, most were transplanted "Yankees" from up north that have been coming down to Florida since Andrew Jackson ran the Indians out almost two hundred years ago. I'm a seventh generation Floridian and a vanishing breed.

As usual, I had overexerted myself on my bike and sat down to rest on one of the benches that was already occupied by an elderly gentleman. For sure he was old, as I myself was on Medicare and he looked ancient to me. A worn handmade walking stick rested on the bench beside him and he reached to retrieve a brown paper bag as I settled back and began to dig in my pocket for a tissue to wipe my face.

We sat there ignoring each other for several minutes, looking out across the waters of East Lake Tohopekaliga and I was considering moving on when he turned and stared at me in childlike candor.

"You from around these here parts?" he asked.

"I live over there across the lake near Boggy Creek."

He nodded his head as if he knew exactly where it was.

"You rode that contraption all the way over here? Hits a wonder you didn't git splattered on the highway the way these folks is a trying to kill each other nowadays."

I explained that I had loaded my bike in my little truck and carried it over to the lakefront so I could ride along the bike path for exercise.

"Women nowadays ain't got enough to do with all these here labor-savin' doodads. Idle hands are thus the devil's workshop," he lamented, looking around at the crowd of pudgy women. "Used to be woman's work was never done, men's neither. Times thus has changed and not for the better. Not to my way of figgerin."

I decided it would probably be useless to try to explain that having nothing to do was in little way related to the need for daily, vigorous exercise.

We sat for a few minutes, each looking about the crowd, saying nothing more until I finally felt the need to defend myself against his accusation that I was lazy and had nothing better to do.

"Well, I for one stay pretty busy, most all the time. I have a twelve acre orange grove, what's left of it after all these freezes. I live in an old house and I don't have a lot of these labor saving 'doodads.' My house used to not have any plumbing or electricity. It's over one hundred years old."

The old man stared at me again with renewed interest but still said nothing.

"I still sleep in the room I was born in and that wasn't exactly yesterday. Not many of these people along this lakefront can say that, or anywhere else in Florida," I bragged.

That really got his attention.

"Who wuz yore Pa?"

"Clint Bass. I'm Clint Bass's oldest daughter. There were four of us. I have an older brother, Van, and a twin we all call 'Buddy,' and a younger sister, Kay."

He didn't say anything for a few minutes and I lost hope that he might know my family. He talked like a Florida Cracker.

He finally nodded his head and said "I knew o' yore daddy, Clint, and Roy and Eller. One o' yore aunts married Irlo Bronson, man that highway over there wuz named after."

"That's right. Aunt Florrie, my daddy's youngest sister. The oldest one, Aunt Bertha married Henry Partin. They used to own all that land between here and Kissimmee. They've about sold all of it to the developers and moved out onto Uncle Henry's pastures on the way between here and Kenansville. Around Canoe Creek."

"Don't fault 'em fer that, wantin' to git away from this rat race. They wuz Mann Bass's young'uns weren't they?"

I was elated. Here was someone who actually knew of my grandfather who had been dead since the turn of the century. Here he was sitting on a park bench right beside me among all these newcomers and tourists.

"Where you from?" I asked, hoping to know more about this rare find.

"Down south o'here a ways. Granddaughter brung one o' her gals and her grandyoung'uns up here to that Disney thing. I told 'em to jest drap me off here in St. Cloud and I'd hang around 'til they got back. She weren't too keen on the ideer but I stuck to my guns 'til I convinced her I could wait 'em out."

I don't think he had any idea how long he'd have to "wait 'em out" while his family got their money's worth at Disney World but I decided right then I'd not be wasting the old gentleman's time nor mine if I spent some of the day, visiting with him.

"Do you mind if I go back home and get a note pad and my tape recorder? I'd like to ask you some questions about the past, if you don't mind. I seldom meet one of my kind around here, especially one that knew my grandfather. I won't be much more than thirty or forty minutes. I'll bring us something cold to drink." I decided to pack my lunch, too. I knew now his must have been in the brown paper bag in his lap.

I didn't even wait for an answer. He seemed eager to talk and I certainly wanted to hear what he had to say.

"You got a family?" He asked when I got back and settled beside him.

"Four children out in Texas. They were all born here but they've moved away. I was married to Little Bill Barber for twenty-six years but we divorced some time ago. Did you know the Barber family?"

"Guess I did from way back. Little Bill wuz W.I. Barber's boy, weren't he? Used to be tax assessor here fer years and years."

"That's right." I sat, waiting for him to go on but again he settled into silence. I didn't want to push him and we sat there, looking out at the lake.

"The Yankees are thus a'takin' us," he finally said.

"I beg your pardon?" Not knowing exactly what he meant.

"The Yankees are thus a'takin' this land," he lamented, sadly.

"Yes," I agreed, "and the Puerto Ricans, Asians and lots of other races, speaking in languages I can't understand. They say there are about a thousand people coming into Florida every day. A Florida Cracker is getting to be scarce as hens' teeth. I know now how the Indians felt when they saw the wagons coming across the Florida line way back there. I'm beginning to feel just as invaded and pushed aside as they were. They haven't run us out and taken our land like we did the poor Indians but they're buying us up and changing our culture just the same."

"Hit's a shame what we done to the poor old Injuns, ain't hit?"

"You can say that again. All they wanted was just enough of Florida to live on in peace and we wouldn't even let them have that and us with a world of land that few whites had even ridden across. It cost the government a hundred times more to kill them and drive them out than if they'd give them the land and left them in peace. What goes around comes around. Now it's happening to us only they're buying us out and we're greedy enough to let them do it. My mother said, before she died that they wouldn't be satisfied until they'd paved every inch of Florida and she's almost right."

"Well, they've shore ruined this here lake. Look how hits growed up in weeds. These fancy college engineers think they knowed so much, puttin' in them locks and things. And all these other people, a polluting and dumping, no telling what all into our waters. I 'member when this used to be a clean, white sandy bottom along here and not all this old grass. You can't wade hit out, way we used to here."

His remarks took me back to my childhood, for I was brought up around the edge of this lake and the mouth of Boggy Creek.

"I used to fish around this lake with my daddy when the bass were spawning. Fished with a cane pole and bucket of red-horse minnows that we caught with a dip net in the ditches along Boggy Creek Road. Fat chance of catching a red-horse there now. I can't even find an access to the lake now. It's all bought up. I have just a few acres of what my daddy used to own and I can't get to the creek where we used to swim and fish unless I pay for it. They say you can't even get a boat into the mouth of Boggy Creek where we used to swim and bathe in the clean flowing water. There used to be white sand bars down there where the creek emptied into that little cove across there. I haven't been down there since before my mother died and my brothers owned the land on the creek."

We sat for a minute, looking at the polluted lake.

"You know what they call these two lakes now? Lake 'Toho.' The Indians named these two lakes. Means 'Sleeping Tiger'. You'd think, out of deference to the poor old Indians we took it from, they could call it by its name. It sort of has a ring to it, doesn't it? 'Lake-Tow-hope-ka-lige-a.' I think it's pretty the way it is."

"They've changed more than that around here."

"I know. Campbell Station is now Campbell City. And Mill Creek Mall over there was supposedly named after Mill Slough that flowed through there after the marsh was drained. I guess a lot of the new people don't know a slough from a creek; I understand before it was drained they called it the Kissimmee Bog. Couldn't ride a horse across it."

We sat there again in silence, nurturing our grievances. I had done most of the talking but he seemed to enjoy it.

"Things shore have changed here. Bet you couldn't catch a decent mess of fish outa here if you wuz starving to death. Nothing but gars and a few 'gators. Bet there ain't no mallards nor wood ducks in these coves like there used to be. May not could even git a mess o' coot livers."

"That's right. When I lived out in Texas for a while my twin brother wrote me how this country was changing. He said he was beginning even back then, about ten years ago, to feel like a stranger in his own country. He wrote there were still things like the old swamps like Reedy Creek still standing and a few of the big pastures my Uncles and the Johnstons and Overstreets still own but it wasn't home anymore. He said they had turned Boggy Creek into a trash hole and he couldn't even wade around the shore of Macy Island for the beer cans and trash in the water. He had been down to Canoe Creek where he and my daddy used to catch strings of fish that dragged the ground, holding them shoulder high and he fished all day and caught two old gars. He recollected how clean and sandy the bottom was around the edge of this lake where you could wade around the edge and feel the holes the fish had fanned out to lay their eggs in during spawning time."

I just couldn't get the old man to say much. I hadn't even turned on the recorder.

"Did you used to live around here?" I finally asked.

"No, but my Pa did fer a while."

"Who was he?"

He ignored my question but went on. "Left this country quite a while ago but he shore loved hit. Used to come back and bring me when I wuz jest a little boy. I used to bring him back when I got so I could drive. My, the tales he could tell about some of these people and the things that went on around here!"

I held my breath. Lord, I wonder if he knows about the Barber-Mizell feud. It had happened so long ago and involved my children's ancestors. Both my ex-husband's people and my father's people had clashed in a bitter feud back in the late 1860's and I had been unable to find out much about it. People still didn't talk about it when I was a child and now that I wanted to learn more about it, most of the old timers were dead. Even when they were alive they didn't know anything, as their parents hadn't brought it up for fear of choosing sides.

"Did he ever mention anything to you about the Barber-Mizell feud?" I asked cautiously, trying to hide the excitement in my voice.

He looked at me and smiled. "I wondered how long hit'd take you to git around to asking that. You being Mann Bass's granddaughter and a'marrying Joe Barber's grandchild."

Smart old fox, I thought. He knew all the time but was too polite to ask me if I knew.

"So you knew Man Bass was a Mizell and now a Bass?" I asked.

"Any o' the old timers knowed he wuz a wood's colt. Common knowledge that he belonged to John Mizell. Who told you?"

"My folks sat us down and told us before we started to school. They wanted us to know that my grandpa was illegitimate in case anyone brought it up. I guess maybe my daddy was teased by some of the children, calling his daddy a bastard."

"Not anybody that was anybody. Folks around here thought a lot of your grandpa. Had one of the biggest funerals ever held in this county. They say there weren't a broke horse left in Osceola County weren't in the funeral procession."

"Nobuddy teased me about it but a lot of curious people brought it up sort of on the sly and I'm glad my folks told me. I was never ashamed of it. Aunt Priscilla, as I was taught to refer to her, was from good family and so were the Mizell's and my grandpa had no say-so in the matter. Daddy used to say we weren't kin to any of these other Basses around in Osceola County. That Grandpa's half brothers' children that survived were all girls and that line of Bass names died out. Anybody with the Bass name now was from his stepfather's people and no blood kin. He seemed to want me to know that. I often wondered why."

He looked at me and said nothing and I wondered what he knew about the Basses.

"I heard several different tales about why John Mizell and Priscilla Ivey never married before or after the baby came but I don't know which ones are true. It doesn't matter now. My daddy's people were still on the defensive about it when I was a little girl and even a teenager. One of my aunts said there had been a marriage but I can't find any record of it and my grandpa took his stepfather's name. If they had gotten married, he would have been a Mizell. I know that."

"So you's like to know a little bit about the feud?" He finally opened up after he realized I had no axe to grind with either side and he could speak his mind.

"I got all the time in the world. Anything you heard about it and anything your daddy heard."

"Well, honey, Pa didn't hear about hit. He wuz there when hit happened. I got hit first hand from him."

"That ended back in 1870. Was he old enough then to know what happened?"

"I reckon he wuz. He knew old man Mose Barber and the whole family. Knew him when he had his plantation back in Columbia County. Used to fight Injuns with old man Mose."

"Wait a minute! The Indian War was over in Columbia County before 1842. The only fighting later on was down around Fort Myers and even that was in '57. Aren't you talking about your grandpa or his daddy?"

He looked at me with a sly grin. "I got all my senses, young lady. I'm ninety-three years old and my Pa lived to be ninety-five. But he wuz seventy-two years old when I come along. Pa had tough luck with his women folk. Said all his young'uns wuz borned with extra big heads and none of his other wives lived thru the labor. Ma married him when she wuz forty-one. Never thought he'd ever have a son. She wuz a old maid then. I never 'membered much about her. Pa worked some as a cook in the cow crews and when he got older he drove a wagon collecting turpentine for a naval store."

I had him going now. He kept talking as if he was a minister, inspired by the Holy Ghost. He finally paused to say, "Sure is nice to find somebuddy interested in the old days. I try to tell my family and they don't seem too interested in the past. Keep changing the subject. Crazy 'bout thet hell-fired TV and their old 'programs.' Won't miss one episode of *As the World Turns.* I call hit *As the Stomach Turns.* Makes me sick."

I tried to get him to stop and rest but he kept on. He mentioned places that I had heard of as a child and forgotten. Ocean Prairie, creeks called Camp Lonesome, Bull Creek and the crossing on that creek called the Mizell Ford, Jane Green and Jane Green Swamp with the section called the Puzzle where not many men could find their way out. Wolf and Pennawah, Jernigan Tyner Slough and Swamp where twelve men were surrounded in a bend and slaughtered in one pile. He mentioned Limpkin, Turkey Hammock, Camp Hammock, John Swamp, Need's Scrub, Burrel Island, the Gardner Marsh, Dubie Oak and the Double Run. Some of the cypress ponds even had names like Board Cypress where people cut their poles for cow pens.

We paused late in the day to eat our lunch. He ate very little and I fed the rest to the birds. He talked on and on, inspired by my undivided attention and the chance to be recorded.

He was still talking when an old grey Chevrolet pulled up to the curb and honked the horn at him. The obviously tired and happy little children called to him.

"Hurry up, Grandpa, and let's go."

They had the door opened on our side and he responded by getting up, reluctantly.

"I guess I 'bout told you everything I knowed anyways." He hobbled over to the car and turned and smiling happily to me, said, "That's the way hit wuz."

I stood, stunned, not thinking. I noticed a Manatee County tag on the back of the car as it sped off, but couldn't remember if he ever told old me his name. Perhaps I had it down somewhere in my notes.

I took the precious tape and note pad home and began my research. I tried to document everything he told me.

With the help of my twin brother, Need Hugh (Buddy) Bass and what few old timers I could find, it's finally done—a true tale in most every respect. None of the names have been changed to protect the guilty or the innocent. All of the following characters were real people. They lived and died in Florida and they were true Florida Crackers. Some of the characters are out of their time frame in which they actually lived, but the part they played "happened." They deserve to be heard and be a part of Florida Cracker history - our past. So now read a tale and find out just *The Way Hit Wuz.*

The original Barber Plantation, built in the 1830's, was located in North Florida. As the Seminole Indians were pushed to the south, Mose Barber expanded his cattle operation into Central Florida. This illustration from the March 12, 1864 edition of *Harper's Weekly* shows Union forces briefly occupying the plantation during the Civil War.

Chapter 1

The five Indians slipped quietly through the early morning mist. They went single file, stopping now and then to gather and look anxiously at their leader as he scanned the surrounding countryside to get his bearings and then once again push on. The four Indians following their leader appeared to be very young, perhaps fourteen or fifteen. At that age, they thought themselves invincible as all young boys do and their leader had handpicked them for this dangerous mission because of their tender age. They were deep in the populated area of northeastern Columbia County where the Indians had been driven out for several years and replaced by small farmers that had sifted down into North Florida from Georgia and the Carolinas. They were strong and full of life, thinking "tomorrow" was forever and that death came to the very old or weak or an accident that happened to someone else.

Easter Choddy, leading the pack was much older and wiser, knowing full well they probably would not make it back to the big swamp. He turned around and looked at the four braves with a bitter smile as he recalled the old Indian proverb. "Life is the flash of the firefly in the dark. It's the little shadow that runs across the grass and loses itself at sunset."

They had come to kill a white man they had never seen and didn't know. Not just any white man but Mose Barber's older brother, William. Easter had left the swamp, slipped down to Mose Barber's homestead a month ago and found it protected by a tall log stockade. Inside was a pack of dogs, trained, as Mose said, "to smell an Indian a mile against the wind." He quickly decided there was no way to get to Mose. But using his skills developed by years of avoiding capture during the recent Seminole War, he observed that Mose's beloved brother, who lived a distance to the east in Nassau County, had no such protection and was vulnerable to attack. So they would kill him and do it in such a way that Mose would get the message.

Mose Barber had been stealing the Indian cattle for years. Even as a boy in Bryan County, Georgia, he had slipped down into Indian Territory and stolen their cattle, driving them into the Carolinas. After he had helped drive the Indians from North Florida and during the Seminole War, he had pushed down farther into the territory and gathered the herds abandoned by the fleeing Indians. All the Indians hated him but Easter in particular, for the cattle had belonged to his grandfather, Ahaye, Cowkeeper of Latchoway, now called Oklawaha. He had come to Alachua with large herds from Georgia, given to his ancestor, Emperor Brims, as a reward for aiding the British. Ahaye had been a chief in Spanish Florida, ruling the St. Johns River from the Altamaha to the mouth of Turkey Creek. The line had passed through Cowkeeper's daughter to her only child, a son, as was the Indian custom. Easter was of the same family and proud of his heritage,

1

and he was sacrificing his life to get revenge. In a way, he was revenging his race for all the killings and cheating and lies the officials had inflicted on the Indians as they had tried to wipe his race from the Florida soil.

It was June of 1841. Time had run out for the Indians. They had already been driven into the Green Swamp northeast of Tampa but a few had fled north into the Okefenokee on the Florida-Georgia line. Rarely they would make their way into what is now Osceola National Forest, hit a secluded trail past High Springs, slip slightly west of Gainesville, then called Hogtown, past Ocala and Bushnell, into Green Swamp. But this path ran through western Columbia County, several miles from where Mose Barber's brother lived and the settlers in the area had become complacent and felt safe from attack. All except Mose Barber. He knew how much he was feared and hated by the tribes.

The four young Indians were around six feet, not an uncommon height for a Seminole. They appeared strong, wiry and amazingly healthy after years of living in the open air with constant exercise just trying to stay alive. Easter was shorter and stockier and a shade short of being handsome because of a large Roman nose. Their eyes shined brightly in the moonlight and their faces honest and intelligent.

For the past four years the young bucks had grown to manhood in the swamp. During the height of the war, the Indians had murdered the people of Roanoke, burned the town and fled to the swamp. Military posts quickly sprang up on the Suwannee River from Cedar Key to the big swamp where the river originated. Fort Gilmore was on the west side, near Blounts Ferry, and Fort Moniac on the southeast near the St. Marys. Surrounded by the white man, their backs to the wall amid the snakes, alligators, mosquitoes, and on rotten, floating earth that trembled when they walked, they had found enough solid ground to build their chickees, a thatched roof hut on poles, high off the damp ground. It had been difficult to prepare the jerky for this journey, hidden deep in the swamp where the white man could not see their fires and the tall trees blotted out the sun so they could not dry it and it would rot before they could store it.

They had held their Green Corn dance as was usual in the spring, killed a deer and drank its broth to appease Yo-He-Wah, their devil that brings pestilences and calamities. It was supposed to have been the first deer of the season but they prayed to their god, Ishtoholo, that he would forgive them as they had been eating deer the year around just to survive.

They had paddled out of the recess of the dark, mysterious swamp, slipped under the tall trees of maples, bald cypress, gums and pumpkin ash to the outer edge where they poled under a canopy of grey moss and around tangled masses of vines and sunken logs until they found the beginning of the St. Marys River.

In their haste and anxiety they had not paused to enjoy the beauty of the swamp as the full moon peeped now and then on the wild orchids and the mass of ferns and blue flags. They poled down a deep, narrow stream that flows to the Cumberland Sound and into the ocean in tiny swirls and eddies, its origin lost to most men back in the primeval swamp.

The full moon had gone behind a cloud and it began to look like rain. They

2

cursed their luck as they knew the lazy little stream could turn into a raging torrent after a heavy summer rain.

When the river made a deep bend, they let Easter out on the southern shore with the only gun and dragged their dugout, or pickle, onto the opposite bank under a low hanging, moss-draped limb that dipped near the water. The dugout was surprisingly light, though twelve feet long. A cypress log had been buried in a mud bank and left to age for several months, unearthed and dried for a week. They had dug it out with a pit-a-chen-a-lo-gee, a kind of wood chisel, to its present thinness and it glided swiftly and silently like our canoes.

To the southeast of them lay regions of pine forests and flat woods and an occasional hardwood hammock threaded with sluggish little streams. At times the pinewoods were laced with myrtles so they stuck to the cattle trails as best they could.

As the sun began to rise over Jacksonville to the east they ducked into one of the large hummocks, or "hammocks" as the settlers called them, to rest and hide until night. They were delighted to find a wild orange tree that had survived the harsh winters and sucked greedily on its sweet juice, devouring even its rind. They ate their cold meal of dried venison and sofkee, saving a small portion for the dog. She was a thin, pencil-tailed fice that would have been eaten months ago except she was vital to this mission.

They slept as the little pot-see-ton-ees flitted among the magnolias and wild jasmine vines. Like the Indians in most parts of Florida except the Everglades, and the wa-te-laws, or whooping cranes, these tiny yellow and green parakeets have vanished from view.

As soon as it was dark, they struck out again, the reluctant bitch straining at her leash. Bringing up the rear with the dog the youngest buck paused to curse her under his breath and look up at the threatening sky with startling blue eyes and brush the misty raindrops from auburn hair that could not deny his Scottish ancestor no matter how proudly he claimed to be "all Indian." Easter had picked him especially, knowing that he might be able to pass as white if they were attacked and he could escape into the woods. He took another wrap around his wrist with the leather and the boy managed to grab a glimpse of their dark red forms as the moon broke between the clouds.

Easter halted the march to go back to see why the young brave was having so much trouble leading the bitch. She was whining and pulling back on the leash and the boy pointed back behind him just as Easter got a glimpse of the wolf. He was standing perfectly still, sniffing the air.

"Give me the dog," he said in Hitchiti, the native tongue. "When you get a clear shot, kill him."

Ordinarily Easter would not kill a wolf. The Indians revered him as a hunter and watchdog but in this particular situation, Easter had plans for his hide.

At his first opportunity the young boy dropped to his knees, arrow ready and it struck home with a thud, the wolf giving a short, sharp yip as he struggled on the ground and then lay still.

The carcass was quickly removed of its hide which was rolled up and given to the young boy. Easter continued on, leading the bitch. Soon they struck the ruts of a wagon trail and knew they were nearing their destination. It was beginning to rain now in earnest and was several hours before dawn so they found a shelter of sorts in a sandy scrub. They could hear the wind overhead in the trees. The sky was turning black and they could not see their hands in front of their face. Here they finished what was left of the food as Easter laid out last minute plans for the attack, praying that the wind would stay to the south so it would blow the scent of the bitch in heat and the wolf hide toward the dogs at the homestead.

They lay to rest as the rain pounded the earth and the bitch snuggled against them. Water formed little puddles around them and was soon running down a cow trail through the scrub, carrying small sticks and dried leaves with it. Easter knew now that the St. Marys would soon do the same only it would be carrying floating logs and green limbs.

Easter slept little through the rest of the night as he lay and listened to the young bucks snore, snuggled together in a heap with the dog like a litter of puppies. The rain slacked off and a few stars came out and he knew dawn was not far away. So he awoke the sleeping boys and they sneaked closer to the homestead. The wind was still from the south as he motioned for the boy to take the bitch and the wolf hide on around to the south side of the scrub. There he was to stay until he heard the shot and then head for the clearing.

"If you hear more than one shot, we've been attacked so drop the bitch and run away and hide. When we have killed the man you will hear our cry. Pay no attention to the dogs. They will be barking at the bitch and the scent of the wolf hide and think it is a she-wolf in heat."

He motioned to the other three to come with him.

"We must keep the wind in our face and remember, kill only the white man. Do not harm the woman or children, or burn the house."

Back at the homestead Susan stirred and sat up in bed. Her husband, Will, was snoring soundly, oblivious to the racket outside in the yard. The rain had cooled the air and he was bundled up like a baby with the sheet pulled over his head. The dogs had become restless and began to whine. The largest brindled cur and bulldog mix snarled and jumped on a smaller cur that quickly turned belly up and crawled under the house. Susan could sense they were upset about something.

"Will, wake up," as she shook him gently, "Somethin's got the dogs all riled up."

Will opened his eyes and looked about. "Huh?" he mumbled, half asleep.

"Hits the dogs. They're a'actin' kinda funny like somethin's out thar."

Will raised up on an elbow and listened for a minute and then laughed. "Sounds like they're interested in what I wake up interested in some mornings," and he turned and grabbed his wife and pulled her down on top of him. "Like as not hits some old stray bitch in heat from over at the Norton. Could even be a she-wolf. I saw tracks in the scrub jestiddy."

He lay there for a moment as Susan struggled to get up.

4

"Want to do something?" he asked.

She didn't say anything. She hated for him to approach her like that. Why didn't he come out and say what was on his mind or better still, touch her in some way that would arouse her slows. His way was always so matter of fact and always got her out of the mood instead of putting her in one. Will was never romantic, but he wasn't abrupt or demanding either. She just wished he'd find a different way to tell her what was on his mind.

"I'm kinda sick on my stomach this morning," she complained as she rolled away from him.

"You think you might be 'pectin agin?"

"I ain't come unwell now for over a month. Could be."

"Don't reckon yore in the change, do you?"

Susan panicked. "I don't look thet old, do I?" The thought of looking old seemed much worse than being pregnant with her ninth child. "Do I look old enough for the change o'life to you?"

"Of course not, wife. Yore just as purty as the day we got married. I wuz just a wonderin'. Fine with me, I'd welcome another boy. Guess I'd better put my clothes on and settle them dogs down fore they take off and I have to saddle up and beat 'em back to the house."

"I got to git up myself. Mose and them boys and the niggers 'll be here to pick the cotton and I ain't even got a fire a'goin'."

Susan usually banked the coals in the fireplace where she cooked but it was summer and she had been so hot, shut up in the house because of the blowing rain. There were only two children at home. Leah, knowing she'd have to cook for the crew had kept all but Rhoda, the oldest girl who would be a lot of help to her mother and Andrew Jackson. The baby had cried to go with his mama so that Susan had brought him home also. Leah was Mose Barber's wife. She had a slave to help her in the kitchen and was always good to help Susan. Susan looked around at her primitive surroundings as she thought of how Leah lived. She has such a nice, big double pen house. Mose and William were so different from each other you'd never think they were brothers, she thought. Will never seemed to have any ambition and Mose had too much. But I wouldn't live with that foul-mouthed, hard-driving man for the finest house in the territory, she mused. Her Will was sweet and gentle and a family man. It was common knowledge Mose Barber had a roving eye for the women.

The clay fireplace was at one end of the room where Susan had to cook. It had a fixed horizontal iron bar built in, running from one side to the other about three feet high. There were two S-shaped hooks attached to the bar. From one hook she took a heavy iron pot by its bail and stirred and smelled of the stew left from supper last night and decided it was still good. She built a fire by taking a piece of flint and a pocket knife and, placing gun powder on a piece of cotton, struck the flint with the knife blade, a spark setting the gun powder and cotton on fire. For more light in the cabin she set fire to the end of a piece of "lightered" from a dead pine tree and stuck it between the logs of the wall. The pitch from the fat pine would drop harmlessly on the dirt floor as it quickly burned. She only had one candle and used it for an emergency as we would a flashlight. When water boiled in the coffee pot she dropped a handful of freshly ground coffee in and let it boil up a couple of times until it smelled like coffee and then poured a cup of cold water into the boil to "settle the grounds." She had heard Will talking to the dogs and threatening them with a beating if they didn't settle down. Fat chance, she thought. Will won't hurt a fly. But they don't know the difference. Mose had trained them and they had quickly learned they would be stomped into the ground if they didn't pay attention to what their master said. They don't know my Will, she thought.

She looked around the cabin as she got ready to go outside and milk the cows. She knew Will would have them in their stanchion. He hadn't taken his gun so she guessed he was correct about the dogs. Rhoda was up now.

"Dress the baby and mind he don't git into the far place nor teach the drip from the lighter knot. Never mind, hits light enough, I'll jest put hit out. Take him outside and don't let him pee of'en the porch neither. He's jest 'bout kilt my rose bush by the edge o' the porch." She grabbed a clean roller towel and changed it at the water-shelf as she washed her face and rinsed out her mouth. One of her pet peeves was dirty towels when she dried her face, and they could smell foul and rancid very quickly in the hot and humid Florida climate. She had taken water from a bucket made form the butt of a cedar tree and dipped it with a gourd. The water was stale and had come from a little branch that ran behind the house. William had never gotten around to digging a well.

She stopped behind the smoke house to relieve herself rather than walk all the way to the scrub. An old mama dog, who had dug a hole under the smoke house to hide her litter of pups, had crawled out and was barking in the direction of the milk shed. What now, she thought, still squatting with her skirt up over her knees as she looked in the general direction of the dog's gaze, her bristles standing on her back and growling now. She heard the metallic "sang" of a Cuban musket. After nine years of an Indian War, she would have recognized the dreaded sound anywhere. And at the same time, she saw an Indian, standing on a log, holding the gun. He was grinning at her. Will came staggering out from under the shed, holding his belly and she ran toward him with a cry of terror. A second Indian and then a third appeared, grabbing Will by his arms and plunged a knife deep into his side. She was so close now that his blood splattered on her clothes and he fell into her arms.

"Run wife, and grab the young'uns. Save yorself. I'm done fer." He groaned.

She looked defiantly at the Indians, expecting to feel the knife enter her body but they just stood there and laughed and then gave out their war cry. It was a frightful screeching, blood curdling cry.

"Yo-ho-e-hee."

She saw a fourth Indian going toward the house and ran to save her children. Just as she got to the gate Rhoda came flying out of the door and down the steps, carrying the baby, half dressed, his naked bottom sticking out from under her arms. The young Indian made no attempt to stop them.

"Ma!, Ma!, Hit's Injuns all over the place!" Rhoda cried, frightened out of her wits.

Susan grabbed her by the arm and steered her toward the road through the scrub, crying "Run, honey, run," looking back toward the milk shed but the grisly scene was hid from view and she could only imagine what was happening to her beloved Will.

They had run about a hundred yards and Rhoda, sobbing and crying, stopped and handed little Andrew Jackson to her mother.

"He's too heavy. I can't carry him no more. I'm about to drap him."

Susan took the little boy and they raced down the road, running until she began to have a terrible pain in her side and she could run no more. They stopped in the road and looked back toward the homestead. There was no telltale smoke so the house was not on fire, yet. They walked on until, exhausted, they ducked into a thick gall berry patch on the side of the road and hid from view. Their faces were hot and stained with tears. They squatted in the bushes like frightened, hunted rabbits and listened, holding their breath straining to hear the Indians in hot pursuit. No one came. All they could hear was the pounding of their hearts and little Andrew's whimpering. He finally quieted down, looking anxiously from one to another. Susan's heart quit pounding so hard. She wiped her face and the baby's nose on the hem of her skirt and commanded Rhoda to do the same. She thought how ridiculous it was to be scolding the girl with her Will probably lying dead on the ground and the house probably on fire by now. But she could still see no smoke.

Rhoda looked up at her mother with a face now grown pale and her eyes still wide with fright imploring, "Ain't Pa a'gonna ketch up, Ma? Ain't he a'comin' this a'way?"

"'Terectly, honey. He'll probably be along 'terectly."

Damn it, Mose Barber, she thought. Any other time you'd have showed up 'fore I got the coffee water on. She wondered what was keeping him and the crew. They should be along by now. She realized how much she was looking to Mose for help. And how much she would need him in the days and weeks to come. Nine children to raise now with another on the way. She would come to appreciate his toughness and strength, his dependability in time of trouble. She looked through the bushes in the direction of the cabin. There was still no sign of smoke. I don't suppose there was any way Will could have got to the house and got the gun and run them off, she thought, knowing in her heart she had heard no more shots and even the dogs had quit barking. She wondered why the Indians had spared her house and touched not a hair of her head when she was right there beside them with their knives in their hands.

They sat there for what seemed to be an eternity when she heard the hoof beat of horses coming down the road and thought she recognized the voice of her son, Francis, laughing and talking as if he didn't have a care in the world, totally unaware of the tragedy that lay just up the road and around the bend.

Chapter 2

At first glance there was nothing about Mose Barber that would distinguish him from the multitude of backwoodsmen that had filtered into Florida over the past several years. Shorter than the average man, slight build and bony frame, he was typical of the men of English descent that had migrated down from the Carolinas and Georgia when it was considered safe to bring their families to settle North Florida. He was tough as an alligator, face and hands freckled and weathered from years in the hot southern sun, his body slouched comfortably in the saddle, moving as one with the scrawny little cracker cowpony that was tougher than his rider. They were a matched set. His face, framed by a shock of red hair and obscured beneath a shapeless wide brimmed hat, was nondescript. He was neither handsome nor ugly. But close up and personal the clear blue eyes that darted anxiously out across the flat woods, squinting at the bright rays of the noon sun, were cold and hard and could blaze like those of a wild horse when angered. His nose, neither too short nor too long had a slight offset with a fine scar hidden in the crease of his left nostril. It had been nearly ripped off, not from a horse's hoof at the tender age of three, as he had been told, but by a buckle attached to a strong leather belt in the hands of his mother. His mouth, maybe a shade too thin, turned downward at the corners much more often than upward in a smile. When in deep thought he had a peculiar habit of pinching his nose between the first and second finger of his left hand. At these moments his eyes would seem their coldest and his mouth almost in a sneer. He sported a long reddish brown handlebar mustache that he blackened with soot for special occasions such as church and weddings. In his left hand he carried a new gun he'd just paid twelve dollars for over in Jacksonville. Isiah, his oldest son carried Mose's old flintlock musket that the family had affectionately called "old fart" because it was made by the Bean family of gunsmiths. Besides Francis, Susan's boy, there were five healthy, well-nourished cur dogs that never left his side when out in the woods. They ate better than most families.

Susan brushed aside her sleeping children and ran out into the road, waving her hands and shouting, "Mose, Mose! Francis, hits me, yore Ma!" Even before she could be seen.

Mose and the boys jerked their horses to a sudden stop, peering down the road where he had heard his name. He could see Susan, followed by the two children, the baby with his bare behind and their tear-streaked faces and knew something was wrong.

"What in the hell's a'goin' on, gal? You ain't out here berry pickin' with the half naked young'un, that's fer shore."

By now the children were crying and screaming, drowning out Susan, yelling "Injuns, Injuns."

Mose could barely understand her. "Injuns? Come on now woman, How many did you say?"

"No fooling, Uncle Mose, they wuz all over the place; out at the barn and a'comin' in the house. We wuz lucky to git away. They was right in on top o' me while I was a'dressing the baby." Rhoda's eyes were still wide with fright, just telling of it.

Susan wasn't saying anything, just standing in the middle of the road, face in her hands and sobbing uncontrollably now for the first time–the children, clinging to her skirt. Mose knew something serious had happened to frighten Susan as she wasn't easily shaken and had been through a lot of bad times and come through them, cool as a cucumber. Mose looked down the road toward the house.

"Don't tell me there's that many Injuns sneaking around these parts and nobuddy's seen any sign of 'em. Yore shore they's genuine Injuns?"

Susan had gathered her senses and stopped sobbing long enough to say, "Hits Will, Mose, Oh my God, hits Will."

"What about Will? Where is he off to? He didn't take out after 'em all by hisself, did he? He knew we was comin'." Mose was just a little put out at his brother.

"That's jest hit, Mose, they shot him out at the cowshed and then knifed him jest as I got to him. See the blood all over my skirt."

Rhoda noticed the blood for the first time as Susan had been clutching the baby next to her all the time. She started screaming now and the baby picked up the cry and hue and both the boys talking and asking questions. Francis, who had been down off his horse had climbed back up, ready to dash on down the road to his daddy.

"Hold on a minute son," commanded Mose, grabbing his bridle. The tone of his voice, alone, would have stopped the young boy in his tracks.

"He's dead fer shore. I know he's dead." Susan went on, wringing her hands in despair. "He told me to run, that he was done fer. All he could think of wuz me and the young'uns. He didn't have no chance to git away. No gun nor nothin'. He thought the dogs wuz a'fussin over a she-wolf. I wanted to stay and help but they wuz comin' in the door after the young'uns." She started to sob again and wring her hands.

"How long ago you figger this took place? You've stepped hit off a purty good clip fore you give out, hit looks like."

"We run 'til we got plum tuckered out. The young'uns cried 'til they went to sleep and I kept thinkin' you'd come along with the crew any minute."

"Hit rained us out over there 'fore we got through with my patch. Thought we'd finish up and then come tell you we'd git a early start tomorrer over here. You and them young'uns crawl back into that there gall berry patch and wait for Mrs. Norton to come git you in her wagon. Isaiah, you git on down there and let Mrs. Norton know. Francis, you stay out here in the middle of the road and if you hear them Injuns a'comin', run down the road as fast as you can to lead 'em away from yore Ma. If I don't come back in an hour or so you'll know they went the 'tuther way and you go on over to the Raulersons and tell them to meet me at the crossing. Isiah, you tell old man Norton to come with you. We'll probably need every hand we can git. I'll see you at the crossing. Susan, you have Mrs. Norton take you to my house and let Leah take care of you."

Susan was by his side, hand on his knee. "Please, Mose, I want to go to my house. I need to see Will. I need to know fer shore," she pleaded, grief on her face, begging pitifully.

Mose softened for just a moment. "Now gal, you know he's dead, y'know. No way he could be alive with that many Injuns all over him and him with no gun nor nothin' to fend them off. You ain't got no business a'seein a sight like that and you probably in the family way. You might mark yore child or have a idiot and thet'd be a double tragedy long 'bout now."

Susan looked at him, questioning him.

"Leah told me about the baby. Men gossip about those things too, you know. Now you go on and git some rest. We'll take care of things. Everything that has to be done will git done. Don't want you throwing the baby and gittin' down on us too at a time like that. Rhoda, you make shore yore Mama gits some rest when she gits to my house. She's got about as much business a 'runnin down this road toting little Andrew in this hot sun as a sow does with a side saddle." At that he called his dogs and was off down the road toward the homestead prepared to accept what ever greeted him at the milk shed.

He slipped to the edge of the clearing and tied his horse. Musket in hand, he walked cautiously into the open yard. There was no sign of the Indians. The door was ajar to the cabin and he could hear the rattle and tinkle of metal against metal. He slipped up onto the porch and paused, listening. Whatever it was, it was not interested in his presence. He pushed the door aside and startled the old mama dog, licking the empty iron pot that had contained the stew. Knowing she was not supposed to be in the house, she ran past Mose to the door too fast for him to hit her in the backsides as he swung his foot, just missing her tail tucked between her legs, tits swaying to and fro. The cabin was in disarray. The Indians had ransacked the place, taking what they could carry after eating Susan's stew. Mose noticed the torch Susan had place in the wall was out and even the coals from the fire had lost their glow. Mose began to curse as only Mose could do. "Godamnsorrysonsobitches!" He stomped out of the house. "Sorry sneaking basterds!"

By this time his dogs had discovered the fice bitch, abandoned by the Indians. She had played her part in the massacre by keeping the guard dogs from smelling the Indians. One of his hounds was hung to the bitch and there was the usual snarling and growling. He walked over to the nearest one and kicked him in the ribs.

"Git outa this yard, you basterds!" he yelled "and come behind." All but the one with the bitch ran out of the yard to where he had tied his horse.

"And git on your bellies and stay there!" They lay down beside the horse, head on their paws, looking at their master as he walked to the cowshed. He could see Will's feet sticking out from under the lot gate. The cows were still in their stanchions, their hind legs tied together and their calves lowing behind the pens. Will lay naked on his back in a pool of dried blood, eyes staring sightless up at the sky. He had been scalped, shot once in the gut and three arrows were sticking out of his pelvic area. His most private part had been amputated. Mose made no attempt to count the knife wounds. There were too many. Flies had already gathered on his body and it was just a matter of time before the buzzards would have gathered to him. Mose tried to pick him up but he was too heavy.

"Damned," he muttered, staring down at his brother and shaking his head. He closed his eyes and put his head in his hands for a moment. "Godamighty, Godamighty" he whispered. It was as close as he could come to a prayer.

He went back into the house to get the bed sheet that only hours ago Will had been contentedly snuggled under, warm and happy, talking of the new baby. The dogs were on their feet now, expecting a command to go but he yelled, "You know better! Git down you sonsabitches!"

He secured Will in the bed sheet and dragged him into the yard and up the steps pausing to catch his breath. He placed him on the bed and tried to lay him out but his arms were already stiffened and he gave up on an attempt to close his eyes. So he covered him with a sheet off the children's pallet and stood for a moment, hat off as he looked down at his brother's body and then around the room. There were wooden pegs instead of nails, hinges on the door made of hickory, and a dirt floor. The furniture was homemade and the mattresses stuffed with dried moss. He and Leah had started out like this but it was so long ago he had forgotten what it was like.

He looked back down at his beloved brother and said, "You worked like a dawg all yore life, Will and still as poor as motherless white owl shit. Jest cause you wouldn't take nothin' from anybody that weren't y'orn. I stoled the Injuns' cows to git where I've got and now you've paid fer hit in my place. Hit ain't fair. Hit just ain't fair." Something akin to guilt spread over Mose's body but turned into outrage and anger. "I'll kill them sorry basterds. Every sneaking, conniving one of 'em. And I'll take care o' Susan and the young'uns and love 'em like they wuz my own. I'll see yore boys git the start you never had. You got my word on hit, Will, right here fore you and God as my witness. They'll never want for nothin'. I promise." He put on his hat and went outside into the fresh air, latching the door as he left.

His dog was still attached to the bitch and he swore at her as he went over to the woodpile and picked up the axe. The bitch snarled at him as he approached the pair but his dog cowered and lowered his head in submission. He struck the female between the ears with the blunt end of the axe, knocking her unconscious. The male, now freed, ran out the gate toward the rest of the pack. Mose began stomping the bitch until he had stomped her head into the ground, repeating as he stomped "I ain't raisin no half-breed Injun pups even if they wuz from my best dawg. You wuz partly to blame for them a'killin' Will. Yore about as worthless as tits on a boar hog." He dragged her behind the cowshed and buried her body in a shallow grave.

He noticed the door was ajar to the smoke house. It was still full of hams but most of the dried beef jerky was gone from the rack. "Couldn't a'been too many of 'em or they'd a'cleaned Will out," he though out loud, as he took a string of smoked sausage down to stuff in his saddlebags.

"Come on, boys," he called affectionately to his pack of dogs as he rode to the edge of the scrub. The dogs sniffed around the buildings until one finally caught the Indians' scent and took off toward the St. Marys River.

— o —

After eating their fill of Susan's stew and anything else edible on the shelves, the Indians had wrapped knives, clothing and assorted eating utensils in the few linens she owned and tied the bundles to their waists. They had raided the smokehouse but most of the meat was too bulky for them to run with so they took only the small pieces of dried and smoked beef. It was a delicacy anyway. They could find wild boar and deer in parts of the swamp but no cattle ventured far into it. They struck out into the woods in a beeline for the crossing where they had hidden their boat, running single file. Easter was in the lead to start with, but the younger boys quickly overtook him and he let them lead the way. There was really no anxiety or need to run fast so they hit a comfortable stride. It wasn't so far to the river and young Indians could run twenty miles in a day. If expeditious, they could run very fast, like young deer, jumping small shrubs until the pain in their legs became severe and they would stop momentarily to cut a vein in their legs to release the pressure of the pooling blood. Indians were trained to stand pain since childhood so it wasn't the pain itself but a symptom that the blood was pooling and by releasing its pressure they would be able to run equally as fast the next day with little discomfort.

Easter had already decided that the woman and children would run into the woods until they could run no more and squat in the bushes like hunted animals. They probably didn't get far, he decided. White women are soft, he thought. And she had a young child to carry. He remembered when his own mother had been chased to the swamps by the soldiers when he was four or five, she could not keep up with the rest of the band so she dug a hole and buried him up to his neck so he would not wander away, leaving him until her return.

It would be hours before they could alarm the community. So, the young Indians ran mostly from the sheer joy that the killing had been successful and they were headed home. They needed this to release the tension that had been building for days.

But there was no joy in Easter. He still had a premonition that they would not live to get back to the swamp. We cannot win, he thought as he ran farther behind the young boys. There are too many of them and they just keep coming. But he was free for the moment and he knew he would never surrender. As he ran, he thought of his hero, Osceola, dying in prison in South Carolina, decapitated and his head hung on the bedposts to frighten naughty children. And Coachoochee, the Wildcat, who had escaped Osceola's fate by starving himself until he could crawl through a high window to freedom and continue the fight for another four years, only to finally have to surrender and be moved to a distant land.

They ran through the dewberries, blue toadflax flowers, crabapples and bamboo vines. They finally reached the crossing. The river was to its banks. As Easter had predicted, pieces of green branches surfaced and then disappeared in the swift moving stream. Once clear and placid, the water was dark, angry and foreboding. An occasional log floated past, switching ends, bobbing and turning quickly out of sight. The young bucks stood in silence, gazing down at the angry water, waiting for Easter to reach the river and then all eyes turned to him. He looked at the swirling water and then turned and smiled reassuringly at the puzzled boys. "I hope you tied the pickle very tight," he asked. They assured him nothing could pull it loose unless the tree came with it.

Easter laughed. "We will lie up as the deer. The water will quickly all flow into the sea and soon there will be little current. You are strong and able to pull against it then. We have food. Swim to the other side and scatter like young turkeys. Let the stream deposit you where it might and then we will meet here when the owls are crying and the deer come out to feed. The white man will never find the dugout." With that he raised his musket high over his head and swam with one hand, keeping the gun held high as he reached the other side.

—o—

Mose and his pack of dogs worked their way to the river. He took his time, careful not to miss a sign that one of the Indians had broken away and hid. Hatred for his prey now overshadowed his grief for his brother and he thought only of the task at hand, driven by revenge and the thrill of the hunt. He stayed well behind the pack of dogs, letting them find the trail. He noticed they did not run in a zigzag pattern as if trailing a wary prey, attempting to throw off the scent. His big brindled bulldog cur led the chase in a relatively straight line and the rest followed easily, pausing now and then to lift their hind leg on a bush or sniff out a rabbit that distracted them for a moment. Once they jumped a white tailed deer that was sleeping in a palmetto ledge at the edge of a cypress pond and it flagged across the flat woods. Two of the curs took out after him but only momentarily as Mose cracked his whip and quickly got them back to the business at hand. He smiled and congratulated himself, as he had figured from the start that the Indians would run in a straight line to the crossing. He had brought all the dogs though, just in case he had been wrong and they had decided to split up and scatter and then several men and dogs would be needed to hunt them down.

Francis, Isiah, old man Norton and Noah Raulerson were waiting at the crossing when he and the dogs arrived. The dogs ran quickly to the bank and sniffed about, realizing that their prey had gone into the swirling water, and looked to Mose for a command. Mose pulled up to the men and got down from his horse, saying nothing, so the dogs took a drink and lay down by his horse in the shade. Their horses were lazily standing on three legs, one hip cocked and then the other, changing legs as they stomped at the horseflies and deerflies that stung like angry bees.

"Been here long?" Noah answered. "We jest scouted around and saw where they'd gone into the water. Looks like maybe four or five of 'em to me."

14

"That's about the balance of 'em, I'd day," Mose agreed. "The dogs trailed 'em purty straight over here."

"Gonna put the dogs on the other side and see can they pick up the scent across the river?" asked Norton

"Has a hawg got a ass?" Mose asked indignantly. "Of course my dawgs can pick up their scent. That's what they been trained to do."

That or git kilt a tryin', Francis thought to himself. Mose took a minute and looked about as the rest of the crew sat and waited for his decision. It was his brother's killers and his dog—his hunt and he'd have the final say.

"I reckon not." Mose finally decided.

"Ain't we a gonna run 'em down and kill 'em, Uncle Mose?" Francis pleaded. Most felt sorry for the kid and didn't come back with some reprimand for disputing his word.

"Yeah, Pa," Isaiah suggested. "Wouldn't take us long. Not with our dawgs," he added, seeing a frown come on his father's face.

"Yeah," old man Norton put in again. "We could track 'em down an flush 'em out one at a time. Jest like killing deer." He hadn't had so much excitement in years and was eager to get on with it.

Noah sat still, chewing and spitting his tobacco. He waited for Mose to speak.

"I know you boys are eager to git them killers, especially you Francis. Ain't no man here any more eager'n me. 'Specially after seein' what they done to Will. But we sic the dogs on 'em and the first time they open on the scent them Injuns will figger what we're up to and head for the river like a bunch of otters. Dogs can't trail nor walk on water. We'd play hell gittin' mor'n a couple of 'em thataway and I want every son-of-a-bitchin' one of 'em, dead! That the way you figger hit, Noah?"

"Yep." Noah figured. And so it was settled.

Mose looked at the two young boys and said, "Isaiah, I want you and Francis to head on back to the house and tie Will's dogs and see did I let them cows out o' their stanchions. I can't 'member if I ever did or not and take care of what else around there needs taking care of. Don't you boys go in the house and disturb nothin'. I got Will laid out in there and I want him cleaned up and fixed up fore anyone else sees him. And I'll kick both yore asses 'til yore noses bleed if'n you don't do jest as I tell you. I don't want no argument outa you young fellers. You hear me?"

Both boys lowered their heads and nodded. They knew better than to open their mouths when Mose spoke this way even though both were dying to go to the ambush with the men.

"Let's git right back on our horses and make hit look like we was a goin' straight on back case some o' them basterds is watching."

They hadn't gone a mile before Francis said, "I'm a gittin' so hongry my stomach thinks my throat's been cut."

"Me too," Isaiah complained.

"You boys both have a holler leg. The food never hits bottom," said Noah laughing. "I member how hit wuz when I wuz their age. Don't really seem so long ago." He looked at the sun. "Hit is a gittin' on around there towards the shank o' the afternoon and I 'spect some o' you boys missed dinner."

"Yeah, yeah," said the boys in unison.

"Come to think on hit, probably ain't none o' us et since early mornin'," Mose said. "Lets git on around and git thet pond on them Injuns so's they can't see our smoke and cook us somethin' to eat."

They all began to pull food out of their saddlebags as Isaiah and Francis gathered wood for the fire. While the fire was burning down a little, they cut palmetto fans to put the food on so that each of them had his own "plate." The men got out their own little individual coffee boilers made from a precious tin can as each boiled his own coffee to his liking. Soon thick slices of bacon and sausage were cooking on a sharp green stick, stuck into the ground.

"Ain't nothin' like good old white bacon and taters," said Francis, as he smelled the bacon drippings sputtering on the coals. Ordinarily the men would "noon" after the meal in the middle of the day but they knew they had work to do and the sun was getting on around behind the ponds, so they could not partake of the usual custom of a siesta after the meal. The scraps were fed to the dogs and the men untied their horses.

"Here, Isaiah. You take my horse. Them dogs'll follow him. You boys git on around 'fore we take off and mind you do exactly as I told you. Tell your Ma's I'll git Mrs. Osteen to come over and lay Will out properlike. I'll be home around comin' o' day and if'n I ain't there, better come lookin' fer me and bring somebuddy with you. You boys head straight fer home soon as you check on Will's stock."

They left Norton holding the horses when they got to the Osteen's. Mrs. Osteen was cooking supper and asked them to stay and eat. They told her what had happened and she said she'd grab a bite and get on over to Will's before dark.

"Them pilferin' Injuns made a mess o' the place, Mrs. Osteen, but you don't pay that no never mind. I'll come over early in the mornin' and bring somebuddy to straighten things up. You got plenty to do and we need to get out the call. Mrs. Norton and some of the ones around our place has probably already got hit started, but I guess if you ain't heered over this away, we need to git goin'."

Mose was talking about the way the pioneers spread the news for help with the sick or dead. They would issue a special "call" that could be heard from one homestead to the other that alerted the community and then the exact news was quickly spread. A body had to be put into the ground in the summer time as decomposition began quickly and nobuddy wanted to miss a funeral.

"We orter be able to scratch up a preacher by noon tomorrer," Mr. Osteen volunteered.

Jim and Will Osteen lost no time in getting their guns and powder and shot and started out to the barn to saddle the horses.

"Who you got out there with you and Noahy?" asked Will. "Looks like old man Dewey Norton."

16

"Thet's him," said Noah.

"Hells bells," said Will, "He's so deef he ain't heard his own self fart in twenty year and he can't hit the broadside of a barn."

"Yeah," said Jim, laughing and shaking his head. "Bet he couldn't hit a bull in the ass with a banjo."

"Well," said Mose, "Any port in a storm. He wuz the nearest neighbor and we'd ask his wife to take Susan and the young'uns over to my place in their wagon. Least we could do wuz let him come along. I'll put him where he won't do no harm"

When the Osteen brothers were ready to ride they headed toward the river again.

"'Member thet smaller crossing we found the day me and you found the bee tree, Will?" Mose asked.

"Yeah," said Will. "Where we cut down thet big old gum tree. Got a couple o' buckets of the purtiest honey I ever saw. Yeller as gold. Sure was good eating."

Little more was said on the way to the river. When Mose had killing on his mind, he put it in that and nothing else and he knew the time was getting closer when he could draw a bead on his brother's killers. D.H. Lawrence once wrote, "The essential American soul is hard, isolate, stoic and a killer." And he had described Mose Barber to a tee. Mose never was one to hang back when he decided a man "needed killing."

As they neared the swamp, the country changed from oak hammocks to the flat woods. There were fewer cypress ponds and only sparse patches of low scrub oaks and oak runners. They stopped to water their horses about a mile from the crossing, tied them to some sturdy scrub oaks, untied their shot bags and powder horns, checked all their equipment twice and, satisfied every man was prepared to do his part, walked toward the crossing.

"Roosted a big bunch of turkeys in these tall cypresses where the river makes that bend down yonders," said Noah, "Kilt three big old Tom gobblers. I wonder if'en they's still using this side o' the river. Anybody seen ary sign around here lately?"

"Come to think on it, Noahy," said Dewy Norton, "I ain't seed no sign of a big bunch like that this side o' the river nowheres fer some time. I did see where a bunch dusted in the scrub this side of Mose's place a while back."

Mose, day dreaming of getting his brother's killers, came back to life and looked hard at old man Norton who still had a large family to feed. "What you doing hunting that close to my place, Norton. Can't you find nothin' to shoot over on yore side?"

"Tell you the truth, Mose," said Will Osteen, trying to smooth things over, "Game's gittin' scarce all over this country and people's still moving in. I fer one'll be glad when we can pull up and move farther south. Now with this Injun trouble gittin' stirred up again, I don't know."

"They tell me the game's so plentiful down farther south the turkey's will fly in and roost on the end of yore gun barrel and you a sitting on the blind–then shit on the barrel and you a holding the gun."

"Them Seminoles'll shit on you and rub it in after they done shot you, got yore scalp and took yore gun," said Noah, "I fer one am gonna give 'em a little more time to clear out."

As they neared the swampy area near the river, they walked past laurel oaks, sweet gum, black gum, bays, cypress and cabbage palms. They stopped under a big bald cypress and Jim Osteen pulled out a small canteen of shine and passed it around. Everyone took a swig but Mose. He never touched a drop of alcohol since his first drunk. He didn't like the feeling of not being steady on his feet and a clear head. He wanted to feel in control at all times and had refused a drink ever since. But he understood the men's need to relax a little before settling down in the crossing. Some men didn't enjoy killing Indians like he did and needed a stiff drink to bolster their courage. And some men didn't know when to quit drinking once they took the first drink, and Mose was one of those. He didn't want anyone to know he had no control over alcohol and would drink it until he was totally soused. So one drink was too many and a thousand not enough in his case. They chewed their last plug of tobacco. They didn't want to have to spit and have the tobacco juice float down stream to alert the Indians as they neared the crossing.

They entered an open place near the river where the swampy area looked as if it had been cleared by man. The water wasn't as deep and the run of the river narrowed. The bottom was hard, white sand. Game had used it for time eternity to cross the river to the other side and had dragged down the sandy banks and kept them clean of underbrush. Here the footing was sure and swift.

The sun was almost down and the moon was rising in the cast over Fernandina like a big yellow guava. The river had gone down dramatically and was almost back to its usual lazy flow. They had a wide-open view of the run of the river as it made a bend and disappeared into the big swamp a few miles up stream. It was a perfect place for an ambush. The Indians would have to slow their movement across the shallow, sandy bottom and would be concentrating on avoiding being stuck on a sandbar.

Mose positioned old man Norton and Will Osteen above the crossing. Will was an excellent shot and would cover anyone Norton missed. Noah Raulerson and Jim Osteen were below the crossing and Mose took the middle. They were all off center of the middle of the stream but well within range.

"Noahy, you and little Jim take the first two, I'll git the third, Norton, you and Will git the two at the end and we'll all reload and take out what's left. No need in us all a'shootin' the same man."

They soon settled down, muskets on ready. They had taken their powder horns off their shoulders, shook a measure of powder down the muzzle of their gun. From their shot bags, they pulled a twist of dried black moss and stuck it down the muzzle on top of the shot, packing it down tight with their rod. When ready to fire they would drop in a cap they had kept ready in their mouth. It would be wet and stick to the dry powder. Then all they had to do was pull back the hammer and pray the musket would fire. In order to shoot again this procedure had to be repeated as rapidly as possible and it took quick reflexes and years of practice to become an expert at reloading.

An hour passed as they waited patiently. As darkness came, so came the mosquitoes out with a vengeance. Soon they were biting their hands and the sides of their faces and had to be brushed off as silently and with the least movement as possible. They pulled their hats down as tightly as they could to cover their foreheads and still be able to see or hear. They were beginning to feel the need to stand up and stretch and were wondering what had happened to their victims when they heard the sound of movement down stream. Pulses quickened as hearts began to beat faster. The adrenalin was flowing and they were alert and ready for the job they had waited so patiently to finish.

The five Indians were talking softly to each other, relaxed, as they poled the last few miles to the swamp, against the slow moving current. They were almost home, free. Even Easter, sitting in the back of the dugout, using a paddle to steer the canoe, had begun to relax a bit. Everything had gone so well and perhaps he had been wrong and they would make it back after all.

As they entered the shallow crossing and were all pushing diligently to stay clear of the sandy bottom, Mose stood up as the rest followed his signal and all fired as planned. The Indians recognized the glint of light as the moon shined on the metal of the musket barrels but were too late to react as they felt the shot enter their bodies. Easter, in the back had been Norton's target and was only nicked in the shoulder. He stood up, gun in hand to find a shadow or some kind of target in the darkness, but Mose and Noah had already reloaded and before the leader recognized the outline of a man, he felt the shot go deep in his chest and thought briefly of the flitting firefly as he saw the flash of Mose's gun. His life flickered out like the little shadow that runs across the grass, losing itself at sunset.

Chapter 3

In the first of many graves of what is now Macedonia Cemetery, they buried William Barber the next day at Creole Ridge. Most of the Barber Clan and many of his neighbors were there. The "call" had gone out the minute Mrs. Norton had heard the news and quickly the surrounding community had responded. Present were the Osteens, Raulersons, Albrittons, Thigpins, Hughey and Dan Norton, Asa Wilkinson, John Canady and all the allied families. The four Williams brothers, H.H., John, Roland and William, had come in the night to relieve Mrs. Osteen and "sit up" with the body. Mrs. Osteen had bathed the mutilated body as well as she could and covered him again with a sheet, cleaned the cabin and waited for one of the men to bring clean clothes to dress him. His head was propped slightly so his hat could cover his bare scalp and Mose reassured the rest of the family he looked "purty good," remembering the sight that awaited him the day before out in the cowshed.

William's three oldest sons, Francis, Champion and Samuel, ages twelve, thirteen and fourteen, and Isiah, who was Champion's age, Mose and his brother Sam, were the six pallbearers. Elizabeth Thompson, who had been widowed by the Indians five years before and left with four small children, tried to sing "Shall We Gather at the River," but broke down and Abner Sweat's father had to finish, alone, with the fiddle. The preacher, new to the settlement, droned on and on in his attempt to save all the unclaimed souls present. It was seldom he got the opportunity to speak to such a large congregation of "sinners." Now, Mose, who liked church and never missed an opportunity to attend, especially when there was a "sing and a dinner on the grounds," listened patiently to the plea for salvation and the threat of eternal damnation in hell-fire, but after forty-five minutes of repeated ranting and raving on the subject, he tried to catch the preacher's eye, the spittle drooling out the sides of his mouth and his Bible raised high in his hand as his clenched fist pounded the air, shaking with spiritual fever, oblivious to Mose or poor Susan who was white and ready to faint. They were all tired and many had missed sleeping at all the night before. Mose walked to his side, held his hand up in front of the preacher's face and asked Elizabeth Thompson, now fully composed and just as ready as the rest of the congregation to get on with it, to sing. This time she rendered a beautiful solo of "When They Ring Them Golden Bells." The preacher, a little more subdued, did his usual thing with the crumbled petals of a rose. "Ashes to ashes and dust to dust," and before he could take off again with the closing prayer on another sermon, Mose asked his brother Sam to say a prayer, which was short and to the point and then took the shovel and threw in the first shovel of dirt on the casket. The rest of the men followed suit and soon a mound of earth was packed firmly over the grave. Then the women and children filed past, placing small bouquets and sprays of homegrown and wild flowers on the grave of damp, dark soil.

There were the usual hand shakes and hugs and crying and then Francis and

Champion assisted their mother to a chair beneath the mulberry tree in the front yard as the women began to spread the table for a late dinner. Mose again took control and said the blessing, lest the preacher get turned loose with an excuse for another attempt at saving souls. The crowd grabbed their plates and dug in. The talk turned to Indians. Mrs. Osteen had lost a brother back in 1839 about two miles east of Alligator (near present Lake City). Mose knew this killing was a different type but held his tongue.

"I wuz right thar," she said. "I happened to be visiting and helping wash and stack taters. Me and Orie and the young'uns run to the Mizells. Little James got an arrer in his shoulder. Ain't healed good yet. Simon Dell, you know the one wuz arrested for selling shine to the soljurs? Well, he wuz a'helpin' James out at the barn. He run to the house to look for a gun and couldn't find hit hid 'hind the door so he stuck a broom handle out the winder and them Injuns thought hit wuz a gun and run into the woods fer kivver. By the time they sneaked back he'd found the gun and got off a shot, but one got him in the chest with his arrer."

"Yeah," put in Mr. Osteen, not to be upstaged in the story telling. "He eventually got alright."

"Hell, Pa," said Will Osteen "He'd drunk so much o' his own shine his liver had done burned into a rock and when that arrer struck hit, hit broke off and didn't go no further."

Everyone enjoyed a hearty laugh. It helped break the tension. As the talk flowed on, Mrs. Osteen went on with the story, glaring at her husband who had interrupted her tale.

"They left James's place and went to Asa Robert's about a quarter down the road but Asa had heered the commotion and run over to his brother Zachariah's place. The Injuns set far to the place. Burned barn and all and stole Asa's only horse. The whole family pulled up stakes and high tailed it back to Georgia, on foot."

Mr. Osteen, insulted now that his wife would take the limelight from him, got into high gear and wouldn't be stopped. "Back in November of 'thirty-eight, that same year, they's a Tippons family from Jacksonville got purty near wiped out over near Ocean Pond. Other side o' the lake from Olustee. They wuz a'comin' to visit them Mizells. Old man David Mizell wuz her pa. About seven o' them Mikasukee Injuns slipped around and hit 'em jest as they got to the clearing, in sight o' the house. Shot John Tippons of'en his horse, dead as a doornail 'fore he hit the ground. Then took their tommyhawks and split Nancy Tippons's head open and two o' the young'uns. Old man Dave and the rest of the family wuz a'watchin' hit all from the house. Said old Tiger Tail hisself threw the youngest gal, Cornelia, up in the air and wuz gonna knife her. She laughed at him up thar and hit scairt him, so he drapped her on the ground. Musta thought she wuz daft in the head or sumthin'. They's scairt o' crazy people, you know. Didn't touch a hair on her head."

Mose remembered the incident. He had gone over to the Mizells to give his condolences and thought he had received a rather cool reception. Mose had always felt inferior to the Mizell family, socially, and felt they all considered themselves just a little better than the rest of the settlers. The Mizells had been a wealthy clan back in North Carolina and though the wealth had dwindled away through the years, they had retained the "old family" culture and Mose had always felt beneath them with their "high falutin' ways," and rightfully so. This was one thing that drove Mose to attain wealth and a certain social position in the community. That and the fact that his wife, Maria Leah, was better educated and socially more refined and culturally above him as well.

After the meal the women folk cleared the table and Susan was put to bed for a nap. The men gathered at the barn and most of them, Mose being an exception along with the preacher, partook from a jug of Will's homemade moonshine and rehashed the Indian hunt for the benefit of those who had failed to hear the story and the remainder who enjoyed hearing it again, as its telling got better and better as the shine was passed about.

As the shade of night was falling, the neighbors packed up to go home or else stay over with some other neighbor rather than go home at night. Mose gathered up his family and then went into the cabin to tell Susan goodbye.

"I'll be back tomorrer and pick that cotton. I'll fix up a place out at the barn fer Nigger Rich to stay for a few days and help the boys. I promised Will right here on this very bed I'd take care o' you and these young'uns and I mean to do thet. I'm a' gonna build you a bigger house and git you all closer to me and Leah where we can look after you better. I don't want you a'worrying 'bout nothing. You hear?" The swagger had gone from his voice and for a rare moment, he seemed truly contrite and earnest in his affection. Susan thought he seemed more like her Will than he ever had.

"I know you will Mose, I trust you to do jest that. I won't worry as long as I've got you and Leah to look after us. But me and the young'uns will do our part. You know that."

"I know," said Mose "I know," and he slipped out to his family and headed home in the moonlight.

He was bone weary and needed a good night's rest. He dropped the reins of his little cowpony and let him go, as he knew the way home. There were two wagons full. Leah with her house slave, Dulcie, her foster parents, the Davises, little one-year-old Betty, asleep in her arms. There was Nellie, almost a young lady, who held little George, and Isaac, who was seven, and Isiah, James Edward, little Mose, Margaret and Archibald. They were all like stair steps, one year apart, ranging in age from fourteen to one year. There had been four years between the last two and she thought she was through until Betty came along. She would have no more, she felt sure.

Mose felt himself dozing off as they made their way home. How the years have flown, he thought. He and his father, William, and three brothers had come to Florida almost ten years. Ago. Mose had been born near Augusta, Georgia not long after the turn of the century but his family had moved to Bryan County, Georgia, when he was a young boy. In 1814, Isiah Hart took the little settlement of Cow Ford on the

Atlantic coast and renamed it Jacksonville. Mose grew to emulate everything Jackson did. Jackson became a land speculator. Mose was determined to have lots of land himself—a plantation and his own slaves and lots of them; a beautiful wife he could be proud of, and take control of them as Jackson had his troops. When settlers were encouraged to move into north Florida after the Indians were run out during the first Seminole Indian War, Mose moved his family across the line, not realizing he and his family, like many other settlers, were urged to do so to create a buffer between the Indians and the wealthy plantation owners over in Georgia. In the spring of thirty-three, they formed a wagon train of ox-drawn wagons and carts and made their way down through south Georgia to Traders' Hill east of the Okeefenokee. From there, they followed the natural highway between the swamp and the St. Marys River that made a bend and turned north before it flowed to the ocean. When they crossed the St. Marys they found a natural spring and above it on a hill where it was dry, they had built a cabin. It was only a one-room with a dirt floor similar to Susan's. It had only one door with loop holes on each side of the door so they could stick their guns out and fire at the attacking Indians should they wander up that far.

At first, Leah was petrified. She hated it. Mose had assured her all the Indians had been run out. She could scarcely take a trip to the outhouse in broad open daylight for fear an Indian was lurking behind every bush. Every creak of the shutters at night or the crackle of the fire made her jump nearly out of her skin. But she began to relax as she helped fight and repel each Indian raid and soon lost her fear of the wilderness. Except for the panthers. The scream of the Florida panther is a hair-raising sound. Thought to be aggressive, fearful takes were handed down about them and if anyone wanted to keep a child's attention after supper, all he had to do was start one of these tales and he'd have to walk with the entire family outside with a lighted torch for them to take care of their nightly trip outside or else they'd wet the bed. The favorite one was about an isolated pioneer woman whose husband was away from home. A panther climbed on the roof and started scratching, trying to claw its way in for food so she had to build a fire and burn all the furniture to keep the cat from coming down the chimney and eat them all. There were many versions of this that hardly a household of children had failed to hear at least one of them.

Mose and Leah had a baby and three small children just a year apart when they moved into Florida. Soon they built a larger house with a detached kitchen. The children climbed a ladder to sleep in a loft. The girls would get up first to help with breakfast while the men and boys dressed. A well was dug so they didn't have to carry water from what was soon to be called Dick White Branch that ran into Big Creek. Trees were cut and stumps pulled out with oxen. A tree too large to cut was girdled. A circle was cut around the trunk, removing the life-giving bark and it was left to die and then later burned. Mose turned his cattle free to roam, as there were no fences except around the homestead and crops to keep the cattle out.

There was a large Indian attack and a brother killed, so William moved farther east into Nassau County and Mose built a stockade around his homestead. It consisted of a barnand a cowshed with several pens. Mose raised corn, sweet potatoes and cowpeas to round out a diet of beef, pork and wild game. He protected his fields with rail fences. They were "horse high, built strong and pig tight." The first ones were worm-laid. The rails were laid on the ground, end to end at angles with alternating lengths six to eight feet long and then ten feet long, then rails placed on top of them until the fence was the desired height. Where the rails lapped, they were propped with poles on both sides and a stake driven on either side about half way on the bottom to keep them from falling down. But Mose found the bottom rails would soon rot on the damp ground and he changed his pattern and built them with a sturdy post and rider.

The women had a garden in the back of the house and had their flowers and vegetables for the table but they did not work in the fields in the "money" crops, as women of quality did not do field work unless they were widows or spinsters. It was considered a damning indictment of their husband's laziness or mismanagement to see a woman helping in the field as long as she had many children and a home and husband to care for.

Leah at first had to card and spin and weave and make all the children's clothes, cook and tend the fire, watch the children, milk the cows, scrub the clothes and floors and a multitude of other chores from daylight 'til dark. And she took time out to have a baby every year. Mose made the children's shoes at night after having spent his day plowing, planting, mending fences and working cattle. Sometimes he came home so late at night she would have to hold a torch so he could tend the stock at the barn. Once she got burned on top of her foot where the hot rosin dripped on it and it became infected.

Relief came only when the children got old enough to help and the Davises came down from Savannah and brought a couple of slaves. Then the house was enlarged again.

The children didn't attend school but were taught at home. Leah and Mrs. Davis taught them to read and write and Mr. Davis their numbers.

Deer and bear meat were the primary sources of protein until Mose stole and raised enough cattle to supply the family with beef. At first there seemed no end to game and Mose used a deer hunt with brothers Sam and Will, as an excuse to get away from home.

The boys were not taught to build a fire, ride a horse, kill or skin a deer or a multitude of manly chores. They simply absorbed the knowledge of doing these things by watching them done by adults. It was a gradual learning process that naturally followed growing up in an environment such as existed in the backwoods and was not considered "work," which has grown to be a dirty word with many children today. Then it was known as living or surviving. It was just a way of life and accepted as what a child did, along with the rest of the family. An accomplishment to take pride in and a badge of having "growed up."

When they got big enough, they went with Mose and learned to shoot, trap and rid the clearing of varmints. Possums and foxes got the chickens; bears got the cattle, hogs and sheep. They got the varmints, skinned them and sold the hides and got even.

Discipline was rigid. "Old Ring" was the barnyard dog that whipped and controlled the other dogs and got to lay beneath the family wagon in the shade. Mose reminded the family that he was "Old Ring under the wagon" and no one was to question his authority, even Leah.

Life went on. Once a pack of hungry wolves followed them home one night and Mose, unable to shoot them all, pulled up to the smokehouse and fed them all the hams available so the family could make their way into the house. Once he found a calf buried in the scrub and a big yellow panther standing guard over it. But when it growled at him, he stomped his foot and yelled, "Scat your cat!" And it turned and ran away. Once Mose got an arrow in his shoulder when hunting strays, too far from home.

One of the worst things to happen was a freeze on a Sunday in February 1835, when the temperature got down to seven degrees and century old orange groves got wiped out. In 1840, Mandarin oranges, planted from Chinese orange seeds from New York, were struck by blight, and Mose topped them in an effort to save them, but all died.

The community grew.

A preacher started coming once a month. There were "sings" and an occasional "camp meeting." Soon there was a school and in the spring and fall, all men were "warned out" for six days to work the roads so they could remain passable.

In hard times, they ate mostly corn. It fed the livestock, made cornbread, hoe cake, mush and moonshine. Any left over was shucked and put into a corncrib to be shelled as used.

They made their own tools, built their houses, barns and outbuildings from wood cut and sawed from the land. They raised their food, made clothes from vegetable fibers and sheep they grew and raised and doctored themselves and their neighbors when they grew sick. It was a hard life.

Lately a stage service had been operated by James Harris. It ran from Garey's Ferry at Middleburg on Black Creek, called Big Creek back then. It went through Barbers' Bay, by Barber's Station where Mose operated an inn of sorts. It soon became the first postal service in the area and Leah's foster father acted as postal clerk.

Soon Mose was making money and felt like he was at last getting somewhere.

Mose dozed as his horse followed the wagons to the barn. He began to build on his dream. No telling how many cows the Indians left running loose and unbranded down south of the Withlacoochee, he thought. He thought of all the wide open grasslands down around Central Florida he had heard of from the soldiers that had fought down there in the Indian War that was dragging to a close. I've got to git down there and start branding them before the Raulersons, Osteens, Canadys and Albrittons git down there, he thought. There's no end of what a man can do if he's got a mind to do hit. The average Florida Cracker was thought to lack drive and like nothing else but the comfort of home and kin, but Mose and a few like him were forever looking for greener pastures and home was just a place to hang his hat. "Why hit won't be long until I'm as rich as six foot up a dun bull's ass and then I can tell them Mizell's to kiss mine any day of the week."

Chapter 4

Though Mose knew a lot about the lay of the land to the south he knew little of the history of this wild land called Florida. He knew it had been named by Ponce de Leon, but that was about all.

When Ponce de Leon landed at the mouth of the St. Johns River in search of the fountain of youth and gold, he found only death instead. He had arrived during Pascua Florida, the Spaniards' Easter Festival of Flowers.

Mose didn't know it but white men had been in Florida for three hundred years before he and his family had come, but there had been little change in its interior except for the northern border in all that time. The English knew it as Carolina, charted just below St. Augustine. The French called it Louisiana, and the Spaniards, who owned it the longest, called it Florida, so that was what it came to be called. All three nations had scrambled for it for control of the Gulf of Mexico, but for all but twenty years of the three hundred, it had belonged, in the most part, to Spain. As it turned out, she claimed to control it, but in actuality, controlled very little of it except her seaports. After her initial exploration and failure to find gold, she settled along the coastline and let the Indians have the interior with the swamps, mosquitoes, snakes and alligators. She never attempted to settle it but merely contained it. She developed St. Augustine because France had established Port Royal nearby, and she occupied Pensacola because France was beginning to put plantations in Louisiana. With the Indians in north Florida she could contain the English in Georgia. But she could not control the Indians, only try to pacify them.

The Seminole Indians that had been in Florida when Mose came were not the ones that greeted the Spaniards. The Seminoles came much later and drifted down from Georgia in several waves of invasion years later. By the seventeen hundreds, the aboriginal tribes that were here when the Spaniards came — the fierce Calusa, Ais and less belligerent Timucua, Apalachees and Yustegas — had begun to die out from wars among themselves and with the Spaniards but especially from diseases brought in by the white man. Many were sent to England or the Carolinas during the Queen Ann's war as slaves or prisoners. There came to be a particular void near the northeast border where the Timucua had ranged from the Atlantic Ocean to the Aucilla River and where the Yuestegas lived near the Suwannee. This void threatened to let the English in.

To the north were the five civilized Indian tribes. The Cherokees in the mountains of North Carolina and Tennessee and the Creeks in East Georgia, along with the Muscogees. The Muscogees were also in Alabama and western Georgia and the Choctaws from The Tombigee River to the Mississippi and the Chickasaws west of them. Their cultural advancement set them apart from the plains Indians who were mostly hunters and warriors that wandered from place to place. These eastern Indians farmed the land, had their own alphabet, printing presses, log houses and a democratic government. They were, perhaps, too democratic as they could not hold themselves together. The chiefs did not rule but were there to advise and persuade. They were happy people, contented with their lives. And then the English came.

With them came the traders. The French came too, but the English, especially the Scots, proved better traders. They had a cheaper supply of goods and more freedom from government control. They began to make life more comfortable for the Indians. They married their squaws and had half-breed children that were better educated and made excellent chiefs with strong ambitions, when they were loyal to their mothers' people, which most were. But along with the conveniences, supplied by the traders, came changes in the Indians' life style. Deer began to disappear after the exportation of thousands of deerskins for leather. The Indians began to rely more and more on the English and the English exploited them because of their childish and trusting nature. The Indian chiefs loved pomp and ceremony and the English made them "Emperors," giving them presents, medals and recognition and all the time grabbing their land and kept pushing steadily westward through treaty after treaty.

Certain factions sprang up among the Indians that resented the chiefs giving up their lands. Customs dictated two kinds of chiefs–those who made war and those who governed in time of peace. When the war chiefs were called upon to go to war they would estimate how many warriors they needed, gather red sticks for that amount needed and each eager warrior would file into the chief's tent and take a stick until they were all gone and then the army had been selected. So the faction opposing the encroachment of the white man came to be called the Red Sticks and the ones who tried to live in peace and let the settlers keep acquiring land were known as the White Sticks.

As the Spaniards noticed the ever-increasing void left by the vanishing aboriginal Indians at Florida's northern boundary, they took advantage of the division and unrest among the tribes in the southern states and sent Diego Pena into Georgia and North Carolina to urge the Red Sticks to break away and settle that section of Florida. The Indians that moved down south to Spanish territory were soon known as "wanderers," or *Siminolies*, by their Creek and Cherokee brothers. The white man soon began to call them Seminoles.

In 1763 when England captured Havana and exchanged it to Spain for Florida, many of these Seminoles went to Spain. Those who stayed held fiercely to the land.

For twenty years, England held Florida and during that time it developed in the interior more than it had during the two hundred years Spain controlled it. In 1767, Andrew Turnbull settled New Smyrna with over one thousand Greeks, Italians and Minorcans. The British built large plantations and welcomed any English-speaking settlers across her borders. The Seminoles began to resent the white man again as he encroached into Florida.

When, after much vacillation on the part of the Creek Nation, they sided with

28

England during the Revolutionary War, and when England lost the war to the Americans and pulled up stakes and went to the British Isles, many Indians felt betrayed and abandoned and feared the new Americans. When an element of Creeks surrendered the lands of North Georgia as far as the Oconee River to appease the new Americans, many more Indians came down into Florida, especially when England turned it back to Spain for her help in the revolt. Many of these were land loving, militant Seminoles, led by the peculiarly talented half and quarter breed chiefs and sub-chiefs.

So again Spain held the coast and let the Indians have the interior. But as the plantations, built by the British, began to grow into weeds and many times were taken over by buccaneers, Spain began to encourage the Americans to come in and settle the land around the plantations rather than lose them to the weeds and the Indians.

Of course, there were certain conditions. The land grants by the Spaniards were under strict control of Spain. Fifty acres were granted to the settler with an additional twenty acres for each additional family member and slave. They also had to agree to baptize their children into the Catholic faith and abide by its rules and swear allegiance to the King of Spain. Many of these independent settlers took the faith with a grain of salt and swore allegiance to no man.

Unrest grew between the American and the Seminoles, but for a while, there seemed to be plenty of room to go around. But again, during the War of 1812 when the ever-appeasing White Sticks sided with Andrew Jackson, over ten thousand additional Indians fled in anger to Spanish Florida. At the Battle of Horseshoe Bend, Andrew Jackson beat the Creeks and their lands were ceded to Georgia. An additional five hundred headed for Florida. Spain now had over fifteen thousand militant warriors to control her northern boundaries. The most militant of these were the Mikasukees. Spain once again tried to control the advancement of white settlers into her land.

The first Seminole Indian War started in 1816 and lasted two years. Colonel Daniel Newman of the Georgia Volunteers tried his hand at flushing the Seminoles off the Florida-Georgia line but the guerilla warfare of the Indians proved too much for the recruits and the soldiers' uniforms of sky blue wool proved too hot for the Florida climate. However, most of the Indians finally fled east of the Suwannee River and the war died down.

The Indians kept saying they wanted no more than to live in peace with the white man. They believed the land belonged to no man and was for man's use as long as he lived on earth and no longer. Their main prayer was that they would not succumb to the white man's manners, laws and power and many felt they were superior in many ways to the new breed of Americans.

Actually, the land and cultural differences were not the main source of contention. In 1802, the United States had passed a law that no more slaves could be imported into the country. Therefore, slaves became a valuable commodity. For years, slaves had run away from the plantations across the border and fled to safety to the Seminoles in Spanish Florida. They were taken into a form of slavery by the Indians but were called maroons and given a sharecropper status. All they really had to do was repay the Indians with a certain amount of their crops and they could live in peace. Many had superior knowledge of farming and could speak the English language. Indians soon began to marry the women and these half-breeds became Seminoles. The influential plantation owners kept pressuring the government to return their slaves.

By 1812, the settlers, now firmly planted in northern Florida, granted themselves self-rule with a little help from General Andrew Jackson. Jackson hated the English, Spanish and especially the Scotch traders who had married the Indian women and raised the militant Indian chiefs. Above all, he hated the Indians and the Seminoles hated the white men, having lived in peace in Florida outside the control of Spain for so many years.

In 1819 when we supposedly bought Florida from Spain for five million dollars, no money ever exchanged hands as the property owners claimed they had incurred damages equal to that much during the time between 1812 and when we actually were to pay for it in 1821. This all because of the terrible Seminole Indian War that was to come.

In 1830 now President Andrew Jackson was instrumental in the passage of the Indian Removal Act, giving the Indians three years to sell out and move to reservations set aside out in the West. Davy Crockett, who had fought the Indians but lived among them, was the only delegate from Tennessee to vote against this act. About half the Indians, now tired of being pushed about, gave in and agreed to sell out and leave, if they could take their cattle and slaves with them. After a visit to the western lands to check out the living conditions, many of the chiefs balked at the removal and the treaties went nowhere.

With Jackson's help, the Georgia Legislature passed laws confiscating Indian land, nullifying Indian laws and prohibited them from assembly. When the Supreme Court declared the Georgia law unconstitutional, Jackson said, "If that's their decision, then let them enforce it" and defied their ruling and continued removing the Indians. Of course, it was the large plantation owners who were behind it all in order to regain their slaves.

Perhaps things would have worked out had it not been for Osceola. He had been born William Powell in the Chattahoochee area about the same time as Mose. He got his Indian name from a combination of the black sacred drink "asse" and holy chant the warriors gave as it was consumed during the Green Corn Dance, or Bosketan, in the spring. Billy Powell passed the drink made from the Yaupon or holly tree. Rich in caffeine, it acted as a mild diuretic, laxative and emetic. The Indians used it to empty their stomachs, believing they could think better on an empty stomach. As they drank it they would chant the holy chant, "o-ha-la, o-ha-la" hence the combined name "asse-o-ha-la" or "Crier of the black drink."

Osceola was tall, light skinned and 90 per cent white. He loved to dance and was very good at sports. He had come to Florida in the second wave of Red Sticks after the War of 1812 with his mother who was the granddaughter of James McQueen, a Scottish trader and a Creek woman. Polly Coplinger, as she was called, was a Muscogee by birth and had been married twice; first to an Indian and then to William Powell. Osceola swore he was the son of the Indian and claimed to be full of Indian by birth but his light skin gave him away.

As a youth, he hung around Fort King, or Ocala as it was to become, and was considered to be intelligent, cooperative and courteous by his friend, the Indian Agent Wiley Thompson. But as time went on, Osceola felt the agent did nothing to further the Indians' cause and began to call him a "government agent" instead. As Billy Powell, *nee* Osceola, became more and more belligerent and caused dissension by urging the other Indians not to go west, he was thrown into jail until he agreed to behave himself. Osceola never forgave the Indian agent for the humiliation of having been put in irons. While appearing to have settled down, he worked secretly against the government in the removal.

In 1835, Chief Charley Emanthla sold his cattle and was preparing to go with the others. Osceola waylaid him, killed him and scattered his money on the ground, leaving the chief's body for the buzzards. In December of the same year, he ambushed Thompson and a Lieutenant Smith taking a stroll outside the fort, cut off Thompson's head and took it to Green swamp. That same day, Major Francis Dade, eight officers and 100 men were also ambushed on a march from Fort Brooke (Tampa) to Fort King by Chiefs Micanopy, Jumper and Alligator and 180 warriors near Bushnell. Both attacks had been planned secretly for a year. All but three of the soldiers were killed and two of these were seriously wounded. The Second Seminole Indian War was on.

Mose and Leah had been in Florida a little over two years at this time. Although the war area was defined as that area from Black Creek near Jacksonville, on to Alligator and the Suwannee River, Mose's homestead was right on the fringe and many an Indian wandered up to their house. Mose and Leah would position themselves on each side of the door and repulse every attack. Leah proved to be a better shot than Mose and he threatened her within an inch of her life if she ever told.

The Indians were finally driven south into Green Swamp, nine hundred miles of trumpet creeper, leopard frogs, alligators, snakes and mosquitoes. It made the Everglades look like the Garden of Eden. From there they fought.

This was when the trek from Green Swamp to the Okefenokee began. Mose soon got tired of fighting the wayward Indians that wandered into his place from a little hole in the wall. He soon built the large stockade of logs around his homestead and enlarged his house into a double pen. This was done by merely building another room structure across from the original and connecting it with a passageway down the middle between the two. Then extending the passageway on out to the dining area and kitchen. This was similar to the so-called dogtrot houses, only the passageway was not opened to the outside. As his marksmanship increased, he soon began to be known as the man who ran the Indians out of the bend of the St. Marys River.

Details of the war would be another book. Forts sprang up that soon became some of the towns of today. Some of the well-known generals of the war went on to become leaders of one side or the other in the Civil War. General Jessup was making headway at becoming one of the most popular officers until he tricked Osceola and several other leaders into surrendering under a white flag of truce and was relieved of his command. Zachary Taylor had the dubious distinction of importing bloodhounds from Cuba at one hundred and fifty dollars a head to hunt down the Indians in the swamps. The problem of this brilliant strategy was that the dogs couldn't tell the difference between the Indians and the sweaty, unwashed skins of our gallant soldiers.

The unsung heroes were the militia of the Florida counties that fought off the Indians and were never paid for their trouble.

The Indians split into small groups and fought independently. The Indian women went to war with their men. They made camp in the dark, in the gloom of the swamps. They scavenged for food and taught their children to play in silence. They all went hungry. They fought, but could not win. They could not turn to their Creek brothers. Since their split, they had spoken different dialects and as they interbred with Negroes, their skins became darker and although they had basically the same culture, they became two entirely different races.

When Osceola was tricked into surrendering under a flag of truce, taken prisoner and jailed in St. Augustine, he was found to be suffering from malaria, tonsillitis and chronic debility. He died in 1838 in South Carolina. Some say he died of a broken heart.

The Wildcat, or Coachoochee, was taken with Osceola, but escaped from prison and carried the war on another four years. Unlike Osceola, who hated war, Coachoochee loved killing and looting. War excited him. A small man, bright, playful and attractive, swift as a deer, he carried out hit and run raids up and down the St. Johns River to as far south as Lake Okeechobee. He would hide and laugh at his enemy as they stumbled and fell in the mud.

But even the Wildcat's spirit was soon broken by the army. He was captured near the Kissimmee River, arrested and taken to Fort Pierce to be shipped by boat to Tampa in July 1841. As a young man he had bragged that his father had told him he was made of the sands of Florida and when buried the Seminoles would sing around his grave. He had often said he would rather be killed by the white man in the Florida swamps than go to die in Arkansas. But it was not to be. Colonel Worth threatened to hang him if he didn't send for the rest of his band and surrender them too. Worth reported that the proud Indian stood up and said, "When I was a boy I saw the white man afar off, and was told he was my enemy. I could not shoot him as I would a wolf or bear, yet he came upon me. My horses and fields he took from me but he said he was my friend. He gave me his hand in friendship; I took it, he had a snake in the other hand, his tongue was forked; he lied and stung me. I asked but for a small piece of land, enough to plant and live on far to the south. A spot where I could place the ashes of my kindred. A place where my wife and child could live. This was not granted me. I am about to leave Florida forever and have done nothing to disgrace it. It was my home. I loved it and to leave it is like burying my wife and child. I have thrown away my rifle and taken the hand of the white man and now I say, take care of me!"

As tears streamed down his face, he sent for his band to come in and surrender.

The war officially ended in 1842, shortly after William Barber was killed. General Worth reported to the War Department that 3,824 Indians had been shipped to the west and 300 more were in the Everglades. It was another Vietnam. In terms of money and lives, it was one of the costliest of any of the Indian wars. The estimated cost was $40 million. More than 1,500 military personnel, not including the volunteers and civilians, were killed. And the Seminoles never surrendered. There was only a cease-fire. And it would throw Florida into a depression.

Chapter 5

One of the first things Mose did after he got William's cotton in and settled in his slave, Rich, to help Susan at her place, was to take the boys camping out in the woods at various locations around the territory. This was not a pleasure trip as the boys would soon learn, and, no, their father and Uncle Mose had not taken leave of his senses as first suspected. There was a method in Mose's madness.

They went out for several days, built a fire and walked around it with abandon. Mose wore a pair of old Indian moccasins and the boys were told to pull off their boots and make lots of footprints. At one site, he dropped a wallet of corn, a broken arrow at another and left a piece of flint at a third.

Soon the word was out that there were more Indians in the country and they were probably getting ready to go on the warpath. His purpose was twofold. The local inhabitants would not venture far from home in order to protect their homesteads and the would-be settlers from out of state would stay put for the time being.

It didn't hurt also when the Jacksonville *Times* put out an article about William's murder, written by a correspondent from the New York *Herald*. It was dated June 8, 1941. It also appeared in the *Herald* on June 14 entitled "Florida Indian Troubles."

After about a week he called the boys in early one morning and announced they were leaving "on the dew" the next morning for a trip down south. Champ, Isiah and Francis were ecstatic. But the neighbors would soon be appalled at hearing he had left his family defenseless with a murdering pack of Indians in the territory. He told both Susan and Leah they had nothing to fear. "You can both shoot better than any man and you got a pack of dogs that won't let an Injun within a mile of this place." He had to tell Rich what was up as he balked at staying alone at Susan's to tend the stock and watch over the place while they were gone.

The whole family set to work getting things ready to go. They looked like an army of worker ants. The young boys didn't sleep a wink, much too excited to sleep. They were going on such a wild adventure! They had all three been helping cow hunt since they were big enough to sit a horse well, but had always had to help out around the camp and had not been allowed to go on the actual roundup. The next day, bright and early before the dew dried, the cowhands were on their way.

The word, cowboy, came from Revolutionary days and didn't look a thing like Mose and the boys. It applied to the armed Tories who tinkled cowbells to lure farmer-patriots, who had lost their cows, into the bush where they could be ambushed. The western cowboys were a far cry from the southern farmers as were the Florida cowboys. But the name stuck and was carried on down to Spanish Florida and applied to anyone who worked cattle there, as well, as it had also spread out west.

The woods of Florida were full of little Spanish cattle, first abandoned by the Spaniards and now the Indians. The Spaniards had been superb horsemen. Many of the cowboy terms had come from the Spanish language. The word, "dally," where they wrapped a rope around the saddle horn came from the word, *dar la vuelta,* or "to make the turn," as did the word "chaps" and many other terms.

The Cracker cowpony was of Spanish origin as well. Of course, many of the well-to-do planters around Tallahassee and Madison County had fancy Tennessee walking horses and trotters but for the most part, they could not endure the wild Florida terrain and the little Spanish horses had long been acclimated to the Florida climate. The horses were small, never over 800 pounds and most times less. Many times the primitive saddle had a rope girth and stirrup straps and the horse controlled by a rope bridle. Saddle sores were common. Add all the trappings they carried along with a fully-grown man and one wondered how they survived. Saddle pockets with two week's rations of cold biscuits, sweet potatoes, salt pork or smoked sausage, coffee, salt, and a coffee boiler. There was a rolled-up poncho of a four by six foot piece of wool or a cotton blanket for a bed roll and sometimes, but not always, a cover of *gutta percha* or oil cloth to keep his blanket dry from the damp ground at night and as a "slicker" in the day from the heavy Florida downpours. There was also a mosquito bar made of calico net and narrow sack full of corn for the poor creature, separated in the center and hanging down on both sides of his neck. An anchor rope was tied around his neck and rolled up and tied to the saddle and another rope rolled up for tying up dogs and yearlings also hanging from the saddle. Most of the time, though not in Mose's case, a jug of shine for "medicinal purposes" was tied on "somewhere." It's no wonder folks said the only thing tougher than a Florida cowboy was the horse he rode.

The Florida cracker cowboy looked much different from the Spanish nobleman that first punched cattle in Florida. He wore flat-heeled boots. High-heeled boots never came in until after the Civil War. That is, if he could afford boots. Many of the cowpunchers wore brogan shoes with no socks. If they hadn't been in the saddle for a while, they had to toughen up a blister on the anklebone for the first few weeks in the saddle. He never wore gloves, as did the Spanish dandies. He said it robbed him of his feel for the rope. His hat, often homemade of palmetto fans, protected him from low hanging branches, his face from flies and mosquitoes, while taking a lunch siesta, or "noon," as the crackers called it, he used it to fan the fire and dipped water and drank out of it. He even wore it indoors while eating or dancing. About the only time he took it off was for church or to sleep.

He didn't wear the Spanish rowel spurs, either. His were filed down to a gentle shaped rowel. The spur heel band fit over the back of the boot while the spur strap fastened across the instep. The heel chain not only kept the spur from riding up but if he was lucky enough to have a real chain, it jangled when the cowpoke strutted about the camp or in town. Like his hat, they came off only in church or in bed.

The shirt was homespun and the pants pretty well finished off any similarity to the gaudy Spaniard. They were generally of wool to ward-off, and quickly dry from, the frequent Florida showers — winter or summer.

So Mose and the young boys appeared as they headed south that summer morning to gather wild Florida cattle and put Mose's brand on them before the other settlers gathered courage to leave home and risk being scalped in the process. Only Mose, the boys and his slave, Rich, knew there was no imminent danger from the Indians. They could be careful, take their time and get the job done without opposition.

Wild Spanish cows roamed the woods along with deer, turkey, and bear. They were considered fair game like gold nuggets in the streams out west. There were plenty of cows without brands but if Mose saw one branded and it didn't belong to a friend, he wasn't above changing the brand, especially if it was a young heifer and had years of productivity ahead. Actually, branding cattle was considered a natural resource and everyone did it. The practice was to persist in Florida until the turn of the century when men began to fence their pastures. So Mose started building his cattle empire through this practice and it would also be the cause of its doom.

Mose used cow dogs to hunt the wild cattle that would run ahead of the men and horses and squat in the thickets and swamps. Mose would "sic" his dogs on them and run them out onto the hill of dry, open land so he could rope them. Sometimes he would drive them by whips and dogs into homemade cypress pole pens and in due time there would be a series of pens stretched across the Florida piney woods for anyone to use. If a bull was too wild or cantankerous to rope or drive, Mose would shoot him rather than let him run wild because he could influence the cattle and cause the entire herd to spook and run.

If there just happened to be one or two head or to save the often-tired dogs, one of the boys would elect to go in after them. Francis usually volunteered to go. The pineland bogs were a pasty soil, half sand and half mud over hardpan. Part resin and part watery mud that oozed under his horse's feet with a sucking sound as his horse stepped, beating out a rhythm. He loved its characteristic smell. It was part tang and part sweetness. The tangy smell came from the leaves of the bay trees and wax myrtles that were in full bloom in June and the sweetness from the legume flowers and the sweet shrubs that bloom under the pines. The woody, yellow St. Johns wort, white bay violets mixed with magnolia daisies and wild iris leaves, the pitcher plant and the yellow and sometimes purple butterworts.

Francis was not aware that it was what he saw and smelled that filled his soul with peace and a rush of sudden euphoria. He was a sensitive boy and would have been the last to try to share it with Mose or the other boys. He only knew that he felt rested and full of energy when he came out of the bogs.

The boys grew strong and proficient in their skills. Sometimes Mose would let them "head and heel" a cow; one roped the horns and the other caught the cow's two hind feet as they roped and dragged her down, stretching and holding her tight at each end while the third boy would sit on her, as Mose put on his mark or brand. In the pens, all three boys would simply run at the scrawny little cows, pull them to the ground and hold them while Mose did the marking and brand-ing.

It was a fun-filled trip and they spent hours telling and retelling their experi-ences to the family when they came back home for the Fourth of July. Of course, they had only touched the surface of vast pinelands to the south and as they became more skilled in their task, Mose planned to venture even further into the Florida wilderness.

But it was time for celebration and nobody missed a Fourth of July. Except for Christmas, it was the most festive time of the year.

For the past two years the three families, including brother Sam, had gone to Olustee to a big Fourth celebration on the edge of Ocean Pond for a fish fry and horse races and a frolic that generally lasted through the night. There were the usual political speeches and fistfights but mostly it was time to visit with friends they hadn't seen for months or maybe since the year before.

The third of July dawned hot and dry. Mose and the gang were well on their way on the Bellamy Road that ran from Jacksonville towards Alligator. Ocean Pond was on the way. Grandpa and Grandma Davis stayed home with Susan and little John, George, Nancy and Andrew Jackson. Susan wasn't feeling up to it and the heat was too much for the old people. They tried to bribe Isaac into staying, promising presents at Andrew Jackson's birthday party coming up, but there was so much crying and begging akin to a downright tantrum that he knew wouldn't be tolerated, that, after he promised to mind Nellie and Lydia and not "run wild" he was allowed to go.

The going was rough. There were numerous boggy swamps and ponds mixed with white sandy spots called sand soaks that could bog down a wagon more deeply than the wet areas. Sometimes the entire party would have to dismount and push the wagon out. But there were many strong backs and they were in a festive mood.

When they arrived, a fairly large crowd had already gathered on the lake's edge for the night and neighbors, living twenty and thirty miles away, visited old friends. Two of the local saloonkeepers, David Ridgeway and Jordan Swindle, had set up a makeshift bar and were selling whiskey by the drink. Leah asked Mose to try to unhitch the wagon as far from the "saloon" as possible.

Leah was dressed in a long, calico dress with tight sleeves, wide padded skirt that hid her feet and a high-necked bodice. Mose had on his black frock coat with imitation linen pants. Since this was the biggest public social event of the year, Mose was determined to look as prosperous and genteel as anyone else. On this, Leah and Mose agreed. Appearance mattered to them both. To Leah it came nat-ural. To Mose it was a façade that was hard to maintain. Leah had always made him feel inferior socially, or at least, unpolished. Publicly he was proud of her social graces and natural Spanish charm, but he belittled her in private and, worst of all, in front of the children. He never failed to remind her that she never even knew who her "pa was" and that if it hadn't been for John and Nancy Davis, who had become her foster parents, she'd probably have ended up in an orphanage "no telling where." And he was always reminding her that if he hadn't come along, "taken her to raise" and then took her folks in, they'd all be in the poor farm by now. Leah, in her infinite wisdom, understood Mose's need to be accepted as a gentleman and his drive to "be somebuddy." And she also understood that he loved her as deeply as he could ever know how to love another. He had just been abused as a child and never taught to love anyone as he grew up. And Mose was very proud of her in a large crowd such as had been assembled and quickly started visiting around to show her off. No one ever snubbed Maria Leah Alvarez Barber because they knew her charm and genteel manners were genuine and she wasn't just trying to "cut the lady" like so many other women.

Leah had been born in St. Augustine. The legality of her birth was in question. Her mother had lived and worked in the home of Don Geronimo Alvarez at 14 St. Francis Street, the house that many claim to be the oldest house in the United States. It had served the Spanish as a hospital for the friars in 1599. Geronimo Alvarez's mother had been Teresa Menendez, a direct descendant of Pedro Menendez Marquis, the Lieutenant Governor of Florida in 1570, Lieutenant Governor of Cuba in June of the same year and the Governor of Florida in March of 1577. He gained these titles from the King of Spain at the insistence of his Uncle, the Adlantado Pedro Menendez de Aviles who had no heirs. When the English took over Florida for that twenty years in 1763, the Menendez family "gave" the house to a Jessie Fish to hold in confidence until Spain could get back control. After Spain returned, the Don bought back the house, claiming it in the name of his mother as his birthright. His first and only wife, Antonio Venze, died after only ten years of marriage in1798, and in 1813 Ana Maria Dolores moved in as his "housekeeper." While living there, Ana Maria gave birth to a boy and a girl. Maria Leah was named Maria Leah Alvarez, but she was never told who her daddy really was. Maria Leah's mother died when she was ten and she was sent to Cuba to be tutored and whisked out of the home. It was there that the Davis couple, elderly and childless, found her and brought her back to Charleston. It was there that Mose met her and married her when she was sixteen.

She grew into a beautiful woman. She wore her straight dark hair in a bun at the nape of her neck. Even after years with Mose on the Florida frontier, she still had a regal bearing and the birth of nine children had not ruined her figure. Her skin was milk white and she guarded it from the Florida sun with a hat and gloves and long sleeved dresses. Her eyes were large and soft as a doe deer but sparkled with mischief and she found humor in everything. At their first meeting she laughed so much Mose thought her shallow and foolish, but quickly learned she was extremely intelligent and her emotions ran deep. He loved her but was jealous of her superior ways, nevertheless, and was constantly "putting her down." Not only because of her Spanish nobility and her tutoring in Cuba, but the Davises were also gentility from Virginia. Maria never picked up the Georgia and Carolina Elizabethan English so prevalent in the settlers from the mountains and lowlands of these southern states. She was constantly striving to polish Mose and keep her children from becoming "Crackers," but it was a losing battle. Mose considered her his possession as he did his children and horses and dogs and when asked, sometimes in true amazement, from strangers where on earth he got such a beautiful and polished wife and especially how he kept her, he would reply, "Jest keep her pregnant and barefoot and don't give her a goddamn thing."

The Fourth got off the next day with a bang. The day was hot and humid. Children played in the shallows of the lake in the brackish waters. Some built little miniature towns of wet sand. Green twigs became trees, and streets were laid out by small fingers making wagon ruts in the sand. A few of the more active children caught minnows in the cup of their hands and transported them to small water-filled depressions along the beach of the lake and then dug canals with their big toe to let them swim back to the lake, watching their frantic flight as they swam to safety. After lunch most, tired from playing and visiting, were put down for a nap so they could stay up late for the dancing. After a long "noon," people began to drift by and Mose and his large family stayed put as friends strolled by to visit. The Mizell family came by making the rounds. First came David Sr. He had known Mose's family up in Georgia and Mose had a great deal of respect for the old man. It was David Jr. he didn't care for. There had been several disagreements up in Georgia and down in Florida over cattle. David Jr. was a stern disciplinarian and as strong-willed as Mose. But David Jr. had been "raised" and not "jerked up by the hair of his head," as had Mose, as the saying went. Mose resented his "high handed" ways. He made Mose feel inferior and David knew it. David Mizell was particular about his children, who they associated with and their education came first. He stressed manners and deportment above all else. Leah valued these things too, but Mose, in his effort to control her, had subconsciously gone the opposite way. He stressed obedience and hard work and now with her nine and all of Susan's children, she just gave up. She found little time for lecturing on the social graces and the children more or less ran wild.

Mose was on his good behavior, "bowing and scraping" and politely passed the time of day with the Mizells. David Jr. and his wife, Mary, stayed a little longer to visit as the children became acquainted, eyeing each other from a distance. But David stood with two-year old John Randolph in his arms while the other four children waited politely at their parents' side. They watched, wild-eyed, at the antics of Mose's gang as they ran and played back and forth. Finally, David William Mizell smiled at little Mose and Edward and little Will and asked if he could play mumbly peg. "Please, may I, mother?" he begged Mary.

She looked at her husband and he nodded a stern affirmative but minded the young boy not to get dirty. "It's almost time for the speeches and you mind your manners." Mary eyed Isiah and Arch as they tripped Sammy and jumped playfully over him, rolling about the ground like three playful puppies. Mary stood in awe of so much unleashed energy and wondered how the poor woman could cope.

"Surely these aren't all yours?" she asked Leah.

Leah sat demurely with little Betty on her lap, seemingly composed and not the least disturbed by it all.

"Oh no, they aren't all mine. I only have nine. Some of these are my husband's brother's children. He was killed last month by the Indians, you know, and his wife, Susan, is expecting another child and in mourning as well. We brought them along. We will be raising them as our own anyway. We now have seventeen in all. We left some at home."

"Oh, my word" was all Mary could say. "Oh, my word!" The thought of so many children under one roof made her speechless. "Where do you manage to put them all?" she finally asked.

"Oh, we don't live in the same house, or at least not for long. We're building a home next to us for Susan and her family. We hope to have it finished by the time the baby comes. She just stays with me when Mose is away from home."

Mose quickly jumped into the conversation lest Dave Mizell started asking a lot of questions as to where Mose had been going. "I understand you've moved your family on down south a ways?"

"Yes, father wanted to move down to Micanopy below Hogtown. I wanted to go on to Palatka, but we think it wise to stay north of there for a while. I understand even though the war has been declared officially over, Indians are still about and we don't want to take a chance with the family. There is such an undesirable element moving into this territory, away from the large plantations, that we wanted to get the children in a better environment."

Mose stiffened, wondering if he considered him as part of the undesirables. Probably so, he thought. "Aren't you afraid o' even going down to Micanopy? It ain't been long since they flushed the Injuns outer there." Mose tried to talk as Leah had told him but it proved too hard and he gave up. This was in the territory he had been gathering cattle and he wanted a little more time. Maybe I'd better push on a little more to the south, he thought.

"I think we're very well protected down there. We've got Fort Wachoota to the west, Fort King to our east and Fort Drane to the south. Most of the Indians have all scattered down into Green Swamp and below. Father had thought of going on down to Fort Gatlin or maybe Fort Christmas but that's way too off base as far as I'm concerned. It's a little too unsettled just yet."

"Better safe than sorry," said Mose. "I thought we wuz all safe way up here and then you see what happened to our brother, William."

"Yes," put in Mary, "And all those little homeless, fatherless children."

"You needn't bother feelin' sorry for them young'uns," bristled Mose, "Leah and me'll see they come up proper and well cared fer. They still got a good Ma and she's a fine woman."

About that time, Champ and Francis came running into camp, chasing two young girls, barefoot with their hair stringing down in their faces. They had been in the lake and the hems of their dresses were wet and held above their knees in wild abandonment. Short on their heels was Isaac holding his bottom, begging, "Ma, I gotta hockey! I gotta hockey!"

Mose calmly turned to Nellie and said "Take thet young'un to the bushes 'fore he messes his pants." About that time Isaac turned to his mother and Nellie and

41

said, "Too late, Ma, I thought hit wuz a fizzie."

Leah calmly told Nellie to get some clean pants from the wagon and go clean Isaac up. Poor Mary Mizell just stood and said, "My word. My Word."

David decided it was time to go but turned to Leah and said, "We feel we have our hands full with five. I don't see how you cope. Of course, we are still young and our family is not complete. I'm sure others will follow but we are hoping to space ours so that we will have adequate time for their training and education." With that, they bid Mose's family a good day and left

Good day to you too, you high falutin' bastard Mose thought to himself as he tipped his hat politely. Mose turned to Leah. "Wife, you want to go listen to the political speeches? Hit's a fixin' to rain like a cow pissin' on a flat rock," as he looked up at the threatening sky.

Leah elected to stay near the tent Mose had made by stretching a piece of oil cloth over a pole laid between the forks of two trees and sent the oldest children with Mose.

Mose joined the crowd, gathered about a platform to listen to Robert Raymond Reed, the new Territorial Governor. Jacob Summerlin was campaigning for Territorial representative for the next year and Mose was impressed with his views. He was a big cattleman in the area and was stressing cattle shipment to Cuba from southwest Florida as soon as Tiger Tail and his braves had been cleared out of that area. Statehood was a hot issue and Mose was deeply opposed to that, knowing it would bring in more settlers. He'd like to keep as many people out of Florida as he could.

The fish fry was a big success. The fish were fried in a large kettle, normally used for making syrup. Jake Summerlin had donated beef and David Platt the hogs for those that didn't care for fish. William Scott, Thomas Dexter and the Mizells had supplied the fish.

That evening Leah went with Mose to the frolic, taking the entire family. A level area along the south shore of the lake that was free of cypress knees had been fringed with lightered splinters stuck in the ground. Pine needles had been spread about tables of rough sawed pine so the hems of the ladies' dresses would not get dirty as the ground became trampled. As darkness settled, the light shined through the feathery topped cypress and their gray gnome-like knees provided an eerie background in the firelight. Leah's favorite dance was the cotillion. There were eight dancers, four of each sex. Later on, the dancing would become less organized with male and female at random around a much larger circle but for now, with the couples present, it was sets of sedate men and women and little, if any, confusion. Now and then someone would forget and go the other way or swing the wrong corner but they generally danced in a preset pattern, circulating the "floor" in a clockwise direct. There would be a designated caller. Sometimes one would spell the other when he wanted to dance. The crowd was so large and there was so much noise it was impossible to call and dance at the same time. Only the musicians had chairs. The fiddlers with their cheap, often hand- made instruments carried the tune. Each would have a partner sitting at right angles to him, beating the strings of the fiddle as his fingers formed the notes and he played. This was done with a couple of brown sedge straws that made a "toong, toong" beat. Someone would also beat the spoons. Tablespoons were held between the fingers of one hand so that they beat together in a sort of native rhythm. There were plenty of empty jugs to blow as the evening moved on. All adding to the beat of the music.

As soon as a tune was struck, the caller would start out with an "honor yore partner, lady on the left and balance all. Swing yore partner, corners, too, then promenade all." Some dancers had no rhythm and quickly got out of step. For some of the elderly, there would be too many instructions as "sashaying, ladies floating and balance your partners."

As the older dancers became confused, they were quickly directed in the right direction by the younger ones. On and on the fiddlers played *The Girl I Left Behind Me, Hell After the Yearling, Weekly Wheat, Pattie on the Turnpike* and the favorite, *Leather Britches.* By the time the caller had yelled out "Right hands to your partners, gents to the center and ladies take your seats," most everyone was soaked with perspiration and a few had been looking from the caller to the fiddlers, wondering when they were going to wind down.

Leah soon tired and was thankful for the open spaces and fresh air as the bodies began to "ripen" from so much sweat. When Nickabod Raulerson, Noah and the Osteen brothers began to feel no pain from many swigs from the shine jugs, she called for Isiah and Sammy who looked imploringly at Mose. He gave in and decided that they could stay with him and Champ and Francis.

"Hits time they learned to frolic," he told Leah. "Next year Lydia and Nellie can stay." Then Arch put in to stay with the boys.

"Right now you young'uns go on and go to bed with yore Ma and Aunt Leah. And you older ones help her put the young ones to sleep. I don't want to hear no fussing and whining about hit or you'll git your asses whupped right here in front o' everybody."

So the fussing subsided as they headed back in the darkness of the wagons.

By midnight, the frolic was in full swing. There were few young girls left but the young boys danced with the older women and no one seemed to care. Mose didn't mind the drunks but touched not a drop of the "squeezings." Soon only the hard drinkers or avid frolickers were left. Contact with the opposite sex was brief but in a "swing yore partner," many of the men took the opportunity to grab the lady and squeeze her up as tight as they could sweeping her feet from the ground and trying to press her breasts to their bodies for a brief encounter.

Oren Simmons had worn his high-heeled shoes for the specific purpose of stepping on toes and kicking the shins of those men he didn't particularly like and his favorite victim that night appeared to be Clay Bass. He seemed to get a keen delight in stomping on Clay's feet or kicking his shins at every opportunity. Clay quickly got agitated and finally had enough and lit into Oren. Cat Padgett, Oren's buddy, came to Oren's rescue and the frolic came to a stop long enough to break up the fight. Clay was quickly escorted to the sidelines to cool off. He quickly had some sweet young thing "gathered up" and was making eyes at her. Then Oren started his shin kicking in earnest. Cat found this highly amusing every time Oren scored. Clay escorted his partner to the side and disappeared into the darkness only to come back waving a pistol.

"Ain't no Simmons nor Padgett, seed nor breed, gonna shove me around!" he threatened.

Noah and the Osteen boys quickly subdued him and confiscated the pistol, lest he accidentally shot someone. They knew he meant no actual harm to the two men. This time Mose and his brother, Sam, cornered Oren and Cat and told them if they bothered Clay one more time, they could accompany them out in the darkness, away from the merry-makers and thrash them within an inch of their lives. They were ruining a good frolic with too many interruptions.

Clay's little girl friend accepted his apology and soon the dancing was in full swing again. Someone had brought a rather plump girl of questionable reputation that seemed to be without a chaperone. She was willingly letting every male have a vigorous hug against her ample bosom and a quick feel of her backsides every time they made contact. Around the circle she floated in wild abandonment as the men hollered and stomped their feet and tried to hold her as long as they could before the next one grabbed her. Eventually all the grabbing and pulling had loosened the string that held up her drawers and they slipped down around her ankles and were sweeping the ground. She stopped just long enough to pull them off and threw them on the sidelines. Champ and Francis, joining in the spirit of the thing, picked them up and started throwing them back and forth to each other until they landed on the head of the only fiddler still able to play.

Mose said, "That does hit," and took the boys to bed.

Chapter 6

On their way south on the second trip, Mose and the boys, looking for a spot to camp for the night, came across what appeared to be an abandoned homestead but saw smoke coming from the chimney and knew someone was probably cooking supper. The fields, once cleared, were covered with chinquapin bushes and little live oak saplings almost twenty feet tall. Grass grew up between the crepe myrtle bushes that had been planted with loving hands by some young housewife and mother, eager to make a home. Some industrious husband and father's dreams had died here, maybe along with him and his family sometime during the war. Mose cautioned the boys to hang back and he rode slowly into what was supposed to be the front yard, now just a trail through the weeds leading to the front port.

Mose yelled "Haloow the house." Mose knew it was dangerous just to ride up to a man's place, unannounced.

Two young boys stuck their heads out from around the front door. They appeared to be maybe ten or twelve at the most. The tallest stood defiantly at the door, holding a gun and the smaller was behind him with his fingers crooked in his belt loops.

"Yore folks at home, son?" Mose asked, eyeing the gun.

"Naw, ain't no buddy cheer 'cept we'uns," answered the one with the gun, it still leveled at Mose.

"When do you 'spect 'em back, son?" Mose asked coming a little closer on his horse.

The boy stood his ground and waved the gun. Mose looked around at the fading light and wondered where their folks could be. There was no evidence that livestock had trampled or eaten the grass, growing even higher where there had evidently been a barn of sorts at one time. There was a strained silence for a few moments as the two young boys continued to peer anxiously from the doorway and then slowly walked out on the porch, eyeing the young boys in the background, still on their horses.

"My folks ain't a'comin' back, Mister. Nobuddy lives 'cheer but me and my brother, Possum."

The younger boy stuck his head from around his older brother and smiled. He does look a lot like a grinning possum, Mose thought. Mose grinned back and got down off his horse. By now the boys had come up to the yard and they, too, got down, letting their mounts feed on the tall grass.

Mose walked up to the edge of the porch, spit his tobacco and sat down near the rickety steps.

"So you boys are goin' hit alone? How long you been a livin' thisaway?" He noticed that their ragged shirts and britches were far too short for their thin arms and legs, but their faces were clean and they appeared in fairly good health in spite of being so thin.

"I don't recollect how long hits been, nigh onto a year, I guess. Maybe two year. We done lost track o' time."

The youngest boy had never said a word, just standing and grinning like a Possum. He had been eyeing the horses.

"Hit used to be us and my Ma and Pa and five sisters. Come down from the Carolinas. We wuz a'gittin' along fine even with the few Injuns that wuz about. Never give us no trouble. Then Pa went off a'lookin' fer our hawgs and come home and come down with chills and fever. Ma filled him full o 'tarter and quinine, but he jest got sicker. Then Ma come down with hit and blamed if she didn't up and die 'fore he did. Both died and left us young'uns to fend fer ourselves. We cried and cried but hit wouldn't bring 'em back. Two o' the girls took hit, but they both got over hit. We tried to stick hit out but the girls didn't like hit here in these woods to start with, so they struck out fer Jacksonville to my aunt's. Man cum by here last summer to tell us they made hit there all right and tried to git us to come with him. But Ma and Pa worked hard fer this here place and Possum and me decided we weren't gonna give hit up so easy."

By now the two boys were out in the yard with the young boys, talking a mile a minute.

"That thar yore horse?" asked Possum, finally loosening up and finding his tongue.

"Hit's my Pa's, least hit wuz 'til last month. He got kilt by the Injuns. Now hit's my Uncle Mose's," he said, lookin' at Mose, not quite sure who it belonged to now as he had not questioned that Mose had taken control.

The boys introduced themselves and Mose asked if they could camp there for the night, already getting under way to staying by unsaddling his horse.

"You 'uns make yorselfs to home. Ain't much but yore welcome to stay." He was looking at Mose's saddlebags, bulging with food as he took it into the cabin and laced it on a clean, pine table. "We done et."

"Guess you could eat agin," Mose said.

The oldest boy was Jack but he hadn't asked Mose his name or where he was from. The boys knew you never asked a man his name or any other personal questions when you meet him on the trail.

"We come from the south fork of the St. Marys River," offered Champ.

Mose had started supper while the boys visited and fed the horses. The bedrolls were brought to the porch that had been swept clean. Mose put Champ to work with the hammer, tightening some loose boards on the porch lest someone get up suddenly in the night and fall through. He soon had a large repast of sweet potatoes; cornpone, ham and blackberry jam ready.

"I know you boys said you' done et but I bet hit's been a while since you tasted blackberry jam. Fly in and help yourselves. We got plenty. Might as well help us eat hit up fore hit spoils and we have to feed hit to the dawgs."

"I ain't had no preserves in so long I plum fergot they tasted so good," said Jack, gobbling down about three day's supply.

Mose liked to see them eat like little hungry, starved coons. He decided he and the boys could kill game and make out until they got back home. They could get jam any time back there.

"What you boys been a'livin' off of?" he asked no one in particular.

Jack, the oldest spoke up. "We kilt rabbits with Pa's old gun and even got a deer long as the powder and shot lasted. Then we got onto trappin' turkeys, rabbits and some quail." He went on to tell them they had four sacks of Irish potatoes planted "across thet field over yonder" but they only got one small sack back. The English peas they planted turned yellow and died. The sugar cane that volunteered froze and a bunch of stray cows finished that off when it tried to come back. A man had come by the past winter and they had cut some water oak pins for him for timber rafters for a penny a piece. He seemed pleased with them and "paid us our full share plus a little bit more," the boy said proudly. With the money, they bought some grits off another man.

"We're a' makin' hit," said the smallest boy.

"Possum here looked a might peaked fer a spell but he's picked up lately." Mose looked at his sturdy son and two nephews and shook his head.

"You boys take the horses down to the branch and water 'em and then tie 'em up good fer the nite. Then feed them dawgs some o' that dried 'gator tail. We best be gittin' to bed. Hits gonna be a long haul tomorrer. Hot as hit is we're all likely to git bar caught 'for the day's over with."

Possum's eyes got big as saucers at that last remark and Champ explained to him that "getting bear caught" was just an expression that you had become too exhausted to work, and they all had a big laugh. The two hosts pulled their bedding out on the porch so they could sleep outside with the rest of them. Mose started telling tales of Indian fighting, killing panthers, bear and so forth with Champ urging him on. As he finished another tale and fell silent Champ would say "Uncle Mose, tell us about the time—" and Mose went on until the boys were all snoring soundly. He lay in the darkness listening to the horses fighting and stomping the mosquitoes. The hound dogs, tired from the day's journey, were stretched out asleep under the porch, yelping softly as they dreamed in their sleep. He had seen many homesteads just like this one the last few weeks, as he was cow hunting with the boys. Some worse than this one. Florida was far from the "Land of Flowers" now. Half plowed fields lay bare except for weeds. Trees so eagerly girdled and left to die so they could be cut down for clearing still stood, row on row, stark and white and bare. Close by would be a half-finished frame for a house and sometimes several graves in the back yard, their occupants probably massacred or died of a fever. Some homes were just ashes, their rail fences and out-houses covered with vines, rotting down. There or rather here, thought Mose but for the grace of God goes me. And things were getting tight around his place too, what with the depression, and so many mouths to feed. I need more slaves to help me with the work. The boys jest ain't big enough to help out and I ain't a gonna ask the women to help. "Ain't fittin'," he murmured out loud.

Mose had quickly learned that farming in Florida was a lot different than farming in Georgia and the Carolinas. These boys' father had evidently not learned that, planting Irish potatoes and English peas. Mose quickly learned to grow sweet potatoes and cowpeas that were better suited to heat and sandy soil. Water poured through the sand and simply disappeared. Apples that had grown readily in Augusta had failed the year around and even corn had often stunted and failed to make more than tiny little cobs. Even the insects were a different variety and winter failed to kill them back, so they multiplied faster than the crops. The only solution was to plant half the crop for the insects and the other half for the family. Mose was a little better off than most of the other farmers as he had learned to hunt and rustle cattle. But even beef wasn't bringing what it used to and hides were down. The price of everything else was going up. The only thing that hadn't gone up was taxes. At least he owned enough land so he could farm and grow something to eat. He lay in the darkness, listening to the frogs croaking down at the branch and an owl screeched way off. In the distance, he thought he heard a 'gator bellow. I bet it gets pretty lonesome for these two little fellows, he thought and began to remember what it was like when he was a little boy and was soon snoring like the rest of them.

They ventured deeper south this time. It was July and out on the hills the sumac and goldenrod were beginning to bloom. Little birds laced through the trees and squirrels chattered. Scrub jays shrilled. The dogs treed a bear but Mose wouldn't let the boys shoot it. He explained that bears mated in July and August. The little cubs will be born in February. Now the meat would be too strong to eat.

"Wait 'til about next May, we'll git that feller," he promised them. Mose preferred bear meat to venison, beef, or pork but already they were getting scarce in his neck of the woods.

They reached the big scrub south of Fort King. Its white sand looked like thin rifts of wind driven snow. In Florida, the sand alternates from white to cream colored continuously but in irregular patterns. They were two different kinds of sand, originating from different places. The white sand came from sand dunes of ancient seashore. The yellow came from marine currents when Florida was covered by this ancient sea. Because of the sandy floor of the scrub, all the vegetation looks stunted. But there was a sharp contrast to the gnarled, crooked and dwarf-like plants—separated by bare, open spaces. One species will not invade the territory of another. In the true scrub are sand pines, short and thick Chapman's evergreen oaks and rosemary, stagger bushes and saw palmettos, contrasting sharply in the snow white sand. In the cream colored sand are the taller, long-leaf pines, towering over turkey oaks, black jack and post oaks.

Mose thought nothing would stay in the scrub with such sparse grass but he was surprised to find small groups of wild cattle feeding on the narrow leafed grass under the long leaf pines in the pine islands, completely surrounded by a sea of white sand.

According to the few inhabitants they encountered, there was still some danger of stumbling on an Indian so they kept their eyes open and stayed alert for an attack.

The boys felt safer at night, sleeping in their bedrolls under the stars because the dogs were close by, and would sound the alert in plenty of time. But as the chill of the morning dampness set in, they would look out at the lurking shadows of trees and imagine they saw all kind of things they didn't want to be there in the mist of early dawn. Even in July and especially after a rain, the air was damp and cool and a light cover would feel good. Being so young, Mose had to curse them once or twice to get them awake and they would roll out with a low moan, saddle weary and not used to riding the long hours. Half awake, they would feed the horses, their eyes darting anxiously into the mist. Their shoes would be damp and their heads stopped up from the moisture, but they shivered many times more from nerves than the dampness. After breakfast, Mose insisted the battered tin cups be washed and stored away. On the little cowponies there was a place for everything and everything had better be in its place. Mose did not tolerate anything being left behind.

As the day began to dawn, palmettos and scrub oaks gradually took form and the fear of Indians burned away with the mist. The sun would rise hotter and hotter and by nine the sweat would be running down their faces and there would be the smell of saddle leather, horse dung and lathered horses mingled with their own. Then all they would think of was a long "noon" under the shade of a tree by a narrow branch or small slough.

It was the time of year that had the longest days and Mose hunted cattle from "can't see until can't see."

By August, the trips had gotten longer and farther south. They had gone down to Fort Mellon where they ran into the Jernigan brothers, Isaac and Aaron, and Owen Simmons. These men had fought in the recent war and were scouting around, wanting to find a place to bring their families waiting back in Duval County. They had come down with a bunch of cattle belonging to Samuel Sloan, bringing their few slaves and were farming on an island at the edge of Lake Toho-pekaliga. They lived on the mainland and each day they would bring the slaves over to farm by dugout. They were bragging about the fertile soil on the island.

"You don't even need a hoe," said Isaac. "You jest kick a hole in the ground and sprinkle in a couple o' kernels o' corn and stomp hit in and step back and watch hit grow. Don't need no fertilizer or nothin'."

"What about the Injuns, they givin' you any trouble down there?"

"We have a run-in with some occasionally. Jest last week I wuz a'comin' back by myself across the lake and I saw three Injuns in a dugout a'comin' right at me. I headed to shore and run into a swamp on the west side o' the lake and hid. Climbed me a tree. I got way up in the top of one o' them big cypresses and his in the moss. I sat 'em out 'til they quit lookin' fer me and when hit got good and dark, I slipped out as quiet as I could. My shoes got to squishin' and stickin' in the muddy water and makin' so much noise I cut the string and took them off and jest left 'em a lyin' there and lit out fer Fort Gatlin. Run all the way, barefoot as a yard dog through the 'metter patches and lightered knots. My old feet are still so scratched up I jest now got to where I can git on a pair o' shoes. Next time I'm a gonna git me a pair o' boots thet don't fill up with water like shoes do. Man got to come down here with the right equipment."

"You say Sloan's got cattle down around this lake?"

"Yep," said Owen Simmons. "He's made me a deal to look after 'em fer him. I'm a fixin' to bring the family down here soon as I'm sure the Injuns are all gone. You thinkin' on the same line, Mose?"

"I been thinkin' on hit. This is as fur as me and the boys has got. I don't think I'll git my wife down here fer quite a while. I had a terrible time convincing her jest to move cross the St. Marys. But the more I see o' this country, the more I like hit. I had some bad luck, lost my brother and I've took his family to raise. We got eighteen young'uns now and that's lots to pull up stakes and come down here with, but I think same as Sloan, hit's a good place fer the cattle business-wide open."

"We best be gittin' back down to home," said Isaac Jernigan. "You git down our way and we'll show you the country."

"Me and boys got to be gittin' back home too. 'Preciate hit anyways, but we'll try to git back maybe next year. Hit's gittin' on towards cane grindin' up in my neck o' the woods."

Mose and the boys turned north and started working their way back toward Columbia County. Once, they camped at the edge of a lake under a large stand of giant oak trees whose branches swept the ground. The lake was edged by giant cane and at dusk a flock of black birds roosted in the cane, singing their shrill melodious songs.

Champ said, "I wish them bird's would stop makin all thet racket."

But Francis loved their songs. As night fell, the notes became lower and more widely spaced and as Francis became drowsy, their soothing whistles fell quiet in the darkness and he fell into a deep, troubleless sleep.

They killed a deer to take to their new-found little friends they had spent the night with the third night out on their way down. Mose had wanted to bring in a few head of yearlings to put in the crivis and fatten on the cane patch after it was cut in September, but he wanted to stop by and check on the two young boys and make sure they understood they had a home in Columbia County if the winter got too rough.

"One or two more won't make no difference," he told them when they had left that morning.

But the door to the cabin was shut and he could find not a trace of the two children when they reached the little cabin and the weeds had grown where their small path had been. Isiah, Champ and Francis talked Mose into staying over a couple of days but they had to get on with the yearlings and were running low on supplies.

"Reckon what happened to 'em, Pa?" Isiah asked as they headed north the next morning.

"No tellin' son, but my guess they made hit this fur wherever they are they're a makin' hit right on. We'll probably run into 'em one of these days."

But they never saw the two young boys again.

Chapter 7

Leah loved Mose—after all, he had been the only man in her life and she was a true and faithful wife as the Bible dictated. But she always felt a sense of relief when he left on his long trips. He was so demanding and stern. His personality overshadowed hers and she felt smothered at times. She felt almost as if on a holiday even though there was much more responsibility during his and the boys' absence. There was no overseer in those early days but there was a hired man that worked between the two homesteads and Mr. Davis and the slaves. The slaves liked her and really worked better for her in the long run. She wasn't so hard on them as Mose and they probably felt the same sense of relief when he was away as she did. Three of them had belonged to the Davises and knew her well. Mose had found three more abandoned by the Indians and he soon realized why, when he couldn't get them to work, so he traded them to Zephaniah Kingsley, who was in the business, for two older and more reliable ones. He had gotten Rich in the bargain and for some reason they had both taken a liking to each other. Mose talked with Rich more than anyone else, even Leah, and Rich seemed to understand his desires and troubles. Rich had been mistreated as a child and understood the demon that dwelled with his master.

And Leah had Susan. She and her sister-in-law worked well together. Susan got a big kick out of Leah's dry humor and the fact that she let Mose's harsh words and crudeness roll off her like water from a duck's back. Mose irritated Susan and she longed for the time she could get her own house.

The cousins got along fairly well except for Archibald and Samuel. Samuel, who was just a few months younger than Isiah was a little miffed that he didn't get to go to the woods with the other boys. After all, he could do the work just as well as they could. He couldn't understand that Mose needed time with Will's two teenagers to break them in to his way of doing things and the three boys he took with him were almost more than he could handle. Sammy would have been just one too many to train. His time would come. But Sammy sort of took it out on Arch from time to time.

James Ed, and Mose Jr., eight and nine, got along well and played together. Isaac, age six, was in a no man's land, wedged in between the two boys and little George, whom he considered a crybaby.

On this particular day Nancy, Isaac and little George were under the edge of the porch playing with the doodlebugs in the dry sand. The house was set up high off the ground in the highest spot on the hill. The sandy yard was swept clean with a broom and what sand was tracked into the house was swept through cracks in the floor of the hallway. Soon there was a clean hill of dry sand under the house and it was a doodlebug's heaven. They were little skinks that swim in the sand, making little miniature sinkholes. The children would cup their hands under the

51

depression where a doodlebug could be seen, throwing the sand in the air, one grain at a time, like lava spewing from a volcano. They would hold the strange looking little creatures in their hands and watch them wiggle and try to escape back into their holes.

They were strange looking creatures about the size of a gnat with wedge shaped heads and a recessed lower jaw. They had tiny front legs that folded into grooves on their body. The children would gather a good amount of them in a jar of sand and then add ants and watch them fall into the tiny funnels and be attacked by the doodlebugs.

James Ed, and little Mose had killed a big fat water moccasin near the branch and noticed she was fatter in the middle than elsewhere and decided to cut her open to see what she had swallowed. They had expected to find a rat or small bird. Much to their surprise, they found 24 baby snakes coiled in a clear sac on each side of her backbone. They punctured one of the sacs and the little baby moccasins came crawling out, fully capable of inflicting a serious bite, all 24 of them. Not realizing danger, they ran back to the shed and got a hoe a piece and set to work to see which one could kill the most baby snakes, both barefooted and vulnerable to a bite.

Children had no toys in those days. They entertained themselves with whatever seemed amusing in the environment and so the saying went that "Idle hands were the devil's workshop."

Leah had put Arch and Sammy to work breaking in milk cows. Now these were not Jerseys or Holsteins, but common range cows that had been gentled around the homestead. Any cow that appeared docile after being in the crivis for a time was penned and taught to stand still to be milked. They were kept in a crivis, a large enclosed area so they could graze during the day. At night, they were separated from their calf, put in a stanchion, a sort of stock their heads fit into that held them in one spot, and generally their hind legs tied together so they couldn't kick when they were milked. Then they were turned back to the calf to get the remainder of the milk and the process was repeated the next evening. It took a lot of milk cows to feed all the children and make butter and pot cheese. The milk was almost void of fat, called "blue-john" because of its blue-tinged color and so butter was a prized commodity.

To break them, the boys put a cow in the horse lot and each followed her around with a long stick, rubbing her between the hind legs until she became accustomed to the feel of a strange touch between her legs and quit kicking. Then they'd let in another and repeat the process. When they had one tame enough, they'd put a rope around her head and one would hold her and put a pole sideways between her legs while the other tried to milk her. Sammy got to thinking of the other boys out in the woods with his Uncle Mose, having all that grown-up fun and started pickin' on Arch. He got his rain slicker, got right in the gate and covered himself, waiting for Arch to drive more cows into the lot. Now, though the cows were fairly tame enough to try to milk, they were still wild cattle. Sammy lay perfectly still under the slicker, waiting for Arch to drive the cows in and when he heard the lead cow come in the gate with Archy behind them, he jumped up, thinking the cows would spook and run back over Arch. But the lead cow did the unpredictable and jumped over Sammy, knocking him down in the dirt and of course, the rest of the cows followed suit and jumped over him, stepping all over him. He had sand in his eyes, his clothes were torn and both the boys got a whipping.

That night they sat at the supper table and glared at each other. Sammy surreptitiously stuck his tongue out at Arch and quickly looked down at his plate, shoveling in the cowpeas.

"There's somebuddy at this table thet's ugly," said Arch out of the clear blue. "He's so ugly he'd run a buzzard off'n a gut wagon."

"Why, Arch!" said Leah, "What a terrible thing to say. I'm sure no one at this table is that ugly."

The two boys glared at each other and Sammy spoke up, "I know somebuddy thet ugly. He's so ugly his Ma carried him around after he was borned with his head stuck under her arm and his naked behind stickin' out in front. Everybuddy thought he was borned with one eye."

Margaret began to giggle and then Rhoda. Susan and Leah, inwardly amused, struggled to keep a straight face. Even Rich, waiting the table, began to snicker. But Leah and Susan composed themselves well enough to send the boys to bed without finishing their supper and they were having blackberry cobbler. Both boys vowed to get even.

And the next day Sammy got Arch alone, tripped him and rubbed his nose in fresh cow manure. They fought like two little banty roosters. Arch, being younger, was getting the worst of it so he broke loose and climbed the ladder to the hayloft. When Sammy started to climb up after him, he pulled down his pants and began to pee on him. Sammy, not to be outdone, ran and got his slicker and hat and started back after him but with each step up the ladder, Arch would let fly and Sammy would cover up and wait until he was sure Arch had run dry. When he finally decided Arch could do no more and got to the top, Arch was laying for him and had saved a little bit back and as Sammy looked up, he peed right in his eyes. Sam's eyes began to burn terribly and he ran to the water trough to try to wash them but they kept on stinging and Leah had to put milk in his eyes to neutralize the acid.

"Arch, what on earth possessed you to do such a thing. I'm so ashamed at you. You tell Sammy you're sorry right now!"

"I couldn't holpe hit, Ma," Arch cried. "He got me down in the lot and rubbed cow doody in my eyes and hit hacked the far out'a me."

"Yeah, and look what he done to me yestiddy, got me run over and nearly kilt in the cow lot," cried Sammy.

"Jest shut up," said Susan. "You probably deserved it and you're both a' gonna git hit."

And so they did. But the boys had settled their differences after that and began to get into mischief together, now friends and almost brothers under the skin. Sammy had learned a lot of respect for his cousin Arch.

The boys behaved themselves after that for a few days and everything settled down to normal. The next day Margaret, Rhoda and Nellie flitted about, running errands while Rich and Dulcie helped Susan and Leah make soap out in the yard under the shade of the chinaberry tree. Soap was normally made in the spring from the pile of ashes left over from the winter fires but there were so many dirty hands to wash, it was a continuous operation at the homestead.

The ashes had been shoved into a trough lined with corn shucks and water poured in. As the water dripped through the shucks and ashes, it formed lye which was put in a big wash pot and boiled. To make the soap soft, lard from rendered hogs was added–about two pounds of lard to a gallon of lye. When the mixture turned to jelly, it was poured into a large crock and cooled.

Rhoda and Nellie had finally tired and gone behind the smokehouse to make a playhouse but Margaret still flitted about, wanting to help but managing to get in the way. Actually, she was bored. Early that morning she had slipped out of the big feather bed she shared with Margaret and Nellie and gone out into the hallway and onto the covered walkway that led to the kitchen and sat down by the top steps that led out into the yard. A mockingbird was hopping about in the crepe myrtles and making a fuss with another bird about a worm. She leaned back against the big cedar posts and thought about what she could do to break the monotony.

She was shook from her daydreaming by Dulcie, her Mama's "house nigger," who had been out in the kitchen starting breakfast. She scolded her for not having her shoes on. Leah had tried to make ladies of her and Nellie. She was succeeding with Nellie who was a couple of years older than Margaret, who was still a tomboy. She still liked to run barefoot and feel the cool white sand between her toes in the early morning. It was before anyone realized that the ground itch the children got going barefoot was connected to hookworms. Actually, most of them didn't even recognize a good case of hookworms and many children in the south died of the parasite or its complications.

Leah came out of her bedroom about that time and put fresh towels on the roller. She saw that Margaret washed her face and she combed her hair for her, pulling her hair back so tight she could hardly blink. Then she took her into the kitchen and put her to work, churning.

Margaret looked out the kitchen window. The pink glow was gone toward the east and the sun was beginning to shine bright and hot. The earth had a good fresh smell. Down at the stables she could see one of the slaves leading a fresh young colt around by the halter, getting him used to the feel of it. The hand had taken the horses from the stable one at a time and brushed them with a currycomb. She did so wish she could be out there at the barn with the horses rather than in the kitchen, churning, but she knew her Mama wouldn't hear of it. She loved horses as much as Mose and the smell of the dust and horse's dandruff as it was brushed away. A flock of white geese crossed the yard by the horse lot, waddling their way to the branch. The big old Dominicker rooster was crowing just to hear his own voice on the clear morning air. It was going to be a good day, she thought.

The cream thickened in the churn and it got too hard for her to turn. "Go on, I'll get someone to finish it. You go get the other girls up. We're going to make soap today," Leah told her.

After she woke Lydia and Nellie, she went out to the outhouse and on the way back she picked a bouquet of crepe myrtles and honeysuckle and put them in a crock on the kitchen table. By that time, Dulcie was putting ham on the table and the hungry little boys were coming in for breakfast.

"I hope your Uncle Sam comes by soon. We need to order some syrup barrels so we can have them for September. The cooper was all out of hoop iron last time we checked."

"We're just about out of flour and I wonder if your daddy is going to try to get some more from Jacksonville," Leah said. "If this depression doesn't let up I don't know..." as she looked at Susan and Mr. Davis. They all knew that money was getting hard to dig up.

"What's a depression?" asked little William.

"It's somethin your Pa and I had been in since you wuz hatched," said Susan and they all laughed, though it really wasn't a laughing matter. Prices were down and they knew it had something to do with the Union Bank failing over in Tallahassee but only Mr. Davis really understood how it came about. He blamed it on the war.

"Soon as you boys finish feeding your faces I want you to run down and keep the rice birds away from the rice field."

Raising rice was another drudgery and hardly worth the time for what they got out of it. Mose usually bought rice over in Jacksonville but with times getting hard they were trying to raise some. A small field was laid off in broad shallow drills about a foot apart and the seed strewn like grass seeds and covered lightly with a hoe. When the little seedlings came up, water was let in from the little near-by branch. This was called the "point-flow." At mid season when the stalks were almost full height, another flooding was called the "lay-by-flow." In between the two flows, the fields are drained and weeds and grass were pulled up or chopped by a hoe. When the heads began to fill out the ricebirds would come by the thousands to eat the grain and someone had to keep them run off. They never managed to save but a piece of the patch. The birds were easy to scare at first and Mose had built a scarecrow but they soon got used to that and now the children had to run around the patch, waving white rags to keep the birds scared off.

Spinning makes a big racket and Leah could not spin at night because it kept Mose awake when he was home, so she and Susan had sat up well past mid-night one night trying to get all the wool spun while he was gone. She didn't try to dye the wool or cotton she spun, but let it stay its natural color. She was a very good weaver and took pride in her work. Wool was harder to weave but was good for the cold North Florida winters. It dried faster than cotton and wouldn't freeze when wet. She made collarless homespun shirts and aprons, blouses and skirts.

They tried to buy the nice material for her dressier clothes and the boy's pants.

And of course, keeping the clothes clean was another matter. It was a never-ending job. Rich would fill the big old iron pot with water and build a roaring fire under it. The clothes were rinsed first in cold water on a battling bench. Each individual piece was lifted from the cold water onto a bench and battled with a short paddle and turned over and over. Then Dulcie and one of the girls would rinse, battle and rinse again. The stains were scrubbed out with lye soap and then boiled for about twenty minutes. The clothes were worked up and down, taking care every crease was touched to get out a week's supply of dirt and perspiration. Every bit of dirt or sweat left in the clothes would rot the cloth in the humid weather so the battling and rubbing did more good than harm. The clothes were lifted from the wash pot and put in a tub at the end of the battling bench and rinsed with fresh water that Rich kept coming from the well. By the second rinse they were shaken out and hung to dry while completely wet. It took a long time to dry in the rainy season and some days they were lying all over the house and even out to the barn to dry. The small children would have a bath in the warm rinse water and the hot water from the kettle was used to scrub the floors, especially the ones on the open porches where the dogs lay and the greasy kitchen where most food was fried.

And so went the Barber household while Mose was away. Susan and Leah knew that Mose would come home, tired and cranky and find fault with everything that wasn't done to his satisfaction and say not one word of praise for a job well done. It was their cross to bear.

The boys had been about as good as they could be for some time and then just before their brothers came home with the cattle they got into trouble again, only no one knew what had happened.

Someone had to butcher almost every day not only for the house but to feed Mose's pack of dogs as well. One day Sammy and Arch took the hides from the freshly butchered steers, dragged one of them out to an open spot away from the clearing and lay down under it, bloody side up. It wasn't long before the buzzards came and after several unsuccessful tries each finally managed to grab one by the legs and ran with them to an empty chicken coop. They repeated the process until they had four of the birds caged up. It had been an all day job. That night they slipped out of bed, caught the hapless buzzards, and tied big bundles of corn shucks to their legs. They took them over by the slave cabin and knocked on the door and yelled, as they ran behind the shed. Just as the Negroes opened the door and peered out, they set the corn shucks afire and turned the buzzards loose. The slaves stood petrified as the buzzards flew skyward like big balls of fire, zooming over their quarters. They woke up the entire household with their screeching and moaning, trying to explain to the white folks that the world was coming to an end.

Leah put the boys to work, trying to run the old rooster down so they could eat him. He had gotten too old to fight off the new, younger one and had started roosting in the chinaberry tree at night. They had all taken turns, trying to slip out and catch him but no one had been able to, so Leah told Arch and Sammy they could run off some of their meanness by chasing him until he became exhausted and they'd put him in the pot along with some of the older hens. Leah had already told Margaret her little banty hen had to go. She had been laying out by the crepe myrtle bush but lately there had been no little eggs forthcoming and only one was saved for her to hatch. It had been gathered and left in the egg crate for weeks. So Margaret began to gather it every night and put it in the next and then come running in, showing it to the family, exclaiming that her little hen didn't have to be eaten after all as she had started laying again. Dulcie and Grandma Davis went along with her game, never letting on that they knew what she was doing and so her little chicken was saved from the pot.

Several days later, Rhoda awoke to the lowing of cattle. Mose and the boys had come home in the night with a bunch of yearlings after she had gone to bed. It had rained for hours that afternoon and the men had come in early from the fields. There had been an early supper and it was still raining. Showers were taken under the eaves at the back of the house and they all washed their hair in the soft rainwater. The cold water and wet hair had chilled Rhoda to the bone and she had crawled in bed with the other two girls and they had told ghost stories and made up fairy tales and then gone sound asleep while it was still light outside, with the rain coming down on the roof.

Chapter 8

The ribbon cane that had been planted in February was ready for harvest. September had arrived with a slight cold snap early on. It promised to be a cold winter. Mose was afraid of a killing frost and the word was passed around. If you had cane to grind you'd better get it over to Mose Barber's because he was wanting to get his in.

A cane grinding was a social occasion. Those nearby came early and spent the day and a few spent the night that lived far enough away for it to be inconvenient to go and come. Last year a bad stretch of stormy weather had knocked the top-heavy slender stalks to the ground and made them difficult to cut. It was during the time Indians were still causing trouble in western Columbia County and Mose could not get enough cooperation from the surrounding community to get all of his cane in and some of it had ruined. He couldn't afford to let this happen now with all the extra mouths to feed. An early frost could harden the leaves and make it difficult to strip them from the stalks. So if anyone wanted to exchange having their cane ground for helping Mose cut his down, they'd better let it be known, otherwise he was putting his in the first of the week.

Cane joints from the year before were planted deep in the ground. Two of three rows of cane were laid parallel in a deep furrow and covered with a plow at the end of February. Shoots came up from the eyes on each buried joint and grew taller and taller through the spring and summer. At harvest time, the leaves were stripped from the stalks and piled up for fodder. These were fed to the little "dick" yearlings Mose had brought in from down south. These were little castrated bull calves that fattened better than bulls, as Mose said, they had their mind on "grass instead of ass." The stripped stalks were cut at their base and stacked in piles, loaded on wagons and hauled to the cane mill. If left too long in the field the cut end of the cane stalks could turn sour, especially if the weather turned off hot.

The grinder on the mill had been oiled and the wooden "sweep" pole and "lead" pole taken from storage and connected at their proper places. The old boiler was turned upright and washed clean less it still contain some of the smell left over from having been used back in the winter to scald hogs. Barrels that ordinarily are used the rest of the year to catch rainwater were scrubbed and covered so the staves wouldn't dry, shrink, and leave cracks to let the sweet green cane juice leak out on the ground. The wooden paddle spoons and the skimmer were dug from their storage place, washed and made ready under the shed by the boiler. Tons of wood were cut and piled near the shed. It usually took two or three cords for each ton of sugar, which was the most important by-product of the sugar cane.

Mose let the neighbors grind first and then his brother, Sam, and during this time, he could relax and enjoy the euphoria of being a good host and the importance he felt by allowing his friends the use of the one good mill and kettle in the community. He and Will had discovered the abandoned mill and kettle near a plantation down below Picolata at the height of the Indian raids and taken it home.

Everyone had left with their syrup except his brother and a few close friends who had stayed on to help him get his in and they were ready to get on with his grinding.

Early that morning, Margaret, always the first to crawl out from between the covers, noticed that Nellie had beat her up and that the kitchen was already full of people having breakfast. Mose and the hired man, Jim Gunter, could be seen outside in the dim morning light with the slaves at the shed and her Uncle Sam and Champ were at the mill. The barrels at the mill were covered with a loosely woven cloth to strain the bright green juice as it poured down the wooden trough. It was still so dark outside she could see only half the circle walked by the mule as he went around and disappeared in the pale misty morning light, made half his circle and disappeared again. Champ and Samuel were feeding the cane stalks into the mill as the juice poured from the grinder down the trough and into a barrel. The mule was fastened at both ends to a long, fifteen-foot cypress pole called the "sweep." At the butt end of the "sweep" a smaller pole was attached at a right angle and a long line tied to its end and then tied to the mule's halter. At his rear, he was hitched to a harness and singletree, very close to the other end of the "sweep" so that as he pulled on that end of the sweep, the line from the small pole, attached to his head, pulled him forward and he was kept turning in a continuous circle. The middle of the long "sweep" rested on, and was connected to, a crusher roller so that as it went around, it turned the roller, that in turn, engaged another roller. The cane stalks were fed between the two crushing rollers. This usually crushed the stalks of about half of their juice. The crushed stalks were then fed to the livestock, along with the leaves. Nothing was ever wasted on the farm.

Then the barrels of juice were carried to the shed where they were strained through another cloth into the kettle. When the boiler kettle was filled within two inches of its rim, the fire underneath it began to burn and dark foam would form on top of the boiling juice. Nellie, a towel pinned over her hair, was already hard at work skimming the scum from the kettle. The skimmer was an eight and a half inch piece of metal with perforated holes that let the hot juice through but trapped the dark scum. It was attached to a long wooden handle so the person doing the skimming did not have to stand so close to the boiling liquid. The scum that was full of impurities was discarded into a bucket and was either made into moonshine or fed to the hogs. As the juice boiled down, Francis and Isiah were busy scraping the sides of the kettle with wooden paddles to keep the juice from scorching or turning into candy. As the morning progressed some of the workers were relieved, especially Nellie who had gotten hot and almost fainted. Adults had gathered about the kettle, dipping sticks into the candied particles at the topside of the kettle and handing them to children waiting patiently for the "candy" to cool. There was much gossip and visiting among the adults that formed a protective circle to keep the children away from the boiling kettle.

Finally, Leah and Susan sent word to quit feeding the children so much scrapings lest they get the "scours," a form of diarrhea. It took from three to four hours to boil just one batch. The liquid had to be kept at a rolling boil at the right temperature so the wood had to be fed properly under the kettle and sometimes water poured on it to reduce the heat to keep the kettle from boiling over. The green juice soon turned into a rich caramel color and Mose, Sam and Mr. Davis would confer as the proper time to pour it up before it began to turn into candy. The kettle held about 80 gallons of juice and out of that came eight to ten gallons of syrup. This was put into containers to cool, taken to a table and ladled into small syrup buckets and stored. They usually made about three batches a day. The last juice was made into sugar. Mose usually made four to six barrels of sugar in all, making a couple of barrels from a batch.

At the end of the last batch each day, a small amount of syrup would be left at the bottom of the kettle and boiled down into candy. The hot sticky liquid would be poured into buttered platters and allowed to cool until it could be handled, formed into large balls, rolling it around in the hands, and then before it got hard, couples with greased hands would stand opposite each other and pull it back and forth in ropes until it turned into a creamy white taffy. It was looped on a platter like a loose braid of hair and allowed to cool. Then it was cracked into pieces and consumed by young and old alike. This was known as a "taffy pull" and gave shy, would-be suitors the chance to gaze into their partners' eyes at such close proximity, touching hands that would not other wise be allowed to be touched. Many young folks came just to the taffy pull.

The women gathered in the kitchen or parlor and the men stayed around the dying fire at the kettle or down at the barn where the language got rough and as the shine flowed, the tales got wilder. They would tell jokes and even repeat tales they had heard before. They were generally about their work, hunting trips or horses. Never about women — not in public as men now do at a bar.

Mose always had a favorite tale and he had a flair for embellishing one. He loved center stage and he had a habit of standing on one leg, bending the other back and forth at the knee, tapping his knee with his left hand as the other flew about in the air. Mose was left-handed.

Noah Raulerson had a new tale to tell about a recent visit up to Waycross, Georgia, to an unusual foxhunt. This wasn't the common kind of foxhunt with the fox in the lead, the dogs close behind and the hunters following on fine horses, jumping hedges and so forth. A bunch of hunters would take their favorite fox hounds out on a moonlight night; each put a dollar in a pot and turn the dogs loose. The first dog to get the fox earned his owner the pot. Of course, the money was important but the main part of the entertainment was to get stationed about the countryside, usually alone, and listen to the dogs bay as they ran, pickin' up the scent. Each man had his favorite foxhound and he recognized his dog's voice above all the rest. It was music to his ears. Usually a foxhound or coon dog was a poor man's prized possession. There was an old saying that you might get away with "messing with" a man's wife but keep your hands off his dog! And the meanest man in the world wasn't the one that beat his wife or young'uns but one that would "pizen" his neighbor's dog.

Noah was telling his tale. "First thing off the dogs had to take the edge off by gittin' in the damnest fight you ever seen. Of course, I was proud as could be of my old Bugler dog. Never got a hair turned back on him. They soon settled their differences and got down to business. I set myself down around the edge of a swamp not too fur from where a part of the Okeefenokee commenced. There was a nice little strand running 'twix these two little cypress ponds. Guess I musta been there 45 minutes more or less with my head propped up agin a stump, good and comfortable like when I heered old Bugler open. God, thet was purty! Has thet dog got a voice! Hit near bout made my hair stand on end. Then the balance got the scent with him. They circled back and forth, north then east and then I heered the row a'comin' right towards me. It was a race between old Bugler and Ike Jernigan's blue tick. I had goose bumps all over me. Now I know how a runaway nigger feels when you set the dogs on 'im. I tell you, I'd hate to be that there feller. They got so close I grabbed my gun and wuz a gittin' ready fer Mr. Fox. I wuz a countin' thet money already. They got about fifty yards out, my heart poundin' and mouth dry and durned if they didn't circle back and run t'uther way. Directly I heered a gun go off and the dogs stopped and I figgered hit wuz all over. I wuz fixin' to leave to go see who got the fox when I heered a couple o' dogs over around the bend of the swamp, a'comin' back to me. I grabbed my gun and hardly got set 'fore I heered the bushes rattle and come a bar, bout the biggest I ever seen not mor'n ten feet away and I barely had time to pull the trigger 'fore he seen me. I aimed the gun and pulled the trigger and old Bessie she spoke to me. Thet bar stopped dead in his tracks and the two dogs right behind him. I didn't recognize neither one o' them dawgs. Come to find out they wuz strays wuzn't even in on the hunt. Ike Jernigan got the money but I got the best mess o' bar meat a feller ever had.

"Jim, I hear you're a purty good hand at breakin' horses."

"I ain't no slouch," Jim bragged. "Thet's what I wuz a doin' when Mose here hired me. Least I had been. Got fired."

"You wuz so damned good at hit what'd you git fired 'bout?"

"Well, this man I wuz a workin' fer had a peg leg. Lost hit a fightin' with old Andy Jackson. But he wanted to run everything. I couldn't do nothin' he weren't out there a watchin' me or gittin' right in the middle o' it, peg leg and all. One day he wuz a holdin' the rope right out in the middle o' the pen fer me to ride this young colt. I wuz a ridin' him around and around in a circle and he lit out and got to runnin' and buckin' and I started spurrin' him. The old man wuz a holdin' his own with the rope but we got right up next to him and he drapped hit. I thought the little horse wuz gonna jump right over him when he throwed me. Went way up, made a awful twist and I didn't know where thet horse went to. I wound up straddle o' thet old man's neck, and spurred him a half dozen times 'fore I realized I wuzn't still on the horse."

The tales got rougher and rougher. Rowland Needham spoke up. "I had the funniest thing happen to me over at Jacksonville. Went over there to visit a sister o' mine and went by to pick up two o' my nephews at school. They'd played a joke on the teacher and she was keepin' them in. They're 'bout half grown young'uns and I think she's a little scairt of 'em. Anyway I wuz standin' out in the school yard with her and a couple of half-grown gals waitin' fer the boys' time to run out. Lawrence, the oldest one, he's a skinny, pigeon-toed, red headed boy, finally cum fryin' outa thet school house, jumped off the porch, high as a bird and spread his legs apart and ripped a big one he'd been storin' up for the best part o the day, I figured. He hollered real loud at his brother, 'Ketch thet one and paint her red and put her in a bottle and I'll give you a nickel fer it.' Well, thet pore little school teacher didn't know what to do, but them gals got to snickerin' and turned red and she'd turned all kinds of colors and finally broke down and started laughing with the balance of us."

About that time Mose heard Arch and Sammy snickering along with the crowd from the shadows of the barn and said, "What you boys doin' up this late?" and decided it best for the party to break up and all get to bed.

When it came time for the sugar making things got serious and Mose saw to it that most of the visitors had gone home. He allowed no tomfoolery because everything hinged on all the right moves or the sugar could be ruined. The fire had to be just right, more so than for the syrup that had a little margin for error. The sugar could be ruined in a split second. Sam, Mose, Grandpa Davis and James Gunter would sit around the kettle, faces becoming more and more serious and fewer words spoken as the syrup boiled down. There came a time when no one took their eyes off the kettle unless they looked at Mose or Grandpa Davis. The syrup had turned into boiling gold. Champ, Francis and Isiah stood with their axes ready to sink the blades into the burning logs and drag them from the furnace under the kettle at an instant's notice. Rich had a long, wooden rake standing ready to rake out what coals were left after the boys got the logs out. When the sugar was ready, all heat had to stop from beneath the kettle. The action would start with just a glance or nod from Grandpa Davis to Mose, both veteran sugar makers. Mose would yell, "I think thet's 'bout got hit," and all would stand aside as Mose and Sam started dipping the golden liquid into a trough that ran from the kettle into the sugarhouse. James Gunter had already run ahead to the little house to see that for sure the trough was positioned into the barrels and yell when they were full. The work was done rhythmically like beating time to music, dipping, pouring in unison with perfect timing to keep the sugar flowing into the barrels. The sugar was brown and moist since not all the molasses was removed, but actually each sugar crystal was as white as the sugar we have today.

It generally took two days to make enough sugar for the two families. After the sugar was made, the boiler was washed and dried and coated with tallow and turned upside down under the little shed until hog killing time in February. The long cypress "sweep" and "lead" poles were detached from the mill, stored in the barn and the mill covered from the elements until the next year.

Chapter 9

Early Tuesday morning after the Christmas festivities, the mail coach stopped at the Barber's homestead. Mr. Davis was the postal clerk and that's where everyone got their mail in that particular section of the country. The mail coach left Jacksonville every Monday bound for Alligator, and then left Alligator every Friday at eight a.m. and got back to Jacksonville late Saturday afternoon. Mose's place was about halfway between.

A letter had come addressed to Mose and since a letter was a big event, everyone gathered about the table to see what it was about. "Probably from Ben," Mose said, as Leah opened it "I hope ain't nothin' wrong. I sent word I wanted him and George to start down here with my cows from Augusta. I'm a fixin' to push 'em on down south o' here, maybe on down even to the central part of the state. They ain't doin good up there. Too crowded and we've run out of pasture. What does he have to say?" addressing Leah who was reading the letter. Mose had not learned to read well enough to read a strange handwriting.

"It isn't from Ben," she said. "It's from a Mr. Zephaniah Kingsley over at Jacksonville. Isn't he the one you traded those slaves with for Rich?"

"What in the hell does he want?" Mose was excited. Mr. Kingsley was about the richest man he knew.

"He wants to meet with you concerning a financial proposition of great importance to you both," she said.

The children, sensing the excitement, all asked who this man was and Mose told them. He owned land from the mouth of the St. Johns River all the way down to Lake George, which was thirty or forty miles above Fort Mellon. Mose figured it to be at least ninety miles plus three or four plantations. His home was a mansion and he was supposed to have "tons of jewels and gold" stashed about. He had traded in slaves and some say he still ships them in from Cuba, Mose told the children. He used to stand on the balcony of one of his mansions at the mouth of the St. Johns and looked for his slave ships to come in with the slaves, and kept them chained in the basement until they had tamed down.

"Ain't that agin' the law?" Isiah asked.

"Not unless you git caught at hit," said Mose.

"I wish we could get some more slaves," said Nellie.

"Then you could really 'cut the lady,'" said Margaret. "I bet you'd just sit around dressed all day and do nothin'."

"With slaves come responsibility," said Leah. "And work," she added. "Don't you girls ever forget that in case you're fortunate enough to marry a man that has them."

"That's right," said Mose. "Slaves are a big investment like fine horses, they'll up and die on you if you don't take good care of them, and then you've lost a lot of money."

"We need to get an answer off in the mail when it comes back through her Friday," Leah told Mose.

"You say he wants to meet at his house on the third o' January?"

"Doesn't give you much time. You'll need a new shirt and I'll have to clean up on your coat."

"I don't want to look too prosperous, but I don't want to go lookin' scroungy neither."

Mose was in a state of high anxiety and anticipation now. He knew he had no money to offer in any kind of financial dealings and wondered what on earth the old man wanted with him. He had heard of all the chambers full of gold and gems with guards standing outside and realized the man didn't need money.

"Write him hit'll be late in the day on the third, wife," and Mose spent several sleepless nights trying to guess what the man was up to. "Them boys pull in here from Augusta with my cattle, you tell them to put 'em in the crivis overnight until I git back to help drive 'em out, you hear?"

Well before it was light on the appointed day, he and Rich set out toward Jacksonville for Kingsley's plantation, Laurel Grove, on the St. Johns River. They stayed on the old Indian trail to Cowford. Soon they left the pine flats with their saw palmettos and scrub oaks. When they hit the marsh, they turned south and rode along the bank of the river. Here and there were clumps of Spanish bayonets that had been planted by the Spaniards long ago as defensive entanglements around their missions. Along the riverbanks were clumps of white bay trees, large live oaks, dogwood, holly in dense forests with sandy ridges covered in pines and blackjack oaks.

Just as dusk was beginning to settle like a veil on the land, they turned a curve, to see what appeared to be a settlement near the banks of the river, nestled among a huge oak hammock. Dogwood and holly abounded. At the gate of the driveway, leading to the house was a small old man of about seventy on a tall white horse, his face obscured in the twilight by a huge Pancho Villa type Mexican hat. As he rode closer in the twilight, smiling at Mose, he caught the glint of silver shoe buckles and his bright green coat of silk glistened like the back of a young tom turkey in the fading sunlight.

"Greetings, my friend. You are Moses E. Barber, I presume. I think we met once long ago when I traded you that young man you have with you for a couple of unruly slaves I lost money on."

"Your servant, Bwana Kingsley," Rich said, taking off his hat to the old man. Rich had really never liked the man. He had been pretty hard on Rich when he was younger and he knew the man "liked black women" and that didn't set well with Rich, either. Rich knew that his place was very secure with Mose and wasn't worried about Mose leaving him behind in any kind of trade.

Kingsley was a short man who looked even smaller on the big white horse. Mose towered above him even on his little cowpony.

Kingsley was an uncle to Whistler's mother and was born in Scotland. He had come to America in 1780 with his father who had received a 3,000-acre land grant. When an adult, he traded in slaves, which he chained to sturdy oak posts in his home called Belleview. It was a large two-story frame house with four Chinese pavilions, one at each corner with a small central tower where he stood and watched his slave ships come in. He kept the frightened, often raving natives, chained until they could be taken to his plantation on Drayton Island in Lake George some 90 miles to the south. Here they were pressed into the hardest kind of slave labor but fed and not mistreated otherwise. They soon were toughened and trained well enough for field hands. This training increased their market value fifty percent of other slaves and he also got his rice, sugar, cotton and other vegetables to market for nothing. He had had a few cattle but they had vanished along with the Indians in the war.

Mose rode his horse to the side of the big white horse and offered his hand to Kingsley.

"I hope your travel was not too strenuous," he told Mose.

"Hit's all in a day's work fer me," said Mose. "Rich here ain't used to sittin' a horse all day but I'm sure he was glad to git to come back fer a visit," eyeing Rich and daring him to look the least bit doubtful. "He'll probably be stove-up for a day or two. This cold weather don't bother me none. I jest sit on old Jackson here and let him do the work."

They were winding down a drive leading to the big house. Mose was leading Old Ring, his favorite dog, by a rope as a pack of Kingsley's hounds ran out to greet them. Ring immediately started growling, his shackles turned up in defiance and stopped and raised his leg on a well trimmed bush. A huge burly slave ran forward and grabbed Ring and more slaves appeared from nowhere to take the horses and show Rich to the barn while another grabbed Mose's small satchel with his new shirt and cleaned coat rolled up inside. Kingsley inquired of the Indian problems and told Mose how much he regretted the death of his brother. Mose told him they were thinking of reactivating Fort White and he wished they wouldn't because more people would be coming into the territory and they didn't realize there was still movement of Indians from Green Swamp to the Okeefenokee.

"I'm afraid more people are going to git kilt if they do," Mose predicted.

"My man will show you to your room. We will have supper shortly and you can freshen up a bit from your travel as I go tell them to start laying it for us."

He motioned forward and the old slave went up a winding stairway, Mose following behind, in awe of the splendor he had not even begun to imagine. The old slave was as black as coal. His face shined like a pool of hot tar and his shoulders stooped from years of hard work. One of the lucky ones, Mose thought. No telling how long he's had him. Mose had noticed he spoke in the Gullah dialect and wondered if he understood any English at all.

The stoic old slave was waiting outside his door after Mose had washed in the basin of warm water and dried his face and hands on a clean linen towel. He had changed into his new shirt and cleaned frock coat and felt presentable, anyway.

Downstairs, Kingsley led him to a large parlor where a servant brought drinks and Mose refused, saying he never touched alcohol, so a nonalcoholic drink was brought instead. Mose looked around at the magnificent room full of massive mahogany and teakwood furniture, oriental rugs and heavy silk drapes. There was another staircase leading to the second floor with a balcony above that evidently overlooked the river outside.

"Just you and your wife live here alone now?" Mose asked, thinking of all the wasted space.

"No," said Kingsley, "I live here in this house, alone, and my wife lives in the house adjoining this one. She's a negress, you know and the law forbids us to live together under the same roof. I have my house and she has hers, called Madam Anna's. She is still a beautiful woman to me—a princess from Madagascar from a long line of African kings. Her name is Anna Madgigine Jai, but I call her Jaibut. You will meet her tonight and I'd appreciate it if you would address her as Madam Anna."

Mose made a mental note of that. He looked at the old man with his sparkling eyes and wondered if he bedded with his black wife anymore and if he really ever loved her as Mose did Leah. I don't know how a man can love a nigger woman, thought Mose.

The old black servant appeared again as quietly as he had left and announced that supper was waiting in the dining room. He wondered if the black wife would join them at the table and to his surprise, she served the first course. She was well preserved, wearing a silk turban over her hair and richly brocaded robe, covered in plain gold chains. She was tall with a big bony frame and her gray-black skin finely wrinkled. The light shined over her forehead and cheekbones and she had a penetrating gaze.

"My wife, Madam Anna, Mr. Barber," Kingsley said as she neared Mose's chair.

Mose froze, not knowing whether to stand and bow or what to do. He decided he'd better treat her as a hostess and stood and bowed. "Madam Anna," he said as he remembered to do. He was afraid if he wasn't polite, she might conjure up a spell to cast on him. He understood some Negro high priestesses did that.

Madam continued to serve the men a sumptuous repast. Much of it Mose didn't recognize except for the oysters, but it all tasted very good and was much more than five men could eat. He wondered what Rich was getting out in the barn or wherever he was. Rich always ate what Mose did. They never ate together but ate the same food anyway. Mose was sure they were eating food that never touched the slave's lips.

"How do you like the oysters?" Kingsley asked after Mose had devoured a plateful.

"They're mighty good," Mose said, "but not like the oysters we have at home sometime."

"Oh," Kingsley seemed surprised, "How is that?" He wondered how Mose could afford fresh oysters so far from the coast.

"They're really not real oysters. We call them mountain oysters. They're really nuts, cut out o' my little bull yearlings. I hear they have the same effect on a man as real oysters and they're mighty good fried."

This intrigued Kingsley and he asked more and more about the cattle industry. "I must try your mountain oysters sometime," he said.

Mose noticed the fine china, sparkling silver and crystal. He was served coffee in a cup so thin he could see his fingers through it as he drained it to the bottom. The bread was made of flour, hard on the outside and soft and warm on the inside. He wondered what it would be like to be this rich.

After a sweet dessert of some unknown fruit, Kingsley led Mose into another room, apparently his office. Mose had never seen so many different rooms in a house. He was sure he'd get lost if they asked him to leave suddenly. The mahogany desk was huge and so was a leather couch and chair. The walls were covered with books and articles Kingsley had collected through the years and from all parts of the world.

He offered Mose a small cigar from Cuba and Mose wished he had a good chew of tobacco instead, but wondered where he would spit it anyway. They did some small talk about his county, Mose talked of how they had vacated Fort White the year before because of malaria and that the people were still a good 25 to 30 miles apart—a good day's ride even pushing it some. Mose was beginning to wonder when he'd get on with the business at hand when Kingsley finally got around to it.

"I suppose you're wondering why I dragged you away over here?"

"Started wondering that the day I got yore letter. Hit's been a eatin' at me day and night."

Kingsley laughed. "I've been a successful man, Mr. Barber. Of course, I was given a very good start by my father, but I've doubled his fortune, dealing in the slave trade. But that's about a thing of the past. By the time I'm dead and gone it'll probably be illegal to own a slave. I still manage to slip a few in from Cuba and down to Lake George. The freeze in February in '35 wiped out most of my orange groves and the blight that followed did much to rid me of my citrus. I still have a small grove of oranges on my island in Lake George but my household manages to eat them as fast as I raise them, so I don't have any for sale. What I have in mind is getting into the cattle business. I've tried about everything but that and I'm frankly getting bored with nothing to worry about."

"Well, there's plenty of worry in that to go around. And hard work too. Surely you ain't thinkin' of settin' a horse and punchin' cattle all day?"

Kingsley could read the disappointment in Mose's face as he thought, surely he hasn't drug me all the way over here just to buy my cattle. He could have done that by letter or sent an agent.

Kingsley said, "Surely you aren't thinking I brought you all the way to see me just to buy your cattle. I wasn't thinking of buying them or working them either. You must give me credit for more than that."

"Well, I must admit you had me goin' fer a second," Mose laughed. "I figger you've got a right smart laid up and don't have to git out and beat the bushes like

69

I do. Hit's a hard life and I don't want to seem disrespectful nor nothin' but I'd say yore getting' a little smoothed-mouth to be startin' out doin' that."

"Precisely, Mr. Barber. But I've worked hard all my life and I want to keep finding new horizons until I die. I like a challenge. This country is going to be wide open now that the Indians will soon be removed or at lest driven into the swamps where they can't thrive. They tell me the prairies around the Kissimmee on down to Lake Myakka and Okeechobee are open waves of grass as far as the eye can see—much of them like the west except on a smaller scale. It doesn't even need clearing. All that land north west of the big lake will be open from the upper St. Johns, the Kissimmee, Peace and Caloosahatchee Valleys. We can ship cattle from Fort Brooke and Fort Myers to Cuba and ports beyond. But now, what I had in mind was a small outlay of cash from me but more in terms of risk to life and limb on your part, depending on your amount of expertise, with a good return for us both. As you know, I still ply the waters around Florida with my steamers and schooner. My captains tell me the federal government is holding some two thousand Indians at Fort Brooke, awaiting transport to the west. With them are their cattle and slaves they acquired before the removal act. I understand they had to give up the ones they took in after the act was passed, but I'm certain there are a good many of them. They are in a holding area there. The weather is cold and they are going to a much colder spot. They are tired and weary and there's no fight left in any of them. It would be like taking candy from a baby to convince the slaves to board one of my ships with a promise to see that they remain in Florida. We wouldn't be lying to them. They will stay in the state, but they will belong to you. I want the cattle. I will get the slaves for you if you will drive the cattle to my place at Lake George. In turn, I will train your slaves to work your fields if you will mark and brand my cattle and teach someone to care for them for me, if you don't want to take on the responsibility yourself. The only thing I ask is that I have access to the young half-breed Indian women to warm my old bones while I train them and the men to work. I'm sure many of them already know how but will have to be psychologically reconditioned to work a plantation."

No problem, thought Mose, wouldn't make me jealous a bit. I like a woman with milk-white skin. I don't care for the dark meat.

Kingsley was looking at Mose who was thinking and had said nothing. "I think we can pull it off, don't you, Mr. Barber?"

"Call me Mose, Mr. Kingsley. I ain't used to that 'Mr. Barber' bit. What's a worryin' me is I ain't got no money to start a plantation if I had a thousand slaves. They have to be housed and fed and I got to have equipment to farm and build fences and lots o' other expenses. There's a depression going on and cattle jest ain't movin' that good."

"You leave all that to me, Mose. I have an ample cash flow, more than I'll ever need and we can work out a simple loan so that you can build up your plantation and not have to pay me back until you get things moving and you have a working establishment. You can come to me anytime you need an additional loan and advice. I know your capabilities, Mose. I've done my homework well or you wouldn't be sitting in my office right now, considering venturing out on such a large-scaled endeavor, if I didn't have confidence in your ability to make a go of it. I've gathered gemstones from all over the world and one of the greatest thrills is to see them polished and cut into magnificent gems. You are a rough stone, Mose and I'd like to try to polish you into a plantation squire such as this country has never seen. We are going to need men to run this state. Statehood is right around the corner in a few months. You, and your wife, I might add, are wasting your talents in poverty. All you need is a push in the right direction. What you say we get on with it?"

Mose sat, silent in shock. It was better than any of his wildest daydreams and he found it difficult to find his tongue. He sat for a minute, his nose between his two fingers, pondering the magnitude of it all and then finally looked up at Kingsley and smiled. "Yore a smart man, Mr. Kingsley. You think I can do hit, then I know I can. There's jest one question. What's my wife got to do with it? Women don't have no business stickin' their nose into a man's affairs. I never let mine interfere with my cattle operation."

"And rightly so, Mose. A woman has no place out in the flies and dirt and cow dung. But you learn to listen to your wife when it comes to handling your slaves and your social life that comes with a large plantation. I'd say it was almost impossible to run a plantation without a good wife. Your overseer can work them to death but it takes a woman's touch to see that they are fed, doctored and otherwise cared for properly. They are perhaps another form of animal to you, Mose. You think only of the work they will perform. Your wife's gentle nature will provide the human dignity they must feel in order for them to thrive. Listen to her advice. Don't take the bull by the horns, as you cow people say and ignore her contribution or it will be your downfall. Yes, a plantation must have a woman's touch. I've never seen a thriving one without it. Agreed?" He looked at Mose without smiling.

Mose agreed. He must know what he's talking about, Mose thought.

"Do you have men you can trust? No one must know what you have planned or where you are going exactly until you have the cattle on the run. I figure $14.00 a month for a driver. I'll double that. They'll have to know how to fight Indians. I hear Tiger Tail is working from Cedar Key over to Fort White so you'll have to swing over south of Newnansville and Fort King before heading west. You're biggest problem will be around Green swamp before you hit Fort Brooke."

He took a large map from his desk and spread it out. "This was just printed a couple of years ago. The dotted lines are the reservations established in 1823. Of course, there are no Indians there now. Here's a lake where I have a sawmill and rice field. I will give you a letter of introduction and you and your men can rest there. Here's Payne's Landing on the Ocklawaha, Fort King, on down to Okihumpkee and then Peltklakaha. You can cross the Little Withlacoochee here. Stay clear west of there. If you can make it to Fort Dade, you'll be fine. You'll have to cross the south end of the Big Withlacoochee on into Fort Foster. If you turn west here, you can cross the Hillsboro River and it'll take you past the bottom end of

Lake Thonotosassa and into Fort Brooke."

"Where you say they got Injuns and their cattle?"

"I say probably right here on this peninsula. You'll have to scout around and see for sure once you get there. If you come out of there with them, follow the north side of the Hillsboro past Fort Foster and stay off the main trail. If you can find anyone who fought with Zachary Taylor, you'll have someone that knows the country. Just remember to stay out of the Big Withlacoochee and Green Swamp and along the western shore." Kingsley sat back, letting Mose study the map for a minute and then folded it up and handed it to him.

Mose said, "I know a man right here near Black Creek fought with Taylor. I'll swing by there first thing in the morning and see can I git him to line up some help."

"I can get my ship ready to go in two days after it gets in here. It'll be here in three days. It'll take me five days to get around to the bay. I want to get out with the slaves at the same time you get the cattle. It must be done the same night or the authorities will be on the alert and arouse suspicion. Let's make it sometime around the seventeenth of January. My ship's name is the *Madagaster* and my name will be on her side. Just show anyone on watch the paper I gave you and he'll take you aboard. Come after midnight. I can wait for you a few days, but not too long. Someone will become suspicious if I hang around too long, so, keep your men well hidden and back in the woods until we get it coordinated."

Mose stood up and the two men shook hands.

"I suppose you'll want to get an early start in the morning. I'll awake you at five and get you on your way with a hearty breakfast. I'll have supplies on my ship should you need them then. If not, I'll see that your men are paid when you get the cattle to Lake George. Give me a week or ten days and then come back here at your convenience and we'll work out the details for construction of your quarters and the financial arrangements. In the meantime," handing him a pouch, "Here's enough gold to get you started on your trip. We can't afford to let financial difficulties hold you back. The seventeenth, remember?"

Mose smiled and bid him goodnight as he climbed the stairs and tried to sleep. His body rested but his mind whirled with plans, plans and more plans, and he finally drifted into a fitful sleep.

The eastern sky had begun to show signs of light as Mose and Rich rode down the lane toward Jacksonville. Their breath puffed a white vapor into the cold January air. Soon a mist began to rise from the dark, placid waters of the St. Johns and the sky turned pink and then a golden sun streaked through the pines as the pair rode past Black Creek and stopped at a cabin about a mile from where its waters emptied into the river. Two old mangy, cur dogs rose from under the porch of a tiny cabin and barked a warning as the horses approached the gate. Smoke was curling from a large chimney and a tall, sharp-faced youth of twenty opened the door, musket in one hand and a lighted splinter of pine in the other. He peered into the darkness, a shock of carrot colored hair shimmering from the light of his torch.

"Haloow the house," warned Mose as he came to the gate. "That you Needham? Hit's Mose Barber from over on the south fork of the St. Marys."

Needham held the torch a little higher and walked out on the porch, trying to get a better look at the two men on horseback. He stood there for a minute and then laughed. "Well Mose, what the hell you a doin' in this neck o' the woods this time o' day?" He cursed the dogs and said "Git back under thet house where you belong!" The two old dogs tucked their tails between their legs and crawled back to their warm beds under the porch with no thanks or award for sounding the alarm. "Git down and come on in, hits a busting the bark this mornin' and we been sittin' around the far a dreadin' to git out and try to make a mark. Who you got thar wit'cha?" peering in the darkness at Rich, not sure if he was dark skinned or black.

"Hit's my nigger, Rich. Mind if I bring him in, he's not used to sittin' out in the cold. He's my house-nigger."

"Hell no, bring him on in by the far. I had a terrible time gittin' my ole lady to crawl out and fix me a cuppa coffee but we got some a'bilein' in here," as he opened the door.

The room smelled of urine, sweat and rancid bacon grease. "Take thet cheer over thar next to the far," offered Needham. "You musta got a good early start from somewheres."

"Been over spent the night with one o' yore rich neighbors at Laurel Grove."

"Old Kingsley?" Needham waited for Mose to say more but Mose looked at the young girl, pouring a cup of coffee, and said nothing else.

"This here's Mrs. Yates," Needham said. "We jest had a young'un and she's been up half the night. Hit's a sleepin' jest now."

Mose looked at her as he thanked her for the coffee. She was strikingly pretty but clearly of Indian extraction and very young. Mose never missed an opportunity to give one the eye, though. I never pass up one from thirteen to forty, he always told himself. You never know when you'll find one with a roving eye.

"We're a jest a gittin' settled in good. Jest got the bare necessities. Been a livin' with Ma and Pa down the way but Ma and the wife here got to fussin' 'bout how much salt to put in the grits. There got to be a row every morning bout the grits 'til we jest couldn't stand hit no more. Guess hit's alright fer young folks to live with the old ones if'n you can stand the row, but if you can't, you can't and so we up and moved out."

Mose thought of Leah and Susan and the seventeen children and slaves at his house. "Kingsley wants me to ramrod a cow drive fer him. Down south a ways."

"That right?"

"Figger you might want a'git in on hit. Pays the best you ever had and liable to last well over a month. If you kin git away."

"I kin shore use some cash 'bout now. How much you talkin' 'bout?"

"How does $25 a month and mighty good rations sound? I kin give you a advance right now to take care o' the family while yore gone."

The young girl had gone to the back of the room and was changing the baby who had awakened. Mose explained the details to Needham and so it was agreed on. The young girl, scarcely more than a child, was holding the baby near the fire.

"Meet the newest member of the house," Needham said proudly. "This here's John. He ain't a year old. He'll be a sittin' a horse 'fore you can turn around."

The young wife, Malinthy, said something Mose didn't understand but recognized as the Indian language, but spoke to Mose in good English. "How many children do you have, Mr. Barber?"

"They's nine o' mine and eight o' Will's, my brother that jest got kilt last summer. And his wife's 'specting one any day now."

"Can you believe Ma and Pa's got a two year old and Pa almost seventy? Change o' life baby, I guess. One reason Malinthy and her couldn't git along. I guess, her a'goin' into the change and all. Lord have mercy on me, you with eighteen in a few months and me jest a'gittin' started."

"You got a couple o' hands in mind you can bring along on the drive?" Mose asked Needham.

"Know of two o' the best in the world but one o' 'em hits the bottle purty hard and the other quarrels all the time but you couldn't want fer better, drunk or sober. He's jest as easy goin' as kin be and I'd rather have him along drunk than most men cold sober."

"Well, I don't touch the stuff myself but ain't got nothin' agin a man that does long as he gits the job done," Mose told him, and with that he got up to leave. He reached into his coat pocket and brought out the pouch and handed Needham some money. Needham gave it to his wife and smiled and told her not to spend it all in one place.

"See you, come Friday," Mose said as he untied Ring from the fence. The dogs had come out from under the porch.

"Friday hit is," said Needham. "Don't give them old curs no never mind. They won't foller you off," as he watched Rich and Mose mount up and head west.

Chapter 10

Mose and Rich got home late that night but he and Leah sat in the kitchen where Mose had built up the fire and talked at length about his plans. Mose was in a state of euphoria. The magnitude of his plans was frightening to Leah. Most of all she was frightened of the dangerous trip to Fort Brooke and the moral issue of stealing the cattle and slaves, but Mose was so confident that the slaves would be better off at a nice plantation than they would be out in Arkansas "in thet Godfer-saken country." He argued that the Indians had taken the cattle from the Span-iards and they rightfully belonged in Florida in the first place. He made it sound so right she was quickly convinced.

"Just promise me you'll treat them all just like you do the ones we have and I'll help you all I can, Mose. You know I won't go along with treating them like wild animals."

Mose remembered what advice Kingsley had given him. "You know what old man Kingsley told me the other night? He told me to let you handle the slaves when they're here around the house and in their quarters. Said you'd know better how to do hit than an overseer, so that's what I'm a gonna do. He can handle 'em out in the field but they're all y'orn here at the place. Fair enough? There's one thing I got to have understood. When one of 'em needs a whuppin' they're a gonna git hit and I don't want any interference. Understood?"

"Whipping, yes. Thrashing or beating, no. Understood?" Leah said. And Mose agreed.

"We've always treated our slaves as members of the family, Mose, and I know it's difficult to do that with so many more but they can have their own life after they come in from the fields. I've been around Dulcie and Rich long enough to know they've got feelings just like we have. They like to sing and gossip, and have fun just like we do."

"And make love twice as much, if'n I hear right," Mose laughed.

"And I don't want any mulatto children being born here either. Do I make myself clear?"

"You ain't a gonna have no problem with me in that department. I don't know what about some of these little hard-peckered boys like Champ and Isiah and Francis."

"You can just put things straight with some strong talk right from the start and have it understood with your overseer. I'm sure you'll want a better man than Jim Gunter or at least more help than he is."

"Kingsley said we'd work all that out. Hit's gonna be a big undertakin' and will take time but you and me, we can git the job done, wife. I'll jest need your help."

"Haven't I always stood behind you in everything, Mose?"

Mose smiled and put his arm around her. "Let's go to bed, and we'll talk about hit some more under the kivvers."

Mose dug into getting ready for his trip with a vengeance. Benjamin and George had not come in with the cattle but he was glad they hadn't, in a way. He had lots of things to do before Friday and the crivis was brown and dead and the cattle would have nothing to eat after the hard freeze. He, for one, would be glad to see them driven further south where the grass was not burned brown with the frost and they would calve without dying, and would multiply.

He sent Isiah to Susan's to get Francis and Champ and put the boys to work oiling saddles and repairing tack. Susan came over the next day to help Leah cook syrup cake and sweet potatoes and put in supplies for the chuck wagon. All the while Mose was straining for the sound of lowing cattle and wondered what he'd do when Needham arrived with his two men and the cattle and Ben and George weren't there to help. They had a schedule to keep and he couldn't deviate from it but a day or two. He'd much rather give himself a little leeway and get to Fort Brooke early than be pushing it for time. Champ and Francis were to be taken along on the drive but Sammy and Isiah were told they had to stay and help with the place.

"Now who in the Sam Hill you think's gonna help out around here with me and Champ and Francis gone? We still got two places to keep up." But his brother Sam came driving up in the wagon that night, his foot wrapped up in a bandage soaked with turpentine. He had sliced it open with the axe and would have to drive the chuck wagon and would need help around the camp. He agreed he'd watch after the younger boys. Mose promised Susan and Leah they would not take the chuck wagon all the way. "When we start outa there with them cows we're gonna high tail hit and can't have no wagon tryin to keep up. They'll be safe enough."

By Thursday noon, Mose could hear the boys coming with the cattle. He heard the whips crack a good thirty minutes before he could hear the cattle lowing and told the boys to run down, open up the crivis and help the men drive them in. "Talk about timin'," Mose beamed. "I couldn't got hit any better if'n I'd tried. Them boys needed a little rest 'fore they take off agin and they hit it bout right on the nail."

The rations of grits and meal, lard, sweet potatoes, ham, and sausage were packed in the buckboard and the saddlebags loaded and everything was made ready. The day was bitterly cold and the cattle had laid down most of the afternoon. By dark Needham Yates had ridden in with two unlikely looking drovers. They were both young boys, not much older than Isiah and Francis, but both had seen service in the war the past two years and were more experienced than appeared at first glance. One was a short, wiry little runt called Percy, and the other was a tall, rugged looking, red-faced boy that answered to the name of "Whiskey" John. The name was self-explanatory. He had brought his jug along and by the time they had bedded down that night he wasn't feeling any pain. Mose didn't offer any negative feelings about it. He trusted Needham's judgment and figured if Needham said Johnny could keep up, drunk or sober, it was all right with him as long as he got the job done.

Sammy, Isiah and Arch might as well not have gone to bed. They were too excited to sleep. They kept Percy awake until he finally told them, "Dadburnit! Young'uns with the high diddles, anyway. Weren't so cold out there in the barn, I'd roll up my beddin' and move out there—instead of beddin' down here with a bunch o' wiggle-tails. You yahoos git to sleep. Yore asses is a gonna be draggin' out yore tracks 'fore we git to Kingsley's lake."

The drive got off on schedule. The first mistake they made was going within sight of Simeon Dell's place and let Whiskey John restock his jug. About three in the afternoon, he was laughing and singing but doing what was expected of him, driving his share of the cattle. His little cowpony was evidently used to his indulgence and plodded right along, turning back strays and keeping up. Actually, the pony was doing his job and Johnny was just along for the ride.

As the cattle cleared the end of a swamp and headed for higher ground of tall pines and palmettos, a group of Kingsley's slaves had paused with their timber cutting to allow the cattle to go by. Johnny and Percy were doing drag and pushing the cattle along quietly. The chuck wagon was bringing up the rear about a hundred yards behind.

Suddenly Johnny spied the black men standing in a small group, watching the cattle and spurred his horse with a dead run right into the middle of them and pulled the little pony around on his hocks, gun held high in the air and shot one time.

"I'm drunker than a skunk and when I git this drunk I jest hafta shoot somebuddy," he yelled and fired again. The slaves bolted and ran, scattering like a covey of quail into the timber. The two guards, who had been lying under a tree in the shade, asleep, jumped up and started yelling at the slaves to come back. Johnny just sat there; laughing so hard he almost fell off his horse. By this time, Mose heard the commotion and stopped to investigate. The slaves had run to Sam's wagon and were peering out behind it. The guards were soon in a shouting match with Percy who was trying to explain that his friend was drunk and meant no harm.

"I lose one o' them niggers and Mr. Kingsley'll have you in jail" one of the guards threatened.

Mose explained that one of his hands had indeed had a little too much to drink and told Johnny to get his head on straight and told Percy to see that his friend didn't spook the cattle or cause anymore trouble or they could both head for Jacksonville. Johnny wasn't so drunk he couldn't hang his head in shame and was very docile and contrite as he went to the back of the herd with Percy.

The next day, some of the crew went with Mose to push the cattle a little more to the east where they turned them out to graze and the chuck wagon went on to meet them at a designated spot that evening. On the way Sam and the boys jumped a bunch of hogs and the boys, ever the bottomless pits, convinced their Uncle Sam to let them get one to eat. When they all gathered up, Johnny told them they had caught a marked hog, belonging to the meanest man in the territory and if he caught them with it he'd probably shoot them right on the spot. So, they buried the hide and decided to eat it anyway.

Of course, as luck would have it, he wandered by camp just as they were getting ready to eat and being the good host that he was, Mose asked him to stay and eat. The man took one look at the freshly butchered hog, fat from his acorns and said not a word. They had cooked a big pot of grits and laid out the sweet potatoes Leah had baked.

"Smells mighty good. Believe I'll take you up on that," and dug right in.

Percy looked at him right hard and said, "Yeah, and if you say thet's yore hog yore'r a'eatin', yore'r a goddamn liar."

Everybody froze and looked at the man, fully expecting him to grab his gun and start shooting. There was a long silence as the boys looked at Mose in terror. But the man looked at Percy and laughed and agreed no matter whose it was it was might good eating.

That night after he left, Mose told Needham he had certainly picked a couple of crazy boys to bring along. Never mind the Indians and the law—if we make it back alive with those two we'll be lucky, and Needham said for one thing there'd probably never be a dull moment anyway. That man knew that was his shoat but was so lonesome for good company he didn't want to spoil a good evening with a fight over one little hog.

They were soon at Payne's Landing on the Ocklawaha River and were making good time now without the cattle. They knew they were fairly safe from Indians but kept a watchful eye out for Tiger Tail lest he wander over into their territory.

They scattered deer as they rode past the wild blackberry bushes and purple beauties growing under loblolly pines. They flushed quail from the bush clover and beggar weed. An otter scampered to safety from the dogs and into the deepest hole in one of the little branches that ran from cypress pond to cypress pond. The terrain was unusual. It never changed gradually but dropped from the big hammocks to low oak scrubs and then to gall berry flats, myrtles and cypress ponds all in just a few hundred yards. There would be high scrub ridges and the limbs of low growing scrub oaks that could tear a man's clothes like steel wire if he rode too close. There were ty-ty bushes, flycatchers and the ever-present saw palmettos on the higher ground. On the low ground grew the beautiful hammocks of live oaks, hickory, wild persimmons, magnolias and countless other bastard varieties of small oaks and bushes. Then the land would drop off suddenly again into the flatwoods of gall berries, myrtles and ponds ringed with sand weed and much higher palmettos, higher than a man's head while mounted on a horse. These small, clear ponds were full of water and a favorite roosting place for wood ducks and whooping cranes. Some even were deep enough for large fish and frogs and an occasional 'gator.

Mose would shake his head and say, "Lordy, Lordy, I sure do like this country."

"You ain't seen nothin' yet," teased Whiskey John. He told Mose of what it looked like on farther south with long stretches of grassy prairies and marshes. "A cowman's heaven," he said.

They all spent the last night together at the north end of Panasofkee Lake. Here Sam and the little boys would stay and wait for the men to come back with the cattle.

The men pushed on past the Withlacoochee Cove where Osceola and his braves fought and won the first battle of the Indian War, but had lost the war. At mid-morning they paused in silence and looked around where the Dade massacre had occurred. Here Whiskey John explained that he had lost a good friend and he himself would probably have been killed had he not woke up from a hangover that had kept him from the march.

Here the trail headed due south. Green Swamp was to their left and Tiger Tail to their right. They tightened their flanks and kept an eagle eye on the dogs who could quickly pick up a scent long before the Indians could draw them into ambush. They forded the little Withlacoochee, passed Fort Dade, crossed the main run of the Withlachoochee and the Hillsborough near Lake Foster and followed the south side of the river near the north end of Lake Thonotosassa. Here they pitched camp.

Noah and Needham scouted the area and found a large, clear spring a mile or so to the east. There was no Indian sign and the dogs were relaxed as if there was no fresh scent near. That night Mose took out the map and they all looked it over.

"Hit's about a day's ride from here, wouldn't you say, Johnnie?"

"Easy."

"Alright, I want you boys to pair off and ride in jest two at a time. Spread it out so hit won't look suspicious. Get the lay of the land so you'll know what hit looks like and then wait fer me about here on the south side of the river. I'll come in after dark and we'll go over any last minute plans. We could use some fresh horses, but I don't know if there's any available. Maybe Kingsley will know. If not we can make hit back to Sam and the boys and then we can lay around and rest fer a spell. Won't be no rush after that. You boys git a good night's rest. We got a long ride ahead o' us and no tellin' what them cattle will be like, so git some sleep."

The next day, before light, Mose and Noah headed down the trail to Fort Brooke. They had no problem finding Kingsley's ship in the bay and rowed out to it. Kingsley was relieved to see them. The cabin was warm and the night had a chill on it.

"We've been here just a day," he told Mose. "You have plenty of help?"

"We got all we need and good men at that" Mose told him. "They're about a day's ride from here."

Mose scouted around and quietly found where the cattle were held. The Indians were cold and huddled under a shelter. Kingsley had the guards in his pocket. There were two peninsulas that jutted out into a smaller bay. The Indians were on the nearest one and the cattle on the one close to the mainland. It was all arranged with the slaves. Most of them wanted to come with Kingsley.

"Give me ample time to slip out of the harbor before you make your move with the cattle. It will take a while 'fore they're missed in this chilly weather, so you'll have time."

"We'll try to move 'em jest 'fore day" Mose said. I'll need some help to take down the fence." Kingsley said he'd arrange it.

"Like takin' candy from a baby," Mose predicted and so it was.

Kingsley slipped quietly out of the harbor with the slaves and Mose drove off with the cattle and not a shot was fired.

They pushed the cattle as hard as they could the first day and the men worked well, even Whiskey John tended to business and Percy didn't quarrel, for a change. It was well into the night before they felt safe to bed the cattle down. It was still cold and they risked a fire the next morning to dress by and have a hot meal. The dogs were tired and foot-sore and reluctant to get out of a big palmetto patch where they had slept out of the wind.

The next night they were relaxed enough to build a big fire and the men bedded down as close as possible. By the time Whiskey John had finished his shift at first watch and come in to sleep, the wind had picked up and was blowing the smoke from the fire toward the only spot left vacant for him to spread his bed roll. He lay down, bone weary and tried to sleep but the smoke and soot was too much for him. He got up, walked a distance from the campfire and yelled, "Loose horse, loose horse." Now, the men had to carry everything on their horses with the chuck wagon being back at the lake. All the food, dry clothes, saddle bags and to say nothing of the horse being the man's only transportation back home. Without a horse he'd have to ride "shank's mare" as the saying goes. Meaning he'd have to walk, and carry his saddle and bridle and much of his gear. So a loose horse was a serious matter. All hands sprang from their warm beds and dashed toward the horses, finding them securely tied and Johnny was lying on his bedroll way from the smoke, snug as a bug.

"Musta one o' you boys had a nightmare," was his only explanation as the rest of the men tried to find a spot around the fire with him.

When they got back to Sam and the boys at the chuck wagon there was plenty of meat hanging in the camp. There was a deer hanging on a gamboler stick and three turkey hens swaying in the wind by their necks, in the shade. Four swamp cabbage boots lay under a huge oak tree on the beach of the lake.

"Looks like you boys have been a eatin' high on the hog," Needham remarked. "I think I'll run my old lady off and take you home to cook for me, Sam"

They had fried turkey breast and swamp cabbage and since it had warmed up considerably, stripped off their sweat-stained shirts and bathed in the shallow, warm water of the lake. It was nice to laze around and have nothing to do for a full day.

Sometime in the night, the dogs began to growl. The horses stomped and snorted and swayed their rear ends back and forth, straining at their halters. By the time some of the men woke up, the hair was raised on the nap of the dogs' backs.

"Quiet, everybody!" Mose cautioned as he raised his hand in the air and everyone held their breath and listened.

"Cat?" Needham asked.

"Most likely a bar, I'd guess," Noah answered. Mose agreed.

By now they could hear the cattle up and restless.

"Best git to the cattle," Mose cautioned. By now the camp was alerted and everyone beginning to saddle their horses. Arch woke up Francis and Isiah and had them help him and their Uncle Sam hitch the team. They grabbed all the bed-rolls and gear and threw them in the wagon.

"We got to git thet wagon into the lake as fer as we can git hit. Them cattle won't run into water. They'll head t'uther way. Untie them dogs so they can git outer the way. They won't chase a bar."

Whiskey John and Ben were riding watch. Whiskey John immediately noticed a change in the cattle.

"I think somethin's got these here cows stirred up." Johnny said. He rode around to Ben. "Kin you sing in Seminole?"

"Hell no, I cain't even sing in English. What you want to sing fer, you drunk agin?"

"No, I ain't drunk here in the middle of the early mornin. I jest thought if we could start hummin' and singin' a tune maybe we could calm these fellers down' fore they spook and run," and he started singing. "Days a breakin' and I must go, Let me feel o' yore bello-o."

He had just reached the far side of the herd that was now milling and all were up on their feet. They had fed around all day. Rested and their bellies full, they would spook easily and Johnny knew it. He prayed the men would get around on his side to help keep them milling. He saw a big red crumpled horned cow snort and dash from the center of the bunch and, as he predicted, she spooked the herd and they all took off like the roar of a freight train. He made a wild dash to get out of their way, as he knew he couldn't turn them back alone. He spurred for all his might, jumping logs and bursting right through the middle of palmetto patches and over brush. He had just cleared the outside when his little pony stepped in a "gopher hole" and fell to his knees. Johnny went flying over the pony's head and literally dived into the only open, sandy spot on the hill. He lay motionless.

Back at the wagon, Sam had been jockeying around to get the team out into the lake. He knew the cows might dash around the beach of the lake but not into it. Francis and Isiah had huddled under the pile of bedding and supplies thrown helter-skelter.

"Ever been in a stampede, Uncle Sam?" Isiah asked.

"A couple. Hits a bad thing, a stampede. Cows'll spook in the night. Jest one cow can set 'em off and they'll take off like a bat out'a hell and run over anything in their path. I've seen 'em bust thru pole fences like they wuz straw. They can strip a horse's hide and hair offen him clean down to the bone. Hits somethin' you shore don't want to see."

"Why don't they take the dawgs and run the bar outa the country?"

"Cause the dawgs won't run a bar, idiot? Didn't you hear Uncle Sam jest say? They jest hunt cows and Injuns."

"Besides, a bar's unpredictable," whispered Sam. "He might run and then agin he might turn and fight. That'd spook the cows fer sure."

About that time, they heard the roar of the cattle.

"We're in fer hit now," said Sam. "Least wise I think they're a runnin' the other way. Sure as hell hope everybuddy got outa their way."

Out near the herd Mose said, "Let 'em rip! No turnin' 'em now." As the men stopped their horses in their tracks and listened to the thunder, as the cattle disappeared into the woods.

"They'll probably run about three mile and settle down. Weren't many calves in 'em anyways and what there wuz didn't mount to a hill o' beans."

"Hell of a note, Uncle Mose," said Champ. "We come all this way and not a minute's trouble and now look what's happened."

"Can't git all yore 'coons up the same tree all the time, boys," said Noah Raulerson, philosophically.

"Yore right about that," Needham put in. "Can't have hit yore way all the time."

"I knew things wuz a goin' too smooth. Goddamn bar. Hope them heifers run over him and stomped him clear into the ground."

"Won't hafta skin him that way, Mose," said his cousin George.

Everyone had something to say, just to release the tension.

They had started to the camp when Ben came riding up, "What do we do now, cousin Mose?" he asked.

"Not much we can do in the dark. Jest go on back to camp and wait fer light and see how fur they've run."

"You seen Johnny, Ben?" Asked Percy, remembering his partner.

"Not since the stampede," said Ben. "He went around on the other side a singin', thought hit'd calm 'em down some."

"Thet's about the way they run. Let's go on in and make a pot o' coffee and see if'n he comes in. Might be back waiting at camp now."

Sam and the boys already had stoked up the fire and had the coffee on. The men dug around and found their bedrolls to lie on but no one felt like sleep. It would be daylight in a couple of hours and so they went ahead and fed their horses so they could get an early start.

"Listen," said Champ, and everyone cocked their head and looked out into the darkness.

"Horse a comin' back to camp."

"I knew old Johnny'd come a draggin' back in," said Percy, obviously relieved and got up to go greet his friend.

But it was just Johnny's horse. The young drover wasn't on him. The little cow pony came into camp, greeted the other horses and went looking for his feed, dragging the bridle reins on the ground.

"Looks sound to me," said Mose, as they all looked the little pony over. "Not a scratch anywhere I can see," said another.

"Probably got knocked out. He's a lyin' out there somewhere and I'm a gonna

82

go look fer him, " said Percy as he started to get his horse.

"Some o' you boys best look on foot," and the crew took off in the dark, calling Johnny's name.

They had split up around the perimeter of where the cattle had run. The ground had been literally plowed for a radius of a hundred yards. They had stripped every bush of its leaves and even palmettos looked as if a bush hog had gone through them. The sky had lightened so that they could see the outline of what was left of the countryside but a gray mist blanketed most of the area, making visibility limited.

They had searched for the better part of an hour and were about to despair when someone yelled, "Over here. He's over here!"

Everyone ran in that direction to see Johnny, sitting up, rubbing the back of his neck. Percy was by his side and squatting down by his friend.

"You alright, buddy?"

"What the hell happened?" asked Johnny, still dazed.

"Don't look like you got run over" said Percy, feeling of Johnny and helping him to his feet.

"My horse! My horse alive?" Johnny cried, blinking his eyes and looking around with a dazed look, unsteady on his feet.

"Yore horse come back to camp and has done et his feed. Not a hair turned back and yore gear in good shape. Sit down fore you fall down," Percy said, gently, helping his friend back down on the ground.

Johnny reached up and felt of his head. "Where's my hat? Lost my hat."

"Yore lucky to have on yore head," said Mose. "Champ, let's git him up on yore horse and let him ride back to camp."

"You young'uns look around and find my hat and I'll give you all a plug o' ter-backer fer hit," Johnny promised.

Johnny spent the rest of the day in the wagon, sleeping on the bedrolls like he would sleep off a drunk. He complained of seeing double and Mose said he couldn't get back on a horse until he could see better. They soon had the strays rounded up and made camp for the night, Johnny had a headache the next day but insisted on getting back on his horse as they left for Okihumpkee, into what is now the Ocala National Forest.

The scrub had burned in spots after the killing freeze. Its naked white sand glistened in the sun, relieved only where the floor was covered by gray-green tufts of deer moss. There is little clay or humus in the sand as any organic matter quickly dries out and blows away. Only salamanders, gophers and ants can burrow in and it quickly falls in on them. Rain percolates thought the white stuff below the roots of anything that attempts to grow there. The scattered sand pines with their short needles and scaly branches were covered with a pinkish-red lichen and now and then a staggerbush, covered with dense felt-like hairs, had popped up. Rosemary leaves roll up like needles so they can't dry out and an abundance of dried seeds survive; so a little vegetation is preserved. These are usually the blue, funneled-shaped flowers of the prostrate morning glory, rosemary and narrow-leaved grasses. Percy described it as just a part of Florida used to hold the rest of it together but Mose said you'd be surprised to find cattle grazing in it.

As they cleared the scrub they found glittering creeks meandering through the cypress strands and hammocks of bay trees and sweet gums.

Rattlesnakes buzzed in the palmetto patches, sounding a warning to the cattle as their hoofs pounded dangerously near. They jumped black bear and panther but they ran off ahead of the herd and posed no threat to anyone. Deer and quail were in abundance. Tremendous cypress trees, five men could not reach around, lined the shore of the river along with water maples, sweet gums and tall bay trees.

They camped that night in view of Drayton Island on the north end of Lake George. Its two thousand acres were the southern boundary of Zephaniah Kingsley's ninety-mile long kingdom. The cows dropped their heads and started feeding contentedly on the lush grass at the river's edge that grew in the water and had come back sweet and tender from the freeze.

Mose's horse had been off his feed so that he wouldn't eat it but would stand and stomp the ground and shake his head back and forth as if in pain. He got so droopy, Mose had tied him to the wagon and ridden along with Sam and the boys to give the little horse a rest. He decided he musta picked up some kind of poisoned weed on the trail, as his belly seemed bloated. They spent the next day, lying around the camp, waiting for Kingsley's man to show up with their pay and the little horse's belly got bigger and bigger, standing around, tied up. Needham suggested Mose have the boys lead him around and around until he got rid of gas and his swollen gut went down. He thought walking behind the wagon had helped keep the horse alive and he needed to keep on moving, so the boys had been taking turns running the pony around in circles, and sure enough he started letting off gas and finally began to lose his bloated gut. The next morning Mose asked Needham how the little horse was doing and if he finally ate any of his feed.

Needham so aptly described the situation. "Yep, he fought hit, but he et hit."

And Mose knew his horse was going to be all right. He knew when an animal won't eat he's trying to tell you something and when he starts eating again, he's on the mend.

The men were finally paid that afternoon and Mose had spent the rest of the day with the overseer, getting instructions as to what brand to put on Kingsley's cattle so they could alter the ones already on them.

Arrangements were made for Mose to stop at the sawmill on the way back and order lumber he would need to start building the extra quarters and sheds for the new plantation. They spent the last night at the overseer's cabin where he and his big fat wife were enjoying the company and the men were hitting the jug.

He had just finished telling Mose and the men about an incident that had happened when a few soldiers and militiamen had come by during the recent war. Some of the troops had stopped by to pick some of Kingsleys' oranges that had escaped the severe freeze in '35 that had wiped out most of the citrus industry. The island, surrounded by the warmer water, had protected the trees from the severest of the cold. The temperature had dropped to seven degrees and an orange tree of any kind was rare in Florida.

"Any of you boys in the war?" he asked, having had no companionship but wife and the slaves for quite a time and that was the only subject he knew to talk about.

"Johnny and Percy wuz," Needham told him.

"What time Johnny weren't in the guard house fer pullin' one of his stunts," Percy explained.

"You mean one like he pulled back at Kingsley's sawmill," Francis asked?

Mose gave him a dirty look as they hadn't intended to tell anyone about that but Mose had to explain what had happened.

"That ain't nothin'," said Percy. "About the dirtiest trick he ever pulled wuz back at Fort Christmas on our cook. He wuz about as cantankerous an old coot as you ever saw."

"Yo're one to talk Percy," Johnny chided.

Percy went on to tell what Johnny had done. One of the cook's pet peeves was anyone riding his horse too close to the cook wagon. He'd haul off and throw a cup or even a skillet at any one he caught too close to it. "He'd holler at us, 'I bet you shitheads never rode yore horses into your Ma's kitchen.'"

"And he wuz the cleanest man you'll ever see and made the best gut stew," added Johnny.

Percy went on with his tale. They had gotten some flour from Fort Mellon and he had baked a big batch of biscuits to go with the stew. There were always so many that some would be left over and he'd save them for the next meal. He would always put these on top so they'd be eaten first and Johnny got onto this and would dig down deep in the lard bucket and get a fresh one every meal.

"We had jest about got to where we wished the flour'd run out so mealtime would be a little more peaceful. Johnny got back to the cook tent early one night and got a 'tater out of a sack, cut hit up in little pellets and stuffed hit down fer shot. When Johnny ran his hand deep down in the lard bucket that night and the cook started cussing him he grabbed his gun and said to the cook, 'You old fart, you've cussed me fer the last time' and shot the old man in the chest. We all thought Johnny had gone berserk for sure and that the old man was mortally wounded. When that wad of soft 'tater pellets peppered his hide, he fell, clutchin' his chest."

But the men could find no blood anywhere on the old man and it took them quite a while to convince him that he wasn't going to die. The Captain didn't think it was nearly as funny as Johnny did and put him in the guardhouse.

"It's a wonder he didn't git us all kilt," said Percy.

"Listen to you talk," Johnny put in. "I remember when we were workin' up the river here at a cow crew an a couple o' the roughest lookin' characters you ever seen rode into camp and the boss fed 'em and let 'em share the fire. They both looked like they'd just as well shoot you as to look at you and we were all givin' them a wide berth. We all went to bed wonderin' if we'd wake up the next mornin' with our throats cut. We were all tippy-toein' around the next morning like we wuz walkin' on eggs and Percy here couldn't find his muzzle full of corn when he started to feed his horse. He walked right into the middle of camp jest like a little banty rooster and hollered, 'Some thievin' son-of-a-bitch has gone and stole my muzzle!' I jest knew we wuz in fer a big gun battle right there. I had mine in my hand I said, 'Here it is Percy, 'giving him mine. He walked off with it and looked down and saw hit weren't his'n and before he could say another word, I had him outa there. I just knew he wuz a gonna git us all shot."

Mose decided on the way home he'd have to find a way to keep Percy and Johnny in the crew just for entertainment.

Chapter 11

Mose was hard at work, laying out his slave quarters with Leah. He had taken a long look at Kingsley's at both Drayton Island and the sawmill that were two different operations. He sat down with the sawmill manager and figured on the amount of lumber he'd have to have. He was getting it on credit anyway and could return any he didn't use. He really, in all his excitement, didn't realize the magnitude of the task that lay ahead. Most plantations start as a small farm and grow through the years as it makes money, enlarge slowly as more slaves are added to the operation. Mose was starting out on a large scale all at once. He was an excellent farmer but there was a lot he didn't know about managing a plantation. He was already wondering where he'd get an overseer that knew more than he did without letting him know it. Mose always had to be in control or at least let everyone think he was.

Ben and George had gone back to Augusta and into South Carolina. Whiskey John and Percy went back home with Needham, but Mose promised them both a job when he got things going.

About five o'clock one morning just as everything had about been planned out, Susan awoke the household, walking the floor in labor. It was freezing cold. Fires were built and water on to boil and Grandma Davis faced her finest hour. She and Dulcie felt confident as midwives and both fought to take control of the situation. Chores were done and breakfast over and still no stork appeared imminent.

Finally, Susan began grabbing at the door jams for support and it was decided she needed to get into the bed. Fresh washed sheets were ironed with a hot iron and Grandma Davis made sure everyone kept their hands washed that came into Susan's room. There was very little puerperal sepsis, known then as "child bed fever," as there were no internal examinations except in a dire emergency and it was fairly well known that everything had to be clean even if they did not know why.

An axe was placed beneath the bed with the blade up to cut the hemorrhage if one should occur and a knife placed under Susan's pillow to cut the pain. This was Dulcie's idea and Grandma Davis allowed her this one concession. She had assembled the scissors, thread and clovine salve at the bedside. Susan had always, before, sat in William's lap but since he was gone, she was made to lie on the bed with Leah, Dulcie and Grandma Davis taking turns holding her knees steady and keeping her flat on the bed. She kept wanting to sit up, as had been her way before. They kept telling her to lie down and not kick her feet. There were usually four or five women in attendance at a birthing but a doctor was seldom available out in the sparsely populated areas and the women had to learn to do with as they could.

Soon Susan was lying on the bed, legs spread apart, knees and thighs shaking with pain. She was pulling for all her might on the rags that had been tied to each lower bedpost and holding onto them for dear life. It was thought that pulling on the rags helped spread the bones apart so the baby would be born much quicker.

She was in excellent condition, having spent most of her pregnancy at Leah's under the watchful eye of Dulcie and Mrs. Davis. She had dutifully taken a tonic of sulfur and blackberry wine and eaten plenty of vegetables and "laid off the sweets."

Mose and the boys had gone out to the barn and built a fire to await the birth so they had not heard the occasional low moans and encouragement from the other women. The house appeared silent.

"How come so many boys is borned 'fore day? Seems like everyone of Ma's has come about this time," Francis asked.

"That's cause that's when most of 'em is got, son," Mose explained. "Us men work so hard each day, ain't got the time nor inclination, to git one until after a good night's sleep."

That seemed logical to Francis who nodded his head and took the whole thing into consideration with what limited knowledge he had of sex.

About that time a high-pitched scream emanated from the bedroom window.

"Aheeeeee-e-e-e!" It seemed to the young boys at the barn that it would never stop and it really didn't until Susan gave out of breath. On its heels came another and then another and by this time Susan's boys were on their feet.

Mose had to assure them that nothing was wrong. "Women do that now and then."

"I never heered her do thet last time."

"Well, all babies is different they tell me."

"My Ma neither," said Isiah. "I never heered her sound like that. Sounds jest like she's singin."

"I think your Ma missed her calling. She could have been one of those opera stars I heard one time in Charleston," said Grandpa Davis.

"Must hurt an awful lot," said little Arch, his eyes big as saucers.

"I guess you'd squeal too if'n you wuz having to shit a gourd, Mr. Smarty Pants," said Champ, not to anyone in particular. He felt obligated to defend his mother and at the same time was ashamed at the racket she was making.

Susan ripped one more high note and then cut it short right in the middle. For a moment, there was silence in the house and then the crying of an indignant baby, squalling at the top of its lungs. There was great activity inside the bedroom. The cord was cut extra long and tied with a heavy piece of thread. Dulcie had placed a clean cloth on a shovel and scorched it a deep brown in the fireplace. She had cut a hole in it before it was scorched and it had been lying, nice and warm awaiting the birth. The cord was pulled through the hole and there it would stay, next to the baby's navel until the cord fell off. It would rot off in about five to six days. Another scorched cloth, covered with mutton tallow was placed over the coiled cord and a band wrapped around the baby's abdomen so he wouldn't rupture while crying. They all waited until Susan passed the placenta, then called the "afterbirth," and Dulcie placed it in a bucket and took it out to the edge of the porch to Rich and it was buried in the edge of the scrub. She stuck her head out to the waiting men and announced that it was a girl and the entire audience was immediately relieved and disappointed at the same time. They, of course, wanted a boy. The little girl was named Lydia.

Susan was cleaned, fresh sheets applied, given a dose of castor oil and allowed to sleep all day.

Mose went about the business at hand, building not only his slave quarters and sheds but also a new house for Susan and her family. She had already had a set-to with Mose about disciplining her children and told him he could take care of them when he had them working for him, but when they were home she'd appreciate it if he'd leave it up to her. He called her a granite head but secretly admired her for her stand. He liked a woman with spunk.

After he had finished his buildings and Susan's house, Mose laid out his fields he planned to cultivate. They were broken only by a few dense woods and wetlands he didn't consider suitable for farming. These would eventually be utilized for timber and rice. He planned to put in fifty acres in sugar cane, fifty in cowpeas and corn, planted together, and eventually two hundred in tobacco. That posed a problem as tobacco had to be planted in virgin soil. So he would use the tobacco fields as timberland until they could be planted in tobacco. Three hundred acres would be in cotton, the big money crop. Another forty acres were to be in sweet potatoes, peanuts and a small peach orchid. Will's old cabin and surrounding land were utilized as headquarters for his cattle, sheep, mules, horses and hogs except for the ones he planned to fatten up around the house. Peanuts were not for sale but were to be fed to the hogs and the peanut hay to the mules.

It took many trips over to Laurel Grove to work out the details. Kingsley suggested certain rules that Mose had not even considered for the control of the slaves. Certain infractions considered severe enough for a flogging were fighting, injuring the mules and not being clean. Mose had not even considered any of these. Kingsley explained that not only were unclean slaves and their cabins unsightly and smelly, but they also were a source of illness and disease. Slaves were not to work on Sunday except for punishment. They would have two to three days off during Christmas. The only time they would be expected to work at night was for shelling corn and cowpeas, feeding the mules and horses and other livestock and certain seasonal, once-a-year occasions such as cane grindings, corn shuckings, and putting tobacco in the barns.

He also reminded Mose that there were certain territorial rules that applied to all slaves and he would have to abide by them. They were not allowed weapons, could not use signals such as beating drums or blowing a horn. They could not strike a white person even in self-defense. There would be a curfew and one could not be out of the quarters after that unless with a white person or some authorization. They could not travel even in the daytime on the public road or in groups except under these same conditions.

They could not be taught to read or write, although many of them were under the authorization of their masters, and Leah said this was one rule she would be glad to break. Stealing, murder and manslaughter were capital offenses but Mose said this was one rule he intended to break unless it involved murdering one of his friends or family. He couldn't see how killing a good slave for murdering another got you anywhere, when you'd have two dead ones instead of one. Of course, if it got to be a habit then he'd have to go. As for stealing, goods could always be replaced and no way they could amount to as much as a good slave was worth, unless it was one of his horses.

There were certain tasks expected of every able-bodied slave. Each field hand would work fifty rows an acre in length in the spring and double that as the plants got larger and crowded out the weeds. Children began fieldwork at age ten but only then at their mother's side until they became a teen and then they were responsible for a full load. After age fifty, tasks were reduced to half. Besides the hoeing, planting and harvesting there would be ditches to dig, fences to build and mend, timber to cut, new ground to clean, new buildings to build and many, many small tasks.

And then there was the matter of food and clothing for the slaves. Basic food was cornmeal and salt pork. This would be supplemented by sweet potatoes, cowpeas, greens and fruit. Actually, this was little less than Mose's family had eaten, except for beef and fresh game.

Each male slave must have two shirts, two pair of cotton pants each fall. The women--two chemises, two cotton frocks and all, a wool jacket every other year. Susan shuddered at all the weaving but Mose assured her the cloth would all be bought until they could train the older slaves to weave.

Many of them might know how already. "But Mose," she said, "that's more than we're used to having ourselves." And Mose told her all of that would change.

The food would be served from a central cookhouse until families paired off and began to have their own houses and cook their own. A hospital had to be built to take care of the sick. Grandma Davis immediately decided she would supervise that part. Certain diseases such as hookworms, dirt eating and malaria took their toll although there was a certain resistance to malaria to be expected among these slaves as they had been living with the Indians all this time. Mose was soon to find that the main illness was apathy and an aversion to work that took the form of non-specific diseases. Certain health practices besides cleanliness had to be observed. Never leave the cabins before sun up or get wet. Accidents took place in the dark and the cold and dampness could reduce resistance to disease. They were to straighten up and walk tall when coming in from the fields after bending over all day.

There were mules to buy, farming equipment, ropes for plow lines, sack cloth, larger skillets and kettles, blankets, and on an on. Susan and Leah were hard put to think of it all. They were going to have to cut out all the cloth, sew it up and label it for each slave. It would come by the bolt. Shoes and hats came by the box. There would be no frills or collars. The shoes had brass caps on the toes so they would not scuff. They were to be worn only in the soft, plowed ground in the winter and to church. The rest of the time they were to go barefoot.

Leah added one rule to it all and was very adamant about it. Absolutely no slaves sold that broke up a family unless the parents or spouse approved. "They aren't animals like your dogs and horses and they have feelings and love just like we do. Under no circumstances will I allow one to be dragged from this place, kicking and screaming and the ones left, crying and wringing their hands. I'll get my gun and see that nobuddy leaves this place with one. And I want that understood right now."

Mose had never seen Leah take such a firm stand and he decided right then and there he'd better abide by her rule.

Kingsley gave Mose specific instructions for an overseer. "He's different from a hired man," he told Mose. He not only had to work in the fields but also had to be capable of running things in Mose's absence. He didn't have to be particularly intelligent or have any ambition—mostly just desire a place to stay and a woman to warm his bed. Leah reminded Mose the man would have to supply his own woman. He was not to use the slave women.

He must have a particular talent and fondness for controlling other people. In Mose's words, "Be hell on a nigger." But most of all he must never forget who was boss. Moss adhered to the Biblical adage, spare the rod and spoil the child but made sure the slaves were not physically abused. They had to be kept well fed and healthy like any of the other livestock. If turned over to the overseer alone, his plantation as well as the slaves would suffer.

They soon got it all together and Mose picked up his slaves. There were only six breedable women in the bunch and one prized Mandingo. The Mandingoes were the strongest and largest of the breed and brought fabulous prices at auctions. Some were bred to fight to the death for the amusement of the very rich. Large sums of money were bet on them in New Orleans where fights were highly publicized for months ahead. Mose didn't mind the lack of breeders. He only wanted to replace the ones that got too old to work and decided he wouldn't have any problems doing that. Only one of the women was obviously with child and the other five had young children. Some of these appeared to be part Indian and one light skinned. There were about fifty in all and mostly fairly young and healthy looking.

Mose soon found that he would have to put aside his dreams of gentility and leisure as a big plantation owner. He, the children, Susan, Leah and the Davises had to work harder than ever just to hold things together. Just when he was beginning to wonder if they could make a go of it and be able to pay back the large debt he owed Kingsley without being in debt to him forever, the old man died and wiped out the debt in his will. By the second year, Mose was beginning to see signs of making a profit.

It wasn't long before he saw that his plantation must be run like an army with him the captain, Leah the quartermaster and his overseer the top sergeant. The slaves were the privates. The entire family had to learn a certain amount of the

Gullah and Seminole dialect, although Leah set to work, teaching the younger ones English. She also started teaching them the basic skills to read and write. Mose allowed them their voodoo practices and let them beat the drums on Sunday at services. He really didn't care what they did to entertain themselves after work as long as they didn't harm themselves and got along with each other. Because of Leah, a flogging was rare. A whipping was to be hung up by the heels, pants pulled down and spanked with a wide paddle on the buttocks where it only bruised the flesh and seldom broke it. That way the slave didn't have a desire to sit down for sometime and actually worked harder. The slaves called this a "hidin'." "Don't hide me, Massa Mose," they would beg. "Don't hide me!" Most of the time, all it took was a threat from Mose, "I'll whip you 'til you shit like a tied coon!" and a beating of any kind was unnecessary.

Mose found the women harder to control than the men. The men were more submissive, but did not work as hard as the women. He would have preferred a few high-spirited men who worked as hard as the women, but he guessed they all went on to Arkansas with the Indians.

It wasn't long, with Leah's help and advice, before he worked out a good mixture of leniency and severity, much like children. There must be reward in one hand and punishment in the other. Reward was often only a bar of sweet soap and this was usually for a good brushing of Mose's horse.

The plantation and all its inhabitants hummed with activity. Everyone worked to capacity and time flew.

Susan stuck to her home and helped with the slaves in anyway she could but basically tried to keep the life-style she had always had with Will. She did not feel that the undertaking of such a large plantation in anyway affected her status. She was grateful to Mose for taking her and the children in but she knew that none of this actually belonged to her but the little cabin she and Will had shared and even that had been traded for the home Mose had built her after little Lydia was born. She often felt herself somewhere in-between the hired help and a poor relation although neither Mose nor Leah neither one ever did anything to make her or her children feel like anything but family. She secretly dreaded the time the children would grow up and realize none of this belonged to them. She was sure they had never thought about it as they shared and shared alike with anything Leah and Mose's children had, including hard work. She remembered that Mose had told her the day they buried Will, that he had promised Will he would see that her children all got a good start in life and she guessed that was really everything a person could wish for. That was more than she and Will could have done had he lived. He never had the ambition Mose did, but she still missed him and never a day went by she didn't think of him.

Chapter 12

Florida was admitted to the Union on March 3, 1845. She came in as a slave state along with Iowa who was admitted as a free state so as to balance the power between slave and free. The population was almost sixty thousand. According to the constitution framed by the convention of 1838, only white males of 21 years who were enrolled in the State Militia could vote. There were 17 senators and 41 representatives elected by the people. In the executive branch, only the governor was elected by popular vote. The state treasurer, comptroller and attorney general were all elected by the legislature, as well as the Supreme Court judges and Circuit Court judges. Florida had only one representative in Washington and two senators. They also were elected by the legislature. William J. Moseley was governor, David L. Yulee and James Westcott the two senators, and William Brockenbrough was the representative.

Mose ran and was elected County Commissioner in Columbia County and aspired to go further. But the polished gem from the rough, uncut stone Kingsley had such big plans for and Mose dreamed about, died with him. Mose didn't have what it took. He tried to up-date his grammar and had a certain amount of success with that. With his manners, that Leah had worked so hard on all the years, he had less success. But he couldn't curtail his curse words and vulgar, descriptive language. With Kingsley gone to guide him over the rough spots, he had to punt after his death and this attempt was a disaster. To those who knew what a really polished gentleman was, he was a phony and to his friends he became a braggart and "uppity." He was abrasive with his viewpoints and had suddenly become an authority on every subject. Leah was his salvation and it was she who provided the glue to hold everything together. But he gave her no credit for this and no matter how hard she and the children worked, it was Mose's plantation. He was still "Old Ring under the wagon" and he never failed to let everybody know it. As was his style, he was heavy handed with the criticism and nonexistent with his praise. "Please" and "thank you" were there words that he never picked up in his quest for a better vocabulary.

The winter had been dry and was hanging on with a vengeance. They needed rain and Mose was restless. Kingsley had let off a lot of the financial strain when he had died and absolved Mose of his debt, but Mose had borrowed a lot of money to buy land and had a huge mortgage payment to make each year. The drought wasn't helping his disposition.

Susan was in the back yard of her house busy hoeing her greens.

"We could sure stand some rain," she said to Mose as he came through the gate.

"Yeah, they're lookin' kinda puny. You can water 'em all you want and they won't do a damned thing until we can git some rain on 'em." He looked up at the sky. "Hit's as fair as a goat's ass up there and we ain't had nothin' but a little old cat-piss sprinkle in three weeks. The fields are gittin' as dry as a pop-corn fart."

Susan was accustomed to Mose's descriptive vernacular by now and sometimes it was a welcomed change from crying children and the loneliness she felt as a single parent.

"Will liked his greens. He claimed they kept a body's bowels open and kept him cleaned out."

Mose sat on the back porch and watched Susan hoe. Her hips swayed back and forth with each swing of the hoe, scraping the weeds from the greens. He noticed her ample breasts as they bounced against her shirt in rhythm with the hoe.

"Why don't you let one o' them niggers do that, Susan. I got so much help hits a goin' to waste out there."

She went on with her hoe. "I like to take care o' my own garden. I don't want no nigger waitin' on me hand and foot. Hit's enough you got one helpin' me in the house. I weren't raised that way. The Bible says a man should earn his livin' by the sweat o' his brow and Paul said 'them that don't work shouldn't eat.'"

"Well, you ought to feel justified in eatin' those greens. You're sweatin' and workin' hard enough for 'em. But you're a lookin' good, Susan. I was a little worried 'bout you right after that gal young'un come, but you look a hundred percent better. Always had good color and all but looked a little peaked for a while."

Susan never had been pretty but she had a certain earthy quality about her and a vivacious personality. In a way, she and Mose were a lot alike because she never hesitated to say what was on her mind. She had always been rather plump with a square figure and large hips. But she had never looked flabby. Mose had often described her as being able to "bear hunt with a switch." But the death of Will, having to move in with Leah and have a baby had taken a lot from her spirit and she was just now, after more than three years, regaining her sense of belonging. She was weaning little Lydia and once again there was a bloom on her cheeks and a sparkle in her eyes.

"I'm fixin' to drive over to the old home place. Why don't you leave the young'uns and come over there with me. I won't be long. Leah was gonna come along and she's come down with one of her headaches. Thinks she's getting' ready to go thru the change and her not even forty. Come take a ride with me in the new buggy. You ain't ever tried hit out yet."

"I got Deedy a scrubbin' the kitchen right now and I want fer her to do the hallway after she gits thru there. She ain't got time fer these young'uns. That why I got 'em out here on this porch. Lydia's got a runny nose and hit's a little bit chilly."

Mose wouldn't give up. "Put that hoe down and come on. These bigger gals can watch them young'uns and we won't be gone long. I got Rich hitchin' the team. Git your shawl and come on." And Mose turned to go out to the barn as if it was settled.

She put on her shawl and ran over to Mose's house. Leah was lying down in the bed, a wet cloth over her eyes.

"I come to see just how you were feelin'," Susan inquired. "Mose said he

94

wanted you to go over to the old place with him and you didn't feel like it but he asked me to go and I thought you might change you mind if I was along. I guess you're really not able to go, are you?"

Leah never even took the cloth from her eyes. "I've really got a bad headache and feel sort of sick on my stomach. But you go on with Mose. It'd do you good to get away and maybe it'll put him in a better frame of mind. He's been like an old sore-footed bear for weeks now. You won't take any of his bitching and I've had about as much of it as I can stand. Go on. I'll have Grandma Davis keep an eye on the children. Hurry up before he changes his mind and goes off without you. He'll do that if you aren't standing out there."

A.J. and the baby put in a cry and hue when they saw their mother get into the buggy with Mose.

"Git a rag, Rhoda, an wipe thet young'uns nose," Susan said as she settled in. "And don't go trackin' in the house fore hit's dry," and off she went.

Mose was quite attentive on the trip over. He had to go by the field and show Susan all the plantings, as if she was really interested in what was going on and it all belonged to her. They had been penning cattle all winter, using their droppings for fertilizer and were getting ready for the spring planting. They stopped by to check with Isiah and Champ who were overseeing the rice planting. Each was on a horse with a gun handy and a dog each lying around. Mose had trained his dogs to run down a slave, as he had them learn the scent of an Indian, but only one had tried to escape in all this time and the dogs had treed him in less than three hundred yards. It cost $150 to get a slave back so Mose had decided an ounce of prevention was worth a pound of cure. He'd turn one young buck loose and give him 15 minutes head start.

"You hear them dogs comin', you'd better hunt a tree, nigger," and it wasn't long before his dogs enjoyed the game and knew just what they were looking for when Mose sicced them on the trail.

Mose did most of the talking. He could be charming and entertaining when he wanted to be. Susan decided that maybe this was the way he was with Leah when they were alone and he wasn't trying to impress anyone. Maybe that's why she's put up with him all these years. I'm glad I got him told early on about where the bear shit in the buckwheat. He don't try to run over me like the rest of 'em.

They were soon at the old cabin and Mose tied the horse to the fence and went on to the cowshed where William had been killed. Susan went to the edge of the field to visit Will's grave. There were no tears. Time had healed the need for crying. But no man had come along to fill the void his death had caused. She pulled up the few weeks growing on the grave and went toward the little cabin. Susan lifted the latch and went in. It looked so small and shabby. She hadn't realized how small it had been since she'd gotten used to her bigger new home. Mose and the boys had rearranged the furniture and added more. It was actually a bunkhouse now and he had put in floors and real windows. Wouldn't be bad just with me and Will here, she thought.

Mose had put the slaves out at the barn to work hauling the horse manure out to the fields and cleaning the stalls. Susan was sitting by the fireplace when Mose came back in.

"I cooked a many a meal right here, Mose," she said, looking with affection at the old hooks. "I was happy too. That is 'fore Will died." She sat and looked at the black hole and empty space where a fire should be roaring on such a cool day. She reached over and got a knot and threw it on to see if it would catch and burn. It just sat there.

"You're not happy now?" Mose asked. He had taken for granted Susan was more than satisfied with her situation and all that he had done for her.

Susan didn't answer but had begun to cry, softly. It was dark in the room, all shut up without a fire. The knot had finally caught from the embers and was flickering on her face.

"What you need is a man, gal," Mose said and walked over to her and pulled her up to him.

Susan felt empty and sad and Mose was there with his arms around her. She needed someone just then and she reached out to him, hungry for another human being to hold her and comfort her. It had seemed years since anyone had even hugged her. Everyone had been so busy building the plantation and getting the work done that it seemed no one had had time for her and realized how much she had missed Will. She felt as if she had been taken for granted like a piece of furniture.

Mose held her and let her cry and then she tried to step back. Mose reached down and kissed her gently on the cheek, one hand at the back of her neck, not letting her go. She mistakenly took it for a friendly gesture and let him continue to hold her. A feeling of loneliness and longing surged through her body and Mose mistook that for something else and slipped one hand from the top of her head down to the nap of her neck and the other around her waist and drew her to him. She felt safe and didn't try to pull back. He smiled down at her, assured of himself now. His hand that was around her waist slipped further down and cupped her backside and he jerked her even closer to him. She felt the hardness from his crotch and she jerked and twisted away in alarm.

"Mose Barber!" as she dashed for the door. Her eyes were flashing in anger now. "You know me better than that. You shame me!"

"I thought you wuz injoyin' hit," slipping back into his old way of talking. There was no façade to Mose around Susan now, "You didn't pull away nor nothin'. How's a feller to know?"

"I thought you wuz a comfortin' me, Mose. Bein' here where I wuz so happy with Will and all and him yore own brother. I thought you understood how I wuz a feelin'."

"Hell, Will's gone and life goes on. Yo're alive and full of hit. A woman needs a man, Susan, and you cain't deny thet. I got enough to go around and I can take care o' thet department good as anybuddy and you don't have to leave home to get hit."

He grabbed her again and brought her to him, harder this time. There was no tenderness in him. Both hands were around her waist and he held her arms close to her side.

"You let me go, Mose Barber or, I'll holler my lungs out."

"Won't do you no good, Susan. Them boys is spreadin' horse shit down on the fields by now." He walked her backward to the bed and pinned her down. He started kissing her on the neck and face as she tried to wiggle free. He grabbed both her wrists with one hand and pinned them under her as she arched her back and struggled. He started up her leg with his free hand and she brought her knees up against his chest with all her might and wiggled free, falling to the floor. He knew she was strong but he was surprised at how well she fought. He started laughing at her and made no attempt to touch her now.

"Git up from there, Susan, and behave yorself."

She got up and stepped back from him like a cornered animal. Mose just stood there and laughed.

"Alright, so I got carried away and wanted to bed you right here. Maybe hit weren't right. Ain't no woman worth fightin' bout. We been too good a friends to let somethin' like this come between us. They's plenty o' women out there I don't have to fight with and their friendship don't mean near as much to me as yours does. I'm a man and you cain't blame a man fer tryin'."

Susan was sobbing now and began to blow her nose on her skirt and just stand there. Mose held out his hand like a man and offered it to her.

"Am I forgiven? Let's shake on hit and get back home, if I am. I'm sorry if I took things the wrong way. I figgered you be a needin' a little bit by now and might jest be a little bit grateful to me fer all I've done for you but I realize now I wuz lookin' at things the wrong way. I don't want no hard feelings, Susan. I'd rather have you as a friend than most men I know and I don't want this to come between us at this late day."

She could feel the sincerity in his voice and he was actually pleading with her and treating her as an equal. She had never seen this side of Mose before and it calmed her.

She even laughed and said. "Hit ain't that, Mose. I am grateful to all you've done fer me and the young'uns. I couldn't a made hit without you and Leah and everybuddy. And I do git lonesome fer a man and somebuddy to hold me. But fer one thing, yore Will's brother and been like a brother to me fer years. I'll always look on you as a brother and nothin' else. You cain't change that. No yearnin' fer a man will ever make you anything but family. I could no more bed with you than one o' my own boys. I thought you felt the same way. I wouldn't a come over here if I'd knowed you felt any other way. I'll jest pack my bags and git out right now if I got somethin like this to worry about."

They were out to the buggy now and started home.

"You won't ever have to worry about me layin' a hand on you ever again like that Susan. And I'll kill the first man that ever tried to touch you if'n you don't want him to. You got my word on hit." He pulled the horse and buggy up and looked hard at her. "I'm a gonna sit right here until I git a answer. Let's pretend this thing never happened and yore gonna go home and fergit I ever tried anything. I want you to feel safe and secure in my presence. I want you to be my friend. I want that more than anything I can think of wantin' jest this minute."

"And I guess that means more to me than anything right now too, Mose."

And so they went home in silence. Neither felt the need to talk. They were comfortable with the situation. Susan turned to Mose as she started to get down and go in. "In a way I'm glad we cleared the are, Mose. Now we both know where we stand and kin enjoy each other's company a whole lot better," and laughed. And Mose laughed with her as he turned the horse over to Rich who had come from the barn.

Chapter 13

The third Sunday of the month was for church and all-day dinner on the grounds. The nearest church was on the north prong of the Sardis River near Trader Hill where Eastern Columbia County and Nassau County could attend. The only time Mose and gang could not attend was when the St. Marys was on the rise from a heavy rain and they couldn't get across the crossing. Mose loved church and never missed a chance to go. Now that he was getting prosperous, he saw that they were dressed to the teeth as befitted a family of means and had a seat right down in front next to the deacons. Mose was one of the largest contributors of the congregation.

This particular service Mose and the men were working cattle. He had had an understanding with the elders that he made his living that way and had to be gone for long periods of time, out of the county, and since he was generous with his offerings though Leah and the family, he was excused.

There was a preacher known as a "saddle bag preacher," as he rode around the various churches once a month and stayed with different families during the week. The church also served as a school for three months in the fall, when all the crops were in and the children were not needed so much at home.

The church was built on a high sandy knoll in the center of a small scrub patch surrounded by heavy pine timber. From the scrub, the ground sloped away toward a creek to the east and to a chain of straggly cypress ponds far to the west. The east slope was covered with wild flowers. There were great patches of yellow ragged-leaf daisies, mixed in with patches of white quinine flowers. At times of the year, wild tiger lilies would add to the colorful profusion. Someone always picked a large bouquet to put in the church as, inside, it was bleak and bare. The pulpit and floors were the usual puncheons, split and hewed slabs of pine logs turned "smooth side up" and they became smoother only after years of wear. The primitive pulpit was just large enough to hold a Bible, which was seldom used except as a prop for the Primitive Baptist preacher to shake at his congregation. There were no notes or prepared sermons and they were all pretty much the same of hell-fire and finances.

Each preacher felt his sermons were divinely inspired and delivered. But it was difficult for the frontiersmen to follow the strict doctrine laid down by the church. There were not only the many distractions of trying to make a living and stay healthy in this wild land but the effort of just attending services so far away was, in itself, a big hurdle.

Leah had been brought up in the Catholic faith and missed the dignity of mass and even now when the preacher said, "let us pray," she looked down for a place to get on her knees.

But she was determined to see that her children got some form of religious training and exposure to groups that believed in bringing up children "in the admonition of the Lord" even if they did not fit her idea of religion.

And the laws of this church were extreme. Members could be expelled for non-attendance, attending another denomination, failure to be baptized, working on Sunday and many other "sins." The deacons of the community kept a watchful eye on the congregation through the week or month as the case may be. The accused had to acknowledge or deny his "faults" and ask the church's forgiveness.

Back in '38, the church had broken with part of its members over missionary work. They did not believe in "worldly institutions" such as Sunday school, temperance societies, conventions and missions. They maintained they were not authorized by the scriptures. They had become a little more tolerant because of this rupture. Dancing was not permitted but the deacons looked the other way at a frolic. The most common sin was drinking.

"No drunkard should inherit the kingdom of heaven!" This would be answered by any offender with, "Drink no longer water but use a little wine for the stomach's sake," and the attestation he had only taken a "drap or two."

Leah and Susan led the group up the steps, Rhoda close behind, and bolted for the front as she usually did, trying to see what everyone had on and whether their hat was prettier than hers. As they got to their row she turned around to get a better look and see if any of the men were looking at her and Susan got her attention with a couple of quick jabs and a dirty look.

The front row was reserved for the deacons' families but they didn't fill it all so this is where Mose's gang usually sat. Mrs. Osteen, a little brown hen of a woman, sat on the row behind them. She had yellowish brown eyes, brown hair and wore a plain brown dress. She blended into the nothingness of the wooden church bench with Leah in front of her with her milk white skin and raven hair dressed in a sky blue dress, black and white vest and white hat. Mrs. Osteen was typical of the Florida pioneer woman and members of the church. This church in particular. They were civil, showed no signs of immodesty, no ruggedness in their walk or mannerism yet could carry a gun into the woods and kill something to eat if necessary. They took pride in their housework and cooking and were very conscious of their virtue as a wife or a mother and their children's character and deportment. Their husbands were equally proud of their role as a father and husband. They strived to be good providers and were jealous of authority and resented superior pretensions. The pioneer on a whole was a matter-of-fact, hard working, self-respecting and substantial, God-fearing individual.

Jacksonville to the east had her share of thieves and renegades and as the preacher would put it that day "the pomp and vanities of the wicked world with its gaudy approval, jewelry, braided hair and paint of the fallen woman." But the church was filled that day with the other kind.

The men sat on one side of the church, and the women and children on the other. Elizabeth Thompson was asked to "raise the tune" after the usual very emotional sermon and closing prayer and as the congregation turned to leave one of the deacons said, "Just a moment!"

Everyone turned around and waited for the axe to fall. They knew someone was in for it.

The preacher said, "I see we have enough male members here for a quorum and I will accept a motion that we are in conference." The women had no voice and many didn't even know what a quorum was but they were made to attend.

Everyone sat down after the motion was carried. The preacher looked at the congregation for a minute and said, "It's been called to my attention that James and Will Osteen have violated the rules of this church by willfully performing labor on the Sabbath. What is your pleasure?" Fortunately, Will and James weren't there.

Mr. Osteen stood up and addressed the congregation "I'll tell you what happened. I had a bunch of yearling's penned up to work last Saturday and hit come a white rain. Hit wuz a plum toad-strangler and commenced to blow and limbs a fallin' all over the place. My horses and those cattle broke out and we wuz into the night a gittin' 'em back in. We hadn't finished workin them cattle and there wuz no food or water in the pen. Come Sunday mornin' sumbuddy plum forgot to tell them cattle hit wuz Sunday and they'd have to wait until Monday mornin' to eat or drink. My boys saddled up and finished out the work and let 'em loose. I apologize fer my boys and since they wuz my cattle, I'll take the blame for what they done. If anybuddy benefited from the work, besides the cows, hit wuz me."

"I say every tub should sit on its own bottom," said one of the deacons. "Your boys should answer for themselves."

"And I say what the Lord said 'If the ox is in the ditch, pull him out'," said Mr. Raulerson, who was a cowman. There were several amens. Mr. Raulerson had a smooth, silky voice and practically everyone, including the preacher, recognized his tone as the one Mr. Raulerson used just before he hit someone in the jaw. So Mr. Norton meekly seconded the motion and the preacher decided to let sleeping dogs lie and dismissed the congregation.

This same year, in 1845, the Baptists took in a minister who broke with the tradition and the church soon formed a Missionary Baptist Church. The Missionary Baptist Church was a little more tolerant of its members. As long as they drank moderately or at lest with discretion, didn't abuse their wives or children, use foul language in public, neglect their family or work or were unneighborly or made or sold large amounts of moonshine, they were free to worship when they pleased. And one did not have to be a member to attend the church. Visitors were welcome as long as they followed the rules. So, Mose soon saw that a new church was built close by and he and his family joined the Missionary Baptist Church.

This church became the school during the week and all the kids from miles around jammed into one room. There was a fireplace at each end, as fall was when most children attended school. Men kept turns bringing in lightered knots to burn and the boys brought in water. The girls swept the floor and helped keep the place clean. The teacher meted out discipline with a rod. They were taught only the three R's of readin', 'ritin and 'rithmetic. They used a quill pen made from a feather from the wing of a turkey or goose. Ink was from pokeberries, kept in a glass partly filled with cotton. There was no place for books except on benches or the floor. The teacher boarded with some member of the community that was close by. Most boys and girls "finished" school by the time they reached early teens.

Mose kept building onto his house. It wasn't the typical colonial mansion with the white pillars and winding drive bordered by massive oaks one would think of as a plantation home. There were no ballrooms and only a small parlor. It was a two-story frame with a large front porch. The main addition was the bedrooms upstairs. Leah and Mose got into a wrangle about Dulcie and Rich. They balked at moving to the quarters with the rest of the slaves when Mose first got them and he had put off making any kind of move until now. He wanted to enlarge their little house and put some of the boys out there but Leah stood her ground. They were part of the family, and would keep their little homes until they died.

Soon there was a dairy, a smoke house full of pork, beef and venison. A deer hunt afforded a welcomed relief and a chance to get away. There were mule stalls, corncribs, wagon sheds, poultry sheds, slave quarters, gristmills, sawmills and an overseer's cabin.

The mules were the cornerstone of the farm, any farm from a one-mule farm to the largest plantation. As in many hybrids, mules were superior in many ways to the mares and jacks they sprang from. They seldom got sick or went lame and they stood abuse well. A mule could lose an eye and still be used in a team. They lived longer, worked longer in the day, day after day, and ate less. They could be sustained on cornhusks and peanut hay. Mose weaned them at six months, broke them to harness and trained them briefly in a team with a seasoned mule. They loved companionship and easily slipped right into the team. They could be stubborn and kick like a sledgehammer. But they seldom ran away, unlike their mother, the horse. The owners wanted them to act a little coltish, believing then, that they were young and in excellent condition. Mose's motto to his customers was "Don't buy a cheap mule, the good ones will bring back more in return for you money." And Mose made money from his mule trade. But he spent a lot of money on fine horses. Especially stud horses. Mose had always wanted to act the dandy with the best team in the county and the fanciest stud horse around. Mares didn't count, just as any female didn't matter as much as the male.

Like the mules, corn was the main stay of the plantation. It took a peck of meal per week for each slave over ten years old and about half that amount for the young ones. It fattened the hogs, along with the peanuts, fed the mules and plow horses as well as the cow ponies, the yearlings, poultry and sheep. It provided the two large families with grits, corn bread, mush, "pone" and dressing.

He had made Whiskey John his foreman on the cow crew and hoped he didn't drink himself to death before he could help train his boys to take over. So far, it looked like Isiah was going to be his best bet to run his cattle operation and he had big plans for enlarging it down into Central Florida and even down to Lake Okeechobee when the Indian situation was resolved.

Johnny amused himself when he was back at the plantation with the slaves. He would show up drunk at the end of church services and wait for them to come outside. Then he would spur his little cowpony in circles round them so hard he'd break wind, right in their faces and he'd laugh and laugh until the slaves would start giggling. There was a saying among the cowman that "a fartin' horse never tires," so Johnny had picked out the one that seemed to have the most wind to expel and found that he could be used for his amusement when not working cattle. At other times, he'd run his horse up into a group and pop his whip over their heads and watch them run back into shelter. They soon learned he wouldn't strike one of them and would stand their ground and so Johnny soon tired of that little game.

He soon learned their Gullah dialect and he'd catch them eating corn pone with little George or Andrew Jackson and tell them, "Yo' cum back heah and quit playin' wid dem white chillin. You know day'll jest lick that jelly off yore pone and call you a niggah."

Or he'd catch one of the young girls that had just paired off with a young buck and ask, "I thought you and Ham had just jumped the broom last month?"

"Yasuh, did."

"Then how come I saw that sorry rascal down behind the barn last night with thet little Etta Mae he's been hoein' taters with all week?"

But in turn, he would bring them bars of sweet soap and fruit and sit around their fire at night and tell them jokes, teaching them English. A few always were afraid of him, but most learned to look forward to his visits and missed him when he was off in the woods, working cattle.

Mose found less and less time to teach the younger boys to hunt. They were allowed to roam about the countryside, shooting squirrels and rabbits but any meat they brought home, they had to clean themselves, and they got particular hell from Mose if it was shot all to pieces or not cleaned properly. They had to learn to shoot on live game, as shot was not that easy to come by, and he quickly reminded them that God put heads on a cat, squirrel or rabbit for the express purpose of not messing up the meat.

When they got a little older, they were allowed to go turkey hunting. Turkeys are one of the wildest and wisest game in the woods and the hunter's greatest pleasure to track and kill. Although they would roost in oaks and other trees, they usually roosted in tall cypress trees over water where they could hear predators sloshing under them and sound an alarm. If any of the men reported having seen where some had dusted and scratched during the day, they would go back and pick out the tallest trees around, usually a bend in the swamp where a turkey could pitch up for the night. Then they would tie their horses near the swamp and walk under the tall trees until they found bird droppings they were sure belonged to a large bird like a turkey, and wait until dusk trying to decide what tree they had roosted in. The "flop-flop-flop" of a turkey as he takes wing and flies into a tall tree is unmistakable once you have heard it. The boys would be hidden in a bunch of brush close enough to the trees that often they could see the turkey as he settled for the night and usually there was a big flock of them. If there was a full moon so they could see the outline of the birds after they had settled for the night, they would shoot them, then, but if it was dark, they would not disturb them then but let them sleep and go back just before day and shoot them off the roost before they flew out the next day. That way they were assured of plenty of meat for the big family. Many times, they ate only turkey breast, fried for breakfast, and threw the rest in a pot and stewed it for the slaves for soup. If some of the turkeys got away and they didn't get a "mess," they would "yelp them up" by blowing on a blade of grass placed between their lips and tongue. When a turkey is separated from his flock, he "yelps" to them and the others answer back until they get back together.

Once Champ and Francis "roosted" some turkeys and slipped back to shoot them the next morning, only to find that they had shot a bunch of buzzards and had some explaining to do when they came home empty handed after using precious ammunition.

They were taught how to read the animal signs and when was the best time to kill the game. Bears were killed in May before they paired off and mated in the summer. Rabbits were killed only in the months that had an "R" in them, as they contained parasites during the other months. Gobblers were easier to kill in March when they started gobbling during the mating season. In the fall, all turkeys are old enough to shoot. The best time to kill a deer was in July and August. At that time, the young bucks were rubbing the velvet cover from their horns against small sapling pines and their "sign" was easy to read. A heavy deer's track sinks deeper in the sand or mud at the back and a young deer track shows only at the front of the track. A buck paws the ground clean of debris and urinates on it, staking out his territory. This is called his "scrape" and he is easy to find and track down. The deer ruts, or breeds in November and sheds his horns in January. They learned to tell a big cat's track from a wolf or dog track as the dog's paw track shows where its claws cut into the soil. With the cat, only the paw marks show.

Sometimes they would hunt deer at night. This was called "fire hunting." They would shine a deer's eyes and shoot him when he was blinded by the light and afraid to run. They hunted on horseback and one or two of the boys would run along on foot, carrying a frying pan tied to a long pole full of burning splinters of fat pine. The deer, fascinated and blinded by the light, would stand like a sheep, ready for slaughter, his eyes shining in the darkness like a pair of white diamonds and be shot in his tracks. It was important to be able to tell the difference between a deer or cow's eyes. The deer's eyes would be brighter and would glitter. Woe be unto anyone fire hunting that shot a cow by mistake. One night they shot a horse by mistake and hid the evidence. They didn't even know who the poor animal belonged to.

The biggest thrill of the young hunter was not the hunt but bringing in the game and telling how he got it to the rest of the boys.

One morning, Isaac, who had grown more proficient than the rest of the boys, came in while the younger boys were finishing breakfast. He was wet, dirty and his legs and arms scratched. They all gathered around and delighted in his tale.

"Yesterday, Johnny and the boys found some turkey sign in thet bit hammock 'tuther side of the river. He let me go with him and the boys to roost 'em. Some-buddy musta scattered 'em earlier cause they roosted way up in a big live oak and I coursed mine but I couldn't see him fer the moss, even though hit wuz moon-light. Isiah got his'n, but mine musta flew out on the edge of a big Christmas tree scrub. I couldn't see him but I coursed the tree where he had to a lit. By the time we got rounded up the moon had gone down and hit was too dark. So Pa made me go back this mornin' 'fore day and try to find him. I got my gun and old Tip and a sack and headed fer the river."

"What was the sack for?" asked little Andrew Jackson.

"Well, if you'll listen, I'll tell you in a minute," said Isaac, irritated at being inter-rupted in his tale. "I had to cross the river a'comin' and a'goin'. I took my clothes off and put 'em in the sack and swam the river on my back, using one arm to swim and hold my sack and gun up over my head so's to keep my clothes dry enough to put back on."

"Then how come you're all wet now?" asked little George.

"Well, did you ever try to swim a river carryin' a sack and your gun and a big turkey gobbler?" And he led them out on the porch where he held up the largest gobbler they had ever seen. He had a big long beard because the head and neck were still intact.

"Pa's a gonna lick me fer shootin' him all up inside but he's about the biggest I ever seen, so maybe he won't be too mad."

He went on with his tale as he hadn't got to the part of the kill and that was the best part. "I got to the hammock and hit wuz still dark so I couldn't see a blessed thing. I hunted and hunted until I found the tree where Isiah shot his turkey. I thought I knew every inch of that place, we've squirrel hunted there so much but the trees look different in the dark and the ground wuz covered with 'metter patches. I jest sat down and waited in a spot where I thought he had landed. Purty soon hit got light. The skeeters had bout eat me bodaciously up and I'd got all scratched up a slippin' thru them 'metter patches but I noticed this kinda funny shaped thing way up all by itself in a big pine tree. I thought at first hit was a plant or big clump o' moss or maybe a eagle's nest. I eased as close to the tree as I could cause I thought I saw hit move. I got my gun ready and 'putted' real loud jest like Pa taught me and that there feller stuck out his old neck and putted right back. I didn't realize how closet I wuz to him. He didn't even flop when he hit the ground. Old Tip here had him by the time he hit and wuz right onto him."

Isaac proudly held him up for all the little boys to see. He stood and looked at him, waiting so the little boys could admire him and finally admitted, "I guess I sure shot him up purty good and Pa'll probably have a conniption fit, but there's plenty o' meat on them bones." Isaac went off to the edge of the scrub to pick and clean his turkey with little Mose, Will, John and A.J. following close behind in adulation.

Another time, the cow crew had seen where wild hogs had rooted around the edge of the river. Mose had some dogs that were trained to attack wild hogs but hog hunting could be a dangerous sport. Not only was there a danger of cornering a wild boar that could cut a persons leg almost off but the dogs could get cut up pretty bad if they cornered and caught the hog and no one came to catch or shoot him, depending on how large he was. Isaac and Arch had been after Mose to take off and take them hog hunting but he never seemed to find time, so they talked Grandpa Davis into going with them.

Mose had agreed the old man could take the wagon down to the spot where the hogs had been rooting around for food with their snouts because the boys had seen the hogs and reported it was just a bunch of sows with their half grown pigs, called shoats and not a dangerous thing. Not long before, Grandpa Davis had gone with them and they had been afraid to go to the aid of the dogs when they had a particularly big shoat caught and the hog had cut Mose's dogs up pretty bad. They were warned that this time, regardless of what the dogs had cornered, as soon as they "bayed-up" the hogs and they could hear them squeal when the dogs caught one, they were to run into the swamp and catch or kill it, lest the dogs got chewed up again by the old mama sow or a half-grown boar. The boys promised they'd get to the attack just as quick as they could. Grandpa was too old to run to the dogs' aid and he'd have to stay in the wagon.

They found the fresh sign, put the dogs on the tracks and waited. The dogs opened and soon they heard a pig squeal.

"Get in there and catch that hog!" Grandpa Davis didn't have to tell them again. They were out of the wagon and going to the dogs. Just as they got to the hog, they met the dogs coming out and low and behold there stood the biggest bear they had ever seen with the shoat in her arms. The boys dropped their guns and climbed the nearest tree they could scamper up. The one Arch had climbed could barely support him and the bear, protecting her kill, had dropped the pig and was swiping at his heels, barely missing him, the little pine tree swaying to and fro. Both boys began to yell, "Grandpa, bring a gun, bring a gun," and Grandpa Davis sat in the wagon and yelled, "Catch that hog, you little cowards! Beat them dogs off!"

The old bear finally picked up her kill and went off and allowed the boys to come down. The dogs had tucked their tails and run home as Grandpa Davis sat and smoked his pipe, waiting for the boys to come out of the swamp with the hog and the dogs.

Chapter 14

The ten years after Florida joined the union had seen big changes at the plantation. Champ had left the flock before the fifties and soon after came Isiah and Samuel. Arch was beginning to act like a grown man and think of taking a wife. James Ed, Isaac, Mose Jr., George, and little Will were half grown teenagers and doing a man's work. Rhoda had married and Nellie was engaged. Only John, A.J., Betty and Lydia were still clinging to their mothers' apron strings.

Mose was prospering and well on his way to becoming as rich as far up the proverbial bulls rear as he had ever hoped to be. He became proficient in farming practices, having learned how to teach the slaves to break middles, plow extra furrows and grow money crops of cotton and tobacco. They had thrived on a long stretch of good weather with warm nights and adequate rain. The cutworms had been a menace at first but he had learned to turn the turkeys into them and let them pick them off. What the turkeys didn't eat the slaves would pick off. The boll weevils were still in Mexico then. In just one day the creamy cotton blossoms would turn to white at noon and pink in the evening, get deeper and deeper red until they would drop off and pods would take their place. A good hand could pick from five to six acres of cotton and Mose had over 70 slaves now, even though many of them he had raised and they were in various stages of maturity. Ten thousand little tobacco seeds that would hardly fill a teaspoon were sowed into virgin soil and the little nursery plants covered at each cold spell with brush or cloth. The small plants were pulled up and planted in the rain so they wouldn't wilt, "laid back," or spread apart, so their leaves would get larger and their tops and any stray sprouts called "suckers," pinched off. In later summer they would turn yellow, were cut and allowed to wilt, and put into the drying sheds. It took a lot of "know how" to get rich farming, but Mose finally caught on with the help of a good overseer who he paid four hundred dollars a year and furnished him everything he needed to live well.

His slaves had been polished into basket makers, shoemakers, carpenters, cooks and the women taught to sew and weave. Louis Osteen, Calvin Livingston and Will Danthford had taken Whiskey John's and Percy's place as cowhands, along with Isiah and the other boys as they were needed. Isiah ran the cow crew for his daddy. Whiskey John and Percy had married and moved further south to Marion County.

Mose had learned to dress in broadcloth, ruffled shirts and plated buttons. He took Leah to Augusta, where his kinfolks lived and where he was born. To Savannah, and Charleston, where they had a public library, race tracks, dancing assemblies and golf courses. He had greatly improved his manners, polished his speech and learned to curtail his vulgar language in public. But he longed to get back home to Susan where the façade could fall off and he could visit with her like a friend and say what he felt like saying, the way he wanted to say it. His slaves were well adjusted by now and he could relax and enjoy life. They had names like Cuffy, Jolly, Bena and Cato. They had their own cabins with a kitchen, garden, hen house and pigpen. If they raised more than they needed, they could sell it to the surrounding community that came to buy small amounts of things like collard greens, pumpkins and melons. He had sixty-six hard-working slaves, 20 mules and five yokes of oxen. There were 370 acres in cotton, 125 in corn and cowpeas, and he had sent Champ with ten slaves to West Florida, where land was selling for 15 cents an acre, to start another tobacco farm.

He had tried to grow rice commercially but the floods, hurricanes, dry periods, and alligators and crawdads that burrowed underneath his dikes so he could not flood the fields at the proper time, had convinced him it was not financially sound.

And then disaster struck Mose like lightening that could come from out of nowhere during a sudden summer storm.

Grandpa Davis had died in the spring and Grandma Davis right on his heels in just a few months. They were old and it was to be expected. The families had adjusted to their loss. But a much greater loss was soon to come.

One night at the supper table Mose said to Leah, "Wife, do you know we'll soon be here alone except maybe for Betty here, before we can turn around twice. We finally about got everyone raised. That is if I can get Little Mose up without him gittin' kilt or killing some one."

Little Mose was cruel and difficult to manage. Leah had to "watch him like a hawk" around the slaves, or he'd mistreat one. He had always been Mose's favorite and was just like him in many respects and he generally favored him over the rest of the boys and the kid was turning into what would now be called a "troubled teen." It was mostly because he had been allowed to do as he pleased and have everything his way while the rest of them were clamped down so tight and criticized at every turn. None of them could please Mose and Little Mose could do not wrong in Mose's estimation.

Everyone agreed, but no one said anything.

"I guess we've finally about got them raised. I get so worn out at the end of the day, though, even with all this help," Leah complained.

"All you need is a dose of Grannie Davis's spring tonic. If she was here, she'd fix you right up."

"I kinda dread hot weather. Got so the heat just about kills me."

"Why don't you get old Mede down at the quarters to fix you up with something," offered Arch.

"That old witch doctor," exclaimed Mose. "You boys had better stay clear o' that old nigger and his potions. He'll put a curse on you and those Geiger girls from over in Nassau County won't pay no attention to you at church. Your voice'll be gettin' higher and higher and you'll be wantin to wear a skirt."

"That'll be the day," said Isaac. "You ought to see how Archy sidles up to Martha Geiger. He acts just like Pa's young pie-eyed stud horse at the Canada's barn when I took him over there the other day."

"Isaac, watch your mouth around these young girls!" admonished Leah.

"Now wife," said Mose. "Ain't nobuddy at this table doesn't know how a stud horse acts around a mare, or what he's got on his mind when he acts that way."

Living around animals, it was never necessary to teach children about the birds and the bees. It didn't take any of them long to learn about sex.

"I know," said Leah, "but I don't want you forgetting and saying something like that out in public or you might get shot. You don't say things like that around a lady."

"He's been around Pa too long," said Arch.

Mose gave him a dirty look but didn't say anything. He knew he had no defense to offer.

But Leah couldn't get to feeling well and finally went to see old Dr. Rivers in Olustee. He told her all she needed was a "good working out" and told her to go home and eat a mess of poke salad. These were tender shoots of the pokeweed that tasted somewhat like asparagus and was often used as a tonic in the spring.

A week later Mose ran into Susan near the chicken house. She was carrying a gun. A big hawk had been getting her little game chickens and had almost decimated the flock. Francis had brought her a pair several years ago and they had roamed wild, hatching their eggs in the palmetto patches and multiplied. She adored the colorful, plucky little chickens and their wild independent nature.

"Thet hawk's still up to his tricks, Susan?" Mose asked her, eyeing the gun.

"Looks like he's gonna put me out o' the chicken business if we don't git him soon. Got one little hen left on a settin' right now and if he gits her, I might as well give up. I got one right there might be old enough to set," as she and Mose watched the rooster chase one round and around. He finally caught her as she hiked her tail feathers and he grabbed her by the top of the head.

"Jest like a woman, playin' hard to git," Mose laughed.

Susan said nothing but laughed with Mose. Since they had settled their differences that day at the little cabin they were the closest of friends and she felt as comfortable around him as she would have a brother, maybe closer.

"I've been meaning to talk with you about Leah. Looks to me like she's gittin' punier and punier. I think she's fell off some too. I don't care what that old doctor over there in Olustee says. He ain't much mor'n a quack. I think you need to take her sommers else and try to find out what's the matter with her."

"Oh, you women and yore complaints. She draws up every winter and then comes out of it in the spring. She'll be alright."

Susan walked over to him and stood right in front of him and grabbed him by his coattail. "Mose, look at me. Look at me. She's sick and I can tell it. There's somethin' wrong and you're gonna do somethin' about hit or I will. Look at her out there in that rockin' chair."

"She seemed alright to me last night. Said she was jest tired." Mose wouldn't admit there could be anything wrong with Leah. She'd always been as strong as an ox and he couldn't conceive of her being otherwise.

"Well, you go take a good look at her in the strong daylight and then tell me she looks alright. Her color ain't good."

Just to please Susan he walked over to Leah who sat on the front porch with a gun on her lap. He sat down beside her on the porch and leaned up against a post.

"Never did tell you I always figured you were a better shot than me with that old gun."

Leah smiled, "I know I was. I don't think it was a matter of skill. I think my eyes were better than yours. They sure aren't any good, now. I've been trying to catch that blessed hawk out there where I can get a good shot at him. He's flown down here twice and I can't glimpse anything but a flutter. He's swift as an arrow. They don't call them darter hawks for nothing. I sometimes think he's a figment of Susan's imagination except I hear a chicken squawk and see them run from him."

Mose sat for a minute and looked at her. "You look a little peaked. You still not feeling well?"

"I don't seem to have any appetite and I feel tired all the time. I kept thinking I'd perk up but I think I'm going down hill a little bit every day."

"I think I'll load you up and take you up to Savannah and get a specialist look you over. No use fooling around with that doctor over there. He ain't done you no good. No use a' goin to Jacksonville either. We can git over to Savannah with just a little more effort. I don't like Jacksonville anyway. Too much riff-raff over there, and they say hit's fillin' up with free niggers, biggity niggers a stirrin' up trouble."

"I guess if they're free they're entitled to their opinion too, Mose. They pay taxes same as everybody else."

"As far as I'm concerned they ain't got no business runnin' around loose. God put 'em on this earth to work. They've been slaves fer a long time. Don't them people ever read the Bible. White folks have had slaves for all time."

"Mose, there have been white slaves as well as blacks and you know that. The color of their skin has nothing to do with it. Sometimes some of their own people sold them into slavery."

"Wife, you don't know a damned thing about it. So quit runnin' your mouth about somethin that's none of your business." Mose had already forgotten the advice Kingsley gave him until she reminded him it was men like Zeph Kingsley that brought them over for slaves, not God. But as far as Mose was concerned, the matter was settled and he told her to get ready for the trip to Savannah. "We'll have you fixed up and well in no time," he told her reassuringly.

But Leah did not get well. She was never going to get well.

"It's just a matter of time," the specialist told them. And Mose refused to believe him. He took her on to Charleston and got the same diagnosis. By that time, she was worn out and he thought she'd not live to make it back home.

She sat on the front porch and listened to the whip-o-wills in the scrub. Dulcie tried to prepare tempting meals for her but she said "Quit trying to poke anymore down me. I can't keep it down."

The cowpeas broke the ground and the sugar cane came up. The young mulberries and scuppernong grapes bloomed. Little biddies hatched out. Susan had finally killed the hawk. Green briar berries appeared on the bushes and amaryllis lilies sprang up. There was a profusion of dogbane and yellow bells. The things of the earth blossomed with all their promise of another year, but the bloom was gone from Leah's cheeks and she became an empty shell.

Champ and Lydia came down to tell her goodbye. The family had to take turns sitting up with her at night. The Barbers were important, and they even got a letter from the Mizells, who were planning to move from Micanopy to Central Florida, at last. But all anyone could do was watch her die.

She called Mose in at dusk one evening and ran everybody out of the room. "I want to talk to my husband alone," she whispered.

Mose didn't want to talk to her about dying. He kept trying to tell her all she had to do was "start perkin' up and not give up too easy."

"Listen to me, dammit," she finally told him in desperation. "For once I want you to sit there and listen to what I have to say. There are still a pile of mouths out there to feed and Betty isn't yet ready to marry. I know about your women, Mose. I've looked the other way for years. You're a wealthy man and there'll be many others standing in the wings to take my place when I'm gone. I want you to promise me you won't bring another woman into this house until Betty's gone. As long as she wants to, she's to run this home and help you with your plantation—her and Susan. I know there's nothing between you and Susan. Not that I'm giving you any credit for that. If she'd been that kind, you'd had another family started over there but I know her. She's been like a sister to me and to you too. Let her help out and listen to her advice. She's got a lot of good common sense if you'll just learn to let her speak now and then."

She took the Bible from her bedside and made Mose swear on it. She knew whatever he had so sworn he'd stay by it. And so she passed away quietly in the night, at peace with the world.

He never realized how much he would miss her until she was gone. He listened for her voice at night as he came in for supper and could feel her presence at night when he climbed the stairs to go to bed. He missed her warmth beside him in the night.

A few weeks later, they were sitting around the breakfast table and he started looking at little Betty. He had not looked at her for a long time. My God, he thought. She's beginning to look like her Ma. And then he thought. Have I ever touched this child or hugged her or told her I loved her? Not since she was a little thing, I reckon, he thought. Or did he ever touch her then? To Mose his time had been for his sons and his horses and plantation. He had always left the girls up to Leah.

"Come here gal, and give your old Pa a big hug," he said. "You know, you're beginning to look just like your Ma."

Betty came to him obediently. She was just a little afraid of him. He felt the girl, stiff and unyielding against him as he attempted to hug her close. They were both uncomfortable and as soon as he turned her loose she went outside and sat alone on the porch as her mother did before she died. And Mose never attempted to touch her again. It was too late, as they had never bonded in all that time and she was already looking around for a man to give her the love and attention he never had.

The next day Mose packed his gear and took off for Central Florida. He had been planning a trip down there for some time and had been thinking of the Jernigan boys and the possibility of starting another plantation there. The third Seminole Indian War had broken out in '55 and was drawing to a close. It had been provoked by a party of surveyors and was fought mostly down around Lake Okeechobee and Fort Myers. But there were only a few encounters, and the Seminole Nation was basically destroyed. Wildcat, Alligator and a Spanish Negro, John Cavalls, had become dissatisfied with Chief Micanopy in their new home in the west, and having to live near the Creeks that had been moved from Georgia. They migrated to Mexico and there the once brave warrior, Wildcat, died of small pox. The Seminoles, driven to the Everglades, survived on the coontie root, pounded into flour, swamp cabbage from the heart of the cabbage palm, alligator tail, fish and turtle. The soldiers tried to starve them to death but were unable to do so. The Federal government finally decided they had been tricked and lied to so much it would be impossible to negotiate with them. The troops were pulled back and they were allowed to live in peace to govern themselves. They lived quietly and peacefully in the Everglades, still an independent and proud people, wanting only to be left alone—which was what they had only wanted to do in the first place.

With Indian troubles over, Mose wished that Leah was still alive and he could sell out his holdings in Columbia County and start anew where it wasn't so crowded. He felt the need to put the miles between him and the plantation with all its responsibility. He was beginning to feel like an old man and wondered if it had all been worth it. For once, all his money and power meant nothing to him.

He told everyone goodbye that morning and took off alone for Central Florida. "I miss you more than you will ever know," he told them with tears in his eyes. "I got to get away by myself and get over this loneliness."

They had never seen their father like this. They didn't know what to say to this man who had always been so stern and tough and unfeeling. Betty was a little embarrassed but she made an effort to tell him goodbye as he rode away, leaving her and Isaac to run things in his absence.

Chapter 15

For years now his cattle had roamed and thrived down the side of the St. Johns Rivers to Melonville, on both sides. Isiah and the cow crew knew the territory well and had done an excellent job in keeping them marked and branded. Mose had had a woman stashed away at New Smyrna for five years. A Mrs. Cook. But now that Leah was gone, for the first time in his life he felt guilty about the relationship and stayed clear of that area on this trip. He had left his horse at Jacksonville and taken a boat up the St. Johns as far as he could go, taking only his saddle and dogs. There he bought a horse and took off through the woods to Fort Christmas.

At dusk that night, he camped alone in the woods near Lake Harney. As darkness began to fall he thought of something Leah had said while sitting out on the porch back home, watching the sun go down.

"I don't know why, but this time of the day has always been the loneliest time of the day for me. Even when I was younger and thought I'd live forever. I used to think, the day is dying and I will never have this day again, and in a way it has always been like a little piece of my life was gone and I could never get it back. You know, we don't die all of a sudden. We die a little bit every day as each day dies with us. We can have hopes and dreams for tomorrow and keep memories alive of yesterday but reality is today and now it's gone and we don't have any promise from God that we will live to see tomorrow. All he gave us was this day and it's ended and I can't help feeling sad."

"I never thought of it that way, wife," Mose said. Leah was a puzzle to him. He had never taken the time to just sit down and listen to what she had to say before and suddenly she seemed like a stranger to him. He had always spent more time in the past ten years with Susan. They talked about earthy things and he could relate to her better than he could his own wife. In a way, she had been more like a mistress to him except there had been no "hanky-panky" involved in their relationship. Maybe I ought to see if she'll marry me when I get back. Betty would soon be gone and he'd need a woman. Leah had been the rudder that kept him going in the right direction although he had never seen that and didn't realize it now. As far as Mose was concerned, one woman was the same as another except for Susan and she seemed more like a man and a buddy. He decided she'd make a perfect wife for him and he'd ask her when he got back.

He went on to Fort Christmas and was surprised to find that there were few settlers in that area. He turned west at Fort Taylor and rode into Fort Gatlin. It was down here that the Jernigan boys had settled and had tried to farm, along with the Indians, around Lake Tohopekaliga. To Fort McCantock near Reedy Creek to Fort Christmas and back to Fort Gatlin was a triangle of roads and they seemed well traveled. The land was full of clear little lakes and pinewoods. One day he hit the trail that led from Fort Gatlin at the northern tip of the triangle toward Fort McCantock. He veered slightly east and came to a dead end near the northern tip of Lake Tohopekaliga. To the west was an impassable boggy area. To the south was a wet marsh and he could see a small island lying between him and the big lake. To his east was a smaller lake and a boggy creek, that originated just south of Fort Gatlin, and ran into a cove at its northwestern shores. The area seemed isolated and well protected by the surrounding natural boundaries. It was here he decided to build a cow camp, bring down some slaves and start another plantation. He scouted the area to the south below the big lake to Fort Gardner as far south as the Kissimmee River, across the Allapatta Flats and back up the eastern side of the St. Johns from its beginning to Palatka. People had begun to settle the area and Mose went directly home with big plans to come right back, driving his cattle ahead of him and start building. They all immediately wanted to go back with him and see what he was talking about.

He was in a more relaxed frame of mind and Leah was pushed aside in his thoughts as she had been in person. The next day he sat in the kitchen, resting from his travels and making plans. Susan and Lydia were picking mulberries from the big tree he had planted almost twenty-five years ago when he had first moved to Florida. He called to her and she came to the steps leading up to the kitchen. They both sat on the big porch.

"I ain't had time to visit none since I got back. You reckon Francis is going to marry that gal over in Hernando County?"

She told him she didn't like the girl. "I like the one John's got pumped. She's our kind, but I'm trying to change Francis's mind."

John had married Needham Yates' baby sister, Mary, and they were already planning to move to Central Florida. So Susan and Mose began to make plans to have Francis and Champ come south into the new territory too.

"It's getting too crowded up this way anyways and taxes is going up and up. That's virgin territory and just waiting for a young man. I sure do want to get Little Mose off down there and see if I can straighten him out."

"You'd better do somethin quick, Mose. That boy's got a cruel streak in him I sure don't like. Hit worried Leah. She and I talked about hit a lot and I jest about decided some young'uns is born that way naturally, and hit takes a lot o' straightening out to keep 'em from goin' wrong."

"I know, sometimes he seems like some of the young colts I've tried to break. You can break 'em to ride and they'll be goin down the road and take a notion to buck you off or you can be saddling 'em up or messing with 'em and they'll haul off and kick yore brains out or take a bite out o' you when you least expect it. I jest shoot one when he comes out that way but I can't shoot my own flesh and blood. He and I git along jest fine. He knows better'n to mess with me, but I cain't trust him to do what's right around the rest of the community. He's jest got a wild streak in him, somehow."

He looked at her as they talked. My God, she's an old woman. It had been over ten years since he had tried to seduce her in the little cabin. She had been desirable to him then. Is it because she's order or have we changed that much? Her hair was gray and she was wrinkled. Her breasts sagged and her stomach protruded. What do I want with an old woman? I'm wealthy and can git about anyone I want. I could get me a young and pretty wife now. I'm strong as an ox even if I am gettin' a little smooth-mouthed.

He had been all prepared with a speech about how in the Bible a man was supposed to take his brother's wife to wed when something happened to his brother. There didn't have to be any sex involved. With all the children gone but Andrew Jackson and Lydia, there'd be plenty of room. Andrew Jackson was sixteen and he planned to go with John and his new bride with the Yateses to Fort Christmas. At least he had been trying to talk Susan into it for weeks, anyway.

She could even have her own room as long as she ran his home and helped with the social life of the slaves and their welfare on the plantation. This way they could keep the estate in the family and her children could keep on benefiting from it along with his. They all seemed like his children anyway. It seemed so logical but he just couldn't say it. I don't want an old woman fer a wife, he thought. I want a young, pretty one.

Susan had gone back to the subject of the boys and their quest for a wife.

Mose smiled at her and said, "You know these young bucks, Susan. Thet thing gits to bother'n 'em and they think hit's love. I tell 'em love ain't nothin' but an abscess that forms in the brain and busts in the groin."

"Mose," said Susan, looking around to see if anyone had heard him. "You know there's more to hit than that. You're always so nasty minded. How about respect and friendship and havin' things in common?"

"Thet comes later," thinking that's what he and Susan had.

"But that's love."

"Then that means I love you, Susan, but I ain't a plannin' to run jump in bed with you or take you for a wife."

Now it was said and out in the open. But Susan didn't seem taken aback. If anything, she felt relief. She had never changed her mind after all these years and Mose would have probably been just a little bit insulted if he knew she really never, in all her wildest dreams, thought about marrying him.

"Everybuddy else around here's a'gittin' married, I figure you'll be next, Mose."

"I don't see no need in buyin' a milk cow when I can git milk without hit," he told her.

"You jest be careful who you git mixed up with," she reminded him.

It was almost Christmas and Little Mose came in to talk with him one evening and told him he wanted to marry Penelope Alexander. He was barely seventeen. Mose had a fit. "Jest cause the rest o' these young'uns is marryin' off you don't have to jump the gun. I was plannin' to take you down south and git you a start down there. You ain't even dry behind the ears and you wantin' to take a wife and start a family."

Little Mose looked at him and smiled. "I done got one started, Pa."

"You got thet little gal knocked up?"

Little Mose didn't answer but just sat and smiled in his cocky little way.

"Well, no need shuttin' the barn door and the mule done out. We ain't got time to build you a house. Thet Pa of hers is the meanest man around these parts. He'd hog tie you and cut your nuts out jest like one o' our bull yearling's if he found out you been messin' around his baby gal. We better git you married up right away for he starts smellin' a rat."

He told Susan right away. "He's a startin' a family and ain't got sense to pour piss outa a boot with directions on the heel. Jest when I got a little peace and quiet around here I got to take him and his wife and a squallin' young'un to raise. Ain't got time to build 'em a house."

The next day Susan came to him and told him she wanted to take Andrew Jackson and Lydia down to John's after he got settled in Central Florida. She'd go with Champ and Francis with their family when they went. Little Mose's family could have her house until Mose and the boys could build them another. I'll go up and live with Rhoda until you can make the move and they can move right in after the wedding." No matter or argument could change her mind. Susan was just as hard headed as Mose and he knew it. Whatever she decided to do, she'd do.

With the excuse that Little Mose and Penny would be needed to help around the plantation since Susan wanted to leave and Mose needed Isaac along with him on the next trip to Central Florida, they were married right away. Penny's mother was probably suspicious, for women have a special talent for knowing such things, but a big wedding was hastily planned and the big day arrived.

A.J., Isaac, George, Mose Jr. and little Will had left for the wedding. Mose and Betty were dressed and ready to go.

"Run over there and see what's holdin up your Aunt Susan. Ain't like her to drag-ass around like that. Any other time she'd be sittin on the porch, waitin on you. I see Lydia a sittin' out there all dressed to go. Tell her we got to light outa here or be late fer the ceremony."

Betty came back. "She says she ain't a'goin', Pa."

"She ain't a'goin'? What in the hell's the matter, you reckoned? You and Lydia git in the buggy and I'll go talk to her."

She wasn't dressed and had on her old shirtwaist and skirt. "Them dogs o' y'orn tracked more sand on this porch than you can dig out with a shovel," she said as she dragged a box out through the door onto the porch.

"Ain't you a'goin' to the big dick-skinnin'? What's got into you?"

"I ain't got time, Mose. I still got to git a few more things packed."

"Let them niggers pack 'em and go git some clothes on. You're a'takin' them niggers with you, ain't you? I done give 'em to you."

"Deedy didn't much want to go to start with but she decided she'd miss these young'uns even though they are 'bout growed up and left"

"Don't ask her to go, Susan. Tell her she's a'goin'. She ain't got no say so in the matter. Goddammit, won't you ever learn how to treat a slave? You're as bad as Isaac, not wanting to hurt one's feelings. They ain't got no feelings in the first place. Come on and git dressed. Everybuddy'll wonder where you are."

"They won't miss me none, Mose. I'll git to bed, over at yore house. I'll need the sleep anyways as we want to git off on the dew in the mornin' and they'll be a *shiveree* here tonight until way into the early part o' the morning."

"I guess yore right. They'll all stick around 'til the last dog's hung. They always do."

And so, Susan had decided to break with the family and thought this would be a good start, not to show up at the wedding.

As planned, he and Isaac left after the wedding for Central Florida, soon followed by Champ, Francis, Susan, Lydia and Andrew Jackson. They would wait for them at Fort Christmas and help them get settled. And so a new way of life was beginning for them all in a new and wild, untamed land. Mose and his children would continue to live on the plantation but with most of his brother's family settling down in Orange and Brevard County in Central Florida. Mose would find it impossible to break the bond with Will's children and widow and would eventually find himself torn between the two areas to the extent that they blended together as "home" and "family" to him and he could make no distinction between the two. He would soon have an empire in Central Florida that would rival the one he had built in North Florida and he would come to love it even more and feel its pull to come back time and time again. Like a man torn between the love of two women, he would find it impossible to give either of them up until fate would provide the way.

Chapter 16

Isaac, Mose and Champ settled Susan and Francis at Fort Christmas with the Canadys and took off for parts unknown. They inspected the area north of the Fort and Econlochatchee Creek from its origin to the St. Johns River. They headed south across the Totoosahatchee to Taylor Creek, Cox Creek, Wolf and Pennewah. Mose had not been south of Fort Taylor, having taken the trail west to Fort Gatlin from there on his first trip. He was greatly impressed with a wide stretch of grasslands called Ocean Prairie down below Pennewah to a little unnamed creek and swamp that would someday be called Jane Green, after one of his infamous lady friends who would get him and little Mose into a peck of trouble.

Near Jane Green, they crossed Crabgrass Creek, Bull Creek and little Bull Creek, Tyson Creek, Ten Mile and Six Mile Creeks, Little Wolf Creek, Ox Creek, Blue Cypress and the Allapatta Flats, below the headwaters of the St. Johns River, on down to Fort Drum. At Fort Drum, they turned west to Fort Kissimmee, up the river to Lake Kissimmee, around to the Gardner Marsh and that area. They worked their way all around Lake Kissimmee, to Lakes Hatchineha, Cypress and Gentry, and over to the eastern shores of Lake Tohopekaliga. So far, Mose had picked Ocean Prairie and Champ had preferred the Gardner Marsh, but Isaac fell in love with a little piece of land that jutted into the big shallow Lake Tohopekaliga.

"Here's where I want to move down and bring Hattie Geiger."

"How you know she'll come down here? You ain't even asked her to marry up with you yet."

"She'll come," said Isaac. "She'd love it here, I know." Isaac could talk of nothing else.

They tried to cross the marsh and go over where Mose had found his campsite at the north end of Lake Tohopekaliga, but could not get their horses across because of high water. So they rode to the east of the small lake, east of Lake Tohopekaliga, found the Harney trail and went in that way. After spending some time there, they went north and then west across Shingle Creek, hit the Tampa trail back to Fort Gatlin and a little town called Jernigan, named after one of the Jernigan brothers, that was soon to be Orlando. Here they found a family called Overstreet, a Robert Ivey and the Mizells. Isaac did not remember David Jr. or the two Mizell brothers he had met that day during the fish fry at Ocean Pond. Had he remembered them, he would have been too embarrassed to speak. Nor did John Randolph remember him as being the little urchin that came running to his mother with an urgent need to go to the bathroom. David Mizell did, but mercifully was too polite to breach the subject.

Back at Fort Christmas, Isaac was invited by one of the Cox boys to go 'gator hunting. Not to hunt the small five and six foot 'gators that Isaac was used to shooting out of the rice fields to smoke their tails for the dogs. This was supposedly a thirteen foot 'gator and Isaac was excited, to say the least. He had never seen an alligator that large.

"I found where a big'un wallered jest a couple o' days ago" said Harley. "Been meaning to git back and git him."

They went to his barn and put Isaac's horse in his lot. After a big supper of cowpeas and buttermilk biscuits Isaac was warned not to eat too much because they had a long walk ahead of them to get to the 'gator hole.

On the way, Harley told him, "I walked down the creek here, a hunting 'gator sign and come to where hit comes into this swamp. I saw where a big boar 'gator had wallered and crawled down a little false run of the creek. I started trailing him and got into the biggest tangle of logs and myrtle bushes, cat claws, bamboo briars and you name hit. They love to git off in a mess like that. Reason he's growed so big and lived so long. I hated to stop and give up. Thet old 'gator knew where he wanted to go and didn't cut no corners. By the time I had follered his trail to his hole hit was a'gittin' dark and I weren't morn three quarters of a mile off in thet swamp. I cut brush every now and then and pretty well got us a trail marked. He's bound to have a cave there. You got some dry clothes to put on when we git back?"

Isaac assured him he had a changing.

"We'll probably have mud clear to our waist when we git outa here."

Isaac didn't know it but Harley had an inner ear problem and had difficulty walking logs. So, he carried a light cypress pole about eight feet long to help him keep his balance. It had a shark hook at the end with the beard filed off, he used to hook 'gators and pull them into his little frog boat when the water was too deep to get out and put them in. He also carried a machete and had a hatchet stuck in his belt. He had a larger 'gator hook than the one on the end of his pole. Isaac carried the torch and a gun. They were only about 100 yards into the swamp when Harley cut the head off a moccasin amid the tangled logs and thick muddy ooze of the swamp. By the time they had killed the third snake, Isaac was wishing he could turn back but didn't have the nerve to say so. When they finally got to the 'gator hole and about seven moccasins later, Harley cut a pole to attach to the big 'gator hook. The hook was about eighteen inches long, made from a long piece of iron that was bent back about three quarters from the end into a 90 degree angle. It was sharpened so it could be laid down on the end of the pole and driven in. Then it was to be fastened onto the pole at the curve of the hook with two wagon bolts. Harley laid the hatchet, hook and wagon bolts down and was trimming the pole he had just cut, getting ready to attach the hook. He had leaned the gun against a cypress tree. The 'gator hole was about forty feet across and ringed with myrtles and willow bushes. A big cypress tree had fallen across the hole and was laying half in and half out of the water. Isaac had walked out onto the log with Harley's little eight-foot cypress pole with the little shark hook at the end of it and had started, as instructed, probing the bottom of the hole.

"You say he's probably down there sommers," asked Isaac, getting more excited by the minute?

"He's most probably at one side down in his cave," said Harley. "If'n he don't come up in a minute we'll dig down there with this here big hook, soon as I can git hit on, and see can we hook him."

Harley was busy gettin' his pole ready to attach the hook.

In a minute Isaac said, "I think I've hooked something already." He pulled back on the little pole and each time he released his grip, it went back down again.

"Well, thet's a big 'gator and if you got thet little hook into him you'd know hit, hit's probably a cypress root."

"I don't know, Harley. Hit sure feels like somethin alive to me. I swear hit does," said Isaac. He was out on the log, pulling like he was trying to land a fish.

Harley picked up his pole and said, "Wait a minute and I'll come see." He took the big pole he'd just cut and probed down into the water. "You may be right, Isaac" he agreed. "Ain't but one way to find out." He laid the big pole across the log and went back for the hatchet, hook and bolts. Just as he got to Isaac his left hand full, keeping his balance by holding onto a willow limb with the other, and his balance not being what it should be, he fell head long into the 'gator hole. As he passed Isaac he grabbed him around the neck with his free hand and knocked him off the log. When he came up he had dropped everything he had and was swimming for the other side of the hole, thinking only of that thirteen or fourteen foot 'gator. Poor Isaac was in the hole by himself, his legs locked around the log, still holding onto the little pole, blowing water like a big whale. He finally pulled back up onto the log as Harley came out from the hole, dripping wet.

"Now what in the hell do we do?" Isaac asked.

"Well, sumbuddy's got to go back into thet hole and find my hatchet, the hook and bolts. I don't know about the bolts, maybe I brung some extra ones." He felt around and came up with a couple of bolts out of his pocket. "These'll do but I got to git my hook and hatchet back. We cain't drag that 'gator out with the one you got."

Isaac stood there for a minute, looking down at he dark, murky water, still holding onto the little pole, still hooked to "something." "Well, hit sure as hell won't be me," he decided.

So Harley took his shoes off and waded out into the hole, feeling around cautiously as he went. The water was deeper than he thought and he was soon up to his shoulders, probing with his toes in between the logs and trash on the muddy bottom.

"They oughter be round here sommers" he told Isaac. "Now if you got a 'gator hooked on thet pole yore a holdin, you tell me if'n you feel anything move."

"Alright."

Harley was searching for his hook and hatchet and watching the pole at the same time.

"He's a movin'!" cried Isaac. "He's a comin' out!"

Harley forgot his precious hatchet and hook and started for the gun.

"My God, what a 'gator," Isaac exclaimed, as the old 'gator started blowing at

121

him. He was right on top of the water with his head away from Isaac who had hooked him through the tip of his tail. He was trying to hold onto the little pole and yet keep from being jerked into the hole with the 'gator.

"Shoot him! Shoot him!" Isaac was telling Harley, who had just gotten back out on the log with the gun.

"I cain't see his head," yelled Harley. "You're a'standin' in my light." The torch they brought was sticking in the mud at the edge of the hole.

Harley finally maneuvered from behind Isaac until he got a clear shot and popped the 'gator right on the top of the head. Not an ideal shot. The old 'gator came up right on top of the water, turned side ways to Isaac and started rolling. He was tearing up the water, rolling right up against the log they were standing on. Isaac was holding onto the little pole for dear life, determined not to let go, trying to keep his balance. Harley had sat down on the log that was bouncing up and down. He wasn't about to take another plunge into the water, especially with the gun. Luckily for the men, but not for the 'gator, he finally got his head hung beneath the log they were on and Harley stuck his rifle against the 'gator's ear and pulled the trigger. The poor thing rolled on his back, dying instantly.

Harley felt down on his belt and in his pocket and announced he had also lost his skinning knife when he fell in. Isaac had a replacement of sorts but it was smaller and dull. They finally got it sharpened, after a fashion, by rubbing it against the metal of the gun barrel. Harley climbed into the hole, up to his shoulders in water, skinning the 'gator.

Isaac sat for a minute, watching him strip the hide off. "Yore a'goin' at that like you wuz a'guttin' a dawg. Ain't there a easier way to do hit?"

"Not with a dull knife. You got to have yore knife extra sharp. I could ride clear to Georgia a'sittin' on this one and not feel a thing."

Isaac sat, contemplating the matter. The torch had almost burned out and they'd soon be in the dark. "We're two damned fools, and you know hit, Harley. Here we are off two mile in the worst swamp in the whole country. Maybe in the United States, trying to skin a fourteen-foot 'gator in the dark with a dull knife. Are we havin' fun or are we havin' fun?"

They both started laughing.

"This 'gator huntin' is a bitch, ain't hit," laughed Harley, but they both agreed they couldn't think of anything else they'd rather be doing.

After the hide was off, Harley probed around the edge of the hole and finally found his knife but vowed he'd come back someday and find his hatchet and hook. They were too expensive to replace. They finally made it home at midnight, the 'gator hide wrapped around Harley's neck, the tail tied to his belt and Isaac carrying the gun, machete, torch and little pole with the small hook bent all out of shape. They were muddy and tired, but happy.

The next morning, Harley asked Isaac, "You ready to go agin?"

"Tonight?" asked Isaac. He shook his head. "I got a belly full o' stumblin' around in the dark, trying to shine a 'gator's eyes and dodging moccasins there and back."

"No, I mean in the day time. Today. This morning. We ain't got our 'gator hook anyways but we can take off down the creek in my little boat with a gun and see can we find one o' them big holes. They's places down this creek ain't got no bottom in 'em and you stand a good chance o' seein a 'gator in one in broad open daylight."

He finally talked Isaac into going, so they packed the boat with a frying pan, fishing poles and corn pone, threw in their bed rolls and the gun and took off down the creek.

Now this creek was not the wide-open body of water some would think of as a creek with high dry banks on both sides. It was really a part of the outlying swamp. Just a low spot of land with water. It had mostly cabbage palms on both sides, reaching all the way out to dry land mixed in with sweet gum, bays, cypress, and maples, on the edge where it was drier. Under the trees were shrubs, and bushes of myrtles, gall berries, palmetto, cat claws and bamboo briars and a multitude of vines too numerous to name. It was a mile or so across and ran for five miles before it hit another larger creek that ran into the St. Johns marsh. In the center of all this was where the water ran, which was called the "run of the creek." It ranged in size from four to twelve feet across and from six inches to ten feet deep in places where the soil had washed out into very deep holes during a sudden deluge of rain through eons of time. The sides of the "run" were lined with huge cypress trees, their knees rising up like huge wooden stalagmites. The creek was filled with almost every type of animal, fish, reptile and fowl known to Central Florida. The little boat they were in was called a "log-hopper." It had a flat bottom that skimmed along the top of the water and over sunken logs. It was light enough for one man to port it around obstacles and would float anywhere the water was four inches deep. Isaac weighed more than Harley, who was a skinny little man weighing less than one-hundred twenty pounds, sopping wet, so Isaac had to sit in the stern and pole the boat while Harley sat in the bow. They carried the machete, gun, bedrolls and other necessary gear so there wasn't much freeboard in the little boat. They had hit some open places in the creek. Isaac was standing up, his legs braced against the side of the boat, skimming along enjoying the view, when they hit a submerged cypress knee. Isaac came running down the middle of the boat full tilt and fell over the top of Harley, landing headlong into the water. It was only three feet deep, but he lost his hat and had mud in his hair and face. Harley thought it was hilarious, but it took a little bit of laughing for Isaac to find his sense of humor. Harley had painted the trip as a nice, leisurely boat ride.

They stopped to eat lunch along a dry spot on the "run" of the creek and Isaac took off his clothes and hung them to dry on a bush and washed the mud out of his hair. He soon began to enjoy the trip and they stopped at dusk where the creek more or less disappeared in a large, almost lake-like opening deep in a swampy area. The hole was full of alligators. Almost as if trapped in the hole, they pushed through the dark water the color of old tea with only eyes and snout visible. Harley had explained to Isaac that you measure a 'gator by the distance from between the eyes to the tip of the nose. For every inch you see, there's a foot of body below the water. Isaac saw one he guessed must be fifteen to sixteen feet long. Just as they reached the bank a water snake dropped out of a tree a few feet from the boat. Isaac was glad to set his feet on dry land.

They soon had a fire going and had caught a mess of small perch for supper, using kernels of yellow corn for bait. The mosquitoes had come out with the darkness and huge swarms descended on them just as they were enjoying their meal. Harley brought out the 'gator oil and they rubbed it over their hands, face, neck and pulled their hats down as low as possible over their face. Isaac thought they were going to wait until daylight and kill one of the 'gators but Harley began to make preparations for a 'gator hunt after supper. He explained it was much easier to blind them with the light and shoot them. "You cain't git close enough to one o' them big ones to git a good shot in the day. He'll sink and go to the bottom and you won't see him no more."

So they got into the little boat with the torch, little pole with the shark hook on the end, bent back in place, gun and paddles. It was too deep to pole around as there was no pole long enough to reach the bottom of the hole. The dark water was alive with eyes. They would shine one after the other, Harley looking for the perfect specimen. Some eyes were far apart and some close together. There were many red eyes and some white and glimmering like diamonds.

"Them little red ones is too small to mess with. They won't run morn five or six foot. Ain't worth skinnin' less you want to eat one. We'll look 'til we find a pair thet's white and shinning and wide apart."

They paddled around in the sea of eyes and curious sounds. There was the constant croaking of frogs. The peep, peep, peep of the little spring frogs and the deeper, hoarser croak of the big bullfrogs. A pond bird cried out from his roost, flapped his wings and flew out into the night. The water lapped against the little boat and now and then something bumped against it and disappeared beneath the dark, still waters. A large fish broke the water just ahead of the boat and there was a whirl and splash among the lily pads. They finally shined one that satisfied Harley.

"This'n'll go nearly four hundred pounds," he said as he raised his gun and shot him right in the ear that was a little lower, but behind his eye. A perfect shot.

"When he waves to you with them feet, he's a goner!" Harley cried as the 'gator sank, then surfaced right in front of the boat, turned crossways and rolled right up under it. The little boat rocked back and forth and Isaac was sure it was going to capsize.

"Back her down! Back her down!" Harley yelled at Isaac, who was just sitting there, holding onto both sides of the boat for dear life. The 'gator bumped underneath the boat, rocked it again and then rolled from underneath it.

"He's a dyin' hard," Harley exclaimed as they watched the 'gator roll over on his back and his feet came up in the air, toes spread apart and he began to shake all over.

"He's a wavin' to us," laughed Harley and Isaac knew it was finally over.

Coming back to Fort Christmas, Isaac rode up to some whooping cranes. He got down from his horse and watched their antics as they shuffled and danced in a clockwise circle, flapping their wings and lifting their feet with lowered heads, whooping wildly. They were snow white with black faces and a bright red patch of bare skin on top of their heads. One bird would bow his head and flap his wings and leap into the air with stiffened legs while throwing his head to the sky. As if not to be outdone, the other bird responded to this antic by running toward his mate, bobbing his head up and down, wings flapping and then both birds jumped up and down together with stiff legs and their necks arched. They seemed to be dancing for the sheer joy of dancing. This particular pair probably had a nest nearby where the female had laid her eggs in late May and the chicks were ready to hatch. He had seen such nest; a three feet tall mound of bull rushes in a shallow pond where the little rusty-colored chicks would hatch. They were getting scarce up around Columbia County and he hadn't seen birds dance like this since he was a small boy. As he watched, another pair of cranes appeared in the edge of the opening and this pair gave a high, penetrating call in unison, the male trumpeting with his beak pointed toward the sky and the female, a couple of shorter trumps and a few notes higher. They were defending their territory. The intruders leaned into the wind, spread their wings and lifted off, circling on the updraft. They had a seven-foot wingspan and Isaac could see their jet-black wing tips that had not been visible when they were on the ground. The departing pair cast a shadow as they turned and flew away. Isaac stood and watched the other majestic pair of five-foot birds feed off around the end of a pond and disappear.

The rest of the family got a big kick out of Isaac's tale about the 'gator hunt. He had helped Harley tack the 'gator hides on the barn and he was to come get the biggest one before he left for Columbia County. But Susan enjoyed hearing of the big whoppers more than anything else.

Mose and Isaac took Susan on a visit over to Jernigan to meet some of the new-comers. They met the Hodges family, John Sr. and Millie, with John Jr. and his wife, Zilphie Ann. Millie was part Creek Indian, like Needham Yates's wife. Many of the men that had wives of Indian blood had migrated down south, where the settlers were more tolerant of such marriages. Along with the Mizells were Robert and Priscilla Ivey who Mose had met before. He had known Robert's brother, Thomas, before he died and had seen Thomas's daughter at a frolic near Jacksonville and told her Aunt and Uncle that she was looking well.

"Priscilla's going to be an old maid if she doesn't quit bein' so particular about her choice of suitors," her Uncle Robert complained. "She's already going on seventeen and never even had a serious suitor, best we can tell." He had already met Henry and Mary Overstreet, who were getting ready to move to Shingle Creek on the Tampa Trail where Needham Yates's mother, father and baby brother, Jack, had already settled in. Henry's brother had come down with him and they had built the first hotel in town, but his brother had become dissatisfied with the new country and had gone back to Georgia. Mose was surprised that he knew so many of the new people in town. Susan was quite taken with the area east of Jernigan.

She liked the idea of being near a village, but wanted to live out in the country. She loved the clear sandy little lakes and the rich fertile soil. Fort Christmas was too isolated for her.

But when they took her on down into Brevard County to see where John and his new bride, Mary Yates, were going to live next to Needham Yates's family, along with the Simmonses, Osteens, and Tysons, she was in total shock. She couldn't believe how many days it took to complete the long ride and wondered where these people got their supplies. She found out that the closest post office was either Jernigan or across the Allapatta Flats on the east coast at Fort Capron, just north of Fort Pierce. There was nothing in between. Just miles and miles of nothing. She quickly decided she was not going to live way off down there and most certainly not down to the Gardner Marsh with Francis and Champ and she and Andrew Jackson and Lydia would make it someway. Mose laughed at her and told her he'd try to work something out.

And he did. He put Andrew Jackson and Henry Hodges to work driving a supply wagon to the various isolated settlers. Leave it up to Mose to think of such a thing. This way they didn't have to wait for someone to make the long ride to Melonville to buy necessary supplies that came up the St. Johns River. He went with Andrew Jackson and showed him what goods he thought would sell well and what items would be needed the most and soon he had a "K-Mart" of sorts on wheels. It wasn't long before every settler "owed their souls to the company store" and that was Mose Barber. Susan and Andrew Jackson and Lydia soon moved near Sweet Water Branch, where travelers stopped to water their horses and where Susan sold supplies there out of the little house until Andrew Jackson finally married and built a place at Lake Conway. Susan had her home, at last, on a lake in Central Florida.

Chapter 17

In no time Isiah and the cow crew, along with Isaac, little Mose and Mose had moved the major portion of Mose's cattle to the south of the Ocklawaha River into Sumter, Brevard and Orange Counties. Needham Yates had helped Mose build his new plantation on the North east shore of Lake Tohopekaliga and soon he had slaves farming on what is now Rose Hill Cemetery. John and his bride, Needham's sister, ran the farm while Mose was gone, either back to his old plantation or in the woods, punching cattle. He was a very busy man, Mose Barber.

He and the boys got back to Columbia County just in time for the Christmas celebrations. His brother, Sam, had just built a new house and insisted the family gather there for Christmas get-together. The large, extended family had all gathered by Christmas Eve. The boys slept in the hall on pallets. Since there were fewer girls than boys, the girls had the parlor and feather mattresses on the floor. Someone made the remark that there was going to be a war pretty soon what with there being more boy babies having been born than girls.

"It always happens before a war," someone said. "Because when so many young men get killed in the war, there's still enough left over for the girls to marry."

Most everyone laughed at the old wives-tale, knowing full well that the Indians had all been run out of north Florida. They had beaten the English and French and they didn't want anymore fighting. "Them Spaniards never did want any of this land after they found out it didn't have no gold, so there's nobuddy left but us. We ain't got nobuddy to fight 'cept amongst ourselves," and laughed it off. But a few of the serious thinkers didn't think that was quite so funny when they thought of the squabbles brewing amongst the north and south about their slaves. But it'd never get that far, they thought.

The older men slept on the floor as well, letting the ladies have the beds. In the past they had spread hay on the floor about two feet deep and spreadsheets and blankets on top of it. It made a very good bed but one year a spark from the hearth had set the hay on fire and a man's night shirt along with it so now they had made mattresses out of bed ticking and put in fresh hay every year according to the number of guests they had.

The next morning Mose was up early and slipped into the kitchen before anyone else was up—he thought. There was a big fire going in the fireplace and Becky Clements, the hired girl was busy dividing eggs for the eggnog. Mose sneaked up behind her and yelled "Christmas gift!" This was an old Christmas custom. The one that sneaks the "gift" on the other one gets a favor in return.

"Oh, Uncle Mose, you near' bout skeered me to death. I didn't know nobuddy wuz up but me." She giggled and walked right up to him looked him straight in the eye and said. "You know I ain't got nothin' to give you."

"We might could work somethin' out," he said, eyeing the young girl.

Sam and his wife had taken the little girl in before she was old enough to be of any help. Her entire family had been wiped out over in western Columbia County during the Indian War. Many orphans were "farmed out" from one home to another until they were able to work and then used as virtual slaves around the farm. They were never paid, but were given room and board and barely enough to wear and get by. They didn't even know what money was. Becky had been one of these, except she was considered more "family" than most, having been with the couple for so long. Mose had never paid much attention to the young girl. She had always been small, skinny, freckled faced and immature. It seemed she had blossomed out overnight and she was already out of her teens.

Mose sat and drank his coffee, looking at Becky as she dried the egg white from her hands.

Why, she's filled out and as cute as a speckled pup under a red wagon, he thought to himself.

He got up and walked over to her, "You could always give me a kiss. That don't cost nothin'," he said, putting his arms around her.

"Why, you sly old fox," she giggled and stepped back but not too far.

About that time Mary, Sam's wife came into the kitchen. She had come from the privy and had seen Mose's arm around the girl through the window.

"Rebecca," she said sharply, "You get out my white linen tablecloth and set the table for the eggnog." Becky knew she was upset when she called her by her full name. She glared at Mose, who smiled and told her she was getting younger looking every day. This took the edge off the older woman's ire, but she knew what Mose was up to anyway.

Becky spread the linen cloth and set a large porcelain dish pan in the center, banked by holly branches, bright with red berries from a wild holly tree. When everyone was up they would have the eggnog, spiked with a generous amount of fine Kentucky bourbon. Breakfast would be late.

The rest of the family trickled in and Mose watched Becky beat the egg whites, her hips swaying to the click of the silver fork against the bowl.

"That gal, Becky, shore has filled out since the last time I seen her," Mose told his brother.

"Yeah, the wife's been a'eyein' her. She never paid no mind to her 'til the boys started hangin' around. Now she's jest a little bit jealous o' her, I think. Says she's a'gonna cause us trouble and bring down disgrace on the family. She even gits suspicious o' me and me as old as I am. She'd kill me off in no time."

"Not me," said Mose. "Anyway, it'd be a good way to go."

Sam's wife had come back in, dressed to the nines in a black silk blouse with a heavy corded silk skirt. There was a velvet panel down the front and a velvet basque with tiny velvet buttons starting high at her throat, just beneath her triple chin and ran all the way down to the waist, bulging open at her more than ample breasts. Mose thought the outfit looked ridiculous on such a cow and thought of how nice Becky would look in it. She had on a plain gray shirtwaist and skirt with a minimum of frills and buttons. He looked at his Betty in her green and white flowered organdy dress with ribbons and ruffles. I could afford to dress that little Becky in such as that, he dreamed.

The table was soon loaded down with great platters of fried turkey breast, ham and hot biscuits. Becky did not eat with the rest of the crowd but passed among the guests keeping their coffee cups full and their plates full of hot biscuits.

After breakfast, they all started out for church services. The teams and horse-back riders stretched out along the road like a parade. Mose rode in the back behind Becky. He found he couldn't keep his eyes off the girl and she knew it, throwing him sly glances and smiling and giggling.

The services were held outside in the church yard, there being too many to get in the church. It seemed almost everyone was there. Mose was in his element with his fine dress, bowing and tipping his hat to the ladies. He was still a fine fig-ure of a man. He had not gone to pot even though he was in his fifties, having spent so many years in the saddle.

Back at Sam's the coals were unbanked from under the turkey pilaf in the big kettle, outside. That evening there was a candy pulling and a Christmas play was put on by the many grandchildren. Mose tried his best to talk privately with Becky but Mary, Sam's wife, kept her busy and he didn't get a chance to see her the next morning before he left for the plantation. But he certainly made plans to come back. He had every intention of getting to know the young girl better — much better.

But back at his plantation, another girl caught his eye. George Ed had been run-ning things while he had been away and he hadn't been out to the quarters in some time.

"Lordgodamighty," he exclaimed to young Mose. "I jest got a look at that gal of Lottie's. She looks plum white. Have you seen her?"

"No, I ain't paid much attention to these little nigger gals, Pa." Even Little Mose knew better than to fool around with the slave women. Leah had seen to that.

"Nigger gals!" Mose exclaimed. "She's plum white, I tell you. Course we always 'spected she belonged to old Kingsley and Lottie's half Injun. Got to be — may even have some white in her. You jest go look and tell me what you think."

Little Mose went to look, just out of curiosity and agreed with his daddy that if you didn't know where she came from she'd pass for white.

"We need to do somethin' with that gal 'fore she gits knocked up with one o' them Mandingoes. She'd bring a pretty penny over in Monticello," Little Mose told him.

"You know yore Ma never would let us sell any of these slaves less they wanted to go and I doubt Lottie'd go fer that."

"Lottie ain't got any say so in hit, Pa. Ain't that what you always said?"

"Well, we might could convince Lottie it'd be to the best interest of the gal, over there at one o' them high class plantations, bein' the man's mistress and all. I'll talk with her about it."

He told the overseer. "Send Lottie into me tonight after supper and have her bring her little gal in with her. I want to talk to her bout somethin' important like."

Mose couldn't look at anything else when the girl entered the room with her mother. She was about fourteen, short and stocky like old Kingsley. She had straight black hair and skin so fair it reminded him of Leah's. The girl reminded him of Leah when she was a little older than that. The only hint of Negro blood was a dark tinge beneath her fingernails and an every so slight flatness of her nose that gave her a sensuous look. He just looked at her and suddenly his groin came alive. He felt his manhood stir and he became ashamed. In all these years, he had never considered even looking at one of his slaves in that way.

"She still a virgin?" he asked Lottie.

"Yasuh, Massa Mose. She ain't been popped yit. I been savin' her. I thought Miss Betty might want her foe a house niggah. She too purty foe a field hand."

"You sure?"

"Sho', I been wonderin' when yo gonna take notice."

Mose looked the girl over. She took a quick look at him and dropped her eyes. Slaves were taught never to look their master in the eyes. But her brief glance had caught him and he sensed it to be warm and inviting. Just ripe for picking, he thought.

"Send her in, in the morning," he told Lottie and he called to Dulcie. "You see thet gal o' Lottie's gits some decent clothes and a bath and put her to work in the house. Tell old Rich to pass the word around, airy buck messes around her, gonna git fifty lashes--not just a hidin'-- and cut like a bull yearling in the bargain. You hear?"

He called Betty in. "You still thinking of marryin' up like you told me?" Betty was "in love" and considering a June wedding. "How'd you like to have that gal o' Lottie's fer a wedding present? She's almost white. I can't talk Lottie into lettin' me sell her over to one o' them dandies over in Hamilton or Madison County. Course she ain't got no say so in the matter."

"You better not, if she's agin it, Pa. You know how Ma felt and you cain't go agin her. 'Member? You promised."

Mose nodded his head. He knew Betty had not had time to get over the death of her mother and the girl still behaved as if Leah were still there. It was "Ma's house" and "Ma's spinning wheel" and so forth.

Soon word got out about the young girl. James, the overseer at Bob Richard's plantation, came over and took a sneak preview at the girl and agreed Mose could get a big price for her.

"She don't look like no nigger wench I ever saw," he agreed.

He gave Mose some good advice. "They say them gals git hot and they begin to stink. So them white men have 'em wash in permanganate o' potash and hit makes 'em smell plum purty."

"All my people smell good," Mose said indignantly. "I see they bathe regular. Them that works in the house, I see they git extra baths. I've been around a few white women smells worse. I found me one down in Central Florida on one of my trips down there, I had go wash off in a ditch, she smelled so bad. I couldn't hack hit. My people don't stink. They bathe regular."

Mose toyed with the idea of talking to Lottie about selling the girl before she got too old but just couldn't bring himself to think of her belonging to another man. He found himself desiring her more and more, just to touch her and feel of her creamy complexion.

Isaac and Betty and their intendeds were away at a corn shucking and he called Lottie into the parlor.

"I hear tell a nigger can cure a rheumatize in a old man's feet, sleepin' at the foot o' his bed. You ever hear that."

"Yasuh, Massa, I heered it so," Lottie already had an idea what Mose was up to. "Yo' want I bring my white gal in, see she kin cure yo's?"

"Wouldn't hurt none to give hit a try. Jest lie at the foot o' my bed at night. Ain't lost nuthin' if hit don't work out."

So Lottie told little Bena what Mose asked her to do. "But don't be 'sprized he ast yo' to pleasure him, too. He old, but he ain't thet old. You do what he say."

That night the girl came into his room and stood by the door. Lottie closed it and left. Mose was sitting on the side of the bed with his nightshirt on, looking at her in the candlelight. She wore a simple long dress with no sleeves.

"God, she is a beauty," he said under his breath. Other than Leah he had never seen anyone more beautiful. And she belongs to me, he thought.

"Come here," he commanded.

She walked to his side and stood, head down, eyes on the floor. He reached out and ran his hand down her arm. Her skin was soft and her flesh warm and firm. He brought her toward him as he sat there and she stood between his knees and he ran his hand up and down her back and down below her small, hard buttocks. She stood there and looked at him, raising her eyes and looking him right in the eyes, so unlike his other slaves. He could see the resemblance of old man Kingsley and for a second it reminded him he was looking at one of his slaves and she was not pure white, no matter how much she looked like it. But the nearness of her and the innocent sensuality she promised had already taken control of him and there was no turning back.

She could read his desire for her, not knowing really what it was all about, but knowing it had something to do between a man and a woman.

"You craves I pleasure yo'?" she asked.

"Do you already know how to pleasure a man?" he asked her in alarm. Part of her appeal had been because of her innocence and the fact that she was still a virgin.

"No, but Ma says do whut yo' wants. What pleasure yo'?"

He smiled and lifted her dress and pulled it over her head. Her breasts were small and hips like a boy's. But the look in her eyes was that of a seductress and he knew she was willing to do what ever he wanted, because she wanted to please him. He pulled off his nightshirt and pulled her down of top of him as he lay back on the bed and continued to explore her firm young body. She said nothing and suddenly began to tremble, her eyes wide with fear. "Relax," he whispered. His voice shook and he found his fingers trembled too as he continued to explore her. "I ain't gonna hurt you none. Jest close your eyes and you'll find you'll enjoy this. It don't turn out to be near as bad as you 'spect."

She smelled sweet and he could feel the heat of her young body and her scent flamed his desire. He rolled over on top of her and he could see her pulse throbbing at the base of her throat. She reminded him of a little baby rabbit his father had brought into him one time from the field. It was trembling like that and Mose had held it tight and squeezed it in a rush of pleasure and when he released his fist, the little thing lay still in death. He had cried because he thought he had squeezed the life from it, until his daddy finally convinced him that it died of fright.

So, he held back and took his time. He ran his hand inside her thighs, up past her groin and caressed her flat, tight belly. He lightly massaged her nipples until they became hard and erect and little by little, he felt her relax. Her arms had lain still beside her, her hands clinched into a fist. But slowly she put them on his back and he could feel her fingers as she began to run them up and down his spine. Only her thighs were trembling now and her breath was coming as fast as his. He could feel it against his neck. Soon she began to moan and toss her head to and fro' and he realized she was no longer afraid of what was expected of her. She was soon to find out the true meaning of "pleasuring."

Mose knew he needed to be discreet. As the familiarity of having her share his bed lessened his overwhelming desire for her, his guilt at what he had been doing increased, and his fear of being caught in the act all put a damper on the activity. Of course, saying nothing about the fact that Mose was no "spring chicken." Although he'd be the last to admit that had anything to do with the decreasing number of trips Lottie made, bringing her to his room after everyone had gone to bed at night. The problem was, that the young girl had acquired a taste for "pleasuring" and thought it should go on forever. Mose simply couldn't keep up with her and was relieved of the chance to get away when the time came to go south.

On this trip, he kept his mind on business, not even going by New Smyrna to see Mrs. Cook. The only other person he thought about was young Becky Clements. He even felt ashamed around Susan when he found he could not confide in her about his act of indiscretion. He had always been able to talk with her about anything in the world but shame had taken place of desire and he felt that no matter how hard he tried to explain to Susan about the girl's beauty and white appearance, the fact still remained that she was a slave and the stigma attached to her was there--no matter how white she looked.

When he got back to Columbia County, he felt no desire to send for Bena. He rested and cleaned up and rode over to his brother Sam's. He clearly wanted to see Becky Clements again.

Sam had been killing hogs. There was one more left to kill and Mose helped him drag the poor screaming animal out of the pen by the hind leg and stick him in the throat, getting the jugular vein with the first jab of the knife to the left side of the throat, exactly three inches from the jaw bone. The kettle, used for making syrup was full of boiling water. Gone were the close-knit family gatherings at Mose's for syrup making. He no longer had time for such activity and Sam made his syrup and sugar at home now. The hog was dipped in the boiling water, careful not to be in it long enough to "set" the hair so it couldn't be removed. After the hair was scraped off the body, it was hung on a gamboling stick that was slipped behind exposed tendons on the hogs rear legs and the stick hung by a hook to a pole that rested with both ends between the forks of two small oak trees. Then more boiling water was poured on spots that hadn't come clean enough to please Sam and scraped until the hide was white and clean, as if the hair had been shaved off by a sharp razor. Then the guts were removed and cleaned to make chitterlings. The carcass was chopped all the way down the backbone, which was removed and handed to one of the boys who chopped it into small pieces while the hams and shoulders were salted down for the smoke house.

Becky came out of the kitchen with a large white enamel pan to get the pieces of backbone. She seemed pleased to see her "Uncle" Mose and Mose felt an immediate surge of pleasure of warmth of her smile and the touch of her fingertips when she laid her hand on his arm.

"You might as well stay fer supper and spend the night," Sam said. "We're gonna bog this backbone up in some rice. Becky, you git right on it."

He wiped his brow with the sleeve of his shirt and looked up at the sun. "I was gonna maybe butcher me a couple more o' them little shoats but hit's turned off so hot. I'm a little dubious o' tryin to cure all thet meat. We ain't kilt no morn' we can eat right now if'n we have to."

"Me and Isaac's too dirty and sweaty to come into Mary's kitchen," Mose said.

"Good honest sweat don't hurt nobuddy," Becky said. She hadn't left with the backbone but had stood, looking first at Mose and then Isaac. "Women know what a man's supposed to smell like."

Becky didn't know that Mose's feeling of being dirty had nothing to do with his shirt but that he suddenly felt guilty because he had been taking one of his slaves to bed. Becky couldn't hold a candle to Bena's beauty and he couldn't imagine that she could even come close to matching the girl's physical activity in the bed, but she was white and very suddenly desirable.

"Ain't thet gal got herself a beau yet? I thought some old boy'd be a courtin' her heavy by now."

"Not yet," Sam said, apologetically. "She jest turned twenty-one, best we can figure and she'd make some man a good wife. She or the wife one runs 'em off quick as they show up. Pickens are kinda slim fer a gal with no family nor dowry, nowadays."

Mose noticed Becky giving Isaac the eye during supper and was glad he was getting ready to wed the Geiger girl. Isaac had grown into a handsome man. He was much better looking than Mose, having inherited his mother's looks. He was almost six feet with black flashing eyes and a somewhat sallow complexion. His hair was surprising lighter than Leah's, having inherited a gene or two of Mose's red hair. The fact that he was spoken for didn't stop Isaac from looking at the way Becky's full bosom was nearly about bursting the buttons off her homespun shirt-waist.

Isaac went on back home the next morning but Sam invited Mose to stay a while and look at some yearlings he had been trying to fatten. Mose didn't take much convincing to stay, as he wanted an opportunity to get Becky alone.

The opportunity came when he found some excuse to get back to the house and he found everyone gone but the girl. She was washing clothes out under the Chinaberry tree.

"Where'd everybuddy git off to?" Mose asked.

"Mrs. Mary's gone to Sanderson to visit her niece and the rest of 'em are cutting fence post."

"I come to the house to git me a cool drink o' water. Come sit a spell while I drink hit."

They sat for a while on the porch and Mose quizzed her about why she had never married. It seemed the right man had just not come along.

"You need to git out more. I tell you what, I was thinkin' o' runnin' over to Raulersons to git a pair o' saddle bags and try out a new saddle over there. Why don't you go over with me?"

"I don't know, I got to git this wash on the line."

"Let 'em soak a spell. They'll come cleaner quicker and you won't have to rub 'em so hard." He picked up her hands and held them for a minute.

"You ought to have a nigger doin' that anyway. Girl with pretty hands like yours don't have no business gettin' 'em red and wrinkled in thet lye soap."

She stood and let him hold her hands and looked him in the eyes and giggled. Then slowly pulled them out of his clasp, threading her fingers through his as she stepped back and gave him an inviting look.

"Come on," Mose said, as they both turned to go. "If we hurry we'll get back before they even know we're gone."

Becky got her bonnet and shawl while Mose saddled the team.

None of the men were at home when they got to the Raulersons and Mose made some excuse for haste, picked up the saddle and saddlebags and they hit the road in a trot back to Samuel's. They stopped at a branch to water the horses. Mose told Becky he thought he heard something that sounded like a swarm of bees off down the branch, so they tied up the team and went down to investigate.

"Be somethin' if we found a bee tree," Mose said. "Ever help rob one?"

"Once, but I was scairt o' gittin' stung. Wasn't much fun."

It was thick in the edge of the little branch and Mose held a limb back so Becky could get through. Once he took her hand and helped her over a fallen log, and she held onto it the rest of the way.

They found the bees. They were swarming and had covered the side of the branch where the water had washed a tall bank on a curve but there was no bee tree. Just a pile of dark, angry bees, looking for a queen.

They stood and looked at the bees for a minute and Mose said, "We'd better git outa here 'fore they decide to swarm on us." They laughed and ran along the ditch bank for a short while until Becky began to stumble and they decided to rest a spell. He took off his topcoat for her to sit on and spread it on a grassy knoll near the branch.

He looked at her and smiled and she smiled back. He thought he recognized a certain look in her eyes as she kept looking at him, spreading her skirt up almost to her knees. This is going to be easier than I thought, he said to himself. He reached out and drew her close to him and she went willingly, meeting him more than half way. She seemed starved for love and appeared to know what it was all about. For a moment, he wondered where she had learned what she knew and knew so well but at that stage of the game it didn't matter. Soon she was moaning and groaning beneath him as they thrashed about the sweet smelling earth, totally oblivious to the fact that they had wiggled free of Mose's coat and were covered in sand.

Finally, Mose lay back, holding Becky as she settled down and they both caught their breath. This sure ain't the first time she's done something like this. She's romped more than once in the hay with a man. They saw they were covered with sand and started laughing. He rose to his feet and pulled her up and began to brush her off and then turned for her to do the same to him. He shook the sand and leaves off his coat and they started back to the buggy.

He pulled her to him and kissed her. "Look what we been a'missin' all this time," he told her. She didn't reply but smiled and kissed him back again.

"We'd better high tail hit back 'fore Mrs. Mary comes home. You'll have to help me git out the wash and hope hit rains 'fore she finds out how late I got hit on the line."

Becky kept talking a mile a minute on the way home. She didn't want to give Mose the opportunity to question her about where she'd learned so much about making love. If she thought she could get away with pretending it was the first time she would have tried it but she knew Mose got around too much to try to pull the wool over his eyes.

Mose helped get the wash out and even carried in some water and helped her get supper started before the rest of the family came home.

Mose didn't stay after supper but told them he had to get ready for a trip down south and looked at Becky as he told his brother goodbye and said to her "behave yourself, now."

He thought he'd get away this time without seeing Bena but the night before he left, she slipped into his bed without Mose sending for her. He sort of felt sorry for her and let her slip her dress off and crawl in bed with him. He rolled over in the dark and pulled her to him. He could feel her round belly that had been so hard and flat.

He sprang from the bed as if he'd discovered a rattlesnake in it.

"Godamsorrysonofabitch," he snarled, kicking over a chair "Goddamn'et to hell."

Bena was out of bed, putting on her dress when Betty came running down the stairs with the new lamp, Coal oil lamps were the newest thing out. Mose came to his senses when he heard her steps.

"What's the matter Pa?" she asked at the door. "That you in there?"

"Go back to bed, daughter I jest stumbled over a chair in the dark and stumped my toe. Jest lost my temper. I ain't got my nightshirt on yet, so don't open the door. I'm alright."

Bena was crouched on the floor, wondering what to do next. Mose waited in the dark for Betty to close her door upstairs and not saying a word to Bena, opened his door, got behind her and shoved her out and closed the door behind her.

Before he left, Mose told James Ed to see about selling Bena to the highest bidder.

"You asked Lottie and she says hit's alright?"

"Lottie ain't got no say so in hit. Sell the bitch," he said and stormed off toward his new plantation on the shores of Lake Tohopekaliga.

Chapter 18

Mose went south by himself this time. He wasn't exactly in the right frame of mind for conversation anyway, and he thought he might get his act together better if he could spend some time alone, trying to sort thing out.

I sure have got my life into a damn mess, he said to himself when he started out. Mose loved women. The greatest joy in his life was making love to a woman. They came first above the horses, even. The strange thing about it, women loved Mose. He was crude, cocky, and vulgar and could be rough and mean but he had a way with them they found irresistible. And this chemistry increased with age. Of course, his money didn't hurt any in attracting their company, but it was his undeniable charm that kept them coming back for more.

There was Mrs. Cook in New Smyrna, a woman in Palatka, one near Lake George and another at Melonville. When he felt the need for solitude, he'd take off into the wilds of Brevard County and get away from the whole mess. But now he had complications back home with Bena being pregnant and Becky Clements now after him hot and heavy. And fathering a Negro child was something he couldn't get away from. If, indeed, it was his. He had ignored the young slave girl lately and there was a possibility her child belonged to someone else. "Anybody, Lord," he prayed. "Let it be anybody's but mine."

He was glad to see Susan and get to visit with her about Becky Clemons at least, even though he could not bring himself to tell her about Bena.

"Lord God, gal, you look like you wuz sent fer and couldn't come! You been sick or sumpin'?"

Susan did look sick. Her face was drawn and she had lost weight. He remembered how Leah had looked and he felt a quick surge of panic at Susan's appearance. He didn't want to lose her. She meant too much to him.

She quickly explained that John's wife, Mary, had been sick--two miscarriages in a row after little Andrew Jackson was born and she'd been down at his new plantation, helping John run things.

"You know, there comes a time when a woman's too old to take care o' young'uns. God knew what he was a'doin' when he made 'em so they got too old to have one. I though I wuz a'gonna have to tell Mary to move over and let me in the bed with her. But she's finally back on her feet and I'm feelin better each day. Don't worry bout me none, Mose, I'll outlive you."

"You sure? I'll git you to a doctor in Jacksonville if'n you figure you need one. Money's no object nor time neither."

"Feel fine as frog hair. Don't give me no never mind."

And so, she really was all right, Mose discovered after a long visit. She was still the same old Susan and they laughed and talked about all sorts of things. He went to church with her and visited with old man Mizell. David Jr.'s family had increased as planned and his older boys had married. The little town was growing in leaps and bounds. It was the county seat and they had just built a post office and another hotel.

"What wuz you a laughin' about in church this mornin'," he asked her out on the porch that afternoon when they were alone.

"I'm ashamed to tell you. I git these crazy pictures in my head sometimes and at the least appropriate time and can't git 'em out. There I wuz in church and should a been feelin' the presence o' the Lord and I got to lookin' at that big old fat Mrs. Nettles and thet little old tiny skinny husband o' hers and started picturin' how they'd look in bed together. Do you ever do crazy things like that?"

Mose laughed. Leave it to Susan to think of such a thing, when most women are wondering whether they had packed everything they'd cooked for dinner on the grounds or wished they hadn't pulled their corset up so tight.

"You know hits usually only men think about such things. I don't know, maybe some women do but they never tell me so. I've seen couples like that and wondered why she don't shake her night gown out on the back porch some mornin' and her little skinny husband fall out of hit, off the porch and into the yard and break his arm."

It was good to be with Susan and be able to laugh. Why can't I be content to have a relationship with a woman like this and leave them young gals alone, he wished? Life would surely be less complicated.

Down at his plantation on the edge of the lake, the slaves had cleared more of the ridge and were growing a new plant he had brought in from Louisiana that had originally come from Africa. It was called okra. The slaves loved it cooked on top of a big pot of cowpeas. It had a strange taste and took some getting used to but Mose soon found it was delicious pickled. The roads were better now up to Melonville and he found it easier to get his goods to market. He stayed long enough to get acquainted with John's little Andrew Jackson, who they called "Deed" for some strange unknown reason to distinguish him from his Uncle Andrew Jackson in Conway. Over near the lake where Isaac wanted to settle, Owen Jernigan had built a house. He was still taking care of Daniel Sloan's cattle that he and his brother had brought down just after the Indian War. They had moved around a lot. First at Lake Holden and then west of Jernigan near the present town of Umatilla. He had sold that land to Aaron Jernigan's father and squatted for a while at Canoe Creek Island. This became too much for Mrs. Jernigan and they had moved back to Jernigan for a while until he talked her into coming back into Brevard County again.

People like the Jernigans never had much, moving around like they did. The beds were simply thin poles stuck into holes in the wall at the corner of a room. Only the fourth corner had any support. The poles were laced with rope and a mattress ticking laid down. Dried moss was scattered over that and a sheet put over it to sleep on. When the moss got thin they'd simply boil green moss, dry it, pluck the fibers out and fluff it with their fingers until it was soft enough to sleep on. They cooked outside on a fire stand, or make-shift stove made of logs filled with sand up, so high, and the top of the logs covered with just enough clay to keep them from burning. When they moved, this was all left behind and there wasn't much furniture to be moved. They had church only two to three times a year. A preacher named Reeves had just come through as a circuit rider. They lived a more primitive life than Mose and Leah had lived when they first moved to North Florida back in 'thirty-three. They went all the way to New Smyrna for their salt. There was a big kettle there that had been abandoned by the British when they had the territory and salt water from the ocean was poured into it and boiled until it evaporated, leaving the salt. It was the settler's only source and they had to have salt to preserve their meat in the hot damp climate.

Mose went on down to Francis and Champ's near the edge of Lake Gardner and finally worked his way back with the cow crew at Fort Christmas and then made his rounds to see all his lady friends. He wanted to make sure Bena had been long gone and had her baby with all his problems resolved in that department before he came home to face the music. People could say or think anything they wanted but "out of sight—out of mind." He wouldn't have to think about whether it was his or not. Mose was so family-oriented, he wondered whether he could live with the idea he had a son he had never seen and some other man was raising. But he kept shoving the thought aside. Maybe hit'll be a girl. A girl wouldn'd matter. But a son was different.

On the way home he made up his mind to go talk to Sam and Mary about hiring Becky as his housekeeper. Now that Betty and Isaac were married, he needed someone to manage the household slaves. He didn't have time to keep in behind them and he often found things not done. Dulcie was on her last legs and Rich could only piddle around, raking leaves and brushing tame horses. For all practical purposes, he had retired them. Of course, Mary needed help, too, and maybe he could loan her a slave to take Becky's place. He had more than he needed anyway. He was eager to see Becky again.

Little Mose had gone back with him and he had hardly rested up from his trip when Mose Jr. came in and announced, "That white gal of Lottie's done had her sucker."

Mose didn't say anything for a minute but then, trying to not appear too interested. "Who'd they sell her to?" he asked.

Mose Jr. told him, "I though you knew, James Ed never did sell her. Found out she was gonna foal and since Betty wanted her, she decided to keep her here until the sucker got here."

"You mean she's right here on this place?" Mose almost jumped out of his chair. "Godamnit, I told him to sell the bitch."

"Betty told him you told her she could have her fer a weddin' present. Maybe she misunderstood."

"Hell no, I did tell the gal I'd give the wench to her but then I went and changed my mind jest fore I left this last time."

"You never go back on yore word, Pa. Least not to one o' us young'uns. I guess Betty figgered you give her to her then she was hers. She's the one decided to leave her here with her Ma 'til the sucker come. I don't know what difference hit makes," looking rather puzzled at his daddy, trying to figure what he was thinking.

You never could tell with Mose. He sat there with his nose between his two fingers and his eyes narrow slits of flashing light like those of a wild horse. Mose Jr. sat and waited for Mose to say something. He knew you didn't mess around with his daddy when he looked like that.

Finally, Mose asked, "What'd she have?"

"A boy, I think."

"Her an the baby alright?"

"Ain't heered no difference."

"I guess hit wuz plum white?"

"Ain't heered nobuddy say. Reckon hit looked like any other nigger baby."

Mose Jr. was really puzzled now. He sat and waited for Mose's mood to change or something to happen.

Mose decided he'd better change the subject for now. "Well, all them little suckers look white when they first hit the light o' day. They git darker and darker as time goes by."

Mose started talking about trivial things on the plantation and decided he'd slip out and see the boy later on.

Curiosity got the best of him though, and as soon as Mose Jr. was out of the way, he went out to the quarters. Bena was standing at the door. She wouldn't look directly at him as she used to.

"I hear you got yourself a boy, Bena."

"Yassa."

Mose went into the little cabin. The baby lay on a pallet by the door. Mose stared at him and breathed a big sigh of relief. Lottie was sitting on the side of a cot and had stood up as her master came in the door.

The baby was dark--much darker than he expected.

"This Bena's sucker, Lottie?" Mose had to be sure.

"Yasuh, ain't he a fine'un?"

"Who's the Pa?"

"Hit be Nealie's," she said and looked at him, grinning really big, nodding her head. Nealie was the prized Mandingo. She knew that was why Mose had come and what he really was relieved to hear.

"Well, we'll git her and the sucker over to Betty's. I guess she's made arrangements fer 'em both?"

"Yassa. You know Miss Betty. She won' separate 'em. Her Ma wouldn't stand fo' thet."

"That's up to her, now. Bena belongs to her an she ain't got nuthin' to do with hit, you hear?"

"Yassa."

Rich was at the barn when he came by there. The old slave looked at him knowingly and gave him a big smile.

"If yo'd ast me I coulda tole yo Bena's sucka one o' dem rolled-lipped niggas, Massah Mose."

"Well, nobuddy asked you, understood?"

Rich was standing there still grinning at him and Mose laughed. Old son-of-a-bitch knew all along, he thought. "Git my horse ready. I'm gonna ride over to Sam's."

Mose sang all the way over to his brother's which was a pretty good trip at that. A big weight had lifted from his conscience. Without the evidence, he was not guilty.

He could forget it ever happened. It was a near thing, he shuddered. *I wonder what I would have done if hit looked like hit wuz mine. One thing, I won't ever have to decide. I git any more young'uns, I'll make sure I can bring'em home with me.*

He rode up into the yard about mid afternoon. The dogs came out to meet him with the usual clamor. There was a brief dogfight, as was the custom until they all settled their differences. Mose yelling for his to get on their bellies.

Mary came to the kitchen door and seemed glad and surprised to see Mose. "Haven't seen you in a coon's age," she greeted him. They said you'd gone down south. I never know when you're here or there. I jest baked a batch o' syrup cookies. They're still warm. Come on in and I'll fix you a cup o' coffee."

Mose looked down at his hands and she motioned him to the water shelf and poured him some fresh water to wash his hands. He pulled the roller towel down and found a clean spot. When he finished his cookies and had his second cup of coffee he asked where Becky was.

"She's over at Reverend Tindall's at Olustee. Went and swallered a punkin' seed. Got to pukin' around here and tryin' to faint on us and we wrung hit outa her. She'd already suspected she was with child. Wouldn't tell us who the daddy wuz. I don't even know if she knows herself. The shame she's brought down on our house and after all we done fer her."

"Well, I be damned," Mose said, stunned at the news. *Out of the frying pan and into the fire,* he thought.

Mary went on. "Sam, he thought we oughter keep her on, her and the young'un, but I fer one wanted to git her outta the way fore she started a'showin'. The shame and all of hit," she said again.

"Know who the daddy wuz?"

"Not particularly. We all wracked our brain tryin to pick one out but never did come up with a shore nuff good prospect." Mary didn't say anymore for a minute and then looked at Mose and asked, "Weren't yore's, wuz hit?"

Mose didn't say anything.

Mary said, "I noticed the two o' you a eyein' each other the day we wuz a killin' hogs."

"You know me Mary, I give all the gals the eye. Little ole gal's not bad to look at. But do you really suspect I'd be the kinda man, goin around coverin' one o' yore gals on the sly? Right here under your roof?"

"Don't have to fool around in the house, Mose. There's miles o' woods out there," hitting the nail right on the head and never suspected it.

"Well, somebuddy knocked her up. Time will tell when. I don't know what she'll do. Ain't got no family nowheres, them all gittin' wiped out by the Injuns. I jest cain't take her back after what she's done. The shame of it all," for the third time.

"We'll try to work out somethin'. I headed over here to see could I hire her fer a housekeeper. I need one bad, now that Betty's gone. I can git a nigger wench to watch the baby so's she can take care o' the house. You tell the Reverend Tyndall I'll see he gits paid fer his trouble if'n he'll keep her 'til the baby comes. Then I'll take her in."

"What'll people say, Mose, you with a young housekeeper and no other woman in the house with you?"

"Ain't nobuddy's business who I hire to keep my house, Mary. I got enough money I can tell the whole wide world to kiss my ass. Besides, what would look better, Becky in the house with me and my hired men or me in the house the way hit is now with a bunch o' nigger wenches?"

"Well, for one thing, Mose. The whole community knows you wouldn't fool around with none o' your slave women. Nor never let your boys neither. You can thank yore lucky stars you had a wife like Leah to ride herd on you and them boys o' y'orn. Too bad she had to die so young."

"You git to thinkin' bout hit, Mary, she wuz in her forties. Thet's not really young. She had a purty long life."

"Too bad she didn't git to out-live you, Mose Barber and spend some o' this money you been a'hoardin'. Now some sweet young thing's a gonna come along and spend hit when hit when we're both dead and gone."

"That'll be the day, Mary. I don't figger on ever marryin' agin. My boys is agonna git what I leave behind. I've worked too hard and they have, too, to give hit to some ole gal. I'm sittin' purty and I aim to keep hit all in the family." Mose stood up to go.

"Might as well stay. Sam'll be back here in a while, come supper time."

"No, I best git on down the road. I want to git on down to old man Norton's. He's been a'shootin' some o' my turkeys over there near the scrub. Wouldn't mind hit but he's been gittin' the hens and I wuz tryin' to let 'em raise."

"Why, Mose. You begrudge that old man one o' yore turkeys and him yore neighbor and he's on his last legs. Can hardly git around and tend his collard patch. Ain't you ashamed?"

"Ain't the turkeys exactly, hits the principle o' the thing. Hit's sort o' like havin' another man git on yore dawgs. I could stand here and try to explain hit to you 'til I'm blue in the face. Bein' a women you wouldn't understand," as he stormed out of the house.

"You git word to Becky, now, and ease her and the Tyndalls' mind."

As it turned out, Becky came to live with Mose before the baby was born. The New Year rolled around and the preacher's wife had to go to her dying mother and didn't want Becky alone in the house with her husband. Mose took the buggy to Olustee and picked up her and her belongings, insisting that she come home with his so he could see that she was taken care of. He felt she had been working too hard for the preacher's wife anyway and could use the rest. She balked at first, wondering what people would say.

"I don't give a damn anyway," he told the preacher. "People either like me or they hate my guts. There's never been any middle ground. Them that likes me will understand, and them that hates me, I don't give a big rat's ass about anyway."

And so Becky Clements came to live with Mose.

Chapter 19

It was 1860. The Federal Census taker visited the plantation and Mose's financial status was entered as being almost forty-three thousand dollars in real estate and one hundred sixteen thousand in personal wealth. Actually, there was no way to determine how many cattle Mose had now, but he could count the number of slaves at both plantations, along with the ones at his sons' farms. Mose "gave" his children slaves and horses, but he still considered them his. Even his cattle he kept in his brands, registered at the various counties.

Becky had a son, she named Samuel Jeremiah. Mose did not acknowledge the boy as being his, although he had a strong suspicion the child could have been conceived that day they looked for the bee tree by the little branch. He was fairly good to Becky, seeing that she had ample help to run his house and he brought her nice clothes, but did not take her out socially.

That fall events began to take place that would eventually drastically change and shape the course of Mose's life forever. And many other southern planters as well.

It was election year in the nation. As always, the heat of political emotion and prejudice that can distort actual facts about a candidate ran high. It was difficult to reach all the voters in Florida, being as isolated as many were. Mose tried to stay informed. Of course, he and his family were Democrats.

The Democratic Party was split into two factions. John C. Breckinridge of Kentucky represented the Deep South and the southern planters. But a few southern democrats along the Border States and even some northern Democrats were putting up Stephen Douglas of Illinois. Mose couldn't see how someone from Illinois could possibly understand the problems of the plantation owners, so he, of course, was for Breckinridge. The Republican Party had nominated Abraham Lincoln, also from Illinois except for a small group of Constitutional Unionists that were mostly old-time Whigs and die-hards who put in John Bell of Tennessee.

The Missouri Compromise of 1854 had prohibited slavery or the movement of slaves north of the thirty-sixth parallel and west of the thirtieth longitude to stop its spread. This, of course was a red flag, waving to the slave owners that certain political factions were against their owning slaves. To them it soon became evident that it was the Republican Party, and since Abraham Lincoln was their strongest candidate, he was automatically against the planters and their large plantations and his main intent was to take away their slaves. Back in '58, as a senator, Lincoln had given a speech on slavery and one thing he mentioned that everyone remembered were the phrases, "a house divided" and "half slave and half free." To many it sounded as if the nation had to be one way or another—that it couldn't remain the way it was. Lincoln, forevermore, tried to convince his listeners that he had been misunderstood in his speech but, forevermore, he would be remembered in the South as one who encouraged a northern war against the South for the sole intent of freeing the slaves and uniting the nation, at the expense of the slave owners. Actually, Lincoln was a moderate. He could see the economic disaster taking away the slaves in one bold move and breaking up the large southern plantations would bring. He had no intention of setting the slaves free but wanted merely to prohibit the spread of slavery into free states and those that were developing to the west.

Democratic Senator Jefferson Davis of Mississippi fought to have Douglas, Breckinridge and Bell step aside in favor of one candidate, but Douglas would not go along with the plan. He ranted that the South had to make war against the northern abolitionists and Southern Disunionists. Had he listened to Jeff Davis and some of the other clear thinkers, the nation maybe would have been spared the long bloody conflict it was destined to fight.

On November 6, 1860, Abraham Lincoln was elected the sixteenth president of the United States of America. The very next day at Charleston, South Carolina, the Palmetto flag was raised in defiance of the election. Even talk of a southern confederacy spread through out the southern states.

Back in May, Mose had attended a Democratic rally in Jacksonville where the talk ran strong that the Union wanted to deny southereners protection and the security of their slave property. They did not consider Florida as feeling safe to be in the Union. Even those who were not for war realized how undeveloped Florida was and dependent on her one-sided economy. Of the one hundred forty thousand people in Florida, one half of them were slaves. So, if a Confederacy was formed, Florida just about had to join it to stay alive.

Just three weeks after the election, South Carolina held a special legislation to discuss secession and Georgia voted a million dollars to arm the state, while Lincoln went calmly about, forming his cabinet, thinking the south was all "talk." On December 1, Florida's Legislature convened to discuss the pressing issue of secession and Mose caught the train to Tallahassee. It seemed no one was thinking clearly or had all the facts together.

In President Buchanan's "State of the Union" address, he stressed the point that the slave states should be left alone to iron out their problems and that the mere election of Lincoln as President did not justify dissolving the Union. "The day of evil may never come unless we shall rashly bring it upon ourselves," he prophetically stated. But the south was not listening. It appeared, or at least South Carolina did, to have tunnel vision.

On December 20, less than two months since Lincoln was elected, South Carolina seceded from the Union. Bells rang, fires were set in the street and hysteria spread. In nine days, Mississippi became the second state to leave the Union and the next day, on January 10, Florida followed suit. Then came Alabama, Georgia, Louisiana and Texas in rapid succession. South Carolina troops took Fort Moultrie where the Florida Indian warrior, Osceola, had been buried. The American flag was raised over Fort Sumter and American troops led by Major George Anderson were sited there to hold the fort. It wasn't long before South Carolina held all forts but Sumter and mobilized for war, should it come to that. Florida took over the arsenal at Apalachicola and Fort Marion at St. Augustine. She tried to take Pensacola with about twenty men, but left without blood shed when fired upon by Federal troops. Federal forts began to fall like matchsticks. Soon Fort Taylor at Key West, Fort Pickens at Pensacola in Florida and Fort Jefferson at the Dry Tortugas would soon be the only southern bases left in federal hands, giving the Union a means of supplying the blockade vessels needed to keep supplies from reaching the south.

All this happened before Lincoln was even inaugurated. He couldn't have done anything to get rid of their slaves at the moment, had he wanted to. He went calmly about, forming his cabinet and writing his speech that would tell everyone in the nation his real views on slavery. He would say, on March 4, "I have no purpose directly or indirectly to interfere with the institution of slavery in the states where it exists. I believe I have no lawful right to do so." But his speech would come too late. In the mean time, President Buchanan was running the country. It was he who allowed the Confederacy to form and the states to secede. He sat idly by and let the Confederacy occupy most of the federal forts and appropriate government property. In a state of limbo between presidents, no one could agree on what to do about the mess down at Fort Sumter.

On April 11, South Carolina officers in a small boat with a white flag rowed out to Fort Sumter and demanded that Major Robert Anderson evacuate the Fort. He refused. At 4:30 the next morning a signal shot was fired from Fort Johnson by Henry S. Farley and the Civil War was on! There would be no turning back.

After thirty-four hours of bombardment, Fort Sumter surrendered. Lincoln, amazed at what had happened "so quickly," called out seventy-five thousand militia and declared a state of insurrection existed in those states that had seceded. The blockade of Florida began in earnest. The blockade initially proved ineffective and the port of Jacksonville and the St. Johns waterway stayed open so Mose could get his goods to market. And Mose began to make money from the war.

Isaac and his new bride, Harriet and infant son, Joseph, were making plans to move down to the spot at Fenny Point on Lake Tohopekaliga, south of Mose's plantation, east of the Kissimmee Bog. No one in Mose's neck of the woods thought there would be more than a few skirmishes of war and that the Confederacy would endure and the South would be allowed to go on as it always had.

Mose saw some rapid changes around his Orange County property. Owen Simmons built a nice double pen log house at the little settlement of Peg Horn, lying at the edge of the marsh between Mose and Isaac's planned farm. He even had an inside fire pit to cook on. A man named Needham Bass operated a ferry through the boggy marsh between Cross Prairie and Fennel Prairie that lay between East Lake on one side and Lake Tohopekaliga on the other. It took nearly all day to make the trip and many times Mose merely elected to cross the little Boggy Creek that flowed into the tip of East Lake and go by way of Narcoossee to get into Brevard County at Fenny Point. He had bought some of Sloan's cattle, the *88* brand. Needham Yates, and his brother-in-law, Mose's nephew, John, were helping in the cow crew. The

Yates, Overstreets and Tyners had settled Shingle Creek and he met someone he knew in the little community of Orlando.

She was Robert Ivey's niece whom he had met at John's wedding in Jacksonville when he married Needham Yates' sister, Mary. Mose had known her father, Thomas, well. Both of her parents had died and she and her brothers and sisters had been farmed out with relatives. At the time, she was living with her sister, Elizabeth, in Jacksonville and Mose was surprised to see her down in Orlando.

"I've come down here with my brother, Robert, and right now I'm staying with Uncle Robert and Aunt Priscilla. They had plans to open a dry good store, but he's afraid of this blockade and thinks he'll start an orange grove. Right now, we've come to town to git supplies for the new house out at Lake Mann, west of here. We been plantin' orange trees and havin' to water 'em every day. I'm jest helpin' out."

"I figured you'd got married and had a passel o young'uns by now. How come?"

"Right man jest ain't come along yet, I guess. The folks has been after me but I jest ain't found the right one, least ways I ain't caught him yet."

"Sounds like you got one in mind?"

Priscilla looked away and blushed and Mose didn't press the matter.

"You better git you one fore long. We have a war and the pickin's'll git kinda slim."

"Most people around here think it won't matter to much of anything but a blockade. We're too far south fer it to touch us much. I think we've convinced them Yankees we mean business 'bout keepin our slaves. You know, Uncle Robert, he ain't too keen on havin' slaves anyways. He and my pa never did see eye to eye about that. I got plenty o' family down here to look after me anyways."

Mose looked at her hard and smiled. "That's not all a man's fer, Priscilla, and you know hit."

Priscilla blushed, but looked him right in the eye and smiled. "How you do carry on, Mr. Barber," and looked around to see if anyone else heard.

Mose bowed and bid her good day. He liked the girl. He thought of Becky. She had been an orphan and farmed out. And Mose had taken advantage of her. The same thing could happen to Priscilla.

"Times git hard and you need any help, gal, you jest let me or one o' my boys know. I'll see you're taken care of."

Mose rode off, thinking that Priscilla just didn't exactly fit in the Robert Ivey family. She's the type to jump the traces and not want to settle down. The Ivey's were strictly religious, hard-shelled Primitive Baptist. No, the girl just didn't fit, somehow.

John Randolph Mizell came around the corner of the post office with a newspaper under his arm. He was tall and lean, over six feet with sparkling blue eyes that looked even bluer, set in a deeply tanned face. His teeth were perfect and sparkling clean. Priscilla began to feel an old familiar feeling as her heart picked up its beat and she got a sinking sensation in the pit of her stomach at the nearness of him.

"Good morning, Cousin Priscilla," he smiled. Priscilla's grandmother had been a Mizell and cousin of David Jr., John's father. Cousins went way back in the old families and everyone was taught to use the salutation as a form of courtesy. "Your

Uncle Robert said I'd find you here. Wasn't that old man Mose Barber you were talking to? You best stay away from the likes of him, I hear he considers himself quite a ladies man. They say he's bad after women."

"Well, he's always been a perfect gentlemen around me." She didn't mention that she thought Mose charming and liked the wicked way he looked at her. "Besides, he's too old for me."

"That's not the way I hear it. They say he has a young woman about your age living with him in the pretense of being his house keeper and she already has a child by him and probably another on the way before long."

"I heard she was an orphan and the baby belonged to someone else and he took her in so she'd have a way to make a living."

John Randolph changed the subject. "I was out by the lake several times, but couldn't find anyone at home. Looks like it's going to be a nice place. Bet it's cool out there," he said, looking straight into Priscilla's eyes, who blushed and looked down at her feet in confusion.

"A swim would be nice about now," he said, taking her hand and holding it tight. "You wouldn't want to go for a swim about now, would you?"

Priscilla felt the goose bumps rise on her thighs and her nipples became erect against her dress. She said nothing but John was stroking his thumb inside her palm. His touch made her weak in the knees. As he looked deeper in her eyes, a warm tightening sensation crept into her crotch and she felt a swelling press against her pantaloons. She had felt this way when he'd touched her out at the lake that day and she knew it was a "wicked feeling" she was not supposed to feel. She had slipped away with him one hot afternoon before they cleared the land around the lake for the orange grove and gone wading, holding her skirt up out of the water, showing her pantaloons. They had chased minnows around the shore and once he made a grab for her and as she jerked away she fell into the water, getting soaked to the skin. The soft cotton shirtwaist and skirt had clung to her large, ample breasts and molded the outline of her hips as well as her crotch. As he helped her up out of the water, he had pulled her to him and she felt the breath leave her body with a gasp. He held her close and kissed her hard on the lips and she had felt the same sensation she was feeling now and had not tried to pull away immediately but then became frightened and ran home. I'm glad we're out in the streets, she thought. No wonder Uncle Robert tells me it's a sin to be alone with a man.

John Randolph dropped her hand suddenly and stepped back as she heard the creak of the wagon and knew it was her Uncle Robert and Aunt Priscilla, loaded with the supplies.

There was talk of the new Confederacy and the possibility of war. John Randolph was ready to fight.

"Pa says I can form my own company if it comes to that. You know, I've been away at school in Gainesville and I've had some training."

"I hope you're wrong," Robert Ivey said. "Have you been out to the lake where we're building our orange grove?" he asked John Randolph.

"Several times. Looks like it's going to be a nice cool spot during the warm summer months. And a nice place to swim in."

Priscilla blushed again as John helped her up on the back of the wagon, surreptitiously stroking the palm of her hand with his thumb, as before.

"Come by for supper sometimes. You're welcome anytime, Cousin John," her Aunt Priscilla said, as he stood and waved goodbye to them.

"About time you latched onto a nice young man like that, Priscilla. You don't want to spend the rest of your life takin' care o' some other woman's children, now do you?"

"No sir, Uncle Robert," she agreed.

"You ought to o' married that nice proprietor your sister Elizabeth wrote us about, Prissy," her Aunt Priscilla said. Priscilla was her namesake and she called her "Prissy."

"He was a old man."

"Lord, he wasn't mor'n thirty-five, Elizabeth told me. Just in his prime. And she indicated he was pretty well off."

"Well, you didn't see him. He looked old to me and his teeth were gettin' bad. I didn't want him kissin' me."

"Priscilla!" broke in her uncle sternly. "You shouldn't dwell on such worldly things as kissin'. A woman marries a man to make a home for him and bear his children, not to kiss him and act wanton. She should have pure thoughts when she enters into wedlock and obey her husband with no thought of pleasure to herself."

"Well," said Priscilla. "I'll be darned if I'm a gonna marry some old man and have him pawin' over me and breathin' his old rotten tobacco breath in my face."

"That'll be enough of that, young lady," said her uncle and the three of them finished the ride to the lake in silence.

I want a husband who'll make me feel weak in the knees and makes my crotch swell like John Randolph, she thought. He don't affect me like that, I won't marry nobuddy. She began to daydream and think of the day at the lake and think of what it would be like lying in the warm water at the edge of the lake, listening to the water lap over their bodies as she lay, naked in his arms with his warm slippery body on hers, stroking her all over as he had stroked the palm of her hand this morning. She could imagine his sweet breath hard on her neck and nibbling on her ear. Priscilla had watched a stud cover her brother-in-law's mare back in Jacksonville one day when no one was looking, and remembered how he nibbled at the mare's ear and licked her all over the neck, and made her squeal and spread her legs and urinate. If horses make love that way, surely people do too. She felt herself getting warm and flushed and her uncle began to stare at her with a puzzled look as they were unloading the supplies.

Sanctimonious old goat, she thought, echoing Mose Barber's exact thoughts a few hours earlier.

Chapter 20

The war that had started with such a bang, progressed very little the first year. Lincoln had done little to try to prevent the secession of other states. He mustered the Seventh New York Regiment to defend the capital but let it be known he had no intention of attacking Confederate troops. He sent the navy in to form the blockade to prevent the seceded states from getting supplies from the north and hoped that peace would come, somehow.

Virginia invited the Confederacy to make Richmond the Confederate capital. And people began to take sides. Military men from posts all over the country and government employees in sympathy with the South, left their positions and went back home.

There was little activity in Florida and one would hardly have been aware there was a war going on. Most of the Florida boys that had joined up were in Alabama or Missouri where there was very little fighting. Isiah was ramrodding the cattle drives to the market and George Ed was in Jacksonville, shipping cattle from there.

Finally, New York troops entered Virginia and took Alexandria. Jeff Davis, the president of the Confederacy, moved the capital in June to Richmond, but the summer months consisted mostly of enlistments and some drilling of troops and organizing the war. Of course, those that opposed the war kept wishing both sides would back down. The hotheads of the South believed that there would be several large battles in Virginia and they would be victorious and the war would be over by the end of the year.

Then the big battle everybody was waiting for finally happened. It was called the Battle of Bull Run, at Manassas, Virginia. It was here at this battle that Barnard Bee, a Confederate who was soon to fall mortally wounded would shout to his men who were breaking rank, "Look, there's Jackson standing like a stone wall" and "Stonewall" Jackson became a national hero, winning victory for the Confederacy. The whole South had his name on their lips.

The big battle had come and gone and the South was victorious, but the war was not over. The Yankees had not quit as had been predicted.

News arrived around the plantations that General John Charles Fremont had issued an Emancipation Proclamation, confiscating all property of those states in rebellion against the United States. All slaves were to be freed and anyone with a gun found in Union Territory was to be shot, if found guilty by a military court. The South was aghast. "I told you so," cried Mose and his neighbors. "That's what them Yankees planned to do to us all along!" Mose's sons were all chomping at the bits to "go whip them Yankees," but Mose was secretly glad he had some ground between his plantation and the fighting in Missouri. As it turned out, Fremont had no authorization from Lincoln and he had issued his proclamation without Lincoln's sanction. So it was null and void.

In October, a band of a thousand Confederate soldiers landed on Santa Rosa Island near Fort Pickens in an attempt to take control of Pensacola Bay, but were unsuccessful. In November, Union troops took over Hilton Head at Port Royal in South Carolina, but Mose felt comfortable knowing that General Robert E. Lee had taken command of the Confederacy in South Carolina, Georgia, and East Florida. Little did he know that Lee thought it an awesome task. It was a wide territory and difficult to defend. Now, with the invasion of Port Royal, there would be even more incursions into the South. And they began days later when the Yankees took Tybee Island in Georgia, controlling the Savannah harbor and got a foothold to attack Fort Pulaski. Isiah came home with the news from Jacksonville.

"Pa, they say you can see flames all along the coast from Charleston to Savannah. Folks are a'burnin' their cotton and crops to keep them Yankees from gittin' hit. You think we'll have to burn ours, Pa?"

He showed them Charleston *Mercury* whose headlines declared, "Let the torch be applied where the invaders pollute our soil."

Mose decided a lot depended on whether the South could raise a navy. "Remember, Lincoln's running the show fer the north and they got our navy, or what used to be ours. We ain't got no money either. We got to print that. But what the north don't realize is all our wealth. We got all this land and cattle and slaves and a lots o' them people in the north is poor. That's the whole problem. They been jealous o' our land and cattle and slaves and the way we live fer the longest time and they jest wanta take 'em away from us. And that's the truth."

Sometime in September the first action occurred on Florida soil when the Confederates tried to block the passes in the Gulf by sinking four old ships in the channel between Barrancas and Fort Pickens. The Union got wind of this and fired the dry dock and withdrew. Two weeks later, a Union ship launched three cutters with one hundred men on board, slipped into the bay and surprised the blockade runner, *Judah*, cut her lines, set fire to the ship and got away. The Union losses were three dead and eight wounded. There was no official count for the South, but there were said to be several lost.

There was a stab at Christmas celebrations on the plantation. The daughters-in-law were courteous to Becky who was expecting her second baby and no one had said, but it clearly had to belong to Mose. The price of everything had gone up. Salt, hardware, groceries, shoes and medicine were scarce and expensive, but Mose was making money hand over fist, selling pork, sugar, syrup, and cowhides and shipping cattle from Jacksonville to various ports and by rail from Baldwin, just forty miles from Lake City where the Florida Atlantic, Gulf Central and the Florida Railroad had their junction.

Along with the usual Christmas carols, the extended families got together and sang some of the new songs that were out.

"I want to be a soldier and with a soldier's stand, a knapsack on my shoulder and a musket in my hand. And stand beside Jeff Davis, so glorious and so brave. I'll whip the cussed Yankees and drive them to the grave." That was the men's favorite.

The women liked the *Southern Wagon* – "Secession is our watchword, our rights we all demand and to defend our firesides we pledge our hearts and hand. Jeff Davis is our President and Stephens by his side, Brave Beauregard our General will join us in the ride. Oh wait for the wagon, the dissolution wagon; the South is our wagon and we'll all take a ride."

Sam took Mose to one side, "I been a studyin' thet little Samuel Jeremiah. Have you took a good look at thet little boy o' Becky's lately?"

Mose looked at the little boy, sitting under the tree. He had come to love the little boy as his own, what time he had been home.

"What about him?"

"You know who his Pa is, don't you?" Sam asked.

Mose stiffened in anger, surprised that Sam would wait for so long to mention who he suspected. Perhaps he had known all along who Becky had been fooling around with and was a little miffed at his brother for waiting so long to say anything. Afraid Mose wouldn't have taken her in if he had known.

"Whose in the hell is he?" Mose thundered, his anger and apprehension rising.

"Why, he's y'orn, you damned fool. Anybuddy can look at him and see hit. Everybuddy else in the whole damned family says so. Looks as much like you as if he'd been picked outer yore ass with a knittin' needle."

"You really think so?" asked Mose, evidently relieved and suddenly very proud. "Yeah, I guess he's mine."

But Mose made no move to marry Becky.

The New Year brought rapid change on the coast. Florida had always been vulnerable to attack along its shoreline, but some sort of defenses existed at Fort Clinch at Fernandina and Fort Marion at St. Augustine. As more troops had to be shifted to Alabama and Mississippi, the situation became critical and weakened. Cedar Key was attacked in mid-January and the railroad depot, wharf, telegraph office warehouses, barges, freight cars and many boats were destroyed. Soon after, some key forts in Tennessee fell and General Braxton Bragg, advisor to Lee, convinced him that movement of all troops from Florida was necessary, because they could not hold it in the event of an invasion by the navy and that the troops were much needed where the major fighting was going on. Only a few troops were left to protect the civilian population and then only because Governor Milton put up such a fuss. Of course, he was thinking of the possibility of Union troops coming up the Apalachicola River and taking Tallahassee. The Union army immediately smelled blood as soon as all troops left Florida and in March 1862 Fernandina's deep water harbor, Fort Clinch, Fort Marion at St. Augustine and then Jacksonville fell into Union hands. Mose's plantation was only forty miles from the Atlantic coast.

Mose and the cow crew were down south and they immediately came home to help defend their plantation, if possible. On his way, Mose stopped by Lake City, renamed from the old town of Alligator and now the county seat, and signed papers to give Samuel Jeremiah and the new baby girl, Virginia Clements, all that stock of cattle in Baker, Brevard and other counties marked and branded "crop split upper bit and under bit" in each ear, branded *W*, some branded *B* and some *B fleur de lis*. Another bunch with a crop, one half crop in one ear and under slope and upper bit in the other ear and branded *DB* and *SJ*. He also gave them a Negro girl named Jenny, fourteen years old and all the increase of both the cattle and the Negro girl. He gave nothing to Becky, who still remained Rebecca Clements. This was about as close as Mose could come to claiming his children by Becky.

Luckily for Mose, the Yankees stayed on the coast and made no move west toward his plantation. But things were not going too well for the South. Grant had taken Nashville back in February and the people had fled the city for the mountains. The Union army was now in Northern Virginia, North Carolina, Alabama, Arkansas, Mississippi, Tennessee and had taken key positions all along the East Coast at Roanoke Island. Big portions of the Carolinas were under Union control.

So the South was going to have to conscript troops. Something had to be done and done fast.

Robert E. Lee was put into command of the Army of Northern Virginia. When Fort Henry, just south of the Tennessee and Kentucky line fell, a major impediment to Federal advances was gone, which left the whole state of Tennessee wide open. Kentucky was lost. It wasn't long before the Union Army would get control of the Mississippi River, take Vicksburg and cut the western supply lines to the east.

On April 16, the order went out. Every white male from 18 to 35 was to serve for three years with no exemptions—except for government officials, ferrymen, telegraph operators, ministers, printers, educators, hospital employees and druggists.

Stonewall Jackson left the Virginia Blue Ridge and headed for the Shenandoah Valley.

John Randolph Mizell had gotten his company as planned. Company F, Seventh Florida Infantry. He was already in uniform and had just received his appointment as a lieutenant from Camp Lee on April 14. He had already enlisted Crawford Bass, William Cook, the Lee brothers, Charlie and John Prevatt, John Padgett and Bill Hodges.

In May, General David Hunter also issued an Emancipation Proclamation freeing the slaves in Florida, Georgia and South Carolina and, again, Lincoln revoked Hunter's actions. This was the second time that Lincoln, long blamed for starting the war to free the slaves, saved the southern planters from losing their slaves.

In May, Isaac and Archibald, who had married the Geiger sisters, enlisted as privates into Company 2, the Eighth Florida Infantry, at Camp Hunt before they could be drafted and separated. They had both bought new breech-loading Maynard rifles, "Warranted to shoot twelve times a minute, carry a ball effectively sixteen hundred yards."

"Hit's called a pop gun," the man had told them. "You jest load her up, turn her north and pull the trigger. If twenty of these things don't clean out all them Yankees, I'm a damned liar."

Isaac got his trusted slave, Jason, to drive him and Arch to the train at Sanderson. Mose had used Jason to train his dogs because he refused to work for him. He'd turn the Negro boy loose, give him a head start and then sick the dogs on him. One time Jason didn't climb a tree fast enough and the dogs had chewed off one of the slave's heels. So Mose had given him to Isaac for a stable boy. He worshipped Isaac because he was good to him and worked for him diligently with no complaint. Jason told him goodbye with tears in his eyes. The two brothers caught the train for Virginia.

Three days later, George joined Captain Tucker's Company in the Eighth Florida Regiment Infantry, hoping to catch up with his brothers. So far, Isiah and Mose Junior were left to help round out the cow crew. James Ed had consumption and was exempt. He had been helping ship cattle from Jacksonville and had come home, but the Yankees left the port as fast as they had moved in. James Ed went back to Jacksonville to start shipping again. Some of the cattle went to Cuba and for these, Mose received payment in gold.

In June, Robert E. Lee was made Commander of the entire Confederate Army. "Stonewall" Jackson marched into the Shenandoah and almost trapped the Federal troops there. He was becoming legendary and had Washington D.C. on his mind. The fighting became fierce in that area and three of Mose's sons were there.

Isaac quickly got religion in the army. "This war is hell. Shells a'tearin' through the woods and bullets a'whistlin' right past yore ears and you a'thinkin' you'd not hear the one that got you, but you keep hopin' you'll hear the next one, yet, halfway expectin' one to hit you any minute, I started prayin' about five minutes into my first battle yesterday. I told the Lord I wuz sorry fer all I'd done and askt Him if He'd git me through all right, I'd confess all the sins I could think of and give my heart to Him like Ma and Pa had been a'wantin' me to do fer so long. But I got to fightin' and plum fergot the Lord and when hit wuz over I wuz so busy a'diggin' me another hole to crawl into I fergot agin. Then they hit us out in the open and my heart got to beatin' so hard I could hear hit in my ears and I tried to pray agin but this time my mouth wuz so dry I couldn't spit. I kept tryin to say, 'Lord, I don't want to die, please don't let me die.' Well, I come outa that one and got busy a'carryin' all them wounded on stretchers. They weren't mor'n gunnysacks stretched between two poles. The men kept a'fallin' off mine and I had to keep pickin' 'em up and I got bloody all over. When I got a chanct to lie down, I went sound asleep and plum fergot the Lord agin. All hell broke loose the minute I went into the line this mornin' and I realized I hadn't talked to the Lord like I promised and I wuz sure He'd punish me right off by lettin' me git hit. So I told Him, 'Lord, here I am and do with me what you want. I got to fightin' and I told Him I couldn't think of all the wrongs to confess while I was a'tryin' to fight but if He'd spare me one more time I'd give my life to Him right then and confess when hit wuz over. Well, I've fought all day and as soon as hit wuz over, I took to the woods and found me a spot and I confessed every mean thing I'd ever done that I could think of and I sung, 'Here I am, Lord, without one plea but that Thy blood wuz shed for me,' and I thanked Him fer sparing my life. And you know, the peace come over me and I cried and I cried. And I want you all to know that if you hear that I'm dead that you'll know I'm with the Lord in heaven."

That same month Isiah and Mose Jr. brought in a shipment of cattle and Mose Jr. told his daddy that Priscilla Ivey was pregnant and abandoned to face the music all alone with John Randolph Mizell now in Tennessee and the fighting so heavy there was no way he could get home, even with his daddy's influence.

"I told you so, didn't I son? I told you all along what kind o' people them Mizells is. I hope now people'll listen to me about them high falutin' better-than-thou hypocrites. At least I had the decency to take Becky in and give her and the young'un a home. And I weren't even sure hit wuz mine."

"Me, too, Pa, 'except hit wuz caught in my trap," and laughed.

"Ain't no laughing matter, son. He sneaked in there, covered that innocent little gal, and then run off and left her way down there in them woods to raise thet baby all by herself. I knew somethin like that wuz a'gonna happen. I could feel hit in my bones."

That really wasn't the way it happened at all. Mose would have been surprised to have found that it was similar to the circumstances whereby he and Becky had become "proud parents."

Priscilla and John Randolph had finally gotten to be alone at the big New Year's celebration at Lake Mann so the community could admire the new house. It had been one of those rare hot winter nights. With the heat of the dancing and of being so close, they sought an opportunity to slip away in the darkness by the lake. Before she knew it, she was lying in the shallows of Lake Mann as she had day-dreamed so many times, with his young, hot body on hers, their clothes discarded and left hanging on a willow bush. She lay and listened to the water as it lapped against the sand, mingled with the beat of her heart and his labored breathing as each thrust of his hips filled her being with an ecstasy that mounted finally into an explosion in her body she could never have imagined in all her wildest day-dreams.

She had not been caught in the act of their love making but her Aunt Priscilla and brother Robert's wife had suspected something had "happened" and not only watched her like a hawk but kept hinting about when the wedding was going to take place. But John Randolph had discussed his plans with David Jr. and they had talked to Priscilla's brother and decided that because of the war situation and the fact that John Randolph was planning to enlist, a wedding would have to take a back seat. Of course, they didn't know that someone had left the barn door open and the horse was out.

Priscilla was one of those fortunate females that felt no hint of morning sickness and cravings that had always been a daily complaint among the expectant members of her family. This was a condition she deemed absolutely necessary as evidence a baby was on the way. To complicate the situation, she was a big woman, tall and large-boned with wide hips and shoulders. Almost masculine in stature. She had suffered from a hormonal imbalance that allowed her to go months without a menstrual cycle. Her sister, Elizabeth, had taken her to a specialist in Jacksonville who advised her that she would probably get straightened out after her first pregnancy and that it was nothing to be alarmed about. Her Aunt Priscilla and sister-in-law both kept an eagle eye out for any signs of morning sickness, the vapors or an increasing waistline. By the time, April rolled around and John Randolph was gone into the service, they had let down their guard and quit counting. But by May, as the warm summer months set in she began to complain about feeling bloated from the monotonous diet of cornbread, onions and cowpeas and wished they had something else to eat. She blamed her increasing girth on "gas." John had written her and the family from the train in Tallahassee on his way to the fighting in Tennessee and had been swallowed up in the war for several weeks before she and her Aunt Priscilla began to wonder about her increasing waistline. When finally confronted, she confessed about the episode at the lake during the New Year's Eve party. By the time she had a letter from John dated June 2 saying he was taking the train to Chattanooga, she was sure she felt the "quickening" she had always heard of and knew that she was pregnant. She shed gallons of tears as she told her brother about the baby that was moving within her and he confronted David Jr., telling him he must make haste to get John Randolph home so he could marry his sister. As it turned out, John could not come home and she got a long letter from him expressing his love and regret, scolding her for not letting him know before he left. He felt assured he would possibly get home before the baby was due in September and they would marry then. In the mean time, she went to Bonnet Creek, near the Shingle Creek community and hid in her brother Robert's home. David Jr. and Mary were embarrassed about the entire affair and more or less "washed their hands" of Priscilla, but they saw that she received the money that John Randolph had insisted she receive, and David Jr. delivered a beef and what fresh vegetables he could, with a cool "good day" and a hasty "good bye." And Priscilla stayed hid at Bonnet Creek and tried to make the best of it.

Harriet shared her letters from Isaac and Martha, as well, from Arch.

"We are both gettin' ragged and stay purty dirty. You wouldn't let either of us in yore house. I wash when I can, even if hit has to be in a mud puddle. I could shore use some money. They say this is a rich man's war and a poor man's fight. Pa's as rich as anybuddy, but hit ain't helpin' me none."

Arch wrote, "Isaac has turned into a regular preacher. Each time he has to shoot a man he takes aim, pulls the trigger, puts his gun down and says, 'May God forgive me.' But he has a purty good sense o' humer about hit. The other day we met some boys Isaac had been a'prayin' with a'runnin' by us and he said, 'Hey little Dickie, where you all a'goin' in sech a hurry?' and Dickie told us they were a'huntin' cover. And Isaac said, 'I've knowed you fer weeks now, Dickie, and all that time you been a'wantin' me to pray you into the Pearly Gates. Now thet you've got the chanct to git in you're a'runnin' the wrong way.'"

They played poker, chucka-luck and cracked gray backs, or lice, for entertainment. "We bet on 'em like horses. We put 'em on the backs o' our plates and the one thet crawls off first, wins."

Chapter 21

The war went on. Isaac, Arch and George were now seasoned soldiers. They had fought the second battle of Bull Run where they had "whupped them Yankees' asses." They wrote of Stonewall and Jeb Stuart, their favorite leaders. They fared better than most, having spent much of their youth in the woods with Mose. They were good hunters so they quickly caught on to the art of fighting. They knew how to take care of themselves in bad weather. Many of the soldiers became sick and died of pneumonia where the camps were muddy, cold and gloomy. They knew how to cook, having spent so many years in the Florida wilds in a cow crew, cooking for themselves. Other southern boys, pampered and never having even learned to make a pot of tea, almost starved to death as they had to cook their own meals after a hard day of fighting. Some of the boys just went to bed hungry.

Arch wrote home to Martha, "Wife, I've learned to make the best hard tack pudding. You grind up hard tack, add a little flour 'til hit's good and stiff, like pie dough, they say. You roll hit out and kivver hit with a little stewed fruit and wrap hit in a cloth and steam hit. Sure is laripin'."

Many of the soldiers stayed homesick and morale was low. They whined about missing their mothers, but Mose's sons were used to being away from home for long periods of time so they were not as homesick as some of the young boys. However, they all wrote of dreaming of fried ham and baked sweet potatoes, rich cream gravy with hot biscuits and blackberry cobbler with big blobs of rich cream.

On September 26, 1862, Priscilla Ivey gave birth to John Randolph Mizell's son. She named him "Mann" because he had been a love child, conceived on the shores of Lake Mann, west of Orlando. In the lonely months of waiting for his birth, isolated from the "better-than-thous" who were lucky enough to have captured their husbands in the nick of time, she kept her sanity by thinking of the few brief moments in John Randolph's arms.

His father, John, spent the day of his son's birth resting from a small skirmish near the Davis Bridge on the Hatchee River in Tennessee. There had been little action that day all over the fronts except for a federal sea and land expedition that left Hilton Head Island and headed straight for the St. Johns River Bluff, to occupy Jacksonville for the second time.

Braced once again for an invasion, Mose and his daughters-in-law waited. They had not heard anything from the boys in Virginia. There had been a big battle, the Battle of Sharpsburg, so they knew the boys had not had time to write. To top it off, Mose Jr. had been drafted into the service—Company H, Second Regiment, Florida Infantry.

Finally a letter came from Arch. Isaac had been wounded and he was coming home on a furlough as soon as he could travel. Arch was being transferred to another outfit. He might not see either of his brothers again until the end of the war. Isaac was to get a two-month stay at home and Arch and George both almost wished they had been wounded too.

"They say this here last fight was the worst and bloodiest one day of the whole war," Arch wrote. "Them Yankees tried their hardest to whup us and capture us. They had us trapped once or twice, but we got away. Isaac, he ain't hurt too bad, so don't you worry. He'll be alright in no time."

One thing neither of the boys had anyway of knowing was that they had been trapped for good--almost. McClellan, the federal commander of the Army of the Potomac, had the chance to end the war for good and three years of battle and hundreds of thousands of casualties could have been spared on both sides. But he blew it.

Lee had issued his orders on September 9 to Jackson, McLaws, D. H. Hill, Longstreet and Jeb Stuart. Their positions were explicit. The next day, they made their march and McClellan, undecided how to counterattack, gave them time to get into place. But disaster struck Lee. His special order, number 191, fell into McClellan's hands, showing right where everyone was. It was never determined who was to blame. Jeb Stuart blamed D. H. Hill, but Hill still had his orders. Jackson says he burned his, Longstreet says he ate his, but anyway, a Union soldier, Pvt. B. W. Mitchell of the Twenty-seventh Infantry found the orders wrapped around three cigars. They had Hill's name on them! They were rushed to McClellan. As a result, McLaws and Hill had to battle in a bloody, hand-to-hand combat to keep Lee's army from being torn apart. But the bloody fighting gave Jackson time to capture Harper's Ferry and rendezvous at Sharpsburg as planned.

Nature had put a few obstacles in Lee's way also. He had his back to the Potomac River, so he could not retreat that way. In front of him was Antietam Creek, which gave him little protection, but was low enough in spots for the Union Army to cross it. He was trapped. McClellan could have ended it right there. He was moving in with ten times as many men as Lee had. As it turned out, even though he knew Lee's plan and what General Lee was trying to do, the Pinkertons, who had gathered intelligence for McClellan, had estimated Lee's strength at ten thousand men, when, actually, he had only one third that many. So several times the Confederates were whipped or trapped, but refused to give up and McClellan, thinking they had many reserves, waiting in the wings to rush in to relieve them, held back his reserves as well. What McClellan didn't know was that Lee used every man, many badly wounded, every horse and every gun he had in that one bloody day and managed to rally his shattered regiments. Every rebel soldier knew that to be defeated was to be destroyed and they did the impossible. Lee escaped to do battle for three more bitter years.

In October, the Yankees left Jacksonville for the second time. Mose was getting used to their coming and going. At the end of November, Isaac left to rejoin his regiment at Richmond and Harriet, pregnant again with another boy, bid him a tearful farewell.

The Christmas festivities were brief and not so festive. The fighting was getting serious and all the boys were away from home. It was not a happy occasion. Baking soda, black pepper, rice, tea and white sugar were not available for the special Christmas dishes. Current war songs had a less optimistic tone—*Sweet Lorena*, *When this Cruel War is Over*, and *Ye Cavaliers of Dixie*.

Down at Bonnet Creek, Priscilla spent the day helping Martha, Robert's wife, bake a tough old tom turkey, bogged down with cornbread dressing, baked sweet potatoes and collard greens. Mose had come by to see the baby and brought her some "piece goods" and a precious package of needles and thread to make a dress. Needles rusted in the Florida climate and they were often shared by several families. Many women pinned their clothes together with thorns, because buttons were a thing of the past. Many spinning wheels were brought back out and slaves, too old for the field, were put to work knitting the yarn into socks for military and civilian use. Wood looms were built to make cotton and woolen clothing. Mose still managed to get some pieces of cloth from England and traded them for favors with his lady friends. Small ships still managed to slip past the blockade in the night at Cedar Key, up the Suwannee to the mouth of the Santa Fe River, into the Indian River and a few got by the gun placements on the St. Johns Bluff.

Mose had been busy branding and gathering cattle each April and then shipping them to various parts of the country. Isiah's crew drove cattle to the Confederacy from around Orlando up to Lake City and to Jacksonville. Needham's crew drove them from Lake Tohopekaliga south across the Kissimmee Prairie to Fort Brooke in Tampa. Often they were sold to the highest bidder, be it Union, Confederate or Cuban. With the fall of Vicksburg, the Confederacy was totally dependent on Florida beef, having been cut off, by the federal control of the Mississippi River, from western beef. Along with Jake Summerlin, Mose was the principle supplier. They shipped six hundred head a week from April to August.

In January of that year, Lincoln actually freed the slaves in the Emancipation Proclamation. It was legal this time. A few slaves ran away but most of them, having no place to go, stayed on.

Mose Jr. wrote home to his wife at the edge of Jacksonville, "I find this fighting fun. Hit don't take much to kill a man and you git used to it in a hurry. I had to shoot one the other day."

He said they had fought all day behind logs and trees and stumps for cover. He had gotten used to the crying and appeals of the wounded. This one boy he knew had his groin torn open by a minie ball clear up into his body.

"I could see his guts a spillin' out all over the grass. He kept beggin' somebuddy to shoot him and git him outa his misery. I walked right up and put my gun to his head and said, 'Hit'll all be over with in a minute,' and pulled the trigger. I ain't like Isaac. I git a thrill outa killin' them Yankees."

Isaac wrote home, "They say this here Stonewall Jackson's quite a man. He lives by the *New Testament* but fights by the *Old*. And he prays before every battle, jest like me. He's Lee's right hand man and they say Lee can't fight without him. I'm proud to be fighting under two such men. They say this here is the greatest army of fighting men in the world and hits because of these two men. We're a'whuppin' them Yankees now. Right now, we're in Fredericksburg and hit's colder than a dead deer's ass. These poor men, when they git hit they got to lie around wounded with the cold wind blowin' into their wounds and freezin' the blood like red daggers of ice. They lie and beg fer mercy, and I cain't do nothin' fer 'em but pray. This war is hell, wife. Tell Pa to tell the rest o' the boys if they send fer 'em not to go, but to take to the woods instead. Me and Arch and George is seasoned and we know how to fight. I ain't sayin' Isiah ain't tough enough, but a man's got to really know what he's a'doin' to survive now and this here army shore ain't no place to practice. James Ed wouldn't last three weeks in this here weather with his cough."

But in May 1863, disaster struck the army and one of the men that Isaac was so proud of, Stonewall Jackson, died on the tenth of the month. He had ridden out at dusk to scout the front of his army. Coming along the Orange Plank Road in the darkness at Salem Church, Virginia, one of his own men mistakenly shot him in the left arm. It didn't seem too serious but they could not stop the bleeding and the arm had to be amputated. During the fierce battle of Chanchellorsville, he lay in the hospital and, after the battle, in a small house near Grunn's Station, south of Fredericksburg, he died. Weakened from loss of blood, pneumonia set in. It was on a Sunday.

"I always wanted to die on Sunday," he gasped. And one of the South's greatest fighters was lost and although the Rebels did not know it, the war was lost. Lee had lost his right-hand man. One that many rightfully believed he could not fight without.

Another graphic letter from Mose Jr. "We hanged a man today—a spy. The Colonel rode by us where we wuz stopped and asted us why we had quit. We told him a man had come along and give the order to quit a'marchin'. He said, 'I never gave no sech order!' He had us go git the man and he told the Colonel that some colonel had told him to tell the troops to quit. 'I am the only Colonel in this outfit, and I never saw you before in my life. Hang that man! He's a spy.' And so we got a rope and I drapped him to a tree and we tied hit around his neck and watched him kick, his eyeballs a poppin' out."

Priscilla heard less and less from John Randolph, now a Captain, who was a comptroller with his outfit in Tennessee.

President Davis put out a recommendation that all the southern fields be devoted exclusively to the production of corn, oats, beans, peas, potatoes and only those foods for man or beast. No planting of cotton or tobacco. Becky complained that she was going to have to start wearing wool that summer as cotton cloth was impossible to get. She didn't know Mose was giving all he could get to his lady friends.

In June, Lee started north toward Maryland. What he didn't realize was that he did not have the army he had before. Stonewall Jackson was gone; the man with whom he had an unusual mental telepathy in battle strategy was no more. So, he had revamped his high command. Jeb Stuart's superior cavalry had always supplied him with last minute intelligence through raids behind enemy lines. But at Brandy Station, he had encountered the Union cavalry and they had fought him to a stand still. Those plow line Yankee farmers had finally learned to ride a horse! This made the cocky assured Jeb Stuart a little more conservative about riding behind enemy lines in the style he was used to. Also, Jeff Davis, waiting for action that never came elsewhere, had kept garrisons of soldiers in the Carolinas and in the west and could not give Lee every soldier he could spare for this offensive.

It was July 1, 1863. They had just ridden past the pleasant little town of Gettysburg, Pennsylvania. Some of the scouts had gone back to town to see about getting some shoes. Gettysburg seemed to have plenty of shoes and the Rebels were almost barefoot. On the way back, they ran into a Union cavalry and ran back to tell the troops. They thought it was a local militia and could wipe it out in quick order. As it turned out, it was the entire main body of the Army of the Potomac under the direction of General Meade.

Lee missed Jackson. Longstreet, his right-hand man, sulked and fretted at the order to attack and was close to mutiny.

"I don't want to attack right now," he said. "Jeb Stuart's gone off on some wild goose chase and General Pickett isn't here yet with his men. I never go into battle with one boot off."

As a result, Lee lost an opportunity the first day to route the Federal army into retreat. Jeb Stuart came back that night, his men worn out, and Pickett was put in charge.

There probably aren't many school children who haven't heard of Pickett's charge on the third day. His Virginians and other troops from South Carolina--fifteen thousand crack troops—lined up as in review and advanced over one and a half miles of broken ground as the Yankees lowered their rifles and charged.

Arch and Isaac were both taken prisoner that day. Isaac wrote later of the battle, "Everywhere you looked there wuz blood 'n guts. Men far'ed into each other's faces not five feet apart. They wuz going down around me, spinning 'round, throwin' up their arms, and spittin' out blood, bombs bustin', the ground a' shakin'. I got nearly to the Yankee's lines and could see the soljur that shot me. I got hit in the arm. All our officers got shot but one and he told us to run. We run back acrost the field fer nearly a mile, steppin' on bodies. Hit wuz bad enough advancing, but runnin' away and thinkin' you'd git shot in the back wuz worse. We'd never had to run like that from a fight. Lots o' men had thrown away their guns and Pickett was a' cryin'. In a way, I'm glad I got captured. I hate this here war and hit ain't never a'gonna end. We won't give up and we can't whip them Yankees. Hit won't be long 'til we're all dead."

It was the greatest battle ever fought in the Western Hemisphere. The South lost and it was the end of the war for Arch, Isaac and George. They all ended up in Yankee prisons.

It was the turning point of the war. Lincoln came to the battleground where he gave his famous address. As Lee retreated back to Virginia, along with the disillusioned South, he speculated as to why he had lost. There had been inadequate staff work. His subordinate commanders had not followed his orders to their advantage. Jeb Stuart was out of pocket when he was needed the most, so there had been no cavalry. But he secretly told himself the truth. "If I had had Stonewall and Jeb Stuart had been in place, I'd have won and I know it." It was downhill all the way for the South from then on.

Back in the area where John Randolph Mizell had been the entire war, the Confederate army, earlier, had advanced from Knoxville to form a line across Kentucky, anchoring its right wing at Cumberland Gap. The Yankees successfully drove them back to eastern Tennessee. The entire Confederate Army of Tennessee pulled back to guard the railroad that ran from the Mississippi River through Chattanooga, Knoxville and Lynchburg, which supplied Richmond, the Confederate capital.

Once more, the right wing of the Confederacy made a push up to Perryville, Kentucky, only to have to retreat back to the line between Knoxville and Chattanooga again. Soon the Union army took key forts on the Tennessee and Cumberland Rivers and General Rosecrans, a Union commander, backed General Braxton Bragg, the Confederate commander, across the Tennessee River into Chattanooga and down to the east side of the Chickamauga Creek.

Unknown to Rosecrans, the Rebels were concentrating for a battle. Buckner abandoned Knoxville and let Union General Burnside have it and rushed to Chattanooga. Breckenridge rushed Confederate troops from Tennessee and Longstreet left Virginia and started west as fast as the troop train could get him there. Here they fought the "River of Death," the Battle of Chickamauga. That night, General Longstreet unloaded his troops and rushed into the battle, finding a hole in the Rosecrans lines. Had it not been for General Thomas who held the Confederates at bay long enough for Rosecrans to retreat back to Chattanooga, the entire Union force would have been demolished. For this, Thomas won the title of the "Rock of Chickamauga." One third of both armies became casualties and it was a bloody battle to equal or even surpass Sharpsburg.

General Braxton Bragg shut the Union Army up in Chattanooga to try to starve it into surrender. He was so confident that he could take the city by siege that, after two months, he sent Longstreet back over the mountains to try to retake Knoxville. And he had already given orders for General Cleburne's troops to get ready to go help him.

When the siege had started, the Confederates were in good spirits. They had just won the victory at Chickamauga but after dilly-dallying for two months, holding the Yankees in Chattanooga, morale began to fall. Bragg's subordinates were urging him to go on and take the town by force before the Union army got reinforcements.

Bragg was not generally well liked by his men. He didn't take care of them, for one thing. Food was always plentiful at the rear but seldom filtered down to the front where the troops needed it most.

He was a tall man with deep penetrating eyes and had no tolerance for anyone who opposed him. Many of his subordinates complained to Jefferson Davis in attempts to have him removed from top command, but he seemed to be Davis's favorite and stayed on.

162

Unknown to Bragg, Union troops were rushing to the aid of the besieged Federals. Grant, who had just won Vicksburg, had just been made overall commander, and, with Sherman, was preparing pontoons to cross the river above Chattanooga. "Fighting Joe" Hooker brought in two divisions from Virginia two days after Longstreet had left for Knoxville. When Cleburne's troops were loading the train to go help Longstreet, General Sherman crossed the Tennessee and started a drive to push the Confederates away from the railroad near Missionary Ridge and Cleburne's troops detrained just in time to stop him.

Bragg, who was now facing Grant, Thomas, Sherman, Sheridan and Hooker, sent an urgent message for Longstreet to come back, but he never got it in time. The Union forces pushed the Confederates south down the railroad toward Atlanta where they finally managed to stop at Dalton, Georgia.

The last time John Randolph had been heard from, he had been at Missionary Ridge and it was erroneously reported that he had been taken prisoner in that battle. The truth was that he had taken sick during the retreat, weakened from the Battle of Missionary Ridge, and was left by the wayside. It was then that he was reported missing. He entered the hospital on November 25.

At Christmas, his family and friends did not know whether he was alive or dead. Hopefully, they kept saying he was a prisoner.

Priscilla had managed to make a few friends. The new had worn off of her shame and disgrace. To help matters, Vianah Matilda Overstreet, from one of the better families at Shingle Creek, had given birth to a girl, Mary Nancy, on December 4. She and Jackson George Yates, Needham's youngest brother, would not be married until April of the coming year. Jack was in South Carolina helping Isiah and the rest of the "Cow Battalion" get beef to the Confederacy, when he got word she was pregnant. He could not get home to marry her. Just as John Randolph had been in Tennessee when Priscilla gave birth to little Mann. Those things happened and it sort of took the edge off Priscilla's ostracism. Illegitimacy was the least thing the poor Floridians had to worry themselves about.

Priscilla ran into Zilphie Ann Hodges, wife of John Hodges, who was a good friend of the Mizells. They had just had a special day of prayer for the boys at the front. Zilphie's John had been in the battle of Gettysburg and she had a letter from him.

"He says he had been a'marchin' an a' fightin' 'til he was broke down. He wuz knocked down by a bomb and hurt but not so bad he couldn't join the lines the next day. He said they lost a good deal of the Florida boys. Buckins, Jenkins, Hull, Gallaway, Savage, and Newberry. Let me read you what he said about Captain Tom Mizell. 'Our brigade charged them under the heaviest firing that I ever heard. We dug up and built our breast works with our bayonets. I heard that Capt. Mizell was taken a prisoner but I can't tell whether it is so or not.'" She turned to Priscilla and shook her head. "He doesn't know that Tom Mizell was kilt. I'll have to write him." She went on with the letter. "'We are at this time in Virginia and I hope we will never have to go there again.' He's being sent to the hospital in Tallahassee and I ain't heard nothin' from him," and she broke down and started crying. Zilphie took for granted that John Mizell was writing Priscilla regularly and that she was counting the days until he came home so they could be married.

The truth of the matter was that Priscilla had not heard from John Randolph in weeks, either, long before it was reported that he had been taken a prisoner. He had long since quit mentioning the "M" word and most of his letters concerned inquiries as to the health and development of his son. She had begun to suspect "out of sight, out of mind." There had been no words of love or longing for her and she had begun to realize that she no longer thought the same way about him.

Priscilla had done a heap of "growing up" during the war. Most of the settlers had accepted the fact that her little boy had no daddy. Accepted, but forgot, no. She was still not asked to some homes, and parties of any kind were few and far between. As with many young girls of that time, she had been orphaned as a small child, forced into a life of poverty, void of love or tenderness. In John Randolph, she had sought some of this but had found only shame and loneliness. The war had brought only isolation and she felt cheated and totally lost.

Chapter 22

As Susan had predicted and Mose had suspected, Mose Jr. had not adjusted to army life. Initially he was in one fight after the other with his fellow soldiers, sometimes arguing with his officers and then he came down with the measles and subsequently got pneumonia and sent home two or three times. What time he was not sick at home, he was in the hospital at Lake City, so that Mose and Isiah and the rest of the family could visit him. He had thought war would be a continuous experience of getting to kill Yankees and riding to battle on his horse. Instead, he had ended up spending most of it in a hospital bed. As punishment for some infraction of the rules at the hospital, he was put in solitary confinement. When he heard that his three brothers had all been taken prisoner, he decided to get out of the army and Mose made every attempt to see if he could get him released, but to no avail. So, Mose Jr. just simply took off in the woods at Lake City and went home. His poor wife, whom he had neglected for years, wasn't exactly glad to see him. She had been living at the edge of Jacksonville near her parents and many times Mose had come in from a cattle drive and stayed at the plantation with his father, not even going home to see her.

Mose was not at home, having taken a load of slaves south. He had heard that Grant had taken Tennessee and Sherman was pounding on the gates of Atlanta. He decided Tallahassee would be next. Mose Jr. had hung around the plantation but he and Becky didn't see eye-to-eye, so he had gone back to his wife.

Mose had started back for the second load of slaves, stopping off at Lake City to see Mose Jr. and do some business at the courthouse. He put one hundred head of cattle into Becky's name, at long last, and that of the new baby, Hezekiah. He also gave them a Negro slave named Mary, who was thirteen years old. He was surprised to find Mose Jr. missing and started home, thinking he was there. When he found that he had gone home to his family where Becky said "he belonged," Mose started toward Jacksonville to find him but met James Ed on the road. The Union troops were once again in Jacksonville.

"I don't know what they want with that poor old town," James Ed said. "Hit's jest a skeleton of itself, dilapidated with weeds growed up in the streets and houses burned to the ground, their blacked frames standing. Hit's godforsaken."

Mose decided it was just a matter of time until the Yankees packed up and went back as they always had. But it was not to be this time around.

Back in February of '63, some enterprising Yankees had filtered down into Florida. The Floridians had called them carpetbaggers because of the little carpetbags they carried for luggage. As Mose told everybody, "They came down with only their hat and their ass and they've both got holes in them." But there were some land speculators, humanitarians and just plain anti-slavery fanatics. Soon word got back to Lincoln that Florida was full of "many" Union sympathizers. He was urged to create a Military Department of Florida with a man named James Garfield, who was soon to be one of our presidents, as commanding general. He was to try to bring Florida back into the Union. Also, by the end of 1863, there had been feuding among the Confederate leadership. Jeff Davis wanted to keep fighting and Alexander Stephens, a Whig turned Democrat, wanted to negotiate for peace. In December, Lincoln put out his Amnesty Proclamation, offering a general pardon and amnesty in return for a oath of allegiance to the loyal state governments and the Federal government. Mose and other people who had been behind the war with such high hopes at the beginning had tired of the way it was going and wanted an end to it, too. But they were not for the Yankees. Lincoln, with this information, decided now was the time to retake Florida and bring it back to the Union. So, Brigadier General Truman Seymour was soon on his way to invade Florida and take Tallahassee. Ahead of him had come Lincoln's private secretary, Major John Hay, with instructions to set up a loyalist government once Tallahassee fell and Florida was occupied. He even bought a house in St. Augustine and waited for the fighting to begin.

The problem was that there were many people in north Florida wanting peace and many sympathizers along the coastal towns, but the rest of the thinly populated state was made up entirely of sturdy pioneers from Georgia and the Carolinas who were steadfast in their loyalty to the South and vowed to defend it "until the death."

Lincoln's other objectives were to open supply lines for the cotton, turpentine and lumber that was plentiful in Florida and the many slaves he thought he could draw from the plantations and weaken the food supply.

On February 7, the Confederates met the Federal troops coming into the channel at Jacksonville and tried to block the channel, but by the next day they had gotten off a sand bar and had taken Camp Finegan, the largest Confederate post in that area. By February 9, they were in Baldwin, where the three Florida railroads met, west of Jacksonville, and were making plans to march to Tallahassee.

Mose Jr. arrived at the plantation just before dawn on the morning of the tenth, his old horse in a lather and winded. "I rode through the woods all nite, Pa, to warn you. Them Yankees is a headin' right fer here on their way to Tallahassee. This ain't no little skirmish. They'll be in Sanderson by tonight. There's over a thousand of 'em. You can't stand up to 'em, Pa, the best thing fer you to do is run—git out, now!"

Mose went into action, stomping and cursing, "They'll be spread out on either side o' the tracks from here to Baldwin. Don't bother firing the fields, we ain't got all that much a growin' this time o' the year anyways--jest start loadin' up them sows and chickens. Mose, you and Ben drive them heifers out and we'll push 'em ahead o' us on the way. Becky, you'll have to saddle up and help us. Rich, you do what you can but don't git in the way. We'll need you to drive one o' the wagons--Becky, what you got there? You don't need that mor'n a sow does a sidesaddle." He threw the knitting Becky had been working on out of the wagon onto the ground. "Sammy, you git yore ass out there an help them niggers build them cages. We ain't leavin' them Yankees nothin' to eat."

Anything that would roll, be led, or driven, was to go.

"You in a bind there, Ben?" Mose asked as they loaded the last old sow.

"No sir, Mr. Mose. I ain't in no strain."

"Well, git yorself in one, because I'm damned sure in one. Here I am a pushin' my guts out and nobuddy's a' helpin!"

By ten o'clock that morning, they were loaded and headed on the trail that Mose had used so long to go to Central Florida. That's where they had planned to go. Everyone who wasn't on a horse walked. The wagons were loaded down and many of the children rode up behind the adults on the horses. About the only thing left behind were the stubborn mules not yet broke to ride or which could not be led with the horses.

They weren't five miles down the road when some of the slaves bolted and ran toward Jacksonville.

"Let the sonsobitches go!" Mose yelled at Lewis Osteen who had started after them. "They won't be worth a damned anyway and hold us up."

At a fork in the road, they met Major Robert Harrison and his men and were ordered to accompany them to Sanderson to intercept the federal soldiers. "We need every able bodied man we can get to turn 'em back," they were told.

Mose told Becky she was on her own and to head for Central Florida. "Rich knows the way," he told her. "I'll be down there as soon as I can get away."

At Sanderson, they met the Union forces under Colonel Guy Henry, consisting of fourteen hundred men, not nearly the entire force of Union soldiers ordered to take the capital. A small skirmish ensued and the Confederates had to pull back, but slowly, stalling for time until General Joe Finnegan could get into position. When Finnegan arrived, the Union commander was surprised at the show of force from the Rebels, thinking he'd meet only token resistance as he had been told. So, they too, pulled back until they could get with their main force that was on the way.

They pulled back to Mose's plantation. They had come by there on their way and remembered it as being the largest dwelling they had passed since leaving Baldwin. They stayed there for ten days, destroying everything they couldn't use and turned the house into a hospital for their sick and ailing. They quickly spread troops on either side of the railroad tracks from Baldwin to within a few miles east of Sanderson. The federal army had also made raids against Gainesville, Callahan and the surrounding areas. Becky was advised that the Union Army would be marching directly in their path so they turned westward toward the Suwannee, near Old Town where she knew some of Mose's relatives lived and would take them in. She had already decided she could never make it down to Central Florida anyway.

Rather than going on back to Lake City, Finnegan's men pulled back to Olustee where he decided to set up an ambush. It had the most desirable defensive position of any place between Lake City and Baldwin. Isaac's in-laws lived in the town. Arch's family lived six miles northeast of there, just five miles from Harriet and Isaac's place. Mose had been assured by one of the soldiers that they would be in no danger of being molested by the Yankees since they would charge right by the two homes on their way to Lake City, right down the railroad tracks. He and the boys were put to work helping the Confederates fortify the town for an attack. A large swamp lay to the south of town and Ocean Pond Lake, where they had had the Fourth of July fish fry so many years ago, lay to the north. It was an excellent choice for an ambush, because the Union army had to funnel their units between the two obstacles as they rushed toward Lake City.

Rebel reinforcements quicky arrived from Georgia and Central Florida and by Saturday morning, February 20, Joe Finnegan had an army of nearly five thousand troops. Many more than the Union Army was expecting to meet them in Lake City.

About noon, Seymour got word that the Confederates would be waiting for him at Olustee. Knowing they intended to defend Lake City, the Union commander counted this report as "inaccurate." As Seymour advanced, the Confederate cavalry took flanking positions, lining up on either side of the natural obstacles to protect their infantry regiments as they advanced into the center. This gave the infantry cover from any flanking Union forces, because the swamp on one side and the lake on the other, lined with horsemen, kept the Yankees from going around them and cut them in half.

Harriet heard the clatter of marching men and equipment as it went by and got dimmer. She had run to the hayloft and she and Jason had watched until they could no longer see the blue coats. She and the two little boys, Joe and Henry, had decided to hide under the bed at the first sight of the soldiers and Trot, her other slave, had stayed there. Mose had given Trot her name when he found out she was sneaking out of the house at nite and making extra money on the side with the local sawmill crew. She would sell her body and then "trot" home in a hurry in order to be present when the other house slaves woke up. Jason decided to tunnel under the hay in the hayloft, but the Federal troops, bent on battle, had posed no threat and marched on by. She had breathed a sigh of relief and was wondering what she'd tell Trot to prepare for supper when about three o'clock, she was surprised to hear volleys of firing and it began to get louder.

At Olustee, about two o'clock in the afternoon, the Union Army had met the eastern edge of the Confederate cavalry which had bolted west, drawing the Yankees into the trap set by their infantry troops in the middle. The trapped Union force drew back a couple of miles to regroup and give battle. So as it turned out, the main battle took place about two miles northeast of town on a big pine island where the railroad track that ran generally east and west, had to turn north for about two thirds of a mile to go around a big, swampy bay.

Two Union regiments, The Seventh New Hampshire and the Eighth U.S. Colored Troops gave way and bolted down the railroad track and fled right near Harriet's plantation. Soon the main battle was not far from the edge of their cotton field, right smack in their cow pasture. Shells were fired at an alarming rate. The Federal troops were stopped and the Sixth Florida and Third Georgia launched a counterattack. The Federals were being pushed back slowly, but were reinforced by the troops that had bolted initially and the reinforced line held temporarily. There was a momentary lull in the fighting as both sides ran low on ammunition. The Confederates were almost out of munitions when a flat car arrived from the west from Lake City with fresh supplies. The battle raged until dark. Early on, the Union army gave ground until they were almost back to Isaac's fields. Suddenly, off in the distance she could see swarms of blue coats and gray coats, men on horseback, and wagons. There were lots of wagons. Smoke hung over the cypress ponds like an early morning fog, except it was in the afternoon when there is almost never a fog in Florida. And this fog was black as smoke. The blue and gray blended together and at a distance, it was difficult for her to tell the difference between the two sides. The cannons roared like thunder and little Joe stuck his fingers in his ears and started crying. He was afraid of thunder anyway. She put him under the bed with Trot and the baby. He could see that his Mama was white with fright.

Soon the wounded were pouring into the house and she could see that she was needed. She ran to the well for a bucket of water. Not used to so much heavy labor, her hands were red and getting raw, she had carried in so much. She tried to spit on them but her mouth was so dry little was forthcoming. Some of the men were bleeding and broken to pieces.

"Is this your farm?" one of the soldiers asked.

"Yes, it's mine and my husband's, he's in a Yankee prison in Delaware."

The boy's name was Walt and he seemed to be hurting pretty bad. Someone cut palmetto fans and placed on the porch for the men to lie on. She stood by the boy for a moment and thought of some of the things Isaac had written her about the battles he had been in.

"Come back and see me in a little while, will you, pretty lady?" She promised him she would.

Suddenly all hell broke loose as a shell burst right near the house. She had just gone out after more water and she could hear Trot screaming and little Joe crying for his mama. It probably barely missed the barn, she thought. There had been no shells fired near the house and she had felt safe until now. The Rebs were at the cotton patch at the edge of the cypress pond about three hundred yards to the east. They had cut off some fleeing Union soldiers and she could almost taste the smoke of the shells and it stung her eyes. She ducked behind the well. A wounded Union soldier tried to get through the fence near the cowshed but crumbled up like a puppet. She couldn't tell if he had died or just fainted. She cringed on the grass thinking she might be next, but she hadn't heard a shell for sometime and decided he must have been wounded earlier and had only now lost enough blood to stop running. Finally, he got up as she got enough nerve to stand up and start drawing more water. He was bleeding from his mouth and nose. She forgot the water and helped the young boy up the back steps and onto the porch and found him a spot to lie down. She went back after the water and set it down on the kitchen floor and rushed into the bedroom where little Joe was hiding under the bed. He was crying and screaming with his little fingers stuck in his ears. Trot had crawled as far as she could get, right up against the wall with her hands over her head. The baby was still miraculously sound asleep through it all. She sat on the side of the bed and cradled Joe in her arms and scolded Trot and told her to quit screaming, it was upsetting her.

"I can't stay but jest a minute, son. I got to try to help some of these boys. They're hurt really bad. You stay here with Trot and help her with little Henry in case he wakes up."

It felt safe here in her room with her little family and she was tempted to stay but she could hear the activity outside the door and the moaning of men in pain.

Someone had thought to build a fire in the fireplace as the sun was going down and it was getting cold. The fire had been going in the kitchen all afternoon and it was warmer there. Some of the men were drinking tea.

"We need more water, ma'm," someone told her. Can't anyone but me bring in water, she thought and then felt guilty, knowing there wasn't enough hands to help the wounded and dying, much less dip water out of a well. She could at least do that and it took her from the painful task of looking at all the blood and broken bones.

"I ought'a git scairdy-cat Trot out here to help me," but then she wondered what she'd do with the children. Jason was busy out in the yard, unloading wounded from the wagons.

Someone called her from over in the corner of the living room.

"We got 'em on the run, they say, Ma'm," he whispered. His arm was bleeding badly and she tore up one of her nice sheets for a bandage. Heaven knows what we'll sleep on if they start taking 'em off the beds, she thought.

"Shore is nice o' you to help out this a way," he told her as she wrapped up his arm.

"Well, I didn't exactly volunteer," she answered. "It was sort of sent on me."

"Yore mighty brave, anyway," he was just a boy, didn't look hardly over sixteen. She could tell that he was hurting but he hadn't let out a moan.

"Would you like a little tea?" and she got up to go get it without waiting for him to reply. When she got back, he had closed his eyes and as he raised up to take a sip, his head fell back over on her hand. She sat there for a minute and watched in horror as the bright red blood began to pour through the fresh bandage she had just put on. She had blood all over her as she tore up more of the sheet and wrapped it over the spot the blood was coming from.

"Thank you for the tea. I think I'll jest rest here fer a minute," as he lay back and closed his eyes.

She felt fortified now to help with some of the others. What's a little more blood. I'm covered in it now so a little bit more won't matter.

Help had arrived from out of nowhere and the army was even loading some of the wounded into wagons instead of bringing more inside. Some of the more fortunate ones were on their feet, gathered in groups by the fire.

"I swear I never seed much 'fore I wuz hurt. Jest smoke, smoke and more smoke a bellerin' all over me. I wuz a' heppin' a gunner in a bunch o' saplings. We wuz a firing and that's the last I 'member 'til I cum to in here." It was his first experience in battle. Many of these men were not even in uniform, she noticed all of a sudden and had probably been conscripted from the surrounding farms. She thought of the plantation and wondered if Mose and Becky had gotten out of the way. Why the Yankees probably came right by there and that seems the way they were headed when they ran back that a way.

She found Jason and told him to go out to the smoke house and get any of the hams he could find that were ready to cook. "We got a bunch of wounded men and it's going to take a while to load them up and take them into town." She was sure they had a hospital set up in there.

She went into the bedroom and commanded that Trot crawl out from under the bed.

"You get out from under there and come in here and help me start supper."

This was a familiar order so Trot automatically came out from under the bed, bringing the baby and little Joe. But when she got to the body of a dead soldier out on the porch she began to cry and wail. Trot was afraid of dead people.

"Lawdy, Miz Hattie, they'll turn into haints and come back tonight and haint us!"

"Oh, for heaven sakes, Trot, they're as dead as that hog we butchered day before yesterday. They're not going anywhere but on those wagons and into town."

Jason had not come in from the smoke house and she went out on the porch to see what had happened to him. A soldier had stopped by the well just to get a drink and water his horse. "We got 'em plum run outa here all the way to Jacksonville. By tomorrow there won't be a Yankee on Florida soil." She heard him tell some of the men that were loading the dead into a wagon, like cordwood.

She changed her dress and washed the blood from her hands again. She felt as if she could never really get them clean. As soon as they had eaten and fed the children, she left Trot and Jason to help clean up the mess. Most of the badly wounded had been evacuated and someone had built a fire in the back yard to burn the bloody palmetto fans and was trying to wash the blood from the back porch. She hitched the wagon and took a load of wounded into town. She wanted to check on her family.

She was surprised to find that there had been little damage done to the town. At the train, she saw them loading the most badly wounded to go to Tallahassee. With them was an eleven year old boy from Macon, Georgia. He had volunteered with an older brother.

The Federal soldiers were buried in Olustee. They would be exhumed after the war and taken to the National Cemetery at Beaufort, South Carolina. The Confederate dead were buried in Lake City. She still thought of the town as Alligator. That's what she had called it for the most part of her life and she couldn't get used to the name change.

She was glad to see her folks were all right and that Martha, her sister and Arch's wife, was safe. They wanted her to stay but she headed back in the darkness. She knew she had to get home before Trot began to see ghosts in the house and upset the children.

On the way home she could see horses, stiff and still by the trail. Broken wagons were turned on their side like a tornado had ripped through the countryside. A fire was burning down around the edge of a pond. Pine trees had been splintered apart by cannon and there was evidence of destruction everywhere. She was glad she could see no more in the darkness because what she could see just on either side of the road gave her an empty lonely feeling. It started to rain before she got back to the house and she was soaking wet.

Mose Jr. was there. He was waiting for his daddy to come back from where Captain Dickison and his men were camped for the night. Mose had heard that the captain had helped form a "Cow Battalion" to ship cattle from Fort Brooke. The Yankees had torched the port of Fort Myers and still would hold Jacksonville. Actually, the port at Fort Myers had been in poor condition since the last Indian war, but the Union troops had it bottled up, nevertheless. He wanted the captain to use his influence to get Mose Jr. released from the trouble he was in, having deserted from the hospital at Lake City, and get him reinstated back into Captain Dickison's outfit, where he had been before. Mose was going to volunteer his cow crew and as many men from other cow crews as he could find to get cattle moving in larger numbers to the troops in Virginia. The Yankees might soon have the railroads bottled up, as well as the port. Mose Jr. knew the country down there and would be of invaluable help. And the Capt. would realize that, as usual, Mose was pulling Mose Jr.'s chestnuts out of the fire.

"They done got into our coffee, Miz Hattie," Trot whined. Hattie told her that was all right, she'd borrow some from Martha in the morning and Mose could bring her some more in a day or two.

"Not from our place, Hattie," Mose Jr. told her. "Pa and Becky has pulled outa there with all the slaves and Becky's headed south. Them Yankees were a'campin' there 'fore they left a'comin' this a way jest 'fore the battle. I 'spect there's not much left to eat or drink on the place."

Mose came in before daylight and told Mose Jr. to saddle up and come with him toward Jacksonville. "I got things purty well straightened out with Captain Dickison fer you to git back into yore old outfit. You might have to go back to Lake City fer a few days, jest for the necessary procedure and signing of the papers, but he admitted he needed you worst down south, a loadin' them cows mor'n you need to be in confinement at Lake City. Things is gonna work out. He assured me. I got his word on hit. Now you got to straighten up and do yore part."

The Union army had reorganized at Sanderson just long enough to cover their retreat until they could reach Jacksonville. The Yankees thought the Rebs would try to drive them out of Florida and pulled back to Fernandina, Jacksonville and St. Augustine. The Confederates formed a line of fortification at McGirts Creek just twelve miles west of Jacksonville but a quick withdrawal of Union troops was ordered and, except for a garrison to hold the city and the mouth of the St. Johns, the Union army was gone before the Rebs could attack. The Federal navy still had control of the port at Jacksonville.

Most of the troops that fought at Olustee were loaded on cars at Baldwin and sent north to fight at Cold Harbor and Petersburg where Lee was holding on for dear life. On the field after the battle of Gettysburg, seven of his colonels had lain dead and the eighth mortally wounded. Of his fifteen regiments, only one field officer escaped injury and he would later fall at Richmond. Lee had started out through Maryland to take Washington with forty-eight hundred men and started back to Virginia with only eight hundred. Yes, he needed every man he could get.

Mose and the boys gathered at the plantation. The sight of the destruction made them sick. Their way of life had been wiped out in just ten days. All that remained standing was the house, which had been stripped of everything but the beds and the furniture too heavy to carry. Rich and Dulcie's slave sheds were still standing and the barn. The rest of the sheds, the slave quarters and any equipment Mose had left behind, "burned as black as a coon's ass in blackberry time," as only Mose could so aptly describe it.

They spent a miserable night in the old house where he had spent so many happy days with Leah and his young children.

"Hit stinks o' Yankees," he told the crew. There was nothing there to eat, no corn for the horses, not a change of clothes. They headed south, not knowing that Becky was safe on the banks of the Suwannee.

Chapter 23

The Confederates had won a victory at Olustee and morale was high. The Union movement in Florida had turned out to be a myth, but the destruction of Mose's plantation was no myth and neither had been the battle at Olustee. There had been one thousand Confederate casualties. The soldiers of the Confederacy and many of the state's civilians had run the Yankees off much of Florida soil and hopes ran high. However, with the Gettysburg and Chattanooga victories by the Yankees, the Confederate soldiers were shut in by a wall of Federal warships and Union soldiers. The Yankees now had control of the Mississippi, Tennessee and Cumberland Rivers. The Confederates to the west of the Mississippi were cut off from Virginia and without any kind of communication from Richmond. Grant moved north to take command of the army there and Sherman was in command of the Union army wintered around Chattanooga.

In the spring of 1864, he set out to fight his way to Atlanta. General Joe Johnston, replaced the hated Bragg and could be seen riding alongside his men yelling, "Give 'em hell, boys. Give 'em hell." But Sherman kept extending his line to the right some of the times and sometimes to the left and followed the Johnston's retreat from Dalton to Resaca, Rome, Cassville, Allatoona and Kennesaw Mountain at Marietta.

John Randolph had finally let his family know that he was still alive and still with his outfit. He wrote of the retreat from Missionary Ridge.

"Sometimes we didn't even have time to bury our dead, but had to leave them lying where they fell. We had to melt the solder's binding on the two halves of our canteens to make a couple of frying pans to cook in. Our supplies are gone. We are living off the goodness of the people in the countryside. They try to share with us what they have, which isn't much."

On June 23, 1864, in these mountains, John Randolph Mizell was cut off and captured as he camped where Peach Tree Creek joins the Chattahoochee River. The war was over for him, at least.

It took Sherman until September of that year to finally take Atlanta. In the early winter, he made his famous march to the sea. This was the final devastation and rape of the South. Fields of wheat, rye, oats and corn were wiped out. His army formed four parallel columns like the fingers of a hand, spread out across Georgia pointing their way to the sea, some sixty-two thousand men, leaving a trail of destruction. Black smoke could be seen for miles away. They lived on the rich countryside full of syrup, honey, sweet potatoes, pork, sugar, chickens, rice, and corn for their horses. They lived high on the hog, leaving nothing for the Southerners to survive on.

When Sherman reached Milledgeville, Georgia's capital, they held a mock assembly and repealed Georgia's secession from the Union. Large numbers of freed Negroes followed behind the soldiers and millions of dollars worth of property were destroyed or stolen. Valuable heirlooms that had been in the possession of families since they had left England over one hundred and fifty years before found their way into Yankee homes. If the slaves didn't tell where the owners had hidden them, a member of the household might be hanged until they did, with Yankee soldiers often rifling the trunks as a family member lay dying.

When Lincoln criticized Sherman for these practices, he wrote back, "War is hell. If people raise a howl against my barbarity and cruelty, well, war is war and I'm not trying to win a popularity contest. If they want peace for themselves and their relatives, then they must stop this war." He sent out word that if guerrillas attacked his men, he would punish civilians. By the end of December, Sherman had marched two hundred and fifty miles to Savannah. He had destroyed the state of Georgia in just forty days and turned north up the coast through the Carolinas.

Before Sherman turned north, Governor John Milton of Florida again feared for the safety of Tallahassee and called out everyone capable of carrying a gun. Captain Dickison's command formed a troop of irregulars and based them at Camp Baker near Waldo. They made raids against the Yankees up and down the St. Johns River, making room for Isiah to drive a few cattle up through the Carolinas to the Confederate army in Virginia. Mose Jr. had gotten into trouble again and had ended up back in confinement at Lake City. Mose had just about despaired of keeping the boy from being hung. Mose desperately searched the countryside, looking for hands to help Isiah in his cattle drives, taking beef to Lee's men in Virginia and the Carolinas, through enemy territory. One in particular he happened across was a healthy-looking boy from Fort Christmas named Johnny Cox. Mose was surprised to find Johnny working cattle near Taylor Creek with his father, Tom, who most everyone called "Uncle Tom." Uncle Tom was a practical jokester and was full of "stories." Even at an advanced age, he had dark dancing eyes and coal black hair, being of Indian descent. He loved to tease so much it was difficult to know if he was telling the truth or not.

"How come yore boy here ain't in the army, Uncle Tom?" Mose asked testily, angered at seeing so fine a specimen of man-hood enjoying the great out doors and his three sons in Yankee prisons, and a fourth risking his life, driving cattle for the war effort.

"They sent fer him one day last year and he come right back to home. 'Pears he couldn't pass the test."

"He looks healthy enough to me. What's ailin' him?"

"They sed his pecker wuz too long. Hit got in the way and hindered him a'marchin'. He couldn't keep up."

Johnny laughed and shook his head.

"Now Pa, you know thet ain't so. Mr. Barber, he's a' funnin' you. Truth is I got rheumatize in my feet so bad I can't keep up. That's all."

"You can sit a horse, looks like," Mose remarked, looking at Johnny's outfit he was using to drive cattle.

"Best cowhand in the country," Uncle Tom bragged. "An I ain't a funnin' this time."

So, Mose made arrangements to have Johnny join Isiah and his crew on his next roundup to take beef to the Army of Northern Virginia.

In December 1864, the Yankee ship, *Adele,* attacked and destroyed the shipping facilities at Fort Brooke in the Tampa Bay where Mose and Jake Summerlin had been shipping cattle. Now there was no port from which to send beef to the Confederate army. It took Isiah forty-five days to drive a herd north where it would reach the troops. A seven hundred pound cow could lose as much as one hundred and fifty pounds on such a trip and many of these little scrawny cattle didn't weight much more than one hundred and fifty pounds, full grown, to start with. Major William Footman and two hundred of the Cow Calvary tried to take back Fort Myers and rebuild the docks so they could ship from there, but were driven back. Captain James McKay took over Dickison's command of the Cow Guard Battalion.

Something had to be done to be able to ship the beef by boat so Mose and Jake Summerlin and some other smaller cowmen got together and with the help of McKay, built a corduroy road from Fort Ogden to Punta Rassa. On the small point of land, jutting out into the Gulf of Mexico, they built shipping pens and a dock out into the natural deep little port where a small steamer could come in.

Driving the cattle to the pens at Punta Rassa was an extremely hazardous task. The land was often flooded and it was difficult to just find a dry place to spread an oilcloth slicker in order to have a dry place to sleep. Someone had to stand guard against Indians that still roamed that territory so near to the Everglades. Sometimes it could be so dry that two or three cups of water from a stump hole was all that was available for coffee water. Sometimes they were lucky enough to find a 'gator hole, but the stench of the 'gator made it difficult to drink or even bathe in the water.

The cattle gathered on the east side of Lake Kissimmee had to cross the Kissimmee River at Fort Bassenger and those on the west side of the lake were driven through open country to the Caloosahatchee River Crossing. At this point, water poured from Lake Flint over a high rock ledge that made the headwaters of the river. In dry weather, the cattle were driven around the end of the waterfall, making the crossing relatively easy, but if the land was wet or flooded, the entire area was covered with water and the cattle crossing would be a mile wide with about one hundred yards that would swim a horse. Sometimes it would take three to four hours to cross. When they got in sight of Punta Rassa, they reached the corduroy road of crossties, ten feet long and ten feet wide of heart pine laid over a saltwater bog with treacherous patches of quicksand. The cattle had to be maneuvered down this narrow road to the shipping pens. Mose got $14 a head in Spanish gold doubloons for his cattle if he shipped them to Cuba. The war had taken his plantations but he still had his cattle business.

But it was to be struck a bitter blow when, on a drive through South Carolina, with a herd of mangy half-starved cattle, Isiah in early March, disappeared into the raging waters of a small river trying to slip a shipment of much needed beef to a dying Confederacy. Now all but one of his sons, James Ed, were in prison or dead, and James Ed was dying of consumption and unable to do manual labor. But Mose endured.

All of Mose's slaves in Central Florida had fled with a group of carpetbaggers through the woods to New Smyrna. Most of the ones who went to Old Town with Becky had left, as well. Rich had expired two days after reaching the Suwannee River and Mose had lost a valuable friend. Except for his cattle, his world was falling apart. He still owed payment for the land he bought to expand his Columbia County and Baker County plantations. And now, if he decided to work the land, he would have to hire help. Wood was eighty dollars a cord, corn ten dollars a bushel, felt hats one hundred and fifty dollars, dress shoes one hundred dollars, potatoes were twenty dollars a bushel and flour one hundred and twenty dollars a barrel. This could have been great if Mose could have raised all of this on his plantations and gotten his goods to market. A Florida orange was bringing a dollar, but there was no way of getting them to the people that still had a dollar. A Confederate soldier, when paid, and many were not, made eleven dollars a month!

Mose had not heard from any of his boys in the northern prisons. He had finally been instrumental in getting Mose Jr. released from confinement at Lake City for the fourth time, and he was back with Dickison again. This alone showed how desperate the Rebels were for men! A record number of men in the northern prisons were reported as dying of just plain homesickness. Mose knew his sons better than that. He knew they were tough enough to take whatever emotional torture the prison life had to offer, but starvation or exposure to the bitter cold was another thing. He hoped the gold that he had made them sew into their boots the last time they were home would last. There were reports that there were ten thousand prisoners on seventeen acres with no stoves in the quarters or hospitals and that many had no blankets. Many southern boys from Florida had never even seen snow. Escaped prisoners told of the bad food and treatment waiting for those left behind. One lady wrote that she had taken food to a prison and that the men had lined up, begging "bread, bread, bread." There had been some Englishmen at the prison at the time and the officer in charge had been so embarrassed that he had withheld the bread she had brought for a whole day. All of this rode heavily on Mose's mind and he wanted the end of the war more than ever.

Mose had soon learned that Becky was safe with his relatives on the Suwannee and he left her in west Florida while he was busy shipping cattle. At Thanksgiving, that year, he had married her due to pressure applied by his family there. Actually, everything was gone and the house that he had promised Leah he'd not take a wife into had already been "defiled by Yankees," so he decided if she still wanted him after he had lost so much, she must still care for him in some way other than for his money. He didn't know that Becky knew he had gold hoarded in the soil around the plantation. And she still had dreams of building it back like it was.

Christmas of '64 found them back at "home." They had managed to survive on his beef and several bushels of sweet potatoes and corn he had bought from a farmer on the way back from Old Town, greens Becky soon had growing in the back yard, along with whatever crops volunteered in the weed-covered fields.

And who should arrive in the middle of the night in January, but Mose Jr. He had deserted again from Dickison's Company, over at Waldo. He and Mose had a long talk about how the war was going and both agreed that they'd all be better off if it ended. So, he took off through the woods to turn himself into the Yankees at Jacksonville but was captured again the very next day and taken back to Lake City. It seemed that Mose Jr. couldn't do anything right. Mose told Becky he was a "loose horse." But somehow or other he escaped again from Lake City four days later and this time made it to the Yankee garrison in Jacksonville by February 9.

His Confederate military records show that he "spilled the beans" to the Yankees. He and his daddy wanted the war over with. His statement went as follows:

-- Statement of Moses B. F. Barber, Deserter, Rebel Army --

"Says he is a private of Captain Dickisons Co. H. Second Florida Calvary. He enlisted September 18th, 1862. Deserted January 19th, was arrested January 19th and carried to Lake City and placed in confinement. (actually, Mose Jr. had deserted the 10th of January but said nothing of the trip to see his daddy or the many other times he had deserted).

Deserted again January 21st, by running the guard. Laid out in the woods about a week with a party who were avoiding bounty hunters and then struck for Jacksonville. Says there are quite a number whom he thinks will arrive here in a few days.

Thinks there are about fifteen hundred Cavalry at Baldwin of the Second Regt. and Fifth Battalion Commanded by Lt. Smith. Says that Capt. Dickison with two Companies were at Waldo as late as the tenth of January.

Says there is a picket post at the head of McGirt's Creek, one at the stage rail and McGirt's Creek, and at the railroad on McGirt's Creek—and at the ford of Yellow Water Creek at James Ellison's place. There is a courier line from below the fish hole on McGirt's Creek at the log landing to Robert's Crossing. A spy is kept from Cedar to McGirt's Creek at Bryant's Landing to intercept deserters.

Railroad is open from Baldwin to Archer and the Cedar Keys road and from Baldwin westward.

Now four of Mose's boys were in Yankee prisons.

On February 1, 1865, nine days before Mose Jr. turned himself over to authorities in Jacksonville, the United States Congress had approved the 13th Amendment, "Neither slavery nor involuntary servitude, except as punishment for crime, etc."

With Mose Jr. and his daddy doing everything they could to bring about a close to the war, others kept putting up a brave fight. On March 4, a thousand Union troops landed near the St. Marks lighthouse on the Gulf coast south of Tallahassee, bent on taking Tallahassee. A local militia company and a company of very young cadets from the West Florida Seminary in Tallahassee met them at Natural Bridge south of Tallahassee. Because of a series of blunders on the part of the Federal forces and exceptional good luck on the Confederate side, the Yankees were turned back. None of the young cadets suffered any casualties.

By mid-March, General Sherman had completed his path of destruction up the coast of North Carolina. By April, Lee began to see that he could no longer hold on to Richmond and Petersburg with his ragged, starving soldiers. On a beautiful spring day, the yards ablaze with colorful buds and blossoms and the earth full of promise of better things to come from a cold, hard, winter, Jefferson Davis went into St. Paul's church in Richmond, Virginia, to pray and by nightfall, he and his cabinet had fled the capital. He made a wild dash to Abbeville, South Carolina, to discuss the remote possibility of holding the Confederacy together, but his Generals advised against it and before dawn at the exact spot in the same house where the Confederacy had been born, he bid them all a tearful goodbye and headed south.

On Palm Sunday, April 9, General Robert E. Lee, a tall aristocratic, gray clad southern gentleman, tears streaming down his cheeks, met General Grant, the whiskey-drinking-smokeless-cigar-chewing, rough, and rather untidy Union Commander, and handed him his sword. Under an apple tree at Appomattox Court House, Lee surrendered the Army of Northern Virginia to Grant.

Lee told his troops, "I have done the best I could for you, my heart is too full to say more." And he got on his white horse, Traveler, and rode back to Richmond. The first thing his troops asked for when they threw down their arms was "food."

Back in Florida, a few days later, Governor John Milton committed suicide rather than face the reality of a Confederate defeat.

On April 11, Lincoln made a speech to welcome the southern states back into the Union. A 30-year-old John Wilkes Booth whispered to a friend, "That's the last speech he'll ever make."

Booth fanatically believed that the country was formed for white men only and that Lincoln was responsible for turning the blacks "loose on society." What he did not know was that Lincoln had already met with one of the foremost Afro-American leaders and had advised him to go to the islands and back to Africa, because he thought it would take too long and produce too bitter a struggle for the black slaves to be accepted as equal by the white population of America. Booth felt he was just a "Confederate gentleman doing his duty," when he shot Mr. Lincoln in the head as he sat in his box, watching the second scene of the third act of *Our American Cousin*.

The first official announcement in Florida that the war was over was on April 30 when General Joe Johnston notified acting Governor A. K. Allison, that he had surrendered to Sherman and that all hostilities in Florida, Georgia and the Carolinas had ceased.

All Confederate soldiers in Florida were told to report to Jacksonville and surrender everything but their horses and the officers could keep their pistols. They had to sign a parole form just as if they were criminals. The Federal government considered them so. Mose Jr. was one of the first ones home.

By May 1865, it was unofficially all over but the shouting. One president was dead and another on the run. A ten thousand dollar reward was posted for the arrest of Jefferson Davis, as he had been officially blamed for the death of Lincoln. He was captured near Irwinville, Georgia, on May 10 and would be kept in prison, sometimes in irons and without a trial, for a year and then released.

On May 22, John Randolph Mizell was released from Johnson's Island in Ohio. By June, the three Barber brothers were on their way home.

The Civil War was finally over for Mose Barber and his family.

Chapter 24

Mose and Becky finally had five "slaves" — two of them as old as Mose and three that had been born on the plantation. They had all drifted back "home," having found life too harsh out into the real world. The ones born on the plantation had played marbles, run races and hunted 'coons with Mose's young sons and this was the only home they had ever known. They wanted to stay and work and Mose and Becky welcomed them with opened arms.

Becky worked just as hard as anyone, trying to make a success of the farm. That was all it was, a small farm. She had been a good and faithful wife and seemed to accept adversity as well as anyone else.

They repaired the few buildings still standing and added a few more that were absolutely necessary. The fields had grown up in weeds and small saplings of black jack oaks and pines. The fences were down and Mose did not have sufficient labor to clear again, much less maintain such a vast area that he used to keep in working order when he had over one hundred slaves.

In the euphoria of freedom, many of the ex-slaves had no inclination to work as long as they could get food from the Federal troops or the Freedman's Bureau that had been established to look after their welfare. They had been fed and housed for so long in slavery that now, as free men, as long as they could get room and board without working, they were on an extended vacation that had no definite end. They gathered around the military camps, waiting for a daily handout and soon "darkie towns" sprang up in most populated areas of any size. So there was little labor to be had for hire.

Mose was not a young man, although he was in excellent physical shape after long years in the saddle. But he was not up to the backbreaking work that was required to be a farmer, day after day. Isaac was moving to Central Florida, Isiah was dead, James Ed was an invalid, and Mose Jr. had turned into an unreliable cowhand. He was a womanizer, cruel and just a few shades from becoming an outright criminal. He had already caught a bum sleeping in his barn and hanged him from the chimney corner of his living room with his own kerchief he was wearing around his neck. Mose had been summoned by Penny, his wife, and had helped her dispose of the body. Archibald and Martha had moved to the Suwannee River Valley and were operating a ferry. George W. was in Jacksonville. So, Mose, who had been surrounded by six young sons, five nephews, one hundred slaves, plus several white hired hands, was suddenly faced with trying to keep his land intact with Becky and five "slaves." It was an impossible task.

That November, the Federal government removed Florida's Governor Allison from office, slapped him in prison along with some other high ranking officials, and a Yankee, William Marvin, was made the provisional governor. The Federal army, many of whom were black, marched into Florida to take control. The Federal government was convinced that Florida's "Crackers" could not be trusted to care for their freed slaves. Clergymen were forced to pray with their congregation on Sunday morning for President Andrew Johnson.

Typical of the humiliation heaped on the defeated soldiers, a small insignificant order was put forth. Buttons were scarce, if non-existent, in Florida. The coats they wore home from the war were all that many of them had to wear that winter. But they were not allowed to wear anything that had military buttons or anything that resembled the Confederacy. They could disguise the coats but had to take the buttons off. If caught with Confederate buttons on anything, they were marched to the Provost Marshal, usually by the shirt collar by a Negro sergeant, and their buttons cut off, in disgrace. In so many ways like this, the South was humiliated and brought to its knees. This was a way it was forced to bow to its often-vindictive conquerors. There are books full of stories about the rough times the South endured during reconstruction. It would take ten long years before the carpetbaggers and native scalawags would give up and the old-time Southerners could wrest control and govern themselves.

"Do gooders" arrived in the South in droves. Many were sincere in their effort to try to ease the freed slaves into their transition from slaves to freedmen, but many came just to line their pockets. Carpetbaggers ran the Freedman's Bureau and other Federal offices but army officers in the upper ranks were superior to them. Often they interfered in civil affairs, and having no experience in such matters and a vindictive feeling for southerners anyway, made life a hell on earth for the native population. As it is now and has been since men ruled other men on earth, corruption and exploitation abounded. The small farmers fared better than the big plantation owners. They were accustomed to hard labor anyway. But the former slave owners who had never worked in the fields found it necessary to hoe and plow, providing they still had a hoe or plow to work with. Confederate money was no good. Some professional men such as lawyers, bankers and even doctors had to farm to raise something to eat. No one had the money to pay them for their services. One could often see a man out working in the hot sun in his garden in a Panama hat, white shirt and black string tie.

At Christmas, the greens in Mose's garden had been killed by a hard freeze but there were still some fresh milk cows for cream and butter. So cornbread, buttermilk and sweet potatoes rounded out the diet of beef, beef and more beef. Wild game and fish were almost a thing of the past in such a heavily populated county as Baker.

Mose tried his hand at cutting timber because lumber was so expensive and in great demand. He had been able to hire a few ex-slaves who had decided they wanted to work and he had put them to work, cutting cedar logs from the back of his plantation.

"I know you've all got hit in the backs o' yore heads some o' this land's a'gonna be taken from me and yore a'gonna git forty acres of hit and one o' these here mules. Ain't that right? Ain't that what those durn fools at the Bureau's been a'tellin' you?"

Silence and shuffling of feet, not one of them able to look him in the eye.

"Well, you might as well make up yore minds right now, the President ain't a'gonna give you one inch o' this land, nor one of these mules, nor my cows nor sheep nor hogs nor nothin' else I got. Not even a fork nor a spoon nor a plate to eat hit on. Nobuddy's gonna give you a Godamned thing. You want any o' these things you got to git out and work fer hit. You believe in the *Bible*, The Good Book?"

"Yashuh. Ahuh."

"Paul preaches to us in the Bible, 'Them that don't work should not eat.' You wanta eat around here, then go, 'gator, and muddy the water. Earn yore keep!"

So it was no wonder Mose could not keep help. He was just as tough on his hired help as he had been on his slaves. Actually, he could not distinguish between the two. They were still slaves to him.

And then the lumber business petered out. The price of logs fell, especially the cedar logs that had been so high. They could be seen stacked up at McGirts Creek north of Ten Mile Station, later called White Horse, in Duval County, for years and years.

Mose became more and more disgusted with trying to make a living in Baker and Columbia Counties. There were carpetbaggers and Negroes in charge everywhere. He couldn't keep help. People tore down his fences and stole his livestock. He and Becky started arguing over money. By April, he was glad to have an excuse to saddle up and head for Central Florida.

"I got a cow business to run, woman," he told her when she asked what she was supposed to do to make a living while he was gone. "Hell, you got three niggers to raise you sumpthin' to eat and plenty o' clothes to wear, and a roof over your head, you ungrateful wench. What more do you want? And I tell you another thing, you'd better make up yore mind that we're a'packin' up and leavin' this hell hole when I git back this fall. You hear me?"

"Well, I ain't a'goin' down to that hell hole you thinks so wonderful with all them snakes and alligators and mosquitoes, and me a hundred miles from nowheres either. And you might as well make up yore mind to that, Mr. Barber."

"Then jest stay here and starve to death, I don't give a big rat's ass. You been around that sorry Penny 'til you've got jest like her. Why can't you be more like Hattie. She's off down there a'helpin' Isaac git ahead. She don't mind the snakes and alligators and mosquitoes and she's further south than we'd be. Little Mose had a wife to help him out stead o' that sorry-good-fer-nothin' Penny, he'd mount to somethin'. Man needs a helpmate. You know what the *Bible* says, 'His people shall be my people and where ever he goes the woman should follow.' No, you and Penny's got to stay right here and stick yore nose up some Yankee's ass. Well, I'm a gittin' outa here. I'm sick o' this goddamned place."

And so Mose wiped his feet of Baker County and the local establishment and headed for Central Florida with his dogs, his favorite horse, and leading a pack mule.

He took a slightly different route this time. His main objective was to find the cow crew and join the spring roundup but he wanted to talk to Susan first.

He went by way of Fort McCoy and thought of the two little boys he, Isiah, Francis and Champ had found during one of their first trips down below Fort King. He remembered Isiah when he was reaching manhood and he mourned again the loss of such a strong, dependable son. He wondered what ever became of the two little boys and if they grew into manhood as well and were possibly lost in the war. I guess you don't ask God "why" or "when," he thought, just "how."

He turned toward Zay Prairie and past Half Moon Lake, through the big scrub, on down to Lake Dorr and across Disappearing Creek and straight to Lake Conway and Susan.

They sat on the porch and he talked with her about his problems back in Baker County. "Becky's a fightin' her head — I think she wants to kick the traces and git the bits in her teeth, and run wild." Mose talked about women as he did his horses. Susan knew that he meant Becky was rebelling against his authority as her husband. She understood, as he knew she would, and he felt better for listening to her. However, though she thought like a man, she had a woman's viewpoint, too, and she told him not to be too hard on Becky and Little Mose's wife, Penny.

"You can't make comparisons between Hattie and Penny. Isaac loves Hattie and she'd follow him to the end of the earth. Little Mose ain't never treated Penny right and you know hit. She wouldn't be a bit better off down in Brevard County around some cow camp than she is right there in the edge o' Jacksonville. Maybe better off there. At least she's got family and somebuddy that gives a hoot about her. Little Mose don't think o' nobuddy but Mose B. F. Barber and you know hit, Mose."

Andrew Jackson told him they didn't have any carpetbaggers taking over Orange County but they did have some scalawags by the name of Mizell that were just as bad. Taxes had gone up and land was worthless.

"I had to laugh at one of the neighbors over west o' here. She said she had the surveyor there and she had to keep an eye on him fer fear he'd throw in a couple extra acres on her. Then them Mizell's a'runnin' the county could git a few extra dollars to build a road. That's all they talk about is putting more roads and maybe running the railroad down here. I wish they'd leave the country jest like hit is. First thing you know the place'll be full o' Yankees and land speculators."

Andrew Jackson told him he needed to go by his plantation at the Kissimmee Bog.

"John and Mary's talking bout moving on down there with Francis and Champ. I'd go, too, but Ma here won't think o' it and I'm a'gittin' along fine the way hit is fer now."

But Mose decided if he went over into Orlando he and the Mizells might end up "gettin' into hit" and he headed east toward Fort Christmas.

Sunday morning found Mose camped on the side of Lake Pickett and he decided to head straight for church. He knew the cow crew should be working cattle somewhere between Fort Christmas and Ocean Prairie, but one more day wouldn't matter and he just might be lucky and hit Fort Christmas during one of their all day sings and dinner on the ground.

He was right, they had finished up the morning sermon and closing song and Mr. Bryant was saying the closing prayer.

"Lord keep us and bind us, tie our shirttails behind us and throw us in the bushes where the devil cain't find us."

The feast was spread out on the benches under a tree by the side of the church. Mose was hungry for some good home cooking and there was plenty for everyone. Someone had brought a stew of meat with baby carrots, onions and a pot of rice. Mose had two helpings and thought it was the best dish he had ever eaten and inquired around until he found Mrs. Canada who had brought it.

"I'm tellin' you, Mrs. Canada, thet's the best tastin' dish I ever tasted. What on earth was in hit? Hit shore was lairipin'."

She looked at him and smiled, her eyes dancing mischievously at her little joke. "Hit's somethin' I bet you ain't et much of lately, Mr. Barber," she told him.

"And what is thet, Mrs. Canada?"

"Some o' yore own beef" and laughed at her joke.

"You jest might be right about that," he told her and enjoyed the joke along with her. Mose knew that it was the custom for pioneers to kill another man's beef now and then but only when it was necessary for something to eat. What he frowned on was changing brands to increase the herd. To him that was down right stealing and a hanging offense.

He slipped on down to the dessert end of the table and looked over all the pies, cakes and cobblers. He couldn't make up his mind which to take so he headed for a cup of coffee before he made a decision and when he got back Mrs. Henry Hodges approached him.

"I seen you a eyein' all them goodies, Mr. Barber. Why don't you try a piece or two o' one o' my tater pies. I'll cut one fer you. Which one you want? I got kivvered, open-faced and cross-barred, all tater. Ain't nothin' better'n' tater pie."

Mose decided they looked so good he'd try one of each, just so's as not to play favorites.

He went home with the John R. A. Tucker family for the night and sat on the front porch, listening to their oldest son play the fiddle. Yes sir, he was certainly glad to be back "home" with real folks, he told them.

The next morning he crossed the Totosahatchee, Jim Creek and at Long Bluff, he went by to check on old man Savage.

"Why, Mr. Savage," Mose told him, when he rode up in the yard where the old man was hoeing, "I plum almost didn't recognize you. What happened to yore beard?"

Mr. Savage had had a long white beard for years and it had been his pride and joy. Mose couldn't imagine the old man without it. All Mr. Savage had left was just a short bit of gray stubble and his face was redder than usual. Mose decided the old man's skin had been hid for so long under the mass of gray hair that he had been out in the sun and his face had blistered. But Mr. Savage had a different tale to tell.

He spit out his tobacco and started in. "'T'was a freakish accident that done hit in. I'd put a fairly good price on my old gray gelding, me not needin' to sell him or nothin'." He paused to get Mose's nod to agree with him.

Mose nodded his head as expected of him, all the time taking in the dilapidated front steps and rags hanging over the windows for curtains.

"Anyways, man come by the house 'bout a month ago, lookin' fer a good horse an I told him if'n he come back, I'd have my old horse in good shape and he could take a good look at him. Meantime I got the horse up and commenced to feed him corn and molasses to git his hair all slicked up and fill him out some. Bless Pat, the day 'fore the man wuz supposed to come look, he come up with his mane and tail plum full o' burrs and matted all up. Biggest mess you ever seen. I flew in and was a'gittin' 'em out. I had his tail tied up to the rafters o' the barn a pickin' away an decided to rest a mite and lit my pipe. Bout the same time that old horse farted, him full o' corn an molasses, you know." The old man paused for Mose to take in the picture, and nod his head in anticipation. "A big blue flame flashed out, the gas a settin' afar from my match, my beard caught on far and so did the horse's tail. I commenced a tryin' to beat 'em both out but the old horse broke loose and took off and I run stuck by head down in the water-trough and put out my beard. Look at me?" he laughed. "Naked as a jay bird."

"Man take the horse?" Mose asked, laughing.

"By golly, he did. Said the tail'd grow back and in the meantime he'd have another tale to tell."

"You know," laughed Mose. "Wonder what'd happen if the whole world farted at one time?"

"Be one hell of a' explosion, won't hit?" agreed Mr. Savage and the two were almost in hysterics from laughing.

Mose accepted the invitation to stay for dinner, the cracker's noon meal. They were at the water-shelf, washing up, and old man Savage grabbed a rag from a nail and was washing his face.

"Git you one o' them rags and clean up if you like," he invited Mose.

Mose eyed the rags suspiciously and thought of his departed son, Isiah. Isiah would never let Leah wash his face away from home.

"Thet might be sumbuddy's old tail rag, Ma," he objected.

Hygiene facilities being what they were then, many families used wash clothes sparingly. There was usually one for the face and body above the waist and one used on the area below used repeatedly for a week. So Mose declined the use of the other rag, smiling sadly at the memory of his long lost oldest son. He splashed on water and dried on the fresh roller towel.

During the meal, the talk turned to taxes and land.

"I'm too old to try to change things, Mose. I cain't keep up with all I have to do around here as hit is. More overtakes a man than he can overtake, when he gits old."

Mose agreed. "The Bible says, 'Sufficient unto the day is the evil thereof.' Hit gits harder every day, jest to make the day, don't hit?"

When Mose hit the trail the next day, he was sure he'd come across his cow crew somewhere nearby. But just as he crossed Wolf Creek, he ran into old man Monroe Partin's crew with a small group of cattle. Monroe was lame and instead of getting down off his horse to urinate, he simply let it fly over the side of the saddle and it would sometimes run down the horse's withers and the hot sun brought out the odor.

When two crews met in the woods with their cattle, they drew close enough so that the cattle in one bunch could see the cows in the other. When this happened, usually a little scrub bull would come out of the bunch to defend his herd from a bull in the other. The two crews would "howdy," starved for news and gossip and, at the same time, check the other crew's herd for evidence of theft. So they would stand aside and watch the two little bulls fight, as men would stand around and watch a cock fight, or as it was in the past, watch two Mandingo slaves wrestle. The little bulls weren't very large, maybe half as big as most bulls of today and were of varied colors, being mixed breeds. There were roans, brindles, and pied, but seldom a solid color. The men would sometimes bet on the color they thought would win. The bulls' horns weren't as long as our present breeds, or as heavy but they were sharp as needles, nevertheless, and they were wild and fierce and didn't back away from a fight. They would charge out of their respective herds with their heads bowed to one side, eyes bulging and their tongues sticking out, bellowing as if in mortal agony. They would paw the ground, throwing sand and glaring at each other. This posturing was as much a part of their defense as their needle-sharp horns. If one did not bluff the other away, then, getting down to serious combat, they would lock horns, butt their head together like two mountain goats until one turned tail and ran. Rarely, one actually killed the other or mortally wounded him.

As Mose was visiting with the Partin crew, they spied another crew coming across the woods and waited for them to get close enough until Mose decided it wasn't his crew after all but another.

With this outfit was a little retarded boy named Sampson Savage. He had become a little difficult to control at home as he grew into puberty, and had been allowed to more or less run wild. The cow crew had let him take up with them and follow along with them on foot, barefooted. Someone bought him a pair of shoes but he kept losing them so they gave up and let him run through the woods barefooted. They saw that he was fed and shared a bedroll or else he'd sleep on the ground like a little animal. He had become tough and strong physically from living in the wild and running all day but, mentally and emotionally, he was just a little boy. He had noticed the practice of a bull leaving the herd to defend his harem when two herds met in the woods, so he started imitating the little bull yearlings. He'd get down on his hands and knees and meet the herd, bellowing, pawing the dirt with his hands and hooking at the palmettos until his ears would be bloody.

Mose and the boys sat, waiting for the other crew to arrive, when Sampson came out from around the herd, bellowing and pawing the ground. Mose was dumbfounded until someone explained what the boy was trying to do.

"Sumbuddy'd better teach thet idiot a lesson 'fore he git hisself kilt," Mose suggested.

So Jackie Hancock got down off his horse and went out to meet Sampson, bellowing and pawing, in hopes the youngster would see how ridiculous he looked and stand up and act like a human being.

But instead of giving up his fantasy, Sampson matched his opponent bellow for bellow, pawing the ground in wild abandonment and when they were about three feet apart, Sampson gave a mighty leap and caught the cowboy squarely on top of the head and laid him out cold. Then nonchalantly got up and walked back to the herd, apparently unscathed—the victor. It took the better part of twenty minutes for Jackie to come around well enough to get back on his horse and ride on.

And so, Mose did the same. Along the St. Johns River marsh, he passed rookeries of great blue herons, snowy egrets and wood ibises with their immense wing spread. There were elder bushes and willows and, sometimes, acres of soft blue pickerelweeds. In the swamps he'd have to work his way around trees, blown down by the wind, covered with vines, and laced with spider webs, spun by giant brown and yellow spiders, and tough as a fiddle string. The silence of the swamps was broken only by the splash of a deer as it flagged across a shallow run and the occasional cry of a hawk or crows. When he reached the far side of Ocean Pond, he came across a sawmill, and who should he find but little Jane Green. Jane wasn't little anymore, having married James Green back in Columbia County. She had been an orphan like Becky and Priscilla Ivey, but instead of settling down once she found someone to love and protect her, she had left her husband over on the coast near Fort Capron and was following the sawmill crew and selling her favors to anyone who happened to have the price and sometimes giving them away if she liked the man. She was still looking for love, but in the wrong places.

Knowing Mose had plenty of money, or at least he always had, she quickly set a price and he just as quickly agreed. And so, he had made a connection now for female companionship in Brevard County.

The sawmill crew had seen his cow crew just the day before over near Jernigan-Tyner Slough, so he set out in that direction.

On the way he met old man Norton, no close relative of his neighbor to the north who had long since expired. When Mose first saw him, he couldn't believe his eyes. Wonder who in the hell that is? Whoever hit is is as lost as a fart in a whirlwind. But Mr. Norton knew where he was going—he had simply lost his transportation to get there and he was riding "Shank's mare." Mr. Norton was walking. He had walked from Fort Bassenger. It seems he had strayed, alone, too close to Croft Bass's outfit and they had taken out after him with, according to old man Norton's account, "Killin' on their mind." Mose took the old man's account of that with a grain of salt although it was well known in those parts that no one wandered into Croft Bass's territory unless well-armed or with some sort of protection. When Croft's riders saw a lone rider like Mr. Norton, they probably decided to have some fun and started chasing him. His horse had almost given out and it appeared they were going to catch him so he jumped off and rolled over into a very large palmetto patch. The palmettos were high and the roots stood three or four feet off the ground. When they saw that his horse had no rider, they pulled up and began to beat the bushes. When they were unable to find the poor, frightened, cornered man, they got madder than ever and set fire to the woods. Mr. Norton said he stuck his head under the tall palmetto roots, pulled his hat down over his face and prayed, thinking to make a dash for freedom would mean certain death and probably would have at this stage of the game. The earth was damp in the palmetto patch and only the green palms burned. His hair had been singed and his hands burned, but he had survived. He had walked out under cover of darkness, as they had taken his horse. Years later this particular Croft Bass, as there were two of them, uncle and nephew, would cut up a man at Holo-paw and leave the country for Montana. So perhaps old man Norton hadn't pan-icked after all. Brevard County was a lawless county and full of wild and dangerous people. It was every man for himself. Mose thrived on the excitement and here he could once again be "old Ring under the wagon." He had already made up his mind he was never going back to Baker County to live. "I'm tired of suckin' the hind tit, an fightin' my head, a tryin' to make a livin' in Baker County. The damned Yankees can have hit!"

Chapter 25

Priscilla had not heard from John Randolph during the time he was in prison and it was several weeks after he got back before he came to call on her. That past winter she had gone to work as a housekeeper for Crawford Bass—not the one from Fort Bassenger, but his uncle. Croft's wife had died, leaving him a small son to raise, so Priscilla, needing a place to live and a little independence from her family, had jumped at the chance to be self-sufficient. Especially not to feel that she had to accept a handout from old man David Mizell.

The day that John came to see his son, Priscilla felt an initial excitement and became flustered on seeing him after such a long time. After all, although pale and thin from having been in prison, he was still a handsome man. But after the formalities were over and John had picked up his little son and tried to hug him, putting him down when he cried, she began to study him objectively and not without some feeling of hostility. John had started in, explaining his inability to get back to marry her and quizzing her, almost suspiciously as to why she didn't let him know she was pregnant. She became more and more defensive.

"I done told you, John Randolph, why I didn't let you know in time. I didn't even know myself before you left. You had plenty of time to marry me if you had wanted to. You didn't have to wait until I got with child and you had to do it. It seems to me you took off in a hell fired hurry to go fight without even bringing up the subject. Personally, I don't think marriage would ever have crossed your mind unless somebuddy had caught us in the act and made you do it. You told me you loved me and I believed you. I thought marriage always followed what you and me did that day at Lake Mann."

"That is what I've come here today to do, Priscilla. Ask you to marry me and give my son a name. Everyone has told me how much he looks like my mother. I know he's a Mizell and I want to do the right thing by offering you the sanctity of marriage and the honor of becoming my wife."

Priscilla felt her face become more flushed with anger than before and her eyes blazed like a flash of cold steel.

"I've got along pretty well so far, Mr. John Randolph Mizell, Mr. Big. I know you don't love me and never did. I don't want a loveless marriage, leastwise with you and your better-than-thou family. I cared for you deeply and it was a long time dyin'. I don't know but what it really died a sure death until just right now. Our son's almost three years old and he don't even know who you are. Yore family considers me trash and half the women in this country don't even speak to me because of you. You know I come from a good family. We're cousins and my folks were just as much quality as yours are. It's not my fault they didn't live long enough to give me a good home and raise me to stay clear of the likes of you. All I wanted was someone to love and give me a good home. I was jerked up by the hair of the head and shipped from pillar to post. A girl don't stand a chance in this world if she ain't got a Ma or a Pa to stand up for her. She's nobuddy and fair game. I guess I'm as much to blame as you are. I knew I was doin' wrong and should have stopped you but I just couldn't. I wanted you to love me then, but I don't love you now and I don't want you to touch me, you understand?"

She stood and glared at him and he said nothing, waiting for her to calm down.

"Mr. Bass has already asked me to marry him. I never gave it much thought until now but I think I'm going to accept his offer. I guess I had it in the back of my mind to wait until you got home and see what you'd do. I can see now there's no warmth or love in you and I see no reason for us to marry and make both of us miserable."

"What about my son, Priscilla? What's to become of him?"

"You mean our son, don't you John? Mr. Bass has grown fond of him same as me and he'd give the boy a good home. He don't know nobuddy else as it is and it'd work out just fine and dandy."

John was furious at the thought of another man raising his son but he saw it would do no good to try to talk to Priscilla in the state she was in.

"I think I have the right to see that he at least takes my name," he told her.

"I don't know that you have any right. You think that little bit of hand-out I got from you alone gives you the right?"

"I am his biological father, that's what gives me the right and don't you forget it COUSIN Priscilla. More of the same blood runs through his veins than any son you'll ever have by Croft Bass and there are laws that protect a father and son, natural or not. Need I warn you about that?"

"I'm not denying you your son, John. You can come visit him anytime you want. I'll see that he grows up knowing who his daddy is. As to him taking your name, he don't need no name right now other than what we call him. When he's old enough to decide what he wants to be called, I'll let him decide. Right now he answers to 'Mann' and that's all that's necessary."

"Well," John said in a threatening tone, "we'll see. You're wise to not try to deny me visitation rights. I want to see him from time to time and see that he has proper clothing," eyeing the little boy in the thin patched gown. "I know my rights and where I stand in the matter, so don't fight me on this. I can win, hands down."

They were out on the porch now and Priscilla had picked up little Mann and held him close as she stood and watched John go down the steps.

"Goodbye, son" he said as he turned and waved to the little boy. "I'll be back," he said to Priscilla.

Little Mann waved his hand half-heartily and politely said "bye-bye" as he had been taught to do, gazing innocently at the tall blond stranger as he mounted his horse and rode off. Priscilla was crying now, and he put his little hands up to her face to brush away the tears and gave his mama a big "bear hug."

Even as far south as Orange County, Reconstruction had reached its arm down into the south and brought its bitterness, hatred and vindictiveness. There were few rules in the absence of Federal troops and civil government had all but vanished, what little there had ever been. John Randolph had an itch for office and believed cooperation with the radical government was the quickest and easiest way to success, so when offered the office of judge of Orange County, he jumped at the chance. Harrison Reed, then the governor of Florida, himself a Yankee, realizing that some form of fiscal responsibility was needed if the area around Central Florida was to develop in an orderly fashion, had made the appointment. John Mizell, although a native born Floridian and an ex-Confederate army officer, was intelligent, responsible and very ambitious. He became an excellent pawn in the hands of Governor Reed.

John Ivey, son of Robert Ivey, Priscilla's uncle out on Lake Mann, was the county sheriff. A log courthouse had been built in Orlando during the war and in the little two-room cabin with a dirt floor, John Mizell and John Ivey, distant cousins, held court. John Ivey arrested the criminals and John Mizell sentenced them. That is until John Mizell sentenced one to hang and John Ivey was told that was his job and he refused to hang a man.

"I'm a God fearin' man and raised to keep his commandments and I will not kill another man, even in the line of duty, less, perhaps, in self-defense."

John Mizell's older brother, David, who desperately needed the job, agreed to do it.

"I don't mind hanging a man if he's got it comin'. If my brother and twelve of his peers say he's got it comin', then I'll hang him."

So, Governor Reed appointed Dave Mizell sheriff of Orange County. The Mizell brothers and their father, David Jr., joined the scalawag force of law and order.

Politics being what it is, ineptness and corruption existed in Orange County as it does most places from time to time. Mrs. Harris, who lived near Fort Gatlin and was Andrew Jackson's neighbor, was right about the surveyors throwing in another acre or two of land when they came out to survey. Mose found out he had a lot more land than he ever had. There was free range and his cattle could roam anywhere they wanted as the local farmers kept their fields fenced in to keep the cattle out. Just the opposite as it is now. They would occasionally let the cattle in to sleep on their land at night, turning them out to graze in the day. This way, when the cattle got to their feet in the morning, they would spread their manure on the land and it became a cheap way for the farmers to fertilize their land before planting.

There had already been a meeting of the minds and everyone was in agreement that the men who owned the most land could help pay for the necessary roads, schools and other necessities. And one of these men was Mose Barber.

The war had drained most people's pockets and they knew that Mose was bound to have money, having shipped cattle during the war to the highest bidder. And he was still shipping out cattle every fall. So it was open season on Mose and the few men in the country that had land. There was such a thing as the homestead law and that's about the only kind of people that had settled Central Florida—homesteaders with a few acres and no money. The county was glad to have a man like Mose Barber moving in.

He immediately made a trip to the courthouse and confronted the local tax collector. This happened to be David Mizell, Jr., chairman of the board of County Commissioners.

Mose was even madder than ever, seeing who was trying to collect all that tax money. "I ain't a payin' no more'n the next feller. Quinn Bass and Henry Overstreet's got almost as much land as I've got and they ain't a payin' all that kind o' taxes and I ain't either. I'll pay my fair share but no more."

"But your cattle roam from one tip of Orange County to the other, Mr. Barber, and for free."

"And so does every other Tom, Dick and Harry," Mose argued. "I ain't got thet kind o' money. You cain't git blood from a turnip."

"You can sell some of those cattle, Mr. Barber," H. G. Partin, one of the other county commissioners told him, as he stormed out the door.

Mose went back by Isaac's and was surprised at his attitude.

"You might as well pay up, Pa. They'll git hit one way or another." And this was good advice. They started collecting Mose's cattle and selling them in lieu of payment. Mose got a lawyer and found he had no recourse but to pay, as Isaac had predicted, "one way or another."

Mose had already sworn to himself he'd give the land away before he'd pay that kind of taxes and so that's exactly what he did.

Priscilla had married Croft Bass, as she had thought seriously of doing after John Mizell's visit, and the next time Croft brought up the subject, she said, "Yes." So Mose gave part of his place where his plantation had stood to Priscilla and Croft. The rest of his land to the east to the Lake he gave to Andrew Jackson. That day he went to John Mizell's office and announced he was giving his son something he would not do himself, a home and land to make a living on. Of course, John Mizell was livid and for a while, Mose was the happiest man in Central Florida.

Chapter 26

1867 was a good year for Mose, for a change. He had rid himself of his land in Orange County and along with it went his tax problems, he thought. Andrew Jackson and his mother moved from Conway to the western shore of East Lake Tohopekaliga near Crop Prairie and Jack, as he preferred to be called, had planted a seedling orange grove. It was close enough to Orlando for Susan and far enough away from civilization for Jack.

Croft and Priscilla had started a family and were evidently happy with their situation. John Mizell still had his nose out of joint because it was all over the county that Mose Barber had given little Mann, Priscilla's and John's love-child, a house and enough land for a small farm. Of course, the land had to be put in Croft's name. Women were not allowed to hold land if they had a husband. But in a round about way, Mose had given property to two of the women he admired the most and he felt like a king for having done it.

That fall, after the big roundup, Mose had gone back to Baker County and had it out with Becky. There was no formal separation but they "agreed to disagree" and he told her to run things anyway she pleased. The house and land were still in his name but it was to be hers to manage and live on as long as she wanted. Of course, she couldn't sell it but she was so far behind on taxes and payments, Mose knew it would only be a matter of time until it would be gone. He washed his hands of Baker County for good and went back "home" to Brevard County. No one knew he still had gold buried at the old home place that would someday briefly drag him back, but he decided that it was safer there than trying to dig it up and move it the long journey south and, so, for then, he let it lie buried. Only Isaac knew where it was. Now with Isiah gone, he felt Isaac was the one son he could truly trust.

Mose had decided he had things pretty well going his way now. He had his cattle, that were free to roam the length and breadth of Florida south of the Oklawaha River, and he didn't have to pay taxes or buy the land they grazed on. He needed no formal home. Most of the time, he slept out under the stars with a mosquito netting over his head. Actually, from May to September in the south end of Brevard he had to wear a mosquito net over his hat and crammed down under his shirt collar until ten a.m. and after four in the afternoon. He had a headquarters, after a fashion, at Canoe Creek Island and sets of cypress pole pens scattered about the countryside with a shed for cover when it rained.

He paid his crew a dollar a day and board and gave them two beeves a year to butcher for the family. He branded Needham Yates' twenty head of heifer calves each spring and ten head for Lyle Padgett, his second man in charge.

Abe Johnson, William Cook and Jake Summerlin also had pens scattered around the countryside and anyone was welcome to hold and work their cattle there, provided they kept them in good repair. And cypress poles came cheap in Central Florida.

Isaac joined the crew when they worked cattle in his territory. Thomas Johnson, Abe's boy, did the same. Farther south, Champ and Francis joined in. In the big roundup when they shipped cattle to Punta Rassa, everyone went along.

If there was a central location where everyone more or less came together, it was the little community of Sawgrass, which started about three and a half miles east of the present site of Holopaw where the sawmill crew stayed and where Jane Green cooked and held court.

After having left Mose's plantation, John and Mary Barber had built a home at the south side of Ocean Prairie at Crabgrass. From there, Crabgrass Creek flowed in an easterly direction for about six miles until it made a ninety degree turn south for three miles, made a loop and joined Bull Creek. In this loop, Mose had built a set of pens and a cow camp. The junction where the two creeks met and flowed east into the St. Johns River formed a large swamp because of the overflow of the two major creeks and several small ones. A small portion of this swamp was so thick one could not see the sun and it came to be called the "puzzle." Many men could not find their way out of it, and the only way they could be found was by blowing a horn made out of a cow's horn. Someone on the outside would answer with the same and they could work their way out onto dry land. The one creek formed by the junction of all the creeks that flowed through the middle of this large swamp would someday be known as Jane Green Creek, and the swamp, Jane Green Swamp. The swampy areas surrounding the creeks at the loop made a natural cover from the winter winds and formed a funnel for the cattle to be herded into the pens.

South of here, on the north end of Lake Marion, Abe Johnson had his large set of pens and William Cook's were on the south side of Lake Kissimmee at a site known as Turkey Hammock.

Needham Yates and his brother, Burrel, had settled near Lake Gentry, not too far from Isaac on the point that jutted out into Lake Tohopekaliga. There was a set of pens at Isaac's and also at Burrel's, and of course Mose had some at Canoe Creek Island. The cattlemen felt as much at home in the vast counties of Brevard and East Orange as a New Yorker did in his section of New York City. All the major lakes such as Alligator, the two Tohopekaligas, Gentry, Winder, Poinsett, Marion, Cypress, Hatchineha, and Kissimmee had been named. All the creeks, that many times didn't resemble a creek to outsiders, had a name. The sloughs that flow into the creeks had names and many of the swamps as well. Even some of the distinctive cypress ponds were named. Mose could talk with anyone who was planning to go into his territory and tell him where he would be or where to meet him at a specific time and place giving no more than part of a day for error.

This large area was generally Mose's habitat now and he called "home" any-where he took off his hat. He had no reason to go into town at Orlando but he did like to visit with Susan and he spent a good deal of his idle hours at Isaac's and Harriet's. Mose Jr. had rather stay at Needham Yates's home since he and

Needham Jr. had become close friends. He and Jane Green had become close also and that's where most of his money went at the end of the large roundup in the fall.

Isaac had built a comfortable home similar to the one he was raised in up in Columbia County. Harriet, being of good German stock, had taken to the Florida territory with enthusiasm. She stayed busy with her daily chores, not minding the long days and nights when Isaac was away in the woods. She had three children now. Little Joe was seven, Henry was five, and Ellen, three. Isaac had been disappointed in Ellen's being a girl. He wanted a big family of sons to help him in the cattle business just as he had helped Mose when he was starting out. But Harriet was glad it was a girl who could help her around the house when she got older and she had promised Isaac there would be plenty of time for more boys.

Some of the pioneer women did not have it as good as Harriet. It was clearly a man's world and many men took advantage of this fact and gave no quarter when it came to their "woman."

One morning Mose and Isaac had left the camp at Canoe Creek and were going back to Isaac's when they heard a woman's cry, "Hello, over tha-a-r!"

"Did you hear somethin', Pa?" Isaac pulled up his horse and raised his hand in the air for silence. About the time he thought he had been hearing things, Mose heard it.

"You over thar, come y'har!" Not seeing a wagon or horse, they ran in the direction of the cry that appeared to be coming from an oak tree on a rise at the edge of a little marshy pond. And there they found Mrs. Dubie, sitting on the ground, tied to the oak. Isaac was off his horse and by her side in a flash.

"You been robbed, Mrs. Dubie? Where's yore horse and wagon and Mr. Dubie?"

"That there Mr. Dubie done this to me, Mr. Barber," she told him, as Isaac began to untie the rope.

"Hold up a minute, son." Mose told him. "You say wuz Mr. Dubie tied you up and left you like this?"

"Shore wuz. He told me last night he was a leavin' afore day to go to the Laniers to see about some hogs. I put in commencing to beg him to let me go and he said he'd think about hit cum morning, but he got up this morning an wuz a sneakin' out without me and when I cornered him bout hit, he told me I didn't have no business goin'. Said he had some business to tend to and I didn't have no sense 'bout sech stuff in the first place. I been down here in these woods now fer weeks and ain't seed nobuddy 'cept him and the boys and they're gone all the time. All I wanted wuz a chance to howdy with Mrs. Lanier while the men wuz a talkin' business. I follered along behind him fer quite a spell until he caught sight o' me a crossin' that flat back there and he tied me up this way until he could git back and pick me up. Said hit would teach me a lesson to disobey him."

Isaac looked at his daddy, waiting for him to say something. Her hands were tied together by a rope that was tied up on the highest limb of a little oak, just like a monkey on a tether. She had room to stand up and move around but couldn't run away or untie the rope.

"We'd like to untie you, Mrs. Dubie," Mose finally said, "but we can't come between a man and his wife. We untie you and he'd find out we done hit and it'd be the devil to pay. You understand that, don't you? Ain't fer us to say 'bout how a man chastises his wife. We may not agree with him, but hit's his business an we cain't interfere."

"How long you been tied up like this, Ma'm?" Isaac asked as he poured her a drink of water and held the little metal cup up to her lips.

She drank greedily, the water pouring down her chin and looked up at the sky.

"Best part o' the morning, I'd say. He oughter be gittin' back along in a couple a 'ourers."

"You gittin' hongry? We got sumpin' here to eat if you like," Isaac offered. He felt so sorry for the older lady. He'd never think of doing such a thing to a woman.

"Not particularly, but I could stand a dip of snuff. There's some in my back pocket o' my apron. I jest cain't git to hit and me tied up like this."

Isaac took the snuff and pinched her out a dip and stuck it under her lower lip. She smiled and sat back down in the shade of the oak that would, for the better part of a century, be called the Dubie Oak.

She seemed resigned to her fate.

"Guess that'll hold me 'til he comes back fer me, and much obliged. Hit shore hits the spot."

Isaac reluctantly got back on his horse and they started on their way.

"I shore cain't say much about how old man Dubie treats his wife, Pa."

"Hit's his business and ain't fer us to say how he handles hit."

Isaac said no more but he suspected Mose admired the old man for the way he had handled the situation, knowing his Pa. He remembered a similar situation over near Ox Creek. They had gone by the Crosby's homestead. It had been extra dry and fresh water in the woods was hard to come by. Mr. Crosby had a good well and they decided to swing by there and get a cool drink and fill up their jugs for coffee water.

Mr. Crosby and family were plowing 'taters, literally. Mrs. Crosby and the three children, ages six to nine, were pulling the plow and Mr. Crosby was pushing it.

"Mr. Crosby!" yelled Thomas Johnson, "Don't you know yore supposed to use a horse fer that!" And all the men laughed but Isaac. He didn't think there was anything to laugh about.

The old man would stop every eight to ten feet and say, "Whoa" as if talking to a horse and kick a potato or two out from the dirt. He finally drove the plow into a resting position and told his wife and children to hold up.

"You men can laugh all you want. My old horse done took sick and I had to git these 'taters in so's my young'uns can have somethin' to eat. I got to git me some greens into these beds so's my little gal there can have some come winter. She gits to lookin' mighty pale and puny. Somethin' wrong with her blood and she cain't make hit on corn and 'taters." The poor child probably had hookworms and was anemic.

"I got a horse I can let you keep 'til yore's gits better, " Isaac offered.

Old man Abe Johnson felt ashamed and offered his, since he lived closer to the Crosbys.

"I'd shore appreciate hit, Mr. Johnson, and thank you fer your offer, Isaac. Them young'uns thought hit wuz fun fer bout the first hour and then the new begun to wear off and hit got like hard work." He turned to his wife, the sweat running down from under her bonnet and dripping from her chin. "Go draw Mr. Barber and them boys some o' that sweet well water. That's what you men cum fer, weren't hit?"

Isaac was on the ground by the well. "Never you mind, Mrs. Crosby, we can draw our own. You jest set a spell. Looks like you and them young'uns is plum tuckered out."

She walked over and got in the shade of the building and agreed it was getting mighty hot. Then she noticed a hard look from her husband and got up and announced she had to go get supper on.

Mr. Crosby dutifully offered to have her cook for the entire crew "such as hit is" but the men thanked him and started on down the trail.

"I think we got just enough daylight left to make a round before we go in," said Mose. "Now that's the kind a woman to have, boys. I bet when old man Crosby say, 'shit,' she squats and strains. No questions asked."

"And after about ten more young'uns and she gits sick and dies on him like his old horse, he'll have hisself another wife," said Lyle Padgett. "This one's his third, I think, and hit won't take long 'fore she's wore out."

Not all the husbands treated their wives like Mr. Dubie and Mr. Crosby, but it was a hard life, nevertheless, and no place for the fainthearted.

In September, the weather turned bad. Low clouds were scurrying southward across the sky line little puffs of gray smoke. An occasional squall would rip through the countryside and each time, the wind would increase until it stung Mose, Isaac and Little Mose's faces. They were coming back from the fall roundup and Little Mose was anxious to get cleaned up and head for the sawmill and Jane Green. They were bringing in a small group of bull yearlings to castrate into steers and Isaac was looking forward to some real "mountain oysters" that Mose explicitly called "bull nuts."

By the time they reached Isaac's pens the wind was blowing at a gale force and the whitecaps on the lake danced across the open waters and lapped up on the shore like a tide was pulling them in. Jason had already dragged Isaac's little fishing boat out of the water's edge and onto a high sandy ridge. They turned their horses into the crivis with the yearlings and the other horses that were already standing with their tails to the wind and began to brace themselves against its force. Rain had started coming down in white sheets and by the time they had battened down the gates and barn doors, the lake had risen nearly to the oak trees at the edge of the front yard. Harriet had managed to cook in spite of the water coming down the chimney and they huddled at the kitchen table away from the windows as the light began to fade, and it was only four o'clock in the afternoon.

Little Joe cried as he peered out of the window and saw his swing hit the ground and disappear under a huge oak that fell silently as if some giant hand had picked it up and laid it gently down on the ground.

"Get away from that window, Joe," she cried as she jerked him over into the center of the parlor. "That glass can bust outa there and cut yore head off."

All that could be heard was the howling of the wind. They grappled around in the dark and found their bedrolls and rolled them out into the spare room that was in the far side of the house from the direction the wind was blowing. They had to shout to each other. Rain was pouring down the chimney in buckets and she had already used up all of her spare rags and the hooked rugs to sop it up. Even then, some of it was running out into the room in little black rivulets. They finally got the children to sleep in the corner of the room and most everyone had quieted down. It was useless to try to carry on a conversation. In the light of a lightening flash, Isaac saw the cowshed swallowed up in the wind and Harriet thought she saw birds flying by and realized they were shingles off the roof of the barn. The door from the walk to the kitchen blew open and Little Mose and Isaac finally got it fastened down before it blew off its hinges.

Harriet lay down and tried to sleep but she kept getting up and looking out to see if the kitchen was still there and any of the sheds left standing. The men were all snoring as if they didn't have a care in the world. After all, they probably thought, let Harriet worry. It's her house and her responsibility. She could feel the house lift up as if taking a deep breath and then shudder as it rested back down. She wondered if, in the next lift, it would fly up in the air and they'd be carried off and land somewhere out in the crivis.

She finally fell asleep from exhaustion, listening to the scream of the wind and wondering if the house could explode and crush them all in their sleep.

They awoke about day to an eerie silence. The wind had stopped and the rain was gone. Harriet ran to the window and looked outside. Moss and leaves and limbs covered the yard as far as she could see. Trees were uprooted and snapped off everywhere. There goes my shade in the afternoon, she thought. The chickens were running around on the few patches of high ground, their feathers drooping, trying to catch a few bugs for their breakfast. The frogs were screeching even though it was daylight and they were hopping all over the front porch. The lake was right up to the front steps and under the house. She heard the milk cow low for her feed, wondering what had happened to her stanchion and her shed. She didn't need milking, as the calf had gotten to her in the night. The fences were down and all the cattle and horses scattered.

"Maybe I can git enough milk fer the young'uns' breakfast," she told Isaac and grabbed the milk bucket.

"You best look out fer snakes, Harriet," Mose warned her. "They'll be lookin' fer high ground. Let me git my pistol and go with you."

And he had been right. The water moccasins had taken over the barn. He and

Jason killed six in the first half hour. Isaac and Little Mose were out, trying to get the trees off the fence and patch it up so they could catch the horses and pen the yearlings. She sent Jason to pick up some wood to see if she could get a fire started for coffee. The children wanted to get out and see all the damage but she said they'd have to wait until some of the adults could go with them.

"I don't want you young'uns a'gittin' on a snake. They're probably all over the place. It won't take long for the water to go down."

But it took weeks to get the place back in order. For once Little Mose tended to business and stayed and helped, in spite of his much-anticipated rendezvous with Jane Green. Of course, the fact that Mose threatened and shamed him didn't hurt much.

"I swear, Little Mose, if we cut yore head open to see what wuz inside I wouldn't be surprised to see hit wuz stuffed with nothin' but cock hairs."

The sweet potatoes that had been so carefully "hilled" inside the crib for the winter were soaking wet. When the potatoes were dug at summer's end, they were put in the corncrib on the highest, best-drained spot. A mound of dirt was piled up and hay placed on top of it for a bed. The potatoes were put on the hay and covered with corn shucks, tent fashion, and dirt piled on top of them to complete the hill. Here the sweet potatoes would get even sweeter through the winter and each time Harriet needed a batch, which was almost daily, Joe and Henry would go out and dig the dirt from a hole they had started in the hill, careful to cover the hole back up with dirt to shut out the cold. Now the potatoes were all wet and exposed and they would have to be dug out and dried on the porch before they ruined. This would be a catastrophe, as they were an essential part of the diet.

Luckily, the smoke house roof had not blown off, having been protected by the taller barn so the hams and beef jerky were still high and dry. But Isaac decided he'd better build a fire to "dry things out," just in case.

Harriet had survived her first hurricane and she would live well into the next century to see many, many more.

One evening before Mose Jr. left for Holopaw, they felt they had a little spare time to go hunting. Little Joe and Henry begged to go and Mose decided he'd take Joe under his wing, if Isaac could put up with little Henry.

They went off east of the house where they had been seeing turkeys and decided a good mess of fried turkey breast would taste extra good. The men scattered to their selected spots at the edge of a long strand of pines in the bend of a cypress swamp where the tallest trees grew. Isaac and Henry sat on a log and leaned back, listening for the tell-tale "flap, flap, flap" of a turkey's wings in the still dusk, when they heard a snap as something fairly heavy landed on a log and then splashed the water. It was a young deer, probably separated from its mother during the storm. Isaac cautioned Henry to sit very still and raised his gun with intentions of killing him and then lowered it as he noticed its size and wondered if it was sick or fevered from an injury. He had started to settle back and let it go when something caught the corner of his eye. It was a panther, moving cautiously in the edge of the tall grass that grew along the edge of the pond. She would stop, tail twitching nervously, and then slink along with her head dipping to the ground and freeze motionless. Then she would slip closer to her prey. Isaac and Henry watched, fascinated, as the pair vanished from sight around a clump of myrtles. In less than a minute, they heard sounds of thrashing, the shrill short shriek of the deer and then almost total silence. The birds hushed their last minute chirping as they usually do while settling in for the night. In a few minutes, the panther appeared out on the hill by the swamp, her front legs straddling the deer carcass, as she dragged it along the ground by its throat, clutched between her powerful jaws. She dragged it to the edge of a clump of cabbage palms where one lay bent almost touching the ground. She quickly ate her fill and then scratched a shallow grave and buried her kill. Then she climbed upon the bent palm tree, legs dangling on either side, licked her front paws and lay there panting for a few minutes and then yawned, closed her eyes and went to sleep. Isaac and Henry had not moved, frozen in their fascination for the beautiful cat. Darkness had swallowed them up and they had totally forgotten the rest of the hunting party and the turkeys that had been their reason for being in the swamp in the first place. The turkeys had long since settled on the roost.

They slipped out and circled around the cat and met the rest of the bunch, empty-handed.

"Did you course them turkeys, Isaac? I thought they flew up over on your end," Little Mose asked.

"No, but we saw a panther, Uncle Mose! Joe, me and Pa saw a panther kill a deer and eat him!" Henry was finally able to talk about his experience. He hadn't been allowed to say anything in the swamp but he had taken it all in.

"Why in the hell didn't you shoot the sonofabitch, Isaac?" Mose asked. You know she'll git into them shoats fore you git them penned back in."

"I jest couldn't do hit, Pa. Hit were the purtiest thing I ever seen."

"Jest like our old Mama cat at the barn, Joe, catching a mouse. Weren't no difference in how she acted, 'cept she and the deer wuz jest bigger, that's all. But I tell you, Grandpa, thet bigness was a sight to remember."

"You won't ever fergit hit, will you, son?" asked Isaac and Joe was instantly jealous that he had not gone with his daddy to roost the turkeys because Henry had probably seen something he'd never get to see.

Chapter 27

It took almost a year for the powers that be in the local government to come up with some other gimmick to get money out of the cattlemen. Clearly, they could not tax their land, because they didn't own the land. Clearly, they could not tax the cattle, because it would be too difficult to get an exact count of how many the numerous large and small cattlemen owned, and how many were in Orange County as they were never in any given county at any given time. The cattle were basically free to roam to Tallahassee if they so desired.

Human nature being what it is and the Florida cowpokes, being what kind of men they were, they were bound to make mistakes of judgment and get cross-wise with the law. Since Tallahassee had the judge and sheriff on the payroll and they were the ones that set the fines, they'd just simply increase the bail and fines imposed when the cattlemen were brought into court. As it came out, those that could afford to pay, paid through the nose and if they wouldn't pay, their cattle would be sold to meet the court costs. They couldn't keep them in jail. As it was, the sheriff had to take the prisoner home with him and feed him and watch over him, so all but the most hardened criminals were let out on their own recognizance.

The first victim of this new scheme was old man Abe Johnson. They dragged him into court for killing two black men that were working with the sawmill crew. Abe had seen one of them running through the woods north of the mill and noticed that he had thrown something in the edge of a palmetto patch. It had been a skinning knife and small saw. There was clearly fresh blood on both so he skirted around the area he thought they had come from and found one of his beeves, half butchered. He ran the man down and happened to catch another with him and hanged them on the spot.

John Mizell had his brother, David, arrest the old man for taking the law into his own hands. This was something the cowmen were accustomed to doing and the old man felt he was justified in the killing. But the government in Tallahassee frowned on such practices and had sent down a mandate that the local citizens were going to have to start abiding by the letter of the law and if they caught anyone breaking the rules, they were to call for an arrest and not try to take the law into their own hands. David Mizell said that was his job and he had to go by the rules of the game. The fact that it had been two black men made it all the worse, as the federal government cried out that the two had been hanged because the ex-slave owner had no regard for a black man's life. They failed to understand how a cowman felt regarding his cattle. They were often more protective of one of their cows than a member of their own family.

Old man Johnson refused to pay the exorbitant bail and Dave Mizell had to drag him around for three days. Since there had been no witnesses to the crime to have to bring into court to testify, there had been a speedy trial. Old man Abe had proudly brought the bodies back to the mill to let all the other hands see what happened to anyone who stole his cows and gladly admitted that he hanged them, when he had been arrested. Then he refused to pay the fine and David Mizell was ordered to round up his cattle and sell them in lieu of the court costs.

So, old man Johnson, on October 26, 1867, set a precedent and "sold" his stock of cattle to his son, Thomas, for forty thousand dollars. Along with it went a wagon, a team of mules, and a bay horse. It was witnessed by J. W. Johnson. So everybody knew Thomas Johnson was bound to be the next suspect when anything went wrong.

But Little Mose, the Summerlin brothers and Mose had already run afoul of the law.

It had been rumored that Mose Jr. had drowned a man in a water trough over near Fort Capron but no one could produce the body or the name of the victim and he was never arrested for the offense. The way it turned out, he had run into a young boy that had told him about having been with Isiah when he was drowned on the Pee-Dee River in South Carolina and it had been his fault that Isiah had drowned. It seemed Isiah had tried to save the boy from drowning and had gotten the boy to the safety of his horse but had been swept down river himself. Little Mose felt that justice would be better served if the young boy paid for the loss of his brother by drowning as well, so he dutifully drowned the boy in the nearest horse-trough, took the body out into the woods to a well-known 'gator hole and fed him to a big boar 'gator. There had been several witnesses to the drowning but they were not interested in involving the law up in Orange County, so nothing was ever done about it. And no witness could be found, just rumors about the crime.

Back about mid summer of 1867, Mose had been busy rounding up cattle to take on the big drive down to Punta Rassa in the fall. They had brought some cattle from the east coast, across the St. Johns River at the crossing on the north end of Lake Winder, and were driving them to his pens at the "bend" of Sawgrass and Bull Creek. He was to meet the Summerlin brothers there, where they were to join the roundup.

The boys showed up with a young girl, dressed in denim pants, riding astride up behind Edward Summerlin. She looked fairly young, maybe fourteen or fifteen and not bad looking; perhaps a little plump but that was the style. Most men didn't go for skinny women and preferred one that had a little meat on her bones. The brothers didn't offer any explanation right off, so after supper Mose took Edward aside and quizzed him about the girl.

"Where'd you git that little gal, Edward? She looks kinda rough, like she might of been rode hard and put up wet."

"Me and Johnny came acrost her and an old man and woman broke down over there on the other side o' Reedy Creek Swamp. They'd broke a wagon wheel and the skeeters and deer flies had about et 'em up. Johnny, he run the wheel over to Campbell Station and got hit fixed at the blacksmith's, and while he wuz gone, I got real chummy with her. She was a'takin' the old couple to Melonville to her brother-in-law's, I think, and then she wuz gonna ketch a boat to Jacksonville to her sister's. I hold her we wuz a fixin' to take some cows down to a boat and ship 'em to Cuber and me an Johnny might take her on the boat with us if'n she be real good to us. We took 'em by old man Eldridges's and he agreed to take the old couple on to Melonville fer her. He wuz a goin' anyways. I figgered she could help us with the cookin' and you could even use a extra hand if you want. She sets a horse jest like a man."

Having a woman around a cow camp wasn't unusual. Jane Green visited all the time, so Mose let her stay.

The problem was that the young girl took an instant liking to Little Mose and by the third night he was dragging his bed roll away from the camp shed and the young girl was sharing it with him.

Most of the cow camps were just a shed made of cypress poles and a thatched roof of cabbage palms, not unlike the ones the Seminoles had used for centuries. It was often built on high ground and if not, the floor was up off the ground and it was here the man stacked their gear and saddles to keep them out of the heavy dew and rain.

The Summerlin boys didn't exactly like the idea of Little Mose taking their girl away from them but didn't say anything initially, deciding that Mose would soon get tired of her, and Jane Green was expected any day — so they bided their time.

Then one night they all got to drinking, except Mose, who, of course, didn't drink at all. Everybody had finally gone to bed except Edward and Little Mose and Edward brought up the subject.

"Hit ain't exactly fair, Little Mose, you a grabbin' her like a dog with a bone and runnin' off a sleepin' behind the shed with her every night. John and me's the one what brought her along."

"Well, you never said anything about hit, Edward. I know you and John wuz a coverin' her right along the first few nights and I jest figgered hit wuz my turn. 'Sides, wuz her jumped on me like a duck on a June bug. I been down here in these woods fer so long and there ain't nobuddy but Jane to mess with. I figgered you'd be glad to share with an old buddy. You oughter feel sorry fer the needy."

"Yeah, the needy, but not the greedy. Hit's been five or six days now and she ain't even looked my way, John's neither."

"Hit's a long, long time 'til we git to Punta Rassa." Mose argued. "We'll both have a belly full o' her by then. You were figgerin' on takin' her on down there, weren't you?"

"Tell you the truth, I don't rightly know 'bout that. The old man'll have the say 'bout whether she goes or not. He don't usually say much bout what we do on the boat as long as we tend to business and git the cattle there alright."

"She 'pears to be a conniving little bitch and out fer little Edna and nobuddy else. I wouldn't git too tangled up with her if I wuz you."

"You should talk. She's about ready to take up with you permanent like."

Little Mose thought about this for a moment and then said. "Tell you what,

Edward, Jest to show you my heart's in the right place, I'll slack off and let you and Johnny have her fer a while. I 'bout had all I can take o' her fer a while anyways and Jane'll be showin' up here any day now."

But little Edna didn't take to being ignored by her new lover and she began to find fault about the living conditions around the camp and whine and start talking about wanting to go back to town.

Isaac had joined the crew and asked Edward, "How old you reckoned that little gal is anyways? Can't be morn fourteen or fifteen at the most. Wonder where her family is?"

"I didn't ask her. She come willin' enough and she never backed up none when I mentioned part of the deal wuz fer her to share our sack. The last night 'fore we got here me and Johnny took turns at the same time and she knew what hit wuz all about."

"Well, if I wuz you, I'd git her back to where she belongs and wash yore hands o' the whole affair 'fore her Pa or some o' the family comes down on you purty hard."

"She told me she didn't have no family cept a couple of sisters and she come to Fort Brooke from New Orleans. She might be young but she's been around and she knows what that thing is for, I can tell you that."

Then one night she began to hit the jug and got drunk and went on a crying jag. She was falling into the men's laps and making a nuisance of herself.

Mose threatened Edward and Little Mose that they'd better straighten her out or he was going to send her packing.

The next night she got drunk again and Jane Green tried to take her off and put her to bed and she slapped the older woman and started pulling her hair. Jane felt a little sorry for her, remembering what it was like when she was very young and stranded and just stood and took it until she finally had enough and she didn't just slap her back but cold-cocked her and put her to bed to sleep it off.

Mose had had enough by that time and when Henry Sullivan and Uncle Jimmy Yates came by on their way to Melonville, Mose gave her enough money to pay her passage to Jacksonville with a little left over and told her to pack her things and "git her ass on thet wagon." He had had enough and he didn't want any argument out of anybody.

Mose forgot about little Edna with one last thought of "good riddance" and went on about his business of working cattle. But little Edna did not forget Mose and especially Little Mose. "Hell hath no fury like a woman scorned."

When Uncle Jimmy Yates and Henry Sullivan stopped in Orlando and found a place to put the girl up for the night, word quickly spread about the "goings on" down at the cow camp at Sawgrass. Edna donned her plain dress of homespun and came out smelling like an innocent, crushed little rose. Mrs. Robert Ivey took the girl under her wing and erroneously formed her own conclusions of what had happened to her down in the woods. She went straight to her husband and complained that something must be done about the poor girl's plight and she was certain those barbarians had compromised the girl's virginity.

The entire incident quickly snowballed and in just a few hours it was all over town that the girl had been kidnapped and carried off into the woods as a plaything for those vile and wicked cowboys.

Of course, Uncle Jimmy and Henry Sullivan knew the true situation, but David Jr. and John Randolph wouldn't give them the opportunity to put a word in crosswise.

They questioned the girl at length and found that not only had Mose Jr. and the Summerlin boys "violated her," but that Jane Green had been sharing Mose and Little Mose's bedrolls as well. She told that Jane Green had been so jealous of her fresh charm and beauty and Mose Jr.'s attraction for her that she had attacked her, as well, and she had to flee with Uncle Jimmy and Henry Sullivan to get out of a bad situation.

Mrs. Ivey and several of the other matrons of the town formed a committee of six to have Jane Green run out of the country, and the men in question brought to justice.

So Mose Jr., Mose and the Summerlin brothers were served the papers by Sheriff David Mizell and "requested" to attend a hearing by the Grand Jury in October to answer the charges of kidnapping, rape and adultery.

But at the October court old man Eldridge and Uncle Jimmy and Henry Sullivan were allowed to have their say-so. It was finally proven to the Grand Jury that the girl had gone willingly with the Summerlin boys and that she was no better than Jane Green who everyone knew had been selling her wares for months. But the Grand Jury was not convinced that sexual intercourse had not taken place between the accused and either Edna or Jane Green, or both, so adultery charges were brought to bear on Mose and Edward Summerlin and two charges of adultery for Mose Jr. It was not proven that John had been involved with the girl or Jane Green and charges were dropped against him.

Bail was set at three thousand dollars for Mose and Edward Summerlin and six thousand for Little Mose, as he had two charges of adultery against him. William Turner, Mose's attorney, cried out against the ridiculous bail for such a ridiculous charge and Mose Jr.'s bail was graciously reduced to five thousand. The other bail stood.

Of course, these men didn't have the money, and a lien was put on Mose's cattle to cover the bail for him and Little Mose and Edward Summerlin was released into Mose's custody. David Mizell was authorized to gather the cattle and hold them as bail until court could be held in April of '68.

Little Mose went to Edna and spread on the charm. He told her how much he loved her, gave her two twenty dollar gold pieces with a promise for more when he saw her again in Jacksonville. Then he spirited her out of town, on her way to Melonville with a promise to see her just as soon as he could get to Jacksonville to see his children for Christmas.

Mose had a long talk with Jane Green and they both agreed the best thing she could do was leave the country. Jane was to get much more. She insisted Mose mark and brand and register in her name fifty head of cattle before she left and soon was on her way with a pocket full of gold coins to St. Augustine and Asa Wilkerson's. Asa had been a close neighbor and friend of Mose's back in Columbia County and Mose knew he could trust him to keep his mouth shut.

Before Little Mose and Mose took the boat to Jacksonville, so they could see their families in north Florida for Christmas, Mose went to Isaac with a plan.

"What say I 'sell' you my cattle like Abe Johnson done Thomas? I know we got a purty good case now about these adultery charges hanging over me and Little Mose, but you cain't tell about them hellfired Mizells. I git outa this one and they'll git me on some other trumped up charge eventually. Won't no money change hands, but I'll file the papers in Lake City and them Mizells won't know nothin' bout hit. I'll give you a bill of sale, all drawn up nice and legal like, then I can spring hit on 'em if they try to take anymore of my cattle fer fines or bail."

"But what about the rest o' the boys, Pa? They won't like hit much and me a havin' all them cattle in my name?"

"Ain't none o' their goddamned business what I do with my cattle. They're mine, ain't they? We all know hit's jest a piece o' paper. You won't actually own the cattle no mor'n Thomas Johnson does old man Abe's. Won't change a thing. You won't have to do nothin' about hit. I'll take care of it 'fore I leave out up there after Christmas, son."

And so Mose, after visiting with his small children, and a cool reception by Becky, spent some time with George and gave a sad goodbye to James Ed, who was close to dying with "consumption." He signed the bill of sale on January 25, 1868, selling Isaac Barber six thousand head of cattle, "more or less," at the price of twenty five thousand dollars. This included "all the cattle south of the Ocklawaha River with specified marks and brands including the *fleur de lis*, Mose's original brand he had held for so long. He headed back to Central Florida, satisfied about what he had done, gleefully dreaming about the look on the Mizell's faces when they found out they could not touch his cattle.

So Court opened in April of '68 and, as Mose had planned, Jane Green and Edna could not be found, so there were no witnesses against the men. No one had actually seen the adultery take place and the men were released for lack of evidence.

"Mose's" cattle had wintered well and were driven back to Brevard County.

Actually, Mose felt he had recouped enough to pay expenses since the herd had been on much better grazing conditions, having been held for bail. Once again Mose decided he had gotten the best of "them hell-fired Mizell's." He had not mentioned the bill of sale, waiting to spring it on them at a more opportune time.

But the federal government didn't slack up even a little, riding herd on the rich cattlemen. They kept an eye out for the smallest infraction, and then blew it up into as big a one as they could get away with and, of course, the sky was the limit when it came to the powers that be in the Reconstruction government. They held all the cards and they controlled "them hell-fired Mizells." And, they were aided and abetted by such upstanding citizens as the Iveys and other well-meaning settlers who wanted to see law and order in the community, no matter who was calling the shots.

It seems none were exempt. For the better part of the spring and part of the summer, they picked on the smaller cattlemen and left the big ones along, not to appear to be playing favorites. Soon Andrew Jackson, Needham Yates and everyone connected with Mose but Isaac had had their day in court and land or cattle sold to meet the costs. For some reason or other, Isaac was never accused of anything. He kept his nose clean, went to church and stayed close to home with his family and out of the clutches of the Mizells and the Reconstruction government. Yes, Mose had picked the right man to "sell" his cattle to.

August found Mose and the crew working the area around the south side of Lake Kissimmee, pushing the cattle on their way to Punta Rassa for shipment. Little Mose and Mose and Thomas Johnson had made a round down around the south side of the lake, not too far from Turkey Hammock to see if they could pick up some strays they had missed the day before. It was hot and sticky and Mose was cursing the flies that were stinging the horses and made them kick and "hump-up" and lose their stride at each bite. He'd spur the poor old horse and curse him too, as if it was his fault, as well, that he was uncomfortable and making Mose's ride a bumpy one. The cypress ponds were few and far between as the pines thinned out into a prairie and one could see for quite a way.

The three men were scanning the horizon for cows when off to the far right they spotted what looked to be a small herd, gathered together to fight the flies, but as they drew closer, it turned out to be three men driving a bunch of yearlings. They hung back and kept an eye on them for about an hour, knowing they were not some of their crew. But they seemed to be drifting toward Cook's pens at Turkey Hammock, so they got a little closer.

"Can you make out any o' them fellers?" he asked Thomas Johnson. Thomas knew just about every cow crew in the vicinity.

"I can't swear, but hit looks to me like maybe a couple of 'em might be young George Bass and Bill Cook, but I can't say fer shore, Mr. Barber."

"Ain't that young George's bay stud, Pa?" Mose Jr. asked.

"I can't tell from here. My old eyes ain't what they used to be," Mose admitted. It pained Mose to have to confess he wasn't what he used to be in some departments. "Let's git these trees on 'em and see can we head 'em off."

But a sudden summer storm came up and lightning began to crack. The Kissimmee Prairie was no place to be out in the open in a lightening storm on a hot and lathered horse. Many men had been killed in Florida under similar circumstances.

Mose looked up at the darkening sky.

"She's a fixin' to let down her drawers, men," Mose cried and spurred his horse into a gallop. "Let's see can we out run this thing back to Cook's pens and some cover. That's where they're a'goin' anyways. If that's George Bass, I want plenty o' witnesses when I catch him, if he's got any o' my yearlings."

There were cattle already in the pens at Turkey Hammock. Mose had turned his cattle out into the crivis the night before. He, Mose Jr. and Thomas rode straight to the pens and looked over the cattle to make sure none of them had the Johnson or Barber brands. Satisfied, they tied their horses to a tree and joined the group, sitting back well away from the fire where a woman was busy cooking on red hot coals, her face the color of a beet and sweat dripping from the end of her nose. Mose took his hat off to the woman, Eliza Gardner, and spoke politely to Jack Sullivant, Bill Smith and young John Sandusky. Only Jack spoke a "howdy" back to Thomas Johnson and gave a civil, if not enthusiastic, nod to Mose and Mose Jr.

Mose made some conversation about the weather that had run them into camp. He told them the rest of the crew were working cattle about five miles to the east and he planned to come the next day for the cattle he had left in the crivis the night before. All cowmen were welcomed to use the pens to pen their cattle but seldom did they camp together because of the confusion and animosity brought on by so many cowboys of different backgrounds and their likes and dislikes. The man that owned the pens had sole possession of the camp when he was working cattle.

There had been a pause in the conversation and Mose had taken a chaw of tobacco and passed some around for the rest of the crowd.

"We seen a bunch o' cattle jest afore we got here off over to the south. Thomas, here, thought he recognized George Bass as being one of the drovers. You seen him around here lately?"

"As a matter of fact, " said young Sandusky, "George and his brother Dick, and Mr. Cook rode off some time ago to see could they pick up some strays got away from them early this morning. That's probably them. Don't know o' anybody else a working cows this close 'cept maybe some o' yore bunch, Mr. Barber."

"Ain't none o' my bunch," Mose told him.

"They oughter been here by now, less that storm spooked the cattle or they had to find cover," John said, anxiously, peering out into the open area.

"It'd rid the country of one more thieving varmint if lightning struck that George Bass," Mose told him.

"I didn't know you had it in for little George, Mr. Barber," said Bill Smith.

"Yeah," said John Sandusky, "What you pickin' on him fer?"

"I done caught him down around the prairie a couple o' times before and warned him to stop stealin' my cows," Mose said accusingly.

Mose Jr. stood off to one side, twirling a small rope he had taken from his saddle that he used to tie the dogs. John spied the string and began to get a little worried.

Mose went on, "He's been a rogue since he was hatched best I can tell and all I want to do is git my hands on the little bastard one time when he's got some of my cows. I'll wean him from sucking eggs right now while he's young."

"You catch him stealin' your cows, Mr. Barber, why don't you turn him over to the law and let them take care of him," Bill Smith put in.

"Law?" Mose snarled as he spat his tobacco on the ground, "They ain't no law in these parts. Where you gonna take him and the evidence into the law? There ain't no law down here. He's from up there in Orange County where his family's got their noses run up them Mizell's asses. Old man Mizell makes a quick turn and one o' that bunch is liable to git a broke nose. They'd jest turn him loose like they have all the rest. No, they ain't no law, and I'll take care o' things like we've always done down here. Them Mizell's ain't got no jurisdiction off down here noways. This here's Brevard County and their sheriff seldom gits over on this side o' the river. He stays hid about half the time. I'll give you a hundred dollars if you can find him fer me in the next five days."

All the men were gathered around now, drawn to the situation and then young Sandusky started telling about some similar incident that had happened up in Georgia when his father was young.

It wasn't but a few minutes until they spied the cattle approaching the camp and Mose, Little Mose and Thomas Johnson got on their horses and rode out to meet them. They were about two hundred yards from the pens and Mose rode around the cattle as the three drovers held up their horses to see what it was all about. Mose could see some of the cows had an *AJ* and *B fleur de lis* on them. As a matter of fact, nearly all of them belonged to him except for a couple of unmarked yearlings. Mose decided they belonged to him as well.

"What you plannin' to do with them cattle, George?" he asked the young boy as he rode along beside the herd, headed for the pens.

"I figgered on butchering one fer me and one fer my daddy and one fer Mr. Cook here and maybe even one fer Mrs. Peterson." Mrs. Peterson was Quinn Bass's wife's mother. The young boy was clearly frightened of Mose. He was only about thirteen or fourteen and his little brother, Dick, perhaps a year younger. He knew butchering cattle for the table would be more acceptable to Mose.

By this time Mose's eyes had narrowed to small slits in his face and began to shine like those of a wild horse.

"I guess you know them cattle are mine, don't you, George?"

George figured he was in a heap of trouble and was driving the cattle as close to the bunch of men now gathered by the pens as he could. His brother, Dick, had already bolted and gone to the camp, leaving him like a dirty shirt.

"The cattle don't belong to you no more, I hear tell, Mr. Barber. If you can prove they're y'orn, I'll be glad to pay you fer 'em."

Goddamit, Mose thought, somehow or other the people at the courthouse in Lake City had let it slip about the bill of sale. Damn them Yankees. They're all so close a dose of salts would work the whole bunch.

"Why you little smart ass," Mose snarled. "If steam boats was a sellin' fer a twenty dollar gold piece you couldn't even afford to blow the whistle."

They were almost to the men, now. He thought to frighten the boy even more.

"I done told you what I'd do to you next time I caught you with some of my cows, George. We done caught you red-handed this time and in front of witnesses."

Thomas Johnson and Little Mose had gotten off their horses and Tom grabbed George's bridle.

"Let's jerk him off that horse and give him a good whippin', Mr. Barber." Tom was a giant of a man and little George was visibly shaken even here in the relative safety of his friends.

"No" Mose said, "You take his horse over yonder a ways and we'll take him up on that hill yonder. I want to give him a good talking to first. March on up there toward them men, George."

The young boy saw that the three men were heavily armed and didn't offer any resistance. He was obviously glad to be temporarily out of the clutches of Tom Johnson. Mose was dismounted now and took him over to one side and started lecturing him. George was white as a sheet and trembling visibly.

"I thought you promised me you'd leave my cattle alone, George."

"I quit fer a while, Mr. Barber, and then I found out everybuddy else wuz a'doin hit and I figgered I weren't doin' nothin' everybuddy else hain't done, including you yorself. I don't know why you want to pick on me," he whined.

"Yore a young man, George, and if thet sorry Pa o' yore's won't try to teach you nuthin, sumbuddy's got to do hit. Times is a changing around these parts. You know you'll git caught up there in Orange County and you got to slip off down here where you know there ain't no law around and steal my cows. You pick on me, I pick on you. Hit's as simple as that."

By this time Mose Jr. had walked up and was pulling the little short dog rope back and forth through his fingers. The boy had heard how Mose Jr. had hung a man from the chimney corner of his parlor with a handkerchief and got away with it. The young boy looked as if he was going to cry.

Mose went on, "Yore Pa has jest let you run wild like a animal and not tried to teach you any respect fer another man's property."

Even Mose was beginning to feel sorry for George by now.

"I'll tell you what I'll do, son. I'll let you go this time if you'll promise me you'll pack up and git plum out'a this country. You think you can do that?"

"Yessir, Mr. Barber, Yessir," he pleaded. "I can be gone in a week or ten days. Jest give me time to git out o here and pack my gear."

Mose stood a minute, letting the young boy stew and then spit his tobacco and said he'd give him thirty days, but he didn't want to see him in bad company or carrying a gun.

George promised him he could count on him to stick to his word.

"Well, then. Hit's settled," he told the boy and motioned for Tom to bring the boys' horse over to him.

Mose and Little Mose and Tom got on their horses, put Mose's cattle in the crivis and announced they'd be back the next day to pick them up.

"You oughter a let me whup him, Mr. Barber," Tom said. "He'll be after my cattle next."

"I think we taught the little shit a purty good lesson fer one day. That ought to wean him from fartin' in church. Let's git on back to camp before dark," and he took off in a trot to the west.

Mose dismissed the incident, deciding that the men around the pens had been witness to the fact that he hadn't laid a hand on the boy and he felt he had done the country a good deed by trying to scare enough sense into him to make him quit stealing cattle at such an early age. And the boy, too, before he got caught and hanged. He told Mose Jr. that night, "He can steal cows when he gits old and wise enough to know how. He ain't dry behind the ears yet."

They worked their way on south, picking up strays and making about twelve to fifteen miles a day. As they got down south just east of Fort Kissimmee, they crossed the Kissimmee River, keeping their eyes pealed for renegade Indians that could stampede the herd.

Three men stood guard each night until midnight, then relieved by three more until day, and they were all getting mighty tired, as well as the cattle, by the time they got to Fort Bassenger. They rested a couple of days, picked up fresh supplies and waited fer the rest of the Summerlin crew to join them with more cattle.

They reached the headwaters of the Caloosahatchee River with over eight hundred head. It had been a dry summer this far south, for which the men were grateful. They herded the cattle across the river below the falls and were soon at Fort Deneud and across the corduroy road, built back in the close of the Civil War.

They reached the pens at Punta Rassa with seven hundred and ninety one. Just about a freighter full. Each steer had to be loaded individually by block and tackle to the lower deck, and when the bottom was full, they were herded onto the upper deck through a heavy wooden loading chute. They worked far into the night by torchlight until the boat was loaded and her crew ready to head for Cuba.

Mose stood by as Isaac accepted the gold for the sale of the cattle and then Isaac dutifully turned to his daddy and handed it to him.

"Where's this bunch a'goin', Pa?" he asked.

"Some place called LaGrande, in Cuber, son," Mose told him, as he put the gold in his saddlebags.

The crew spent the night at the military barracks at Fort Dulaney, built by the government during the Seminole Indian War in 1856. It took then a week to get back to Fort Gardner where he paid Francis and Champ and three more days on into Isaac's.

They had hardly turned their horses out into the barn where Jason fed them, helped Isaac hang up the saddles, and were having coffee at the kitchen table when little Joe asked Harriet, "Ain't you gonna tell 'em about the Sheriff, Mama?"

The three men turned to Harriet and stared.

"What in the hell did he want?" Mose Jr. asked.

She looked at little Joe, really angry for him bringing up the subject, knowing how tired the men were.

"I weren't gonna bring hit up jest yet. Thought I'd let you men git cleaned up and rested first. He come by here the other day a askin' where I thought Pappa Mose and Mose Jr. and Tom Johnson were. Said he had some papers to serve on the three o' you 'bout something that happened down at Cook's pens. I told him Cook's pens wuz way off down there in Brevard County and what happened, if hit did, weren't none o' his business but he jest ignored that and said this involved George Bass and George Bass wuz from his county and that made hit his business."

"Sneakin' bastards," said Mose. He sat with his nose pinched between his first two fingers of his left hand and said nothing, eyes narrowed and cold as steel. No one said anything as they knew that was the signal that Mose was terribly upset and they all sat quietly, eyeing each other and waiting for him to say something.

"I oughter knowed that sneakin' George Bass'd run right to his old sorry Pa, and he'd run right to Ackies Bass and he'd tell them Mizells a pack o' lies."

Isaac and Mose Jr. tried to explain what had happened at Cook's pens.

Harriet agreed with them that it didn't seem to amount to much.

"But you can bet my money-makin' ass they'll find some way to snatch every goddamned bit o' this gold I got left over from this cattle shipment; if they can figure anyway to git their hands on hit. Bastards," said Mose. "Sneakin' bunch o' thieves."

No one said anything for a minute, waiting for Mose to calm down.

"Well, we might as well clean up in the morning and go in and see Bill Turner and face the music. I wuz really planning on heading fer New Smyrna after resting up fer a few days. Wanted to go by and see Susan anyway, so I might as well figure on stayin' there fer a few days. Hell, hits right at court time and they'll have the three o' us railroaded right into the pen if we don't git up there." Mose seemed resigned to the inevitable.

He went to Harriet and handed her the gold. "You know where to put it, gal" was all he said. Then he went out on the porch and gazed off across the choppy blue waters of Lake Tohopekaliga.

"Ain't yore Pa gonna eat some dinner?" she asked Isaac.

Isaac went over and put his arm around his wife, "I guess this business is enough to kill a man's appetite," he told her as he pulled her to him, hungry for the comfort of her arms and she for his. Little Mose and the boys kept on eating, ignoring the couple as Isaac started rubbing his beard up against Harriet's neck. She started giggling and trying to get away.

"No telling what you brought home in the rat's nest," she told him.

"Probably a big wood's rat, Ma," little Joe giggled.

"You git them dirty clothes off right now, all o' you. I'll have Jason bring in some water. No sleeping in my house 'til you men git cleaned up. I'll git these dishes readied up while the water's heating," as she put more wood on the fire. "You can put them dirty clothes out on the back steps 'til I can git 'em boiled. You might a brought home some lice, or even worse," looking at Mose Jr.

The next morning Mose and Mose Jr., all shaved and "slicked up," headed for Orlando. Isaac had agreed to take word to Needham Yates and see if he could get "ahold" of Tom Johnson and see if he got any word about the "trouble."

And trouble it was. If the two had known what it all was leading to, they would have gotten on their horses and gone as far into Brevard County as they could get and stayed there.

Chapter 28

The little courthouse in Orlando was a popular place that Monday morning. Of course the Mizells were there and all the local gentry and farmers from the outlying areas. Circuit Court was held only three times a year, so it was a big event. Even Susan and Harriet had come. There was a nip in the air, a feeling of fall and Isaac woke up that morning thinking of hunting and roosting a turkey but he knew he needed to be there to support his father and brother.

Bill Turner, the only available attorney, had taken the case on such short notice but had advised Mose it may turn out to be more than he could handle and could snowball into something serious. So he'd better see about getting his attorney in Jacksonville. He was sure he could get a continuance until the following April and that would give Mose time to get better representation.

They had the three men on a felony offense. The grand jury had met the Friday before and Bill Turner had quickly reminded them that this offense occurred in Brevard County and this Grand Jury was illegally selected among the citizens of Orange County. But Judge John Mizell decided that this would come out in the trial to be proved or disproved, as Bill Turner had no proof where the line lay between the two counties. The grand jury had quickly indicted them for "maliciously threatening an injury to a person and property of another and with intent to make a person do an act against his will." Of course, they pled "not guilty." And bail was immediately set for an exorbitant sum and the clerk was advised to instruct David Mizell to "collect the same for the State through their good and chattel lands and tenements for use by the State." Of course, that meant to get all the money they could for the local Reconstruction government. When Bill Turner advised the court that Mose and Mose Jr., his clients, owned no property in the area and all properties were in Baker and Duval County, there had been a buzz among the spectators as each turned to the other with a "I told you so." As it turned out, Thomas Johnson was to have his cattle confiscated instead, this time. And there had been another buzz of "I told you so's." So Mose and Mose Jr. were released into the custody of the local Sheriff, Dave Mizell. But since the Circuit Court judge was already in town and court was convening the following Monday, they were allowed to go to Andrew Jackson's and were released into his custody.

There was such a large crowd and the little courthouse was so small, court was being held out under a massive oak across the street in a vacant lot.

John Mizell, the judge of Orange County, acted as host and stood before the crowd and announced, "The Fall term in the year of our Lord, eighteen hundred and sixty eight A.D. Seventh Judicial Circuit Court of the State of Florida is now is session. Judge John W. Price, presiding."

Judge Price quickly decided that the prisoners and their attorneys were all present and accounted for. John C. Long, the prosecuting attorney, was there and

215

the proceedings were started.

Mose Jr. petitioned the court for a continuance "in that Absalom Cook, his material witness, was absent without his consent and lived in Brevard County, a great distance from this court, he could not proceed to trial."

John Long accused the prisoner of only attempting to delay the proceedings by such a ploy, but the judge granted him the continuance.

Then Mose petitioned the court for continuance since his chief witness William Wolford could not even be reached on such short notice.

David Mizell gave testimony to the effect that he had searched for Wolford but had not been able to serve him on such a short notice and that he, indeed, had not been served.

So the continuance was granted.

Thomas Johnson gave the same excuse and the three were released. Mose Jr.'s bond was set for five hundred dollars and Thomas and Mose released into their own recognizance. They had a right to Thomas' cattle, or rather old man Abe's, as bond for Thomas. And it was well known that Mose had a place in Baker County. Of course, no one knew it was already mortgaged to the hilt but they somehow felt that Mose was not going to skip the country. They all knew exactly who really "owned" the hundreds of cattle roaming in Central Florida with the *B fleur de lis* brand.

Two things that never came out in the proceedings was that the incident happened down at Cook's pens and everybody knew old man Cook lived near there and the court accepted the fact that Cook lived so far "into Brevard County" that he couldn't get to court on such short notice, but nothing was brought up again about this whole affair being held in the wrong courthouse in the wrong county.

Also, it was never asked if Mose Jr. had cattle in Orange County. Of course, he did, but they were not registered in his name. Still "old Ring under the wagon," Mose had registered the cattle in his name, alone, all those years. And although they had been "given" and marked and branded for his sons, they were, nevertheless, still his. And now they were in Isaac's name, but in name only. And Mose Jr. had his own cattle and it was understood that brand belonged to him. But it was a family matter and legally, the State of Florida could not touch them. Everyone knew Little Mose always had plenty of money to squander on women and a good time, but no one in the court questioned where it came from.

They sat out on the porch that night at Andrew Jackson's and cussed the Mizells, the Reconstruction government and now the Basses, but none were ready to pack up and go further south.

The next day, Mose went by way of Joe Story's and bought a new horse and took off for New Smyrna. With Jane Green out of the country, he longed for some feminine companionship, the kind that Susan could not provide. Susan had been supportive in her sympathy for the predicament the family was in. She understood that Mose had only tried to scare the young George Bass into quitting his stealing at such a young age and that Mose was only trying to help the boy. But she did agree he went about it the wrong way.

216

The woods were ablaze with fall colors. The sumac and colic root, with its white and orange flower that looked like an orchid, were blooming along the trail. At every homestead the mulberries were ripe and the trees almost a lavender purple. There was a nip in the air.

Mose caught a schooner at Melonville for Volusia where he bought six yards of calico, ten of denim, linsey and broadcloth and some produce. He had a sack of Irish potatoes, a keg of syrup, meal, grits and a big sack of licorice strings and a sack of apples. He rented a mule and cart and went east to New Smyrna.

When he got back, he bought himself a new Rogers knife and took the boat for Jacksonville.

He skirted around Penny's, knowing she'd ask where Mose Jr. was and he didn't want to have to listen to her tale of woe. He knew his son would eventually show up with something for the children's Christmas, so he headed straight for Becky's and his young family at the old home-place.

The hickory had turned yellow and the blackjack oaks a bright red. The grape-vines at the old plantation glistened like gold and the wind flitted the underside of the magnolia leaves, showing their copper bottom and spilling their red cones, and seeds all over the ground in the back yard. A wave of nostalgia engulfed him as he greeted one of his old dogs that still remembered him. He came out from under the steps with his tail between his legs, wagging his hips that were almost on the ground, in total submission to a man that used to beat him for the least infraction when he was a young pup. Mose reached down now and patted him on the head.

The children came out with Becky and greeted him with indifference. After all, it had been a year since they had seen this old man they were taught to refer to as "Pa."

Mose was in his sixties and Becky only thirty-two. The generation gap could no longer be bridged. It had been widened even more by months of being separated and the loss of Mose's power and prestige in the community. It widened further when Becky realized she was married to a bitter, disillusioned and troubled old man. And Mose saw that she had become an even colder and more distant stranger.

Mose wanted to know how things were going and Becky made the mistake of telling all. She was even deeper in debt and besides that, one of the children let it slip that she had been digging around in the yard, looking for "money."

"You might as well quit yore diggin', Becky. You'll never find hit. And I ain't a gonna pay off yore debts with hit, so you might as well give up that notion. No sense throwing good money after bad."

"What do you intend to do with all that gold, Mose? You cain't take hit with you when you go and yore children need hit now."

"You mean my squandering wife needs hit. You can throw hit out the back door with a teaspoon quicker than I could bring hit in the front door with a shovel. I know that's all you married me fer, in the first place, Becky."

He looked over her poorly kept records and shook his head. "You got to keep yore nose to the grindstone in this business. You cain't afford to pay them lazy niggers and give them room and board to sit on their lazy asses and not turn out a day's work. Goddammit, woman!"

"They won't work fer me like they do you, Mose."

"Then run their lazy asses off and git you some that will. And don't be a feeding 'em so good. They git hongry enough they'll work. You been a pourin' yore money down a rat hole, gal. You'd better draw up that purse string tighter than a bull's ass in fly-time or yore gonna lose this here place, lock stock and barrel. Them Yankees is jest a'sittin' back waitin' to pounce on hit like a spider a watchin' a fly, caught in his web. You're jest a loose horse and I can't tell you a goddamned thing."

There was more or less a truce during Christmas. Becky attended the Christmas festivities at Sam's and Mose went to the gravesite where James Ed had been laid to rest. The place just didn't seem the same to Mose.

"You'd better cowboy up, Becky," he told her when he left "Fish or cut bait." He sat on his horse for a minute, looking around at the old place and finally could stand it no more. He turned his horse toward Jacksonville to the law office of Rogers, Fleming and Daniel who would be his close advisors for the coming year.

When he hit town at Orlando, he was surprised to find the town had built a new courthouse. He was even more surprised to hear that they blamed Mose Jr. for burning down the old one and had issued a warrant for his arrest for arson. The entire county had been hard at work, duplicating the burned records and everyone had been urged to come in and add any documents they could think of. They even had adultery added to the charge for Mose Jr., even though he had been acquitted of that offense.

Mose Jr. emphatically denied setting the courthouse on fire.

"They cain't tack that on me, Pa. I weren't even in this country when hit happened."

"I know you wuz there at St. Augustine with Jane Green and then went from there to see that little sneakin' Edna in Jacksonville."

"And I guess you weren't in New Smyrna with that Mrs. Cook, neither?" Mose Jr. asked, smiling at his daddy.

Mose had no defense against this charge and shrugged his shoulders and walked away.

It turned out that it was the general consensus of opinion among the citizens of Brevard County that old man Abe Johnson had set the court house on fire. Not only had he tried to keep them from collecting his cattle for Thomas's offense, but they had him up on a charge for stealing a man's horse.

Mose Jr. said it didn't matter anyway about that or the adultery charge; he wasn't coming back to Orange County for the trial in April anyway. He was moving on down to where Champ and Francis were and the people around Orange County could look for him all they wanted but they'd never find him down there.

"I don't blame you none, son. But that don't help me out none. I got no place to hide. I bet old man David Mizell can't shit 'til he has that ass-kissing son o' his serve me with a stack o' papers a mile high."

But Mose found that nothing had been added to his charges. He and Mose Jr. and Thomas Johnson were still indicted on the same charge about George Bass. And he wondered how long it would be before they trumped up something else to harass him with.

It wasn't long in coming. In March, they served the papers on John Barber's young son, Andrew Jackson, who had been named after his uncle. They called the boy "Deed." Needham Yates's son, Needham Jr. who was the boy's first cousin had been nicknamed "Need." And when little Andrew Jackson started learning to talk he couldn't pronounce the "n" when he spoke of his cousin Need, but called him "Deed" and that became his nickname to differentiate him from his Uncle Andrew Jackson.

When the boy was twelve, Mose had given little Deed a prize heifer and taught him how to mark his mark in her ear. They had practiced on a piece of orange tree leaf until the boy could mark his own heifer. He put the *AJ* brand on her and she was his pride and joy. She used to come up to the back fence at Crabgrass and Deed would feed her potato peelings from the sweet potatoes. He nicknamed her *'taterpeelin'*. The heifer strayed away when she began to look for a bull and ended up in a herd of cattle that his Uncle Jack had sold to Morgan Mizell, another of David Jr.'s sons. Somehow, no one noticed the different mark in the heifer's ears.

When Deed found what had happened to his heifer he took it upon himself to go get her back.

He had shot up a sight in the past year and at almost fourteen was as big as a grown man. He searched the woods to the north and west of Crabgrass until he found *'taterpeelin'*, who had already had Morgan's brand put on her and drove his pet home and shut her up in the crivis.

Someone saw the heifer in John Barber's crivis and told the sheriff one of his brother Morgan's heifers was penned, evidently for beef in John Barber's crivis at Crabgrass.

David Mizell came down to investigate. Deed told him he and not his father, John, had penned the heifer and insisted she belonged to him but that someone else had changed the brand. But Dave made him butcher and skin his own heifer so they could take the hide with the altered brand back, as evidence. No one was home at the time but Deed and his mother and the smaller children. So, David, not knowing the boy's age, and the true facts, had no alternative but to take the young boy into Orlando and arrest him for rustling.

The Yates and Barber families insisted, had it been any other cow but one of the Mizell's, the sheriff wouldn't have arrested Deed. But, nevertheless, he was to stand trial in April along with Mose.

Mose had less than a month before his trial. His was set for the opening day of court on the fourth Monday in April, which fell on the twenty-ninth. Deed's trial was set for the first day of May. Evidently, the court didn't think it would take long to try Mose.

The settlers down around Crabgrass knew of Deed's pet, *'taterpeelin'*, and were very much in sympathy with the Barbers. People were taking sides all over the county. George Bass was the main source of irritation.

"Deed Barber ain't but a couple years younger than me. If Mose Barber thinks I'm old enough to git hung fer stealing his cattle, then Deed Barber's old enough to go to the pen. I don't see no difference."

The rumors flew. Every one of the Basses thought Mose couldn't get a fair trial in Orange County. They knew where the county lines were and that most of Mose's witnesses lived a good ways down in Brevard, and it would be difficult to drag them into court way up in Orange County. Also, Bill Cook's crew did not get along with the Barbers and they certainly would not be very cooperative in telling what went on down at the pens that August. From what they saw of the situation, knowing Mose Barber came riding up with blood in his eyes, looking for young George, and, knowing him so well from past experiences, they would naturally expect the worse to happen. And when it didn't, they would assume that at the least Mose and Moses B. F. Barber had certainly insinuated that they would carry out their threat at a later date if George didn't get the hell out of the country. The Barbers' reputation was certainly against them.

On April 29, the Wolford brothers, John and Thomas, Needham and James Yates, Quinn Bass, Will Nettles, and A. Waterman came before the clerk of the court and signed a sworn statement that they thought Mose Barber couldn't get a fair and impartial trial in Orange County. Mose's lawyer, Mr. Fleming, of Rogers, Fleming and Daniel of Jacksonville, requested a change of venue and a continuance.

John G. Long, State's Attorney, argued that it would be almost impossible to hold court in Brevard County and since most of the state's witnesses, including George Bass, lived in Orange County, it would just as unfair to George Bass to change the venue to Brevard as to leave it where it was.

Of course, Long was a part of the "click" from Tallahassee and Mose's lawyer, even though he was the best the State of Florida had to offer and that money could buy, didn't stand a chance. Mose got his continuance but the change of venue was denied.

Mose wanted to git it over with but he also wanted to be around for Deed's trial and the law firm was happy to get another chance to dig down into Mose's pocket again.

On May 1, Needham Yates and Andrew Jackson Barber, the boy's uncles, came before the court and acknowledged themselves severely indebted to the State of Florida for Deed's bail. John and Mary did not have the wherewithal to get the boy out of jail so they had gone Deed's bond.

At the trial, 'taterpeelin's hide, foul smelling and covered with salt, was unwrapped and dutifully presented to the court as evidence for the state. Morgan Mizell's brand was still visible. Morgan testified that, indeed, was his brand. Sheriff David Mizell testified he had forced Deed to butcher the heifer at gunpoint and the hide had been in his possession since that time. The prosecution had presented its case.

Several witness testified to the fact that the boy had kept a heifer with that colored hide around his home at Crabgrass and that she had one crumpled horn that grew down close to one eye and had to have the tip cut off. That the heifer had been marked with a crop and under split in one ear and a swallow fork in the other and branded *AJ*. Also, that the pet had disappeared and the boy had scoured the countryside, looking for her. But Deed, being young and his mother being the naive countrywoman that she was, had left the ears and crumpled horn behind when they went with the Sheriff into Orlando. The boy had been in tears, if not in severe emotional shock, after having been forced to butcher his own heifer, and the mother frightened out of her wits.

Under cross-examination, no one could swear that the hide was *'taterpeelin'*s. Lying stretched out and stinking on the ground, outside the courthouse, it looked like any other old deteriorating hide. The only defense that Deed could offer that the cow he was forced to butcher was the same heifer call Taterpeeling, and a pet that had belonged to him, were the ears bearing his mark and the crumpled horn with the tip cut off. They were no longer available. The ears had long disappeared in some buzzard's innards in the wilds of Crabgrasss Creek. And the horns, carried off by some varmint.

The boy's age and good record had no bearing on the case, John C. Long argued.

"It's time the letter of the law starts being observed in this part of the country. You people will never progress until your citizens learn to respect law and order, regardless of how young they start. A boy is held accountable for his actions at the age of twelve."

And so young Deed Barber was sentenced to serve six months at the State Correctional Institution in Chattahoochee.

Fleming told Mose it would do no good to file an appeal.

"We don't have a leg to stand on. Someone should have brought in the head with the ears and horns, when they brought in the hide."

Susan, the boy's grandmother and Mary, his mother were in tears. They might as well have been sending him to Siberia.

"He ain't got no business locked up way up there with a bunch o' crazy people," they wailed.

As it turned out, Mose and his lawyer accompanied young Deed on the journey to Chattahoochee.

"Don't you worry none," Mose assured Susan, "I'll see that he's taken care of and we'll git him outa there, jest you wait and see. If hit takes every cow I got, I won't leave him there."

At Palatka, the boat stopped for supplies and Deed, his hands being tied while on the boat, so he couldn't jump over board and swim, asked for a "chaw." Mose cut off a big plug of tobacco and Dave Mizell took it from him and crammed it in the boy's mouth. Somehow, it cut his lip and it started bleeding. David Mizell said he was sorry and he wasn't used to hand-feeding a young boy tobacco, on choppy waters, but Mose was furious just the same.

"This day, Dave Mizell, you're on yore way to hell." And everyone on board heard Mose, loud and clear.

The party never made it to Chattahoochee. They took the train to Tallahassee from Jacksonville and, with David Mizell's blessings, got an appointment with the Governor. Along with David Mizell's testimony, this time admitting he possibly could have made an error of judgment in his hasty arrest, and the extenuating circumstances of the boy's young age, Deed was sent home with a pardon.

There was loud rejoicing at Crabgrass Creek and Needham Yates's house. Mary, his mother, and Susan, his paternal grandmother were just relieved to have the boy home again, but Needham's wife, Malintha, part Indian, could not forgive and vowed to get even with Dave Mizell.

Poor David, guided by the Reconstruction government, said he was just doing what he considered his duty and carrying out the law to the letter. But all the Barbers and the Yates could see was that he had almost sent an innocent boy to prison. They had moved down into the wilderness of Brevard County to live in peace and quiet and they were tired of being harassed.

The journey to Tallahassee with young Andrew Jackson had taken a lot out of Mose, emotionally and financially, and taken precious time he needed for his own defense.

It had been costly for Deed's father, John, and his uncles, Needham and Jack, as well. John eventually gave J. J. Daniel of the law firm, fifty head of cattle for his part in going with Deed to Tallahassee and representing him before the governor. Andrew Jackson, in October of that year, gave Flemming and Daniel "a certain stock of cattle ranging in the lower part of Orange County near what is known as Crop Prairie; marked split and under the upper bit in one ear and under slope and upper bit in the other and branded *B figure 3.*" There were about forty or fifty head in that herd, "more or less," and Andrew Jackson agreed to keep the cattle and take care of them in lieu of the fact that he still had some legal matters pending. Namely, that he still owed the State of Florida money.

It seems most anyone who had cattle eventually ended up owing the State of Florida money.

Not only was Mose having a terrible time getting witnesses to testify on his behalf in court in July, but he was served another summons for having confined and imprisoned William Smith on the same day he and Little Mose and Thomas Johnson had been charged in the case of George Bass.

It read with a flourish, "Not having the fear of God before his eyes and being seduced by the instigation of the Devil, the nineteenth day of August, eighteen hundred and sixty eight, with force and arms at the County of Orange, William Smith of the County of State, said in the peace of God for the State of Florida, the accused (Moses E. Barber) did forcibly imprison and confine him against his will."

Mose called the piece of paper a "crock of shit" and took it straight to Bill Turner, who said he'd handle it if it ever got past the grand jury, which it, fortunately for everyone, did not. It seems Bill Smith was one of those exhibitionist that had not been subpoenaed for the George Bass case and decided he wanted a piece of the limelight. But it turned out to be that much more to antagonize Mose.

He tried to get Mose Jr. and Thomas Johnson to come in and testify. Mose Jr. emphatically refused to even enter Orange County and the State subpoenaed Thomas Johnson for themselves.

As a matter of fact, the State got the jump on Mose while he was gone with Deed to Tallahassee and had subpoenaed nearly everyone that was present at Cook's cowpens that day. And some that were not. They were William Cook, Richard Bass, Charles Bass, Quinn Bass, William Bass and, of course, George Bass. Also, Absalom Cook, James Padgett, Stewart Tyner, Jesse Lee, Henry Overstreet, Eliza Gardner, J. H. Sandusky and Jackson Sullivant.

By trial date on the second Monday in July, Mose had managed to subpoena Henry Hodges, Needham Bass, and Jackson Sullivant. A. H. Stockton, the clerk, had given the papers to David Mizell to serve on A. W. Shackleford, one of Mose's star witnesses, but had been unable to find him. Shackleford had told William Shiver that he had heard George Bass swear in his presence that he would testify to anything, if it would find Mose guilty. Strangely enough, Jackson Sullivant and Needham Bass had been subpoenaed for Mose but when they showed up for court, they were made to testify for the State, as their subpoenas for the State had the earliest date.

As is turned out, when court convened, no one came forth in Mose's behalf. Henry Hodges, living in Fort Christmas, said he wasn't even there that day and knew nothing about what had happened, which was true.

Flemming tried to get another continuance because Shackleford had not been found and Mose had no witnesses, but the State had cornered the market on everybody. A continuance was denied and Flemming had his job cut out for him.

When they started selecting the jury, Flemming objected to Francis Foster because William Roper had said on the stand that Francis Foster had told him he had already formed an opinion as to Mose being guilty. But Judge Robert Price ignored the request. It seems they had had enough trouble finding men to sit on the jury that weren't witnesses and it was all they could find at the moment.

The twelve men were, A. G. Martin, Benjamin Griffin, William Jones, J. H. Herndon, Jesse Bumby, R. Stokes, A. Tanner, W. G. Roper, R. S. Kirkland, Robert Ivey, D. Hall and Francis Foster.

First came the testimony about the county line, with Flemming trying to have the case dismissed on the grounds that the incident happened in Brevard County.

Long asked William Cook, "Where do the people around this part of the country pay their taxes and do their legal business?"

This was objected to by defense council as secondary evidence and therefore illegal, but it was overruled and exception noted.

Next, George Bass was asked, "Was it generally understood by the citizens of the surrounding county that the place where this affair occurred was in Orange County or not?"

Defense objected to this as a leading question and secondary and not a matter to be proved by public notion, where the lines are defined by law. This, too, was denied and exception noted.

Someone else said it was supposed by the citizens to be Orange County and "no one knows where the line is."

No one had copy machines in those days to show that the line had been changed to run due east from north of Fenny Point where Isaac lived to just south of Crabgrass, across Bull Creek and due east to the coast about Port Malabar. Cook's pens, down at Turkey Hammock as Cook had earlier testified "on the other side of the Kissimmee," were well into Brevard County. No question about it, but Mose had no witnesses to prove it and it seemed no one knew anyway. The people in Brevard paid their taxes in Orange County because they had the St. Johns River between them and the nearest village of Fort Capron, north of Fort Pierce. The line was immaterial to these cattlemen who had no fences.

Mose testified on his behalf. He swore he had not looked on Bass as a prisoner and never put his hands on him nor attempted to prevent him from going where he pleased. "I gave him the best advice I was capable of doing and he agreed and it was all settled."

George Bass agreed that Mose had not laid a hand on him during the entire time. But he swore that they had taken his horse away from him for twenty minutes or so and he felt like a prisoner. But it came out that Thomas Johnson had taken his horse away, not Mose.

"The principal threat that was made was by Thomas Johnson, Mose E. Barber told me to leave the country in thirty days but did not threaten my life."

"Was this against your will?"

Objected to by defense council as leading and without foundation, but objection denied and exception noted.

"It was against my will to leave my native country." Objection made, denied and noted.

Mose whispered to Flemming, "Hell, I didn't plan on him a leavin' Florida, jest git outa Brevard County and away from my cows."

When it finally went to the jury, they failed to agree. They came back into court and were instructed again by having the charge read to them again. They finally said they could not agree. It was evidently on one part of the charge that they did not agree, so they finally decided that Mose was not guilty.

Mose's lawyer thought that was the end of it but the judge did not dismiss the "prisoner at the bar."

The jury foreman, Jesse Bumby, George Bass, and John Mizell had a conference with Judge Price. It was brief and took only a few minutes. Judge Price had nodded his head in agreement the entire time.

"Will council approach the bench."

Spectators went into a flurry of excitement and the judge had to quiet the crowd. Mose could see Flemming, Long and the judge arguing and Flemming appeared more agitated by the minute.

He came back and sat by Mose. "I wonder where they dug this idiot up. He evidently is straight out of the ark," he told Mose.

"What's a goin' on?"

"They're trying to say now that the charges were worded wrong and misleading and that you're going to have to stand trial again."

"Can they do that?"

"Not according to my law they can't, but it appears these men can pretty well do anything they want to do down here."

Judge Price requested "quiet," and asked for the prisoner to approach the bar. Mose stood up and waited.

"It's been brought to the court's attention that the charge brought against Moses E. Barber, Moses B. F. Barber and Thomas Johnson by George Bass were erroneously worded, leaving out one very important charge. The jury has found that Thomas Johnson was absent from the scene when this offense took place and the charge has been dismissed against him. Moses Edward Barber, you now stand charged with 'forcibly confining and imprisoning another person against his will.' How do you plead?"

Mose, stunned, and not wanting to do the wrong thing, turned to John Flemming and looked at him with a blank face.

Flemming shouted at the judge, "I object to this proceeding, your Honor. This is clearly a case of double jeopardy. My client has been cleared of all charges in the original offense and can not be tried again for the same offense."

The objection was denied; Mose pled "not guilty" and a jury selection commenced.

Of course, the community was small and the court was hard pressed to find twelve more men so Herndon, Bumby, Foster and Hall were selected to serve again on the second jury. Flemming objected vehemently. Two of these men were the same men he had objected to the first time and he clearly could see that they were stacking the jury against Mose. John Ivey, the main fly in the ointment at the first trial that stood firm in his opinion that Mose was not guilty, was objected to by the prosecution and discharged. Along with the four previously selected men were, A. J. Vaughn, W. B. Cowart, Morgan M. Mizell, H. S. Partin, Wilson Simmons and J. W. Prevatt. Most of these had served with John Randolph Mizell in the war.

When Mose tried to get Thomas Johnson to come forth as a witness for his defense, since he had no witnesses on his behalf, and Thomas was not charged in this case, Judge Price ruled that Thomas Johnson was not a "competent" witness, although the State had originally subpoenaed him.

The next morning, on October 19, the second trial got under way.

George Bass had his story down pat this time. When he came to the part where Thomas Johnson said, "Mr. Barber, now let us whip him," George said, "Mr. Barber said, no, let us carry him over to among them boys and Moses B. F. Barber says, 'no,' if you do that them fellers will hang him.' I did not say in the presence of Mose Barber and William Shriver that I would leave the country in thirty days if they would not hang me, before anything was said about it. I did not, during this term of court, tell any person that I made the proposition to leave the country if they would say nothing about it, before there was anything said about it. They were all armed. Johnson had a double-barreled shotgun and a pistol. Moses and B. F., a shotgun and pistol. Perhaps Moses E. Barber did not have a pistol. They said they had taken the law into their own hands and were going to execute it. I was not a liberty for at least half an hour. My horse was led off against my will and held in custody against my will."

Mose basically repeated his same story. He testified that he did not look upon Bass as a prisoner and did not treat him as one. "I never put my hands on him or attempted to prevent him from going where he pleased."

No matter what Flemming objected to, Price overruled. And whatever Long objected to, Price granted. It probably didn't matter in the long run, for the jury had their mind made up anyway. As a matter of fact, the jury became bored during the proceedings and two of the men went to sleep. Once, Frances Foster got up and left the box, evidently to go to the privy and came back, never having been accompanied by anyone.

When the judge charged the jury, he was ambiguous in his charges.

"If the jury finds from the evidence that a person was forcibly imprisoned or confined without legal authority against his will, and that it was within this state, then it is your duty to find him guilty." And then he turned around and said, "That he (meaning Mose) must immediately proceed with such a person to the nearest officer of the law and deliver such felon to him. The distance to such officer is no excuse for not doing so."

Every word that George Bass uttered was taken into consideration, but Price charged the jury that, "the statements of the defendant are not evidence and you can't take such statements into your consideration as evidence." And also, what ever went on down at the pens, "the acts of one were the acts of all and it is necessary for the prisoner to show the acts that excuse him." He clearly was trying to convince the jury that Mose was guilty, as if he had to do so in the first place.

While the jury was deliberating, off to one side, Jesse Bumby got up and strolled off for about ten minutes, out of sight of the bailiff or anyone and finally ambled back.

While they were "deliberating," Flemming was furiously writing out an appeal for Mose.

"I have already found twenty instances where the court erred in this case, Mr. Barber. I'll read them to you after the trial. I have them all ready for Judge Price when they come in with the verdict. I already know what it will be."

And of course, they found Mose guilty this time, and Flemming immediately presented his request that Mose be released pending the appeal. This was granted when Judge Price saw the long list of exceptions and court errors. He knew it would not be in his favor to deny it. Besides, there was the question of court costs that Mose had to pay and he was sure it would take time to collect the money.

Mose was presented his bill for all charges made during all the trials and he realized why he had been granted so many continuances. Every witness was to be paid for his mileage to and from the court and his expenses while in town. It was noted that William Cook was paid for sixty miles each time. But the judge accepted the fact that it was still in Orange County, since Cook had sworn that "I live down on the other side of the Kissimmee [River], I do not know if it was in Orange or not." Sheriff Mizell's bill and the bill for A. Stockton, the clerk, was six pages long with every conceivable cost noted. Mose had to borrow money to get out of town. No one in his family had that much cash.

Mose was clearly depressed and felt suddenly old. He was pale and drawn as he rode with Needham Yates and Isaac to Andrew Jackson's to spend the night.

"Hit looks like none of us is going to have any peace of mind until either Sheriff Mizell's run plum out of this country, or dead," put in Needham Yates.

"What good would that do?" argued Isaac. "Hit's not him, hit's them Reconstructionists that's behind all this. They're dead set on law and order and they're not goin' to rest until they've got hit. Trouble is, their idea of what's right and wrong is different from ours. That's all hit boils down to. This country is a gonna change and we got to learn to change with hit. If we can hang in there we can ride this thing out. Git enough of us crackers down here and we can eventually squeeze them Yankees out and take control of our own lives."

"But me and yore Pa'll be dead by then. We want some peace of mind right now."

"Or broke in the bargain," said Mose. "All they want is our money. Hit's as clear as the nose on yore face. I'm tired o' seein' that hellfired sheriff a coming. He's got dollar signs written all over him. Every time I see him a coming into the yard. They ain't a'gonna leave us along until there ain't a cow left in Brevard County."

When Mose repeated this lament to Mose Jr. on their way to Jacksonville, little Mose said, "I done talked hit over with Need. He's figured out a way to git that damned sheriff the next time he steps a foot into Brevard County. We done decided the next time he comes across that line he's a dead man."

"Isaac says won't do no good to git the sheriff, they'll just stick another in his place."

"Isaac's jest a Psalm singin', *Bible* toting, pussy-whipped do-gooder. Him and Arch has been that way ever since they first laid eyes on them Geiger gals. I say hit's time we quit letting 'em shit all over us and rub hit in our faces."

"If you got anything on your mind in that direction, son, jest don't let me know nothin' about hit. What I don't know won't hurt me."

And Mose Barber could not have been more mistaken when he spoke these words. They would come back to haunt him in the months to come.

Chapter 29

When little Mann was seven, John Randolph glibly talked Priscilla into letting him take the boy to Orlando to be educated. Late in '67 she had given birth to another boy, Oscar Renniford, who they called Rull, and had just had another, named Thomas. So, Priscilla had her hands full. Croft Bass had served with John Mizell during the war and had admired the man for his courage and the fact that he was educated. When John kept persisting with the request to have his son educated by a private tutor, he too, bombarded poor Priscilla with arguments as to how much she was depriving her son by being so obstinate. So she finally gave in and let the Mizells keep him, but only for a short school term.

They didn't reckon with the fact that little Mann might be unhappy in such a strange environment and so he refused to learn. The fact that John was married and starting a family of his own complicated the situation. As a matter of fact, he cried so and wouldn't eat until they eventually had to return the boy to his mother.

It was on February 20 when David Mizell left Orlando with little Mann to take him home. He had to serve some papers to Mose Barber anyway, so it was decided to kill two birds with one stone. To make Mann Bass, as he insisted on being called, happier about the trip, he took his son, Will along, and his brother, Morgan.

It was to be a routine trip. A man by the name of Galloway had sold Mose cattle at the close of the war and Mose had paid him in Confederate money, knowing it was worthless. But the man, being slightly behind the times, had accepted it and let Mose have the cattle. Mose had refused to make the money good. Mr. Galloway had first tried to collect on Mose's real estate holdings in Orange County, but soon learned Mose had signed it over to other parties. Then he tried to collect on his plantation in Columbia and Baker County and found that Mose had it mortgaged to the hilt and he would have to stand in line. By the time he tried to collect on Mose's cattle, he had already signed them over to Isaac. Now Galloway was trying to attach the cattle that had originally belonged to him by legal means and had to serve notice to Mose. Of course, it was a hopeless situation. The cattle were long gone, swallowed up into the woods of three counties and the brands changed for five years. But the papers had to be served according to the letter of the law and it was Sheriff Mizell's order to so do.

David Mizell was no coward. He sat tall in the saddle at six feet one and weighed over two hundred pounds. He had served as a private in the Confederacy until poor health had gotten him a discharge and was just beginning to regain his health when he took on the job as sheriff.

To David, it was just a job. He took no particular joy in harassing his fellow citizens, even those that were not particularly admired, like Mose Barber.

"It's my duty to enforce the laws that are passed by the State of Florida and the County of Orange." He was dedicated to his office and loyal to his community-minded father and his politically ambitious brother. David Mizell Jr. had been one of the first settlers in that area and he was determined that law and order be followed to the letter in order for the community to flourish and begin to get some semblance of culture and civil order. He was getting too old to move on and he had a lot invested in Orange County.

Personally, Dave Mizell did not relish the task of going down into Brevard County, looking for Mose Barber. He felt he had no business that far afield but he was legally authorized to hunt for Mose Jr. anywhere in the state. He carried, at all times, papers to serve on Mose B. F., should he find him, to bring him into custody for the arson and false imprisonment charges still out against him. David had his own ideas as to who had actually fired the court house back in '68 and he felt the charges against young Mose, and the other two men, for that matter, were asinine, and knew young George Bass was none the worse for wear after his encounter at Cook's pens. He may even have felt it probably did the young boy good to get scared out of his wits. But David had been hauled into the courthouse once and accused of not hunting Mose Jr. diligently enough, so that was the reason for having the papers on his person when he left home.

The last week in February started on a Monday. The moon would be full in a few days and generally, there would be a change in the balmy weather. "Full moon in February" was always the cracker's dire prediction for a hard winter freeze if one was to be forthcoming, and David didn't want to be out in the woods in bad weather. He wanted to serve the papers and get back home.

No one ever knew exactly where Mose might be, so he started out at Andrew Jackson's on the west side of East Lake, and then dropped little Mann Bass off at Croft and Priscilla's at Mose's old plantation. Next, he went to Isaac's at Fenny Point. From there, he went to Needham Yates's down near Lake Gentry. This proved to be a terrible mistake. Two of Needham's sons were in the back of the house when David rode up, looking for old man Mose. Said he had some papers to give him. They already had killing on their mind before the sheriff got on his horse to ride away. Needham, and Need immediately took off as soon as David Mizell got out of sight and got ahead of the party, headed for "the Puzzle" near the bend at Crabgrass and Bull Creek to tell Mose Jr. that the sheriff was coming that way to serve his daddy more papers to drag him back to court. They knew he'd be coming up the north side of Bull Creek to get to Mose's pens because Needham Sr. had told him that'd be the best way to get there.

"We ain't agonna git no better opportunity than we got now," they told Mose Jr. They decided to double back and catch David and Morgan and the young Will at dusk and ambush them as they were settling in for the night.

"I ain't agonna be no party to killin' that young'un of David Mizell's. He's got him and Morgan with him." Both men promised not to shoot the boy, so Needham went along with the idea.

"It's gettin' dark and we best find a dry place to camp." David told Morgan.

230

They were out on the high ground, siding up the creek. They had passed Billy's Lake about three miles back. There was a nip in the air.

"Big lightered knot fire'd feel mighty good, Pa," little Will suggested to his daddy.

"You know, seems like if I remember correctly, there's a big high hammock on the other side of the creek up here. We outa be gittin' to the crossing 'fore long. Be a might good place to camp."

Need, Mose Jr. and old man Needham were just out of sight, close to the edge of the creek, keeping an eye on the three horsemen. So when they turned and hit the trail going down to the crossing, Need yelled excitedly, "They're aheadin' fer the crossing. Let's git on up and make the crossing and hit 'em from the other side when they're in the middle of the creek."

The hammock lay between Little Bull Creek and Big Bull Creek and the crossing was about half a mile south of their junction to the north. The trail that led down into the creek from the Piney woods was bounded by cabbage palms and tall oaks. The settlers had driven their wagons and carts across the creek at this point until there were two deep ruts gouged out into the white, coarse sand. The wild Spanish cattle and white tailed deer and before that, probably buffalo for eons of time past, had crossed here.

"Looks like somebuddy crossed not too long ahead of us," said Morgan.

"And they were in a full run, looks like to me." David agreed. "Must'a been in one hell of a hurry to get where they were going." He laughed.

The horses splashed the tea colored water as they waded deeper into the main run. But the bottom was of white sand and packed hard from so many hoofs that had crossed there.

"Good place to go swimming, son, if it was a bit warmer weather," David turned around to say to little Will, who was just behind him.

Will had his feet out of his stirrups and up high on his horse's shoulders to keep his boots dry. "Is it gonna swim the horses, Uncle Morgan?" He was looking back at Morgan who was bringing up the rear, Indian file. Morgan started to tell him the water wouldn't get much deeper when shots rang out, and Morgan recognized the thud as one struck something close by, then another.

Will was yelling, "Whoa, Red," to his little horse, trying to calm him as he shied from the gun shots and Morgan yelled for him to come back his way as he saw David hit the water without a sound. He knew the shots had come from across the other side of the creek. Knowing Will was safe, he forgot his own safety and was down in the water, pulling his brother's lifeless head up so he could breath.

They could hear the muffled voices of what appeared to be Indians speaking in Hitchiti, the Seminole Indian language, and one let out a war cry as they heard the hoof beat of several horses riding off. The birds that had already gone to roost were shrieking indignantly at having been run from their perch. Morgan hadn't even had a chance to get a shot off at the invisible targets that had been lurking in the still dusk among the cabbage palms on the other side. His first thought was to get his brother's lifeless body up onto dry ground so he could make an assessment of where the bullet had struck him. He knew he had been hit because David's blood was turning the water a deep maroon as it swirled around the two men.

Morgan could see that he was either dead or unconscious. Not only was David a big man, but his boots were full of water and his heavy coat soaked. The best Morgan could do was to drag him to a small island in the middle of the creek. He yelled for Will to come help him.

"Let's get him up on this tussock," he shouted to young Will who was only ten years old. But they managed to drag David's body up out of the water and stretched him out on his back. Bright red blood had covered the front of his coat. On careful examination they found that one shot had torn through his left arm as he had turned to look back at young Will, another had entered his chest, tearing his aorta and collapsing a lung. It was a mortal wound. A red stain seeped onto his lips and the only sign of life was the sucking sound, as air flowed in and out of his lung through the puncture wound.

"He's still breathing, Uncle Morgan," Will said, hopefully, as he wiped the blood from his father's lips. He was begging his daddy to speak to him and crying and Morgan felt that his beloved brother was dying, but he had to try to do something, as little Will started begging him to go get some help.

David moaned and moved his head, responding to his son, crying for help. This gave Morgan a faint ray of hope.

"Me or you one's got to try to get to Crabgrass through these woods. It ain't far up the creek."

Little Will began to cry in earnest. "You'll have to go, Uncle Morgan, I'd never find the way in the dark. I'll stay with Pa. He'd want me here with him anyways when he comes to. I'm not afraid. I got Pa's gun," as he looked at his father's horse, standing patiently on the bank. David's gun was still in its deer hide scabbard that he had gotten for Christmas.

The big sheriff moaned and moved his head once more.

"Let's cover him up," Morgan suggested and waded over to David's horse and got his slicker from the back of the saddle. "Maybe if we get him warm he'll come to. You jest stay right there and I'll tie your horse up on the other side, if you happen to need him."

Little Will got comfortable with his daddy's head in his lap, his feet barely dangling in the water. Morgan waded across to the other side and mounted his horse and started off.

"I'll get back with help as soon as I can," he promised.

As luck would have it, he met George Sullivan on the trail, told him what happened and George volunteered to go stay with little Will until help arrived.

"I'll stop by the Crosby's and have them bring a wagon down. Then I'll ride on and get a doctor and meet you at their house. Be gentle with the boy, George, Dave might not make it."

Young Will sat alone in the dark and listened to his daddy's labored breathing. Dave began to get restless and started thrashing about.

"Be still Pa, we're out in the middle of the creek on a tussock and you might wiggle off. I can't get you back by myself. Uncle Morgan's gone for help."

David reached up and touched his son's hand and spoke. He didn't open his eyes, but he knew that Will was there.

"I'm bad hit son. I'm not gonna make it."

"Don't talk that way, Pa. Help's a'comin'. Hang on for a little longer."

David moaned and took a deep breath.

"Listen. Listen to me son," he whispered. "I don't want no big trouble over this. I don't want anybody else gettin' killed over me. Tell your Uncle John. You hear? Tell your Uncle John, I'm sorry we come. I wish we hadn't. We didn't have any business draggin' off down here."

David lay still for a moment and then opened his eyes for the first time and looked at his son.

"No trouble," he whispered and slipped back into a deep coma.

Will attempted to arouse him again but David was still as death. Will sat and stroked his hair and wiped the froth from his daddy's lips as his breathing became less labored and there were times when he quit breathing. Will would shake him and tell his daddy to wake up and the breathing would start back up, fast and shallow. The young son felt his daddy becoming colder and he tried to gather his body up under the slicker and tuck it under him. Will was tired, cold, hungry and sleepy and tried to stay awake but finally drifted off to sleep, his chest against David's head, cradled in his lap.

He awoke once when a deer came down to water at the crossing and splashed back onto the bank, waking him with a start. His daddy looked different. There was only dried blood on his lips and his face was a strange blue gray-color. His head flopped at an angle when he leaned down and kissed him on the forehead. It was cold as ice and he knew in his mind his daddy was dead, but he prayed in his heart he was wrong and sat and stroked his hair, crying, "Oh, Pa, Pa, Pa."

He had dozed off again but was awakened by a different noise this time. He listened. The horses were stomping the mosquitoes and were restless, wanting to be fed or turned free to graze. Frogs croaked and peeped and a limpkin cried out from its perch. The moon was directly overhead now, turning the sand silver. He could see through the opening of the crossing. Out on the hill, a horse and rider were coming, but help arrived too late. Sheriff David Mizell was dead.

George Sullivan, old man Crosby and one of his boys loaded Dave's body in their wagon and, not stopping for Morgan to come back, started to Orlando. They met the doctor and Morgan on the trail, and turned them back.

The sheriff was buried by his Masonic brethren from the Apopka Lodge. It was an impressive candle light service and the first of its kind in Central Florida. His body was laid to rest at his home on the shores of Lake Rowena, the first of several gravesites in what is now Leu Gardens at Winter Park.

Of course, many people were grief-stricken over the murder of David Mizell. He had been as popular among the citizens of Orange County as he had been unpopular with many of those in Brevard. But of all the mourners, the most distraught and angry was John Randolph. As a young teenager, he had looked up to his older brother who was taller, stronger and ultimately wiser. When Dave became sick during the war and had to be released from service in '64, he had sent home some of his captain's pay to help finance a trip to south Florida for Dave and his family. The doctor had told him that a diet of shellfish, muscles and turtle meat might purge his body of the cholera that had caused him to become a wasted, shell of a man.

Angeline, Dave's wife, kept the small family going, using the funds to buy a tar processing plant. The Federal gunboats finally shelled it to smithereens, but the family survived and David finally recovered to full health.

After the war, John, better educated and more ambitious than Dave, continued to help his older brother struggle by in anyway he could, and, of course, eventually got him the job of Sheriff of Orange County. Now John felt, in some way, responsible for David's death. If he hadn't convinced David to take the job, he'd probably be alive today, for he was sure the murder had something to do with the Barbers.

As grief turned more to anger, John put his whole being into finding Dave's killer or killers.

As had been predicted, a sudden winter storm at the full moon in February had wiped out all traces of the ambush. Fresh cattle and deer tracks were all that could be found at the crossing.

When the news came out that Sheriff Mizell had been ambushed and killed by Indians at the crossing on Bull Creek, some of the settlers at the lower end of Brevard started carrying guns and barring their doors at night, but many did not buy the story that Indians were once again on the war path. It had been over ten years since there had been any Indian troubles in that area. There were approximately forty-two families in Brevard County and most of them were over on the coast around Fort Capron. The Indians were basically miles to the south of Bull Creek and no one could see any reason for them to have come all that way with the possibility of ambushing a straggler at Bull Creek. If they'd wanted to start killing, they would have gone to the coast.

Slowly, as the days dragged on, things began to settle back to normal and everyone was convinced there were no Indians in the area. No one had reported any sign of them. The search for the killers had proved fruitless.

Over and over, John quizzed his brother Morgan and nephew about what they heard and saw that evening at dusk.

"You sure they were yelling in Hitchiti?"

"I ought to know, I heard it enough back up there in Micanopy. I couldn't understand a word they were yellin' but it certainly wasn't English, was it Will?"

Will remembered only the war cry and he'd never heard anything like it before.

The second week in March, the case began to break. William Bass started the rumor that he had heard the elder Needham Yates's son, Need, singing in Hitchiti.

"His Ma's part Indian, you know. Maybe even half-breed."

Actually, Needham's wife, Malintha Lee was only a quarter Indian, but she had strong Indian features and had proudly taught her children some of the Indian songs her mother used to sing to her. Many people in Orange County were not acquainted with Malintha Yates. She seldom went anywhere but to church when a camp meeting came down to Crabgrass or Peg Horn in Brevard County. She loved to sing and was very religious. She loved the wild countryside and detested town. So, Needham or some of the boys brought in supplies.

"You know, old man Needham's been heard to say how much Sheriff Mizell needed killing."

"I heered he told William Bronson he'd better not come down into Brevard one more time or he'd be shot."

"That Indian wife o' his hated David Mizell for arresting Deed Barber and takin' him to the pen. Mrs. Dubie says she same as told her she wished sumbuddy'd kill him fer hit."

"And the Barbers, too. I heered tell they all wanted him dead. Old man Mose same as told him he wuz a dead man when he cut Deed Barber's lip on the boat at Palatka."

John Randolph had sent word to Tampa, trying to hire David Stewart to replace his brother as sheriff. No one in Orange County wanted the job. Stewart had been a tough sheriff in the Tampa area but his tactics had proved too harsh for the local citizens and he'd been voted out of office for that reason. John Mizell decided he'd be just the man for the job. Stewart sent word he'd like to come and give it a try, temporarily—he was never officially sworn in as sheriff until June 27, 1870, and resigned in January 1871.

When a posse had been formed to help the newly appointed "sheriff" bring in the Yates for questioning, John Mizell instructed them to shoot first and ask questions later, if they tried to resist arrest. He wanted to question them and get to the bottom of it.

"Hit ain't no crime fer my boys to sing in my mother's language," Mr. Yates argued when the posse suddenly showed up and demanded that Needham and his sons go with them for questioning. "I jest taught 'em *In The Sweet Bye and Bye* and a couple a more songs. I been a singin' hit fer years and my Ma afore me and her Ma, too. Ain't no crime."

"Hush, wife, won't do no good. Pack us somethin' to eat. We'll go along willingly," Needham said, turning to David Stewart.

The three suspects were not allowed to take a horse. They lived on the west side of Lake Gentry but they were to walk the entire way to Orlando, taking only their hats and coats. They were surrounded by the posse and marched around the southern tip of Lake Tohopekaliga to the west banks of Shingle Creek before they were allowed to rest. They followed the Creek to E. L. D. Overstreet's new house where he had just moved in with his bride, Spicey.

Visibly upset, Spicy asked her young husband that night, as the posse camped out underneath a large oak near their barn, what the Yates men had done. Vianah, E. L. D.'s sister, had married old man Needham's baby brother, Jack. So "family" was involved.

"They say the people that killed Sheriff Mizell spoke Indian and the Yates boys sing Indian songs."

"So did my grandma and lots of other people. That ain't no proof. I think that's a crime they're making 'em walk all that way and they don't have no proof they done anything. I want you to go tell Vianah right now what's a'goin' on. Surely they'll listen to Jack or at least let him give 'em a horse to ride."

The next morning, bright and early E. L. D. talked to the men and tried to reason with them.

He went back into his wife and told her. "Didn't do no good. Their minds are set. I'll run over to Jack's and tell him what's a'goin' on."

"And I wouldn't trust that Sheriff Stewart no farther'n I could throw him. He looks mean to me. I think he'd just as soon shoot you as to look at you. And that's a whole bunch of Quinn Bass' boys with him. They're all outlaws, the lot of 'em. I jest don't like the looks o' things. I tell you. You go get Jack right now."

"Now what do you think he can do that I can't do?" He was a little miffed at his young bride for asking for outside help in a situation.

"It's Jack's brother and nephews. It's his family and his matter."

But the next morning, Jack was not at home. He had already left on his mail run to Bartow and Vianah begged her brother to go with the Posse and see that nothing happened to her brother-in-law and nephews.

"Jack'd be beholden to you."

By the time he got back, the posse had left with the Yates, and Quinn Bass was having a problem with what they were doing. "You know, El and Spicy Overstreet is right. Here we are making them walk all the way to Orlando and we ain't got no proof they done nothing. That ain't right. Least we could a done wuz let 'em take their horses."

"But, Pa, you know Sheriff Stewart knows what he's doing. He'd been a sheriff longer'n Sheriff Mizell wuz."

No one in the posse knew their so-called "sheriff" was just a hired gun.

"Hell, yes, Pa, he says they'll confess 'time we git there."

They were on the Old Indian Trail that led south to Tampa. When they neared Sand Lake, Stewart pulled up his horse, took careful aim and shot the brim of Needham's hat off. The old man didn't even bother to look up. He just spit his tobacco and kept on walking. The second shot hit the ground at William's feet.

"Don't pay 'em no never mind, son. He ain't got nothin' on us."

This terrorist activity went on for another mile and finally Stewart pulled up the posse and told them all to get down for a rest. Then he called Quinn Bass and William Bronson over.

"He's a tough old bird. We all know he's guilty as sin and that youngest boy's gittin' as nervous as a pregnant nun. Judge Mizell told me if they tried to run, shoot first and ask questions later. I say we shoot the old man and them boys'll confess."

"El Overstreet wuz right, Pa. They don't confess and we take 'em like this and there's gonna be devil to pay. We ain't got no proof."

"But we all know they done hit!"

Quinn Bass looked down and shook his head. "I know they done hit, too. I'm jest agin' shootin' a man down in cold blood."

"It's a matter of execution and savin' the State a lot of money they don't have. That money could do better put to a different use," Stewart argued.

And so, they stood Needham Yates up on a stump and shot him.

"Keep yore mouths shut, sons." He told his boys before they pulled the trigger.

"You ain't got nothin' on us," Need told them, stoic to the end as his daddy had commanded. And so, he was shot also.

They stood William on the same stump. His young legs were shaking and his face twitching, eyes wide with fright.

"You tell us or you'll git the same thing," Stewart warned him.

And William could take it no longer. He had already wet the front of his pants and he could hardly stand up.

"I won't in on hit. Pa and Need and Little Mose. They done hit. They follered Dave Mizell down to Bull Creek and laid fer him and shot him. I wuz with 'em when Dave and his brother Morgan come by the house and they overheard he wuz lookin' fer old man Mose Barber. They took off to git the Barbers, and then circled back. Them Barbers is as guilty as my Pa and Need. They's the ones behind hit. They put Pa and Need up to hit. But I weren't in on hit, I tell you."

The boy was sobbing now, and stood there, helpless and white as a sheet.

"I believe him, " Quinn Bass said. "He wouldn't lie at a time like this."

"Only to save his own hide. He's jest as guilty as the rest."

"You say the Barbers were in on this?" Stewart asked him again.

"They were the main ones. They started the whole thing."

"All of them? You say all the Barbers were behind this killing?"

The boy nodded his head.

"The balance of 'em," William Bronson said.

"There's yore confession, Now we can take him in and git it over with and go after the Barbers."

"There's just one fly in the ointment. This boy knows we shot the other two before they confessed. Dead men don't tell no tales," and Stewart pulled the trigger and shot William dead.

They packed the three bodies in on the gentlest horses and told the authorities the three confessed, but were shot trying to escape. The posse was told to talk to no one about the affair and to say nothing until after the inquest.

The sheriff, John Randolph, and his father, David Jr. had a big confab and all agreed it would be easier to bring the Barbers in if nothing was said to implicate them. They'd never be able to track them down if word got out. They promised the posse they would be notified and could be in on the hunt, but complete secrecy was an absolute necessity. All agreed and were dismissed until after the inquest.

But before the inquest, Malintha Yates showed up with Needham, Need and William's bloody clothing. It clearly showed that all three were shot in the chest, head on.

"See here. They plum shot the buttons of'en this'n," she cried. Deputy Morgan Mizell tried to persuade her to leave the clothing for the inquest but, trusting no one by this time, and especially a Mizell, she took them home after filing a formal complaint.

"What about this, Stewart?" John Mizell asked.

Stewart's story was that the three men had confessed but they had shot them before they had a chance to escape and had saved the State the cost of a lengthy trial. He reminded John what he had said about shooting first and asking questions later. John agreed that they had done the right thing but someone would have to get rid of the evidence from Mrs. Yates.

"I don't think anyone would pay any attention to the woman. She could shoot into any of their clothing and bloody them with any kind of blood. A good lawyer could tear her story full of holes. But it just makes things messy for us. It would be better all around if she was out of the picture. Let's give the bodies time to decompose so she can't dig them up when she no longer has the clothes."

"I'll take care of the matter," Stewart told John Mizell.

He went straight to Quinn Bass and told him they'd all be in a mess if they didn't get those clothes away from Malintha Yates.

"I knowed hit," Quinn lamented. "I knowed hit wouldn't bring nothin' but trouble."

Stewart assured him all they had to do was catch Mrs. Yates away from home and they'd slip in there and get the clothes.

"That old squaw don't go nowhere but to church or a sing. She hates town and never goes no place. She won't leave again 'til the inquest and then hit'll be too late."

"Well, we'll see that one comes down there for her to go to."

And so it was done. The inquest was set for ten o'clock on March 18. It had been hot before the bodies had been buried and Stewart knew by that time they would have been so badly decomposed the evidence would be gone. No one would want to touch them, anyway.

The day of the scheduled sing, Quinn announced he and some of the boys had an errand to run. But his wife started quarreling and throwing clothes about.

"These boys is a'goin' to church. If anybuddy needs to git back in touch with the Lord, hit's them. Me an these gals and little 'uns ain't a'goin' down thar all by ourselves, so you might as well git yore clothes on."

His wife was on one of her "tears," as he called it, so he backed off and started getting dressed.

"Missouri and Ellie, one o' you watch thet bread a bakin' whilst I git my good clothes on. David's out thar a pickin' up lightered knots all by hisself. Dick, you and Arnold git out thar and help him pile 'em up. We'll need a big far a'goin' when we git back tonight and hit a bustin' the bark."

"Ma, you know hit ain't a'gonna freeze and hit the middle of March," Dick said.

"Quit a arguin' with yore Ma and git yore ass out there and go to pilin' up them knots," Quinn told him.

238

Quinn hadn't worked out a plan as to how to get away from Peg Horn but decided he could find someway to slip out once the sing had started. William Bronson was to meet him at the bottom end of Alligator Lake.

"I hope hit don't rain, Ma," Missouri said as they started off in the wagon.

"Hit's as fair as a goats ass up there," Quinn assured them, looking up at the clear, blue sky.

Quinn noticed that Malintha, young Andrew and little Vicky were at the sing and just as soon as the preacher got started on a long, opening prayer full of hell-fire and brimstone, he slipped away through the woods to Alligator Lake. He picked up William Bronson and they headed in a trot for the Yates house at the west side of Lake Gentry.

But they searched and searched and could find no such clothes as Mrs. Yates had brought before Morgan Mizell and rather than go home empty handed, they poured coal oil on the little house and set it on fire. They knew the clothes had to be around there somewhere. They were in the act of burning the barn when Bur-rell Yates, Needham's brother came riding up. He had settled on an island at the southern tip of Lake Gentry and had seen the fire around the lake and came to investigate.

William Bronson had just mounted his horse and the pair were standing back watching to make sure the barn had caught good when Burrel got to them. He suspected immediately that they had set the fires and got off a lucky shot at William, striking him in the lower gut. When Quinn took off, William's horse followed and the pair got away while Burrell stopped to put out the fire.

William Bronson died a painful death the next day and Quinn Bass, having been seen at the sing, had witnesses to testify that he had been there all day with his family. With the evidence destroyed, Malintha Yates didn't have a leg to stand on, at the inquest, and Sheriff Stewart was free to form a posse to get the Barbers. Judge Mizell told him to do it as quickly and quietly as possible and he wanted no prisoners. So, it was open season on the Barber clan and anyone connected to it.

Chapter 30

The inquest on the death of the three Yates suspects was to be held on Saturday, March 18. Judge Mizell, not wanting Morgan to be quizzed about seeing the bullet ridden clothes Malintha Yates had brought in, sent the posse off to start bringing in the Barbers. They were under strict orders to tell no one, not even the immediate family about their mission.

"Ride south and don't bring back any prisoners. Leave only widows and orphans," was John Mizell's orders to Stewart and Morgan, heads of the posse.

Clerk Stockton quickly drew up an arrest warrant for most of the Barber and Yates men. Kill any male over twelve, the posse had decided. Stockton even erroneously included the name of William Bronson in the warrant, trying to cover all dead bodies, forgetting he had been on the other side.

By Friday afternoon, they had already searched the woods and hiding places of lower Brevard County as far south as they considered necessary. They knew Mose and his crew would probably be rounding up cattle in the woods somewhere between Ocean Prairie and Turkey Hammock and were working their way north when they chanced up on a crew of men at Jernigan-Tyner Swamp, in a big bend that "sided-up" the slough of the same name.

A spy, sent out to look the crew over, had spotted Champ Barber and Lyle Padgett for sure and it was decided to surround them and kill the entire Barber crew before any could get away and warn the rest of them.

The twelve men didn't stand a chance. The posse rode up nonchalantly as if another cow crew and had them surrounded in the bend of the swamp before the curious Barber crew knew what was going on.

Little did they know that John Barber and his brother Frances and Thomas Johnson were over at Board Cypress, cutting poles to patch the Johnson's cow pens. When they found the bodies, hours later, Lyle Padgett was still alive, barely, and told them what happened. They high-tailed it for the coast and made their way to Old Town on the Suwannee. There, Frances and John stayed with relatives and Thomas Johnson went to Marion County for the "duration."

Meanwhile, on Saturday, the inquest went off without a hitch. Malintha, Burrell and Jack Yates swore on the Bible that the bodies and clothing of the three suspects had clearly indicated they were shot facing the guns, rather than in flight, as the posse testified. But they had no evidence but their word and six of the eighteen posse swore otherwise. Little Will swore the killers let out a war whoop as the killers shot his father and William Bass testified that he had heard the Yates brothers sing in the Seminole language. It was all cut and dried.

It was ruled the three men, Needham Yates, Needham Jr. and William Yates, having confessed to the murder of one Sheriff David William Mizell at the crossing on Bull Creek, later to be forever named Mizell Crossing, attempted to escape and were shot. Nothing was said about the fact that they had implicated the Barbers. It was a reasonable finding as most everyone believed that the Yates had done the killing in the first place, even Malintha and Needham's brothers.

As for William Bronson, it was ruled his murder was by persons unknown and probably justified.

As for Mose and Mose Jr., they escaped being with the cow crew because Mose's best and only horse had gone lame and had to be turned out to pasture and they had been on their way to Joe Story's to buy another.

They had slipped into Andrew Jackson's late Sunday night, so Mose could see Susan. She hadn't been feeling well and they were lonesome to talk to family. Joe Story lived only a few miles north of Jack's place on the west side of East Lake Tohopekaliga.

Monday morning, Isaac had gotten up bright and early and gone to his Uncle Jack's to put in a sweet potato patch, on shares. Jack had bedded down a bunch of Susan's favorite sweet red potatoes and Isaac had promised to help plant them. They had already gone into heat and sprouted and were ready to be cut and the slips put into the ground. Jason would have gone along but Harriet needed him to help her wash. Little twenty-two month-old Ross had an earache, and she couldn't take him outside until the sun came out and dried off the ground. So Joe, and Henry, age nine and seven, were elected to help Isaac put in the potatoes.

The seed potatoes had been bedded down in a plot of well-pulverized muck out in the hot sun. They were placed as close together as Jack and Susan could place them and covered with rich cow manure. This caused them to go into a heat and sprout about the first week in March and the "slips" or, long shoots, were freshly cut from the mama sweet potatoes and ready for Isaac to plant when he arrived with his cart and young helpers that morning. Of course, Joe and Henry had to have a helping of Aunt Susan's buttermilk biscuits and honey before they could get to work, claiming they were already hungry from having eaten so early that morning.

"Besides, yore Pa and Little Mose is here."

While they were eating, Jack and Mose came in the back door from the barn where they had been inspecting Jack's new stallion he had just bought from Joe Story.

"Grandpa!" Little Joe and Henry cried in unison as they walked in. Mose Jr. had ridden up on the new stallion and tied him to the back gate and came in the door behind them. The horse was still a little frisky and little Mose wanted to saddle and ride him around a few yearlings out in the pasture to see how much "cow" he had in him.

Isaac was surprised to see his brother so close to Orlando, knowing the new sheriff was also looking for him. Sheriff Stewart had been told he has skipped bail on the arson and George Bass thing and had never stood trial. Little did the four men know a much greater charge was hanging over all their heads at the time.

"You're a'gittin' mighty brave, little brother," Isaac smiled affectionately at him and his daddy. He hadn't seen either of them since Mose had left after his trial in

November.

"That new sheriff don't know his ass from a hole in the ground," Little Mose told Isaac. "David Mizell's rottin' away as rightly he should be and I guess I come outa this whole thing smellin' like a rose."

"I wouldn't count my chickens 'fore they hatch," warned Susan. "Something's bound to come up. They ain't let this family alone this long since we come down here. If I wuz you I'd begin to smell a rat and start to worryin' some."

"Sufficient unto the day is the evil thereof," said Mose, quoting the *Bible*. "We're jest a takin' hit one day at a time," smiling at Susan.

Isaac had to brag about how the new baby boy was growing. He was so proud of his son and as all men were then, never mentioned his daughter, Ellen, who had slipped in among his boys.

"Well, I guess we'd better git at hit, boys," he told his young sons. "Them 'tater beds is likely to dry out purty quick from thet big rain the Lord sent us yestiddy."

If the ground was wet, Joe and Henry could drop the slips about two to three feet apart on the beds and Isaac could simply come along behind them and punch them into the soft ground with an old rounded hoe handle and tamp the ground in over them. Otherwise, if the ground dried out and became hard, Isaac would have to dig a hole and the boys put a dipper of water in it and the slips set by hand. Punching them into the hard, dry land would break the slips into and they would never root. It was tedious, dirty and backbreaking work that way, and took much longer.

"I guess we'll slip on over to Joe's and look at some o' them horses and see what he's got broke and ready to ride," said Mose.

"You two be careful. You need eyes in the back o' yore head," warned Isaac.

Harriet had inherited Leah's old spinning wheel and since the winter had been colder than usual, the sheep had produced enough wool for her to try her hand at spinning and weaving some of it. She had washed some of the wool in warm water and lye soap, taking care not to get the water too hot and had let it dry all weekend until it had lost about half its weight.

She had two sets of cards, or combs. Carding broke up the wool and made it easier to spin. One was a "breaking card" that began to separate the fibers and the other the "fine card" that combed the wool into rolls for spinning. The rod they were rolled on was called the distaff, hence the "distaff" side of the family was the woman's side, as she did the spinning.

Leah used a corn shuck for the core of the bobbin and the wool was spun onto that. Harriet was spinning and little Ellen was busy helping her mother by watching little Ross while Jason watched the wash pot. He had helped wash clothes when he was a slave at Mose's plantation and was better at it than Harriet.

Harriet had just slipped a full bobbin off the spindle of the spinning wheel and replaced it with an empty one when the dogs began to bark, announcing the arrival of horses at the back yard.

It was the new sheriff and the posse. They inquired about Isaac. Had they asked for Mose or Mose Jr., Harriet wouldn't have been so obliging but since they were looking for Isaac, she decided no harm would be done and told them where he and the little boys were. They thanked her kindly and innocently went on their way.

Over at the sweet potato patch, Isaac and the boys were busy planting the slips. Each little boy had the tender slips draped across one arm and was dropping them across the raised beds with the other hand. Isaac was coming along behind them, pushing in the middle of the shoot with the hoe handle.

A few weeks before, in an adjacent field, they had put in a corn crop. The field had been plowed with a single pointed "bull tongue" plow a foot deep into the earth and a sharp iron "coulter" had cut the tough roots. Isaac had "laid off" the rows into evenly spaced lengths while Jason plowed an adjacent furrow, and Joe and Henry had dropped in seed corn. A third plow, guided by Jack, covered this row by furrowing along its sides. The little green corn shoots had just popped up through the clods of muck and it would soon be time to "break the middles" by plowing three extra furrows into the ground between the seeded rows to loosen the soil and destroy any of the remaining roots.

Isaac was doing with his sons what fathers had been doing for generations in the south. Teaching them how to grow food to eat, for that was the only way to get it to the table. Else, they would have to do without. There was no produce sold in stores in Central Florida. Only seed and something to plant with.

The posse came riding up innocently enough and asked Isaac if they could talk with him for a minute. He climbed over the fence, not waiting to open the gate.

"You boys stay here," he told them, as they stopped dropping the slips. Isaac decided it was something serious, there being so many men and he had recognized the new sheriff. By the time he got over the fence and walked up to the horses they all drew their guns and pointed them at him.

"We're arresting you for the murder of Sheriff David Mizell, Isaac Barber," Sheriff Stewart told him.

"What?" Isaac asked, stunned.

"The Yates' boy says you Barbers paid them to murder the Sheriff," Quinn Bass told him.

"You know better than that, Quinn. I ain't pointed a gun at nobuddy since the war," Isaac argued.

"Just the same, you been tried by a jury o' your peers and found guilty," said young Croft Bass.

"Shut up, Croft," Quinn told his son, "You keep out o' this."

"I have a warrant for your arrest signed by Judge John Mizell," Stewart told him, showing him the piece of worthless paper.

"This here says Isaac C. Barber. That ain't even my name. Hit's Isaac J. Barber."

"Don't make no never mind," said George Bronson. "We all know who you are."

"Can my boys go with me?" Isaac asked, looking at little Joe and Henry.

"Not where you're a goin'," said Stewart. "Judge Mizell said to take no prisoners."

"Quinn Bass, you oughter know better'n this. You know I ain't done nothin' wrong. I'm innocent. You men all ought to know that."

George Bass came out with his classic statement, "The acts of one are the acts of all."

"And you shut yore damned mouth too, George," Quinn told him. "But the boy's right in a way, Isaac. Yore family's dragged you into this. I'm sorry if you have to pay along with the rest of 'em."

"We got our order," said Stewart, "and our warrant. It's all legal like."

"The hell it is," said Isaac as they led him over, under a tree.

"What about the boys?" Quinn asked. "They're under twelve."

"Let 'em go," said Morgan Mizell. "You boys git on thet cart and ride back to yore Uncle Jack's," he told the two young boys that had joined their daddy, realizing something was wrong.

"Do as you're told, boys," Isaac told them. "You run back to your Aunt Susan's and tell her the posse's taking your Pa to jail fer the murder of Sheriff Mizell. They'll know what to do."

"But Pa-Pa!" Joe said.

"Don't argue with me son, take your brother and get going."

The men stood in silence as they watched the frightened boys drive off.

Stewart turned to Isaac and said, "We'll give you a sporting chance. We'll give you twenty yards out there and if you can outrun us to that pond there and git away, we'll let you go."

"I ain't running like a coward. I ain't killed nobuddy and I ain't guilty. David Mizell was my friend. You're shootin an innocent man and every last one o' you knows hit. You'll have to stand me up here and shoot me down in cold blood," Isaac told them stoically. His legs were shaking and his hands trembled, but he refused to beg for his life.

They took him over to a small oak and wrapped a rope around and around him and the tree, binding him, his back to the posse.

"Am I to be shot in the back like a coward?" he asked them. I have a right to face my accusers like a man and I want everyone of you sneakin' bastards to be lookin' me right in the eye when you pull that trigger."

"Sorry," said Morgan. "Hit's got to be done this way." He knew this time it had to look like Isaac was shot while trying to escape.

They were all off their horses and Quinn asked, "Who's goin to do the shooting?"

No one wanted to be the one to pull the trigger on Isaac. After all, he'd been a friend to most of them.

They decided that all would aim, close their eyes and shoot and then no one would know who had shot him. They lined up like a firing squad. Before they raised their guns, Stewart asked Isaac if he had any last words before they shot him.

"I guess all I'd like to say is that you can tell John Mizell I fergive him and you, Morgan, 'cause I know you're both a'doin' this to revenge yore brother's death.

The rest o' you bastards are after the Barber cattle. That's pure and simple to me and yore a'using John Mizell as an excuse to drive us out and take over. So the whole bunch o' you can go straight to hell as fer as I'm concerned. Tell my wife and young children I said I love them and God be with them."

Isaac was stalling for time now. He knew he was doomed and he hoped that his two young sons could reach Jack's in time for him to ride to Joe Story's and warn his father and brother.

"You boy's ready?" Stewart asked.

"I'm not through," said Isaac. "I got a few more words to say."

"Then say 'em and git hit over with. We got work to do."

Isaac paused as long as he could. "There ain't a one o' you men out there that don't know I'm innocent o' this killin'. David Mizell wuz my friend and I had the utmost respect for him as a man and a sheriff."

"You done said all that," shouted George Bass.

"I think I have the right to ask fer a few minutes of silence while I pray, don't I."

"I grant you that," consented Quinn Bass. "We'll hold up a minute fer you to speak to yore Maker."

The men all bowed their heads in a silent prayer.

Isaac never raised his head as he whispered, "May God have mercy on yore poor souls," and braced for the volley of shots to tear into his back.

The men had just lowered their rifles and were ready to mount their horses when young Arnold and Dick Bass, Quinn's two sons came riding in.

"What you two a'doin' here?" Quinn asked, disgustedly. The two young boys were not to have been a witness to this affair.

The boys stared in disbelief at Isaac's lifeless form, held together only by the rope that bound him to the tree.

Arnold finally found his tongue, "We come to tell you that we think we jest saw Mose Barber's bay horse tied up at Joe Story's corral where he sells his horses. We wuz a'comin' to tell you old man Partin come by and told us he heard they wuz a'goin' to Joe's lookin' fer fresh horses."

His older brother, Dick, sat wordless, his eyes glued to Isaac's body. His face pale as death itself.

"I guess the cat's out o' the bag now. Only thing to do is have these boys in on hit with us," William Bass said.

"I guess so," said Quinn, resigned to the fact that his sons had seen more than they should have. "Here, Arnold," handing him his gun. "Git down and put one shot into Mr. Barber."

"What fer, Pa! He's already dead, ain't he?"

"Do as yore told, son. And you, too, Dick."

Quinn knew that his two young sons had to do this deed so no one could say who killed Isaac. They all had to be guilty according to Stewart so that none would tell.

Young Arnold took aim and shot Isaac as instructed and got back on his horse.

Dick just sat there, getting paler and sicker by the minute.

"Why'd you have to shoot him in the back like a coward?" Dick said disgustedly. He was still on his horse.

"Don't argue with us son, git down and do as yore told."

Dick took one more look at the body, hanging from the rope. It didn't' even resemble a human being now, the blood soaked top coat with pieces of bone and flesh protruding out of it. He turned his head and wretched, vomiting all over the side of his saddle and spurring his horse as hard as he could, both ashamed and disgusted, headed for Harriet Barber's as fast as he could travel.

Mose and Little Mose had been at Joe Story's the better part of the morning, looking over Joe's herd of young stud colts and trying out several. Mose was looking for a colt that he could use in the mud. The winter had been unusually wet and the marshes were muddy and the ponds full of water. Mose Jr. wanted one that could "turn on a nickel and give you a dollar change." He didn't care if he was sure footed in the mud or not. He wanted one that could keep his balance if he stumbled in a "gopher hole" and not fall down. The sandy pinelands were full of holes dug by the dry land tortoises the Crackers called gophers.

Mose had picked out a rather coarse-headed little pony that he liked the stride on, but Joe advised him not to take him.

"You don't want that loggerhead. I don't know why I even got him up. He's got a tough hide and a short recollection. You can spur him to death and you can't train him to do nothin'."

Little Mose had finally decided on one he liked and had changed his saddle and was running him up to the corral fence and turning him back.

"I think I'll take this one, Pa."

Mose still wasn't satisfied. "Jack says that stud you sold him is tough as a 'gator and takes to the mud as well. That's the kind I need."

"Come to think of hit I got a full brother to him sommers in here. Thar he is, thet sorrel with the one stocking foot."

"I guess I could stand one white foot," Mose decided, watching the young colt as Joe caught him and put his bridle and saddle on him. The Central Florida pinelands were covered in lighter knots from the heart of the dead pine limbs that could bruise and cripple a horse as he stumbled over them. A white hoof on a horse was tenderer and easily bruised than a dark hoof and the more stocking feet on a horse; the less a cowman wanted him for a cowpony.

Mose rode the little sorrel back and forth in the corral, turning him this way and that.

"Thet colt and his ma wuz raised right down here on the marsh at the mouth of this little boggy creek," pointing toward East Lake, "They come and went any time they took a notion, right through mud an water acrost to thet island over thar. I guarantee he won't bog you down like a sand-hill horse. He's a marshraised horse if you ever saw one." Joe knew he had just about clinched a sale and was putting the finishing touches on it.

"As fer that one Little Mose has decided on. His ma had a lot o' 'cow' in her and he'll darn shore watch a cow."

When a horse had a lot of "cow" in him, it meant he loved to work cattle and part them in the pens. Some horses would even run up and bite a cow on the rump. Joe was deep into his sale now and spreading it a little thick.

Mose decided on the sorrel colt and had paid Joe. They were both on their horses and Joe was latching the gate when Jack came riding up in a lather.

When little Joe and Henry came to the house, crying that the posse had arrested their Pa, Susan began to cry and ring her hands.

"You best jump on thet horse and run warn Little Mose and his Pa, Jack."

They had seen Dick and Arnold as they came along and decided the posse probably knew where Mose was by then. Jack's new stud was still tied to the gate where Little Mose had tied him, as Jack had been planning to get over to the "tater planting" as soon as he got his morning chores done.

"The posse's got Isaac over at the new corn field where he and the boys were settin' the 'taters," Jack warned.

"What on earth do they want with him?" cried little Mose. "He ain't done nothin'." He suddenly realized what he had dragged Isaac into.

"Never mind that, we'd better ride. They're after the lot o' us," warned Jack again, and not waiting for Mose and his cousin, took off toward the crossing at the creek.

Jack was right. The posse was hot on their heels and the three men had not disappeared into the trees before Stewart and his men came riding up and paused just long enough to see that Mose and his son were no longer at Joe Story's. They hit the trail in hot pursuit.

Joe Story had been correct in what he had sold Mose and Jack for a good "marsh-raised" horse. They made it across the creek and out of gun range on the other side, but Little Mose's new colt was floundering in the mud, bogged down to his belly when the posse got to him and drew their guns. They could see that Little Mose had no chance of getting away as he yelled out that he was their prisoner and not to shoot. He jumped off his horse, covered in mud and walked into the crowd with his arms raised high.

Their horses were tired and they, too, quickly bogged down trying to cross the creek.

"Let 'em go fer now," said Quinn to Stewart. "A bird in the hand, I say."

They made Little Mose walk, one of them leading his new horse and headed for Orlando.

"I say shootin's too good fer the sonofabitch."

"He outa hang—the murderin' bastard."

"I got a better ideer. Why don't we take him up here to Lake Conway and drowned him like he done Jack Roberts in the water trough at Fort Capron, a couple o' years back."

"Yeah, the goddamned sneak thought he'd got away with that, didn't he?"

"He's a yeller' bellied traitor too. I hear he turned all o' Dickison's men in durin' the war. Some o' the very men he fought with."

"Killin's too good."

"Let's put him to the bottom of Lake Conway!"

For once Little Mose was quiet. He was no longer the cocky little banty rooster. He knew they had him fair and square and he had no chance of getting away. So, he decided to take his punishment and die like a man. He was a good swimmer, having learned to swim in the St. Marys River when Champ and Isiah first threw him in and told him to swim out. He'd give 'em their money's worth.

Two men rowed him out into the lake, his hands bound and a plowshare tied to his middle. He didn't wait for them to throw him in. He closed his eyes and jumped overboard.

"May you rot in hell," he yelled as he hit the water.

He surfaced twice, coming up for air, working at the rope that bound his hands. The third time he came up, he had worked the bond free and grabbed onto the boat, rocking it in an attempt to drown the two men. But they beat his hands with the oars until he had to turn loose in pain. He swam under the water, with the plow, toward the opposite side of the lake where the crowd had gathered. He wasn't too far from shore before Stewart and his men spotted him, and they tore off around the beach of the lake, their horses knee deep in water, until they got into gun range. Little Mose almost made his escape, had it not been for the plow tied around his waist. He couldn't free himself in time and was shot just as he reached the shore. They dragged his body up on dry land to make sure he was dead and left him lying there. Some Good Samaritan took the body and gave him a decent burial nearby.

Mose and Jack made it to Henry Hodges where they left their horses and packed enough supplies to reach Jacksonville. They walked to Lake Harney, found a boat and headed down river for Jacksonville.

Chapter 31

As Mose and Jack walked to Lake Harney, making good their escape and Little Mose waited on the shore of Lake Conway for his execution, Harriet spent a sleepless night with Susan and Jack's wife, Violet, waiting for light so they could take Isaac's body home for burial.

When young Dick Bass rode up to tell Harriet that her husband had been shot by the posse that had gathered there earlier that morning, she knew at once by the strickened look on his face that something was seriously wrong. He was sobbing and crying so hard that he could hardly make her understand what had happened.

She and Jason hitched the wagon and started for Jack's, going by way of Cross Prairie, but when she got there, no one was there to pole her and her wagon across and she had to go around on the east side of East Lake to get to Jack's farm near the island.

She, too, almost bogged down crossing the boggy creek, with Jason leading the old horse and carrying little Ellen and no one in the wagon. She waded across, the water to her armpits with the baby astride her shoulders.

It was pitch dark when they came to Jack's house and had to untie Isaac from the tree in the dark, with it misting rain. His body was already stiff, as *rigor mortis* had set in hours before, and they could not stretch him out in the bed of the wagon. So they laid him face down in the little cart Isaac had used to carry the potato slips to the field from the hot bed, his arms and legs dangling down over the sides.

There was no way they could lay the body out, as they usually do in a wake, so the three women "sat up" with him under the barn with Jason asleep in the kitchen in case the children woke in the night and cried for their mama.

The next morning, Jason drove his ex-master and dearest friend home in the cart while the three women and the children followed in the wagons. By that time, they were permitted to cut across on the ferry that was once more in operation.

They laid Isaac to rest, still draped across the floor of the cart. It would be useless to try to get his misshapen body into a coffin. Harriet cut his black coat off and kept the bullet-ridden garment in a special trunk with other mementos, long after she remarried and started another family.

Many widows, orphans and wives, whose husbands were not in evidence, attended the funeral. Few men were brave enough to attend. Isaac had been loved by many people, but his friends were lined up, choosing sides by then, and those on the "Barber" side were afraid of the posse. Those on the "Mizell" side were afraid of Harriet, for she threatened to shoot them on sight if they stepped one foot on her land. Harriet donated the plot where he was buried for a cemetery and it is still used by the Barber and allied families to this day.

When she found anyone near her property, attempting to round up her "shuck eaters," the tame cattle that hung around the barn and crivis to eat scraps from the garden, she took a gun and ordered them off. She couldn't keep them from thousands of her cattle, but she was going to see that she and her children had beef to eat.

In June, when the 1870 Census was taken, Mary Barber, John's wife and six children, Mary Yates, James Yates' wife and six children, and Violet Barber, Jack's wife and five children and Nancy Yates, Need's widow and four children, were all living with Harriet and her four youngsters. The five women and Jason kept the more than two-dozen children fed through that terrible, lawless year that followed.

While Harriet was struggling over her grief over losing Isaac and Violet and Susan were wondering if Jack and Mose were dead or alive, the two men were making their escape along the west shore of the St. Johns River towards Jacksonville.

They hid in some isolated cove or creek during the day and rowed silently by any settlements at night. The only time they dared talk was where the banks were uninhabited. Then they could converse freely.

"You know, Jack," Mose told him. "I been a'thinkin' maybe I'm bein' paid back for what I done to the Injuns. I hated their guts when I first come to this country. Man ain't never satisfied, is he? I guess I had jest about everything a man could want in this life—the love of a good wife, six strong, hard-workin boys. 'Cept for Little Mose. Guess he never did set the world on far as fer as work goes, but he shore give the women and a cow pony hell, didn't he?"

"I guess you could say that."

"Anyways, I had about as nice a plantation as a man could want, over a hundred slaves and the woods full of cattle, and they took it all. I don't see no way to git any o' it back. Man may as well jest leave the country. They's ruin this country anyway."

"You know what galls me mor'n anything else, Uncle Mose, is to see a group o' my friends aridin' up like that there posse did down there at Joe Story's. You could see the hatred and revenge written all over their faces and they had nothin' but killin' on their minds. Why I hardly recognized 'em and knowed most o' 'em fer years. All 'cept that there Sheriff Stewart."

"Thet's what happens when you git a bunch riled up like that. They quit actin' like human beings and turn into animals. Most o' them men wouldn't hurt a fly under ordinary circumstances."

They rowed and drifted along in silence for a while, each contemplating their predicament, attempting to sort out what was left of their shattered dreams.

"Goin back to them Injuns," Mose mused. "I been a'thinkin. You know, they weren't so different from you and me. They had their own way o' life and we moved in here and took over jest like them damned Yankees and carpetbaggers has done to us. All they wanted to do wuz live in peace and quiet and to be left alone. We took their cattle and slaves and run 'em plum outa the country and now thet's jest what's happened to me."

"'Member thet piece in the *Bible*, Uncle Mose, about what goes around, comes around? You 'member how thet went?"

Mose thought a minute and finally said, "My mind ain't aworkin' like hit used to be. Hit went somethin' like 'what is now wuz yesterday and what will be later on has already been and God requires of us that which is past.' I never could really figger out what he meant by that last bit 'til now. I think he meant that we, all the different generations, jest keep makin' the same mistakes over and over. We don't ever learn. We jest keep changing roles. Some of us is the perpetrators for a few generations and then we switch around and become the victims. But the acts don't change a bit. Them that ain't got wants what others has got and in the end, they lose out to somebuddy new. I took from the poor old Injuns and now the Yankees is a takin' hit from me. Sooner or later we all got to move over and make room fer the greedy."

"But, Uncle Mose, I ain't had my turn yet."

"You will, Jack, hang in there long enough and yore turn will come. They say 'every dawg has his day.' That's the way hit is and that's the way hit wuz and that's the way hit'll be agin'. And we all git to play our role."

All hopes for any of those left behind were shattered by the news when they reached Little Mose's old homestead and talked to his wife, Penny. It seems that only John and Francis had made it out alive. They were over on the Suwannee River and Jack decided to go there and hide out until things blew over as they both thought it would. He left Mose at William's old home place where they dug up his gold and he gave Jack enough for him and his brothers to get by on for a while. The gold was buried at the foot of Will's grave, the mound of earth now level with the ground and covered with weeds.

"I think I'll git plum outa the country and start over out in Texas. They say a cowman can make hit in that country, hit's wide open."

When Mose told Becky what he planned to do she began to fume and rave.

"But what about all them hundreds o' cattle down there in Sumter, Orange and Brevard Counties. Some o' them cattle you give to me and the young'uns. Here. And Penny, she's got a right to some o' them too. Leastwise them with Little Mose's brand on 'em. And I got a right to some o' them ain't been give directly to me. I'm still yore wife, ain't I?"

"Not so's a man could tell?" Mose laughed bitterly. Becky had refused to share his bed or have anything to do with him from the time he first rode up with the bad news.

"Them cows is still there fer now if yore a mind to go after 'em I ain't a'hinderin' you. But hit's not safe fer a man like me anymore down in thet country. They're a'ruinin' it anyways."

He kissed the children goodbye and, saddlebags packed for the long journey out west, got stiffly on his old horse and started out the gate for Texas.

"But I thought you loved Florida, Pa," Jeremiah called out to him.

Mose didn't turn around but waved to him as he left

"To hell with Florida!" they could hear him shout as he galloped off down the lane, headed west.

EPILOGUE

What became of Mose Barber? No one really knows. Even Barber family tradition has no answers.

Some say he went to Texas and started over, using his bag of hoarded gold to buy a ranch and cattle.

Some say he went to the edge of the Okeefenokee Swamp, died of natural causes and was buried by his cousin, Obediah Barber.

It has been rumored that he died in a gun battle in the Panhandle of Florida, defending his sack of gold against a band of bushwhackers, and Judge John Mizell sent a black man to dig up the body and bring back evidence that Mose Barber was really dead.

Another story was that a young couple, on the banks of the Suwannee River, claimed they poisoned him. They had put him up for the night and the young wife discovered his sack of gold doubloons in his saddlebags as he slept. The next morning, she insisted he have a hearty breakfast before he left, headed for Texas.

If anything, I'd think he died of a broken heart. His six sons he was so proud of, only two were still alive. The war had taken one of his sons and another had died of disease contracted during the conflict. It also wiped out his plantation and freed all of his slaves. That way of life was over. He tried to start anew down in Central Florida, but Reconstruction took his cattle, two more of his sons and a nephew. Probably Texas was not kind to a bitter old man, alone and unable to adapt to such a different environment.

A fog of investigation into legal documents leaves absolutely no answer.

Before the probate judge of Columbia County on December 24, 1870, Becky declared that "she is widow of Moses E. Barber, deceased late of Columbia County in the State of Florida, departed this life on or about the 27th day of November A.D. 1870 in testate."

But seven years later, on August 17, 1877, a Mose Barber received a deed from his wife, Rebecca E. Barber. He declared he had been in serious financial difficulties as attested by Rebecca E. Barber.

That same year Becky filed for bankruptcy. "She believes the debts and liabilities of her deceased husband greatly exceeds the assets of the said estate and suggest insolvency."

Attorney R.H. Charles held a judgment and execution against the estate for eight hundred and eleven dollars and fifty cents in favor of George W. S. Waldron.

On February 3, 1885, a power of attorney was given George Washington Barber by S. J. Barber and his wife and other heirs to manage and settle up the estate of Moses E. Barber, "late of Columbia County, deceased."

Becky was unsuccessful in her attempt to regain any of Mose's cattle.

In June 1870, as Mose had suggested, Rebecca E. Barber appointed William Turner her lawful attorney to take charge of all her cattle in Brevard and Orange

County and drive them to Lafayette County to A.A. Barber and pay debts that Mose owed to John E. Luten and Turner's attorney fee. But it appears Mose himself also signed the paper in Columbia County, witnessed by H.P. Eastern, Clerk of the Court.

In February of 1871, Becky, alone, appointed, of all people, John R. Mizell of Orange County her attorney, giving him power to collect the same herd of cattle in Orange, Brevard and Sumter Counties. Witnessed by C.R. King and W. M. Ives.

Becky later filed a complaint that all her original papers and records were stolen from the office of Probate Court and destroyed March 15, 1871. However, the two papers she signed, giving power of attorney to William Turner and then John Mizell are still on file today in Orange County Court Records in Miscellaneous file "A through C."

In two years after Mose disappeared, she remarried, and then married a third time to Bill Turner.

Penny, Mose Jr.'s widow, died in poverty at the edge of Jacksonville.

James Ed died in 1867.

Isaac's widow, Harriet, remarried Edward Whaley. They had one son, Alexander. The Whaley family is well known in Osceola County today. Osceola was made up from parts of Orange and Brevard.

Although the bulk of Mose's cattle "South of Ocklawaha River" that Isaac supposedly "bought" in 1868 would legally have gone to his widow, Harriet, there is no evidence that she regained many of them.

Joe, Isaac's son, died in testate in July 1893, leaving only one hundred head of cattle, one black horse, and some debts owed him by customers in a store he ran at Peg Horn. His sons, one of whom was W. I. Barber, my children's grandfather, were "farmed out" among relatives when they became old enough to work. They evidently inherited little, if anything.

Susan is supposedly buried in an old cemetery at the side of the Hilliard Isle Road off Bogg Creek Road, the site of Andrew Jackson's farm where Isaac was murdered and near where Joe Story had his horse corral.

Needham Yates's widow, Malintha, and Needham Jr.'s widow, Nancy, moved westward into that area of land now owned by the Candler Family, known as Johnson Island. Burrel Yates, Needham's brother, moved to Fort Christmas.

Joe Story told relatives that the posse came back and chased him through the woods, but left him alone thereafter for his part in the Barber's escape across Boggy Creek on his "marsh-raised" horses.

Andrew Jackson came back to Orange County after everything died down and lived out his life peacefully. He has many, many allied families in Orange and Osceola counties today.

John Barber died or was killed in Old Town. Deed settled at Flat Ford and his descendants are still in Osceola County. Champ's family moved to Boggy Creek, next to Jack's place. His widow was Joe Ward's first wife.

Francis stayed in Old Town.

There are few "old timers" that don't have a drop or two of Barber blood, or are related to one by marriage.

Mann Bass, son of Priscilla Ivey and John Randolph Mizell, married Mary Nancy Yates, daughter of Jack Yates (Needham's brother) and Vianah Overstreet. At age ten, he changed his name, legally, to Walter, but he was always called "Mann" by his family and friends.

John Mizell remained close to his son. He offered to take him to South America to start a cattle ranch there, but Mann refused to go. Mann died in 1908 of a fever he contracted by drinking impure water from an abandoned well while deep in the woods of Osceola County. At the time of his untimely death, he was a successful man. He was Chairman of the Board of County Commissioners of Osceola County, owned over four thousand acres on the shore of Lake Tohopekaliga including the beautiful subdivision on Kings Highway and along Fish Lake. He also left sixteen hundred head of cattle.

He left eight children; the youngest boy was my father, Clint Bass. So, I am John Randolph Mizell's great granddaughter. In 1942, I married William P. Barber, Isaac's great grandson. Our four children are the product of the contents of this book.

John Randolph Mizell stayed in politics but there is no evidence that he took any of the Barber cattle for himself. However, there is strong evidence that he gathered cattle for his son, Mann Bass, who was eight years old at the time. Mann Bass had a sizeable herd by the time he married at age eighteen. In the 1870 Census, John was worth only one thousand dollars. He married Margaret Crooner and had four daughters--Lena, Lilla, Alice and Luta. He had no sons and begged Mann Bass to take his name. But Mann refused and remained a "Bass" taking that name from his stepfather, Crawford.

On June 12, 1879, John formed the Little River Canal Company for the purpose of digging the Southport Canal between Lake Tohopekaliga and Lake Hatchineha. He moved from Central Florida around the turn of the century and became Collector of Customs of Pensacola, Florida, and then moved south where he was the first Mayor of Pompano Beach when it was incorporated on June 6, 1908. He was listed as a truck farmer there in the 1910 Census. He lived alone, dying November 9, 1913, in Miami, Florida.

Priscilla Ivey Bass lived on Mose Barber's old plantation until her death. Strangely enough, it was six months before the death of her former lover, John Randolph Mizell, on May 29, 1913. She is buried at Rose Hill Cemetery on the outskirts of Kissimmee, where Mose Barber's slaves once farmed and where she and Croft Bass lived. Mann Bass and his wife, Mary Nancy Yates, were both buried in the family plot along with Mann's half brothers and their family members.

Inscribed on Priscilla's tombstone is the message her children wanted the entire community to never forget.

"She Died As She Lived, A Pure And Upright Woman."

An investigation into the mass execution of the Barber and Yates families, without benefit of a trial, resulted in Stewart's suspension and his eventual resignation in January 1871. The investigation uncovered the fact that he was only a hired gun when he led the posse that turned into a vigilante mob and was not officially made a sheriff until June of that year.

Lawlessness prevailed in Orange and Brevard Counties for several years. In 1870, the year the Barbers, Yates's, and those associated with the two families were either killed or driven from that part of the state, the Brevard County Court House was burned to the ground. All records were lost and, apparently, none kept until the 1880's.

Of forty-one murders, only ten came to trial with no convictions. Complete disregard for law and order evidently was the rule.

Just four months after Isaac was killed, Quinn Bass had given his ten children from 100 to 250 head of cattle each.

In February 1873, documents reveal Quinn had sold 11,125 head of cattle to various individuals. Records from that era seemed to have been poorly preserved. There could have been many more transactions not documented. Apparently, this particular family took good advantage of the unattended Barber and Yates cattle roaming the Florida grasslands.

Roads and railroads were eventually built deep into Brevard County. The land where the Cooks, Johnsons and Mose Barber punched cattle and had their cow camps and pens was soon accessible.

A railroad was built from Bithlow to Holopaw, Illiha, Nittaw, Whittier, now called Kenansville, to Locasee, Yehaw, Fort Drum and Lake Okeechobee.

R. T. P. Allen started a trading post on the northwest shore of Lake Tohopekaliga, called Allentown. When the Southport Canal was dug and steamboats could run from Lake Okeechobee into Lake Tohopekaliga, the little trading post was incorporated into the present city of Kissimmee in 1880 and the first house built there in 1881.

Developers soon drained the land lying around the northern and eastern edge of the lake, including the Kissimmee Bog and Cross Prairie. This reclaimed many acres of land surrounding the little town of Kissimmee. Soon, islands in the area could be reached by "fills" and settlers began to move into the outlying lands around the two lakes.

Even to this day reclamation continues. The uninhabited marsh and precious wet lands lying to the east of Kissimmee between the railroad and Rose Hill Cemetery, leading out to Boggy Creek, and East Lake, have recently been filled in. A large shopping area lies where, even just twenty years ago, no one could build or, at times, ride a horse.

Thousands of people live on the lands Mose Barber owned and gave to Croft Bass and his nephew, Andrew Jackson Barber—an area he once considered a desirable location because it was surrounded by inaccessible wet lands. Where has all that water gone?

THE WAY HIT WUZ certainly ain't no more.

BIBLIOGRAPHY

Blassingame, John W., *The Slave Community: Plantation Life In The Antebellum South*. New York Oxford Press, New York 1972.

Blay, John S., *After The Civil War*. Bonanza Books, New York 1960.

Boyd, Mark Frederick, *Florida Aflame: The Background And Onset Of The Seminole War 1835*. Florida Board Of Parks And Historic Memorials 1951.

Brown, Virginia Pounds and Lawalla Owens, *The World Of The Southern Indians*. Beechwood Books, Birmingham, Ala. 1983.

Burnett, Gene M., *Florida's Past*. Pineapple Press, Englewood, Fl. 1986.

Cash, W. T., *The Story Of Florida*. Volume I, The American Historical Society, Inc. New York, N.Y. 1938.

Collins, Leroy, *Forerunners Of Courage*. Calcade Publishers Inc. 1971.

Cotterill, R.S., *The Story Of The Civilized Tribes Before Removal*. The University Of Oklahoma Press, Norman, Oklahoma. 1954.

Crow, Myrtle Hilliard, *Old Tales And Trails*. Byron Kennedy And Co., St. Petersburg, Fl. 1987.

Davis, Burke, *Sherman's March*. Random House, New York 1980.

Foote, Shelby, *Sumter To Perryville* (1958); *Fredericksburg To Meridian* (1963); *Red River To Appomattox* (1974). Random House, New York.

Foreman, Grant, *Seminole, Of The Five Civilized Tribes*. University Of Oklahoma Press, Norman Oklahoma, 1982.

Hodges, Jeannett, *Back Country*. Pageant Press Inc., New York N.Y. 1958.

Johoda, Gloria, *Florida - A Bicentennial History*. W. W. Norton and Co., Inc., New York, 1976.

Keuchel, Edward K., *A History Of Columbia County Florida*. Sentry Press, Tallahassee, Florida, 1981.

Laumer, Frank, *Massacre*. University Of Florida Press, Gainesville, Fl 1968.

Long, E. B. with Barbara Long, *The Civil War Day by Day, An Almanac 1861-1865*. Doubleday And Co, Garden City, New Jersey 1971.

Lutin, Reinhard H., *The Real Abraham Lincoln*. Englewood Press, Prentice-Hall Indiana and New Jersey 1960.

Neill, Wilfred T., *Florida's Seminole Indians*. Great Outdoors Association., St. Petersburg, Florida, 1952

Perdue, Theda, *Slavery And The Evolution Of Cherokee Society*. University Of Tennessee Press, Knoxville, Tenn. 1979.

Perry, John Holliday and Frank Parker Stockbridge, *Florida In The Making*. The Debower Publishing Co., New York, N.Y. and Jacksonville, Florida 1926.

Phillips, Ulrich Bonnell, *Life And Labor In The Old South*. Little, Brown, and Company: Boston, 1929.

Smith, Julia Floyd, *Slavery And Plantation Growth In The Antebellum Florida, 1821-1860*. University of Florida Press, Gainesville, Fla. 1970.

Snow, William P., *Lee And His Generals*. The Fairfax Press, Lincoln and London, 1986.

Sprague, John T., *The Origin, Progress And Conclusion Of The Florida War.* D. Appleton Co., New York, 1948.

Stern, Phillip Van Doren, Editor, *Soldier Life In The Union And Confederate Armies.* Bonanza Books, New York, 1960.

Tebeau, Charlton W., *A History Of Florida.* University of Miami Press, Coral Gables, Florida, 1971.

Tucker, Glenn, *High Tide At Gettysburg.* Bobbs-Merrill, Indianapolis and New York 1958.

Utley, Robert M. And Wilcomb E. Washburn, Editors, *History Of The Indian Wars.* American Heritage Publishers Co., Inc., New York, Distributed By Simon And Schuster, Inc. 1971.

Vernam, Glen R., *The Rawhide Years, A History Of The Cattleman And The Cattle Country.* Doubleday And Co., Inc., Garden City, New York, 1976.

Walton, George H., *Fearless And Free 1835-1842.* Bobb-Merrill Co., Inc., Indianapolis, Ind. 1977.

Wigginton, Brooks Eliot, *Foxfire Books I-III.* Anchor Pres/Doubleday, Garden City, N.J., 1968, 1969, 1970.

Wiley, Irvin Bell, *The Life Of Johnny Reb, The Common Soldier Of The Confederacy.* Louisiana State University Press, 1978.

Wilson, Minnie Moore, *Seminoles Of Florida.* Kingsport Press, Kingsport, Tennessee 1928.

Wright, J. Leitch Jr., *Creeks And Seminoles.* University Of Nebraska Press, Lincoln and London, 1986.

_____, *The Only Land They Knew.* The Free Press, London, 1981.